You Think I Hate You?

Copyright © 2021 Pauline Adolfsson

All Rights Reserved

The characters and events portrayed in this book are fictitious. No part of this book may be reproduced, or stored in a retrieval system, or transmitted in any form or by any means, electronic, mechanical, photocopying, recording, or otherwise, without express written permission of the publisher.

ISBN-13: 9798594481954

Cover design by: Pauline Adolfsson

Prologue

Harry was sitting at the kitchen table, eating dinner with his mother and sister in a comfortable silence when his mum decided to speak up. "I've got some news to tell you," she announced, looking up at her two children with a small smile on her lips.

Harry and his sister Gemma leaned forward in their seats, eyes staring at their mother curiously. "Yes?"

His mum, Anne, brought her fork with spaghetti to her mouth and started chewing on it awfully slowly. Harry could barely take it, but restrained himself from urging her on, knowing it would only take more time for her to say whatever she had to say.

When she had swallowed down the food, she reached forward to grab her glass of water and lifted it to her lips to sip on it. Harry and Gemma were rolling their eyes at this point, knowing this was so typical of their mum. She loved taking her time only to make them impatient and frustrated.

"For God's sake mum, can't you just say it?" Gemma finally groaned when Anne had swallowed another forkful of spaghetti.

Anne smirked at her two children, nodding her head slowly. "Sure, but only because you asked so nicely."

She was like a three-year-old in a grown woman's body, Harry was sure of it. "So?" He said after thirty seconds of silence.

"I've started dating again," she confessed, a bright smile breaking out on her face.

To say Harry and Gemma were shocked would've been an understatement. Their mouths were hanging open while they were staring at their mother with wide eyes. Anne hadn't dated anyone in three years; ever since their dad left them to start a new life. She was devastated at first, promising herself that she would never fall in love again, but now three years later she had apparently met someone new. Finally.

"In fact, I've been on quite a few dates with the same guy, and he's actually coming over tomorrow night. So, would you please make sure you are home then? I want you to meet him."

Harry finally got out of his daze and nodded enthusiastically. "Of course. I've got nothing better to do anyway. Do you know if he has any kids?" He asked hopefully, wanting to befriend new people, especially if it was someone who would be his stepbrother in the future.

"Yes, he actually does. I've never met him personally, though. I just know that he's got a son your age, Harry," she smiled, looking over at Gemma who rolled her eyes.

"Looks like I'm never going to have a sister," she sighed, but you could clearly hear that she was just kidding. Not that she wouldn't love to have a sister. It had been her dream since she was little and started playing with dolls. It didn't matter how many times she tried getting Harry to play with her, he always refused anyway. It wasn't until she grew up that she finally understood why her brother never wanted to play with her dolls.

"Sorry, honey," mum said, pouting, although a small smile was playing on her lips.

"Thank you so much for dinner, mum. I guess I should head up to my room and finish off my homework now. See you later," Harry announced, getting up to dump his plate and glass in the sink before going up to his room.

Once he was seated at his desk with his homework scattered in front of him, he started thinking about who the kid could be. He most certainly lived in town because he doubted his mum had met someone far from here. And since there was only one high school in the area, he probably went to Harry's school as well. However, there were a lot of guys there, so it could be anyone. Despite that, Harry was still very curious and couldn't stop thinking about the mysterious guy for the rest of the evening.

Chapter 1

[Harry]

It was Monday morning, and I was waiting for the school bus to arrive. It was rather chilly outside being late November and all, but I was quite used to the cold these days. It had been raining for seven days straight, so this was nothing new to me. Though, I was starting to freeze a little, standing there in the rain and waiting for a bus that just wouldn't show up. It should've been here ten minutes ago, yet it was still nowhere to be seen.

I wasn't the only student waiting for the bus, though. About ten others were standing here as well, rubbing their hands up and down their arms to keep their body heat. Some of them were even whining, which I was getting quite annoyed by because let's face it; the bus wouldn't show up any faster even if they whined for it to come. It was only irritating and disturbing.

After about five more minutes, the school bus finally appeared around the corner and stopped in front of me and the other students. I wasted no time to hop on and start searching for an empty seat I could sit in. Unfortunately, though, all the front seats were taken, so I had to walk towards the back where all the jocks were.

I hated them, all of them. They were so far up their asses that they barely knew what one plus one was. Additionally, they thought they owned the entire school just because the majority of the students looked up to them, which was really pathetic if you asked me.

"Hey, nerd! What the hell are you doing back here? Go sit in the front with the other losers," a voice I recognized as Niall's, one of the most popular jocks, mocked, making my fists clench.

If there was something I hated, it was stupid remarks like that, especially when they came from people who thought they were cool by saying them. "Go fuck yourself," I muttered under my breath, continuing my search for an empty seat. I didn't miss Niall's shocked face that turned angry only seconds later. However, I wasn't scared of him nor the other jocks. Sadly, though, I was one of few students who dared to stand up to them.

The thing was, they never did anything in return even when I made a comeback or whatever. They were too chicken for that. The only person who ever did something was someone I'd rather not speak of, someone I hated with all my heart because he had made and was still making my life a living hell. Louis Tomlinson, the captain of the football team, the most popular guy at school, and also the one person everyone worshipped, except for me. I was the only one not agreeing with everybody else about how hot, amazing and absolutely fantastic he was and, to be honest, I was proud of it. I liked being rare and not one of many.

As expected, Niall didn't say anything nor did anyone else, so I soon found an empty seat with no problem at all. It even turned out I didn't have to sit beside anyone, which was definitely a good thing. I loved being by myself, if not with my best friend Liam Payne, that is.

Liam and I had been friends for a few years now, ever since things had started getting really bad with Louis. I was glad I had made a new friend I could lean on at the time, otherwise, I wouldn't have known what to do with myself, having no friends whatsoever. From there on, we had practically been inseparable, almost doing everything together. The only thing we didn't share was that Liam would rather obey the popular students than go against them, which I didn't mind too much since I knew there weren't many people who actually would.

About five minutes later, the bus finally came to a halt, and I could get out of it along with the other students. Unfortunately, Liam didn't ride the same bus as me, so I was always alone every morning until I arrived at my locker where he would always wait for me. It wasn't like I minded being alone though, it was just nice to have your best friend by your side.

As I started making my way into the school building, I noticed people rushing inside, probably due to the rain. I contemplated whether to do the same thing or not, but decided against it because I didn't like to rush. I wasn't that late anyway, even though it felt like it took ages until the bus had shown up at the bus stop this morning.

Once I got inside, I shook my head, making my soaked, brown curls fly everywhere. I ran a hand through them but pulled it out again when it got stuck in a large knot. Sighing heavily, I made my way to my locker and took off my jacket.

"Hey, mate," a chirpy voice said, the person slamming my locker shut, almost hitting me in the face as they did so.

"You want to give me a concussion the first thing you do today, huh? Hi to you too, by the way," I replied, rolling my eyes at my best friend who had a bright smile on his face.

"Sorry, I didn't know you were standing so close to it. However, I heard your mum's started dating again." Liam rolled back and forth on his heels, his eyes glinting with what seemed like hope.

"Yeah, but don't get your hopes up. She's already found someone she seems to fancy quite a lot."

Liam had for some reason always had this weird crush on my mum. I always teased him about it, although I thought it was kind of weird. Mum was like twenty years older than him and had wrinkles and all that stuff, so how could he possibly like her? She was way too old for him anyway.

It had now been two months since mum revealed she was dating someone to me and Gemma, and she had been on even more dates with the same guy ever since. Gemma and I were so happy for her. She had finally moved on from dad who left us all those years ago to start a new life. We had even met the guy, Troy, twice now, and he seemed genuinely nice but also quite familiar. I couldn't put my finger on what it was, but his features reminded me of someone. No matter what, I was happy for her, and that was all that mattered.

The brown-eyed boy pouted. "Ah, man! I thought I would actually have a chance now," he huffed, making me laugh so hard I had to cover my mouth with my fist to muffle it.

He shot me a glare, and my laughter slowly died down. "I'm sorry, mate. It's just hilarious how you actually thought you had a chance with her."

Smacking the back of my head, he muttered; "Shut up. I was just hoping, okay? What's so wrong with that?"

Before I could open my mouth to reply, the bell rang, signaling the first class was about to start. I opened my locker again to pull out my Maths books, then turned to Liam who was still waiting for an answer. "It's wrong because you're more than twenty years younger than her. Plus, she's your best friend's mother," I said, rolling my eyes. "However, first class starts in a minute so we should probably go get your stuff if we wanna arrive on time."

With another huff, Liam agreed and we made our way over to his locker that was on the other side of the hallway. I never understood why he didn't just go to his own locker before meeting up with me in the mornings. It would save us a lot of time, but apparently, he liked doing it this way better, which I didn't bother to argue about.

As I patiently waited for him to grab his books, I looked around the hallway to see if I recognized any of the students who had yet to arrive at their lessons. The only person I recognized was Zayn, also one of the most popular jocks at school. He was pressing a blonde girl against the lockers as he played with a strand of her hair that was hanging in front of her eyes. In return, she was beaming up at him, a wide smile playing on her lips.

Not only were the jocks popular and played on the football team, but they were also massive players who shagged different girls at every party they attended. Shockingly, Louis wasn't one of them. He had actually been in a relationship for about two years now with the same girl, Eleanor Calder, who was one of the most popular girls at school. When they got together, people said they were like meant for each other considering they were both so popular. I didn't agree, however. Not that I was jealous or anything, but Eleanor was actually a really nice girl who deserved someone sweet in return, and I knew for sure Louis was nowhere near that.

Liam slammed his locker shut beside me, following my gaze to where the jock and blonde girl were now standing lip-locking or more like tongue-battling. He visibly cringed at the sight in front of him, muttering something under his breath that I couldn't catch.

"Come on, let's go," he said a few seconds later, pulling me with him to the Math classroom across the school.

The bell rang again when we were only halfway there, so in order to not arrive later than necessary, we picked up our paces and jogged the rest of the way there. With our breaths in our throats, we entered the classroom a second before Mr. Storm would close the door and start the lesson.

"You were lucky today, boys," he muttered as Liam and I took our seats at one of the desks in the front.

Neither of us bothered replying. Instead, we tried to catch our breaths as we opened our books to start working. We ended up working intensely for a good fifteen minutes before the sound of the door being pushed open broke the silence in the classroom.

I looked up just in time to see Louis arriving with his hand locked together with Eleanor's. Right behind them, Zayn and that blonde girl were walking with smirks on their faces.

Mr. Storm got up from his chair at the arrival of the four students, his face hardening. "Mr. Tomlinson, Mr. Malik, Ms. Calder and Ms. Edwards, what do you think you're doing, interrupting my class like this?"

The sound of Louis' laughter made me roll my eyes. Of course he didn't care, when did he ever? "I'm sorry, Mr. Storm, but are you saying we're not allowed to attend our own lecture?" He asked stupidly, causing Mr. Storm's face to turn red.

"I don't want to hear a word from you, Tomlinson. If you're late to my lesson you're bound to get detention, which I'm certain you already know by now."

Louis merely rolled his eyes as he went to the back of the classroom with Eleanor, Zayn and the blondie, his eyes catching mine as he passed my and Liam's desk. He gave me a dark look as if saying my presence wasn't making anything better.

I ignored him, though, and kept my gaze on the front where Mr. Storm was glaring at the backs of the four students who had arrived late. After that, everything pretty much turned back to how it was before they got here, except the constant laughter and whispers that could now be heard from the back.

Mr. Storm scolded them a few times, but they didn't seem affected by it, as per usual. This was like a normal day here at Holmes Chapel's high school for me. Louis was loved by everyone besides the teachers and me, and the jocks pretty much owned the school by doing whatever they felt like doing. If we didn't have teachers here, I wouldn't have known what to do with myself, to be honest. Surely, I wouldn't be able to stay here, even if I personally thought it was already bad enough.

When the bell rang, I gathered my books and got up from my chair, Liam following suit. We were just about to exit the classroom when I heard an all too familiar voice mock behind me; "So, how's nerdy little Styles doing today?"

I turned around abruptly, pressing my books tighter against my chest to contain some of my sudden frustration. "Very well, Tomlinson. Thank you for asking," I said sarcastically, sending him a fake smile.

The smirk that had just been on his face faded at my words. Instead, he clenched his jaw together. "How great. Wouldn't want you to feel otherwise, right?" He muttered, a dark glint hinting in his eyes.

Beside me, Liam was fidgeting uncomfortably, sending glances towards the door as if he wanted to disappear from this situation as fast as possible. I wouldn't mind joining him. If only I could escape this. I mean, I knew Louis sadly wouldn't let me go that easily. "No, I don't think so?" I said, raising an eyebrow in an attempt to ridicule him.

He took a step closer to me, pointing his finger at my chest. "You can try acting like a brave little fucker, but you are aware that it won't get you anywhere, right?" He taunted, his voice rather intimidating, although I wasn't fazed by it.

Rolling my eyes, I pushed him away. "You will be glad to hear that's not my intention then."

He let out a grunt, stomping his foot childishly against the floor before turning on his heel and walking out of the classroom, Eleanor following behind him with an exasperated look on her face. She probably disliked this side of Louis as much as I did.

To think we had actually been friends once in our lives was just unbelievable, and I was sure I wasn't the only one thinking that way.

Chapter 2

[Harry]

When I got home that day, I went straight to the kitchen to pull out the ingredients for pancakes. After an hour of working hard in P.E. class, I was both exhausted and starving. I'll admit, my fitness wasn't the best, but that didn't mean I didn't try my best, unlike others. Some people couldn't even jog a lap around the gym without running out of breath.

Louis had been a pain in the ass during that lecture as well, just like always. He couldn't seem to stop minding my business and interrupting me by making nasty remarks. It was just so damn frustrating. Like, what did he even get out of it? Joy for sabotaging my life? Because really, I had done nothing to him, besides not worshipping him for his popularity and falling at his feet. Absolutely nothing.

Pulling out the milk from the fridge, I strolled over to the counter to pour it in the bowl with the other ingredients. Once the batter was done, I grabbed a pan from one of the cupboards and turned the stove on. It took me about half an hour to make all the pancakes, which were about ten. Don't ask me why I didn't just make half of the recipe - that would surely not have taken as much time - but being the good brother and son that I was, I made some for my family members as well.

Just when I sat down at the kitchen table, the front door slammed shut in the hallway. Not even ten seconds later, my lovely sister stepped into the room, a smile playing on her lips. "Hey, bro. Are these for me?" She went over to the plate of pancakes on the counter and smelled them.

I brought a fork of pancakes to my mouth, chewing on them before gulping them down. "Depends on how many I'm going to eat," I winked, earning a roll of the eyes.

"Ha ha, funny, aren't you?"

Gemma and I had probably one of the best brother and sister relationships around. We had always gotten along with each other even if we had small fights every now and then. Usually, it was only over silly things though, like she once thought I had stolen her car keys. But I mean, come on. I didn't even have a driver's license, so of course I hadn't taken them. However, she had whined about it all day and blamed me until she finally found them in her jacket pocket... Man, that was something I probably won't ever forget.

She sat down in the seat opposite me and poured some maple syrup on her pancakes before stuffing a forkful of the food in her mouth. "How w's school t'day, brother?"

I shrugged, sipping on my glass of milk. "Okay, I guess. Louis won't leave me alone, though," I grumbled, looking down at the surface of the table.

Gemma knew everything about me and Louis and our friendship in the past. No one did, except for her and Liam, not even my own mum. Louis had been quite... demanding. He didn't want anyone to know about our friendship because the reason he first befriended me in the first place was due to his low grades. He needed a hand, and I had shockingly agreed to help him, but only because he told me he would pay me for doing it. I would never have done it otherwise, I didn't even like him back then.

However, things changed after some time. Whenever we would meet up in the library or deserted places at school, he would act like a whole other person than when he was around his friends. We would laugh, play awful jokes with each other and just hang out like two close friends. Still, he was afraid of someone finding out about our friendship, so he always used to remind me not to tell anyone. And of course I kept our secret. I had started liking him being there, and I couldn't afford to lose our friendship.

It went on for almost a year, and we only grew closer and closer each day that went by during that period, until he all of a sudden stopped showing up at our meetings. By this time, I had stopped charging for helping him out with his school work. We hung out to have fun, not because one of us was paid to be there. So, when he suddenly stopped appearing, I felt rather sad. I would try sending him a look when we passed each other in the hallways, but he would only look away, pretending as though he hadn't seen me.

Thankfully, I had started befriending Liam by that time, and I had also even gotten myself a girlfriend whose name was Miranda, so it wasn't like I was alone without Louis being there, but I still missed him. He was that friend you could always tell things to because he would listen to whatever you had to say. However, after that, it only got worse. He started picking on me whenever he had the chance to, and I being the strong person that I was, stood up to him even if my insides screamed at me not to. The only thing I really wanted to do was go cry in a corner because I knew then that I would never get my friend back.

And really, that was all I knew. I never got to know the reason why he all of a sudden left me and decided to hate me.

The only thing I did know was that I now hated him as well because, after three years of being picked on, I had lost all those friendly thoughts I had about him back then. Our friendship was long forgotten and to be honest, I was glad about that. Louis Tomlinson was an asshole, and to me, he would always stay that way.

"Hmm, I wish I knew a way to make him stop, but I don't... Maybe you should talk to him though, clear some air and stuff, you know?" Gemma suggested, making me raise an eyebrow in disagreement.

"Are you serious? As if he would even want to talk to me in the first place. Besides, it was two years ago. It's not like it even matters anymore."

She brought another forkful of pancakes to her mouth and gulped them down. "If it doesn't matter, then why do you two still hate each other? Clearly, you're still acting on the outcome of what happened all those years ago," she said matter-of-factly, sending me a knowing look.

I let out a sigh, knowing she was right. The thing was; even though I wanted to know why he hated me, I didn't want to have that talk with him. I despised him too much for that. I would rather not know why he hated me than have to talk to him about a friendship we had years ago that didn't even matter anymore. It was over. Furthermore, I was sure he wouldn't want to talk to me either, so Gemma's idea was definitely not good. "Whatever. I don't care," I said, which was partly a lie because I did care about the fact that Louis was picking on me, but I didn't care about our friendship.

She tilted her head, raising her eyebrows. "Sure about that, brother? Because only a second ago, you told me Louis was bothering you."

Rolling my eyes, I turned my attention to my now empty plate. "I'll get over it eventually. Plus, I graduate next year so after that, I won't ever have to see his face again." Seriously, I couldn't wait for that to happen. Six months were all that was left.

"If you say so," she said, smiling a little.

I put my plate away and chugged a glass of milk down my system before sitting down in my seat again, facing my older sister. "Enough about me. How was your day?" I asked in need of changing the subject. I didn't want to talk about Louis anymore.

She went on about this guy she'd been crushing on for quite some time now, telling me how great he looked with this tan he'd gained after a week in Spain. Apparently, he'd gotten back yesterday morning. It was quite entertaining to listen to Gemma when she talked about him. She would get these heart-eyes while her voice went an octave higher, almost squealing about the boy. Maybe it was because I was bisexual and didn't mind talking about hot guys, but who knows? It could also be because I liked hanging out with my sister.

However, after fifteen minutes, we separated. I went up to my room and she went into hers. Mine was located on the second floor, next to a bathroom that I had all to myself because my room was the only bedroom on the second floor, apart from the guestroom that was located on the other side of the bathroom. The restroom was even connected with the two bedrooms, so I didn't even have to exit my room to go to the toilet.

Once I had shut the door behind me, I flopped down on my bed and fished my phone out of the pocket of my black jeans. Surprisingly, I had received a message from Liam. It shocked me because I hadn't heard it, and I never turned off the sound on my phone since I never brought it to class, so this was rather odd.

Opening the message, I read it over carefully. It turned out he had forgotten his homework at school, and we had an important test tomorrow so he was desperate for me to send a picture of the papers. Chuckling, I walked over to my desk and took a picture of the paper before lying down on the bed again, sending him the image.

After that, I went onto twitter to see if anything new had happened, but nothing interesting seemed to catch my eye until I saw something that made me stop my movements.

@Louis_Tomlinson: Moving to the other side of the city in a week, into a house full of people I don't even know #sucks #notworthit *Retweeted by Ed Sheeran.*

I raised an eyebrow, wondering why he was moving in with someone he didn't know. Was he going to live with foster parents or something? But what about his real parents? Didn't he have any? Shaking my head, I let it slide. It wasn't like I cared anyway, but it wouldn't surprise me if he was going to live with foster parents, because with that attitude of his, his parents probably didn't want him.

Okay, that was pretty rude of me... but it was kind of true.

Putting my phone aside, I ran my hands over my face, suddenly feeling tiredness take over my body. It didn't take more than five minutes until I could feel myself falling into a light sleep, knowing I wouldn't be able to sleep for more than forty minutes since it was only the afternoon, but right then, I didn't care.

"Harry, love, Troy is here, so could you please wake up and come join us at the kitchen table? We've got some important news to tell you." My mum's voice woke me up, making me groan in annoyance.

"Ugh, fine. I'll be down in a minute."

She left my room after that, silently closing the door behind her, but not before reminding me to come down and not fall back asleep again. Well, I had had my forty minutes of sleep now, so it probably wasn't going to happen anyway. I usually had problems falling asleep in the afternoon since it was still bright outside, but today it was easier than it usually was, which was probably due to the rain and clouds that made it quite dark outside.

After rubbing my eyes and fixing my hair so it didn't look too messy, I went down to the kitchen where my mum, her newfound love and Gemma were sitting at the kitchen table, waiting for me. "How nice of you to join us," mum said with a smile when I sat down beside Gemma, opposite her and Troy.

I just flashed her a sleepy smile, nodding my head. "You told me you had news?"

She nodded, glancing at Troy who was flicking his gaze between me and Gemma. "Yeah," he started. "Anne and I have decided that we want to take our relationship to the next level since we've been dating for about three months now and everything feels so great."

I narrowed my eyes suspiciously, wondering what he was on about. Please just tell me they weren't planning on marrying each other yet. I knew for sure that was way too early in their relationship, and I didn't want my mum to fall into the same trap she'd done with my father. They had married too early, and see how that ended up; two kids with two divorced parents.

"Troy and I are moving in together," mum revealed, not being able to hold it back any longer. "We've discussed it for a week now, and we both agree that it's the best thing to do, seeing as we see each other almost every day anyway. So, Troy and his son are moving here next week," she said excitedly, clapping her hands together.

My eyebrows raised at the news because I had to admit I was a little shocked. After what happened with dad, I thought she would be more careful and take it slower with her next partner, but I guess not. Not that I minded. I was happy for her as long as everything worked out the way she wanted it to.

"That's so nice to hear, guys!" Gemma smiled, seeming almost as excited as mum, though I doubted that was possible. "I'm happy for you."

I nodded in agreement. "Me too. As long as you guys think it's a great idea, I'm all in for it. Also, I'm finally going to meet my stepbrother," I said, my lips curling upwards at the realization. I would finally get to know who the mysterious guy was.

"Thank you, guys. It means so much to have your support on this," mum grinned, leaning her head on Troy's shoulder happily.

He wrapped a protective arm around her waist, clearly enjoying mum's proximity. It was then I realized how much they really seemed to like each other. Sure, I had seen them act all coupled up before, but not like this. They practically beamed with happiness and love for one another, and it was definitely a beautiful sight. I loved seeing my mum like this. "Yeah, thank you for being understanding... Um, my son wasn't too happy about it, so it's definitely nice to have you two on our side," Troy said, grimacing a little at the mention of his son.

"Of course," I frowned. Why would we not approve of it? It wasn't like we could do anything about it even if we wanted to anyway, but I mean, who wouldn't be supportive of these two love birds? It wasn't hard to tell they loved each other, and who would want to be in the way of that? Well, apparently Troy's son did.

"When are we finally going to meet him?" Gemma asked, making my mum and soon to be stepdad exchange a look.

"That's a great question, honey. We've wanted you all to meet since we first started dating, but Troy's son hasn't been too keen on it. So, you're probably not going to meet until they move in here on Monday," she said, pouting a little.

Judging from everything I had heard about this kid, he didn't seem sweet at all. To be honest, he seemed like an asshole who didn't give a fuck about anything, and I didn't quite like that. Sure, I couldn't do anything about it, but I had actually hoped for something better. I mean, Troy was so nice, so I couldn't even imagine his son being anything else. It seemed like I was wrong, though.

"Oh," Gemma grimaced, probably thinking the same thing as me.

We all stayed in the kitchen to talk about all plans we had for the future. For instance, where Troy's son was going to sleep once they moved in. Not once did I question the fact that they never mentioned his name - the only thing they kept referring him to was 'Troy's son' - and maybe that was because I never really acknowledged it.

That wasn't even the only thing I didn't acknowledge. I didn't even think of the coincidence that Louis was moving in with someone he hadn't met before and that the stepbrother I had never laid eyes on was going to move into my house. Maybe that was because I was so certain that Louis wasn't Troy's son. However, it turned out I was wrong yet again.

Chapter 3

[Louis]

"Louis, don't forget to make sure you've packed all your things. We're leaving at four in the afternoon, when school and work are finished, alright?" My dad reminded me when I was just about to exit the apartment and go down to the bus stop.

I didn't want to answer him because I honestly couldn't care less about this stupid move, but I didn't want to be rude to my dad either. He was the only one I had after all. "Okay," I muttered before closing the door behind me, jogging down the street to the bus stop that was around the corner.

The place was crowded with people once I got there, which wasn't exactly unusual. I lived in the center of Holmes Chapel, where almost everybody hopped on the bus that took us to the only high school around here. The place was practically bound to be crowded, although it didn't go more than a few hundred people to the school.

What was sad, though, was that none of my closest friends lived around here. They lived on the other side of the city, also the side I was going to move to today. That was honestly the only good thing about moving there. I was going to be closer to where my friends lived. Other than that, there was no good thing about it. At all.

"Oi, Louis!" Someone hollered when I was just about to come to a halt. I turned my gaze up to see Ed standing a few yards from me, a smile on his face. He was a guy on the football team who simply got along with everyone. I seriously didn't know anyone who had something against him. He was just that guy everybody liked, including me.

"Hey, mate," I greeted, plastering a smile on in return.

He stuffed his hands in his pockets, probably to shield them from the cold outside. "I wanted to ask you when practice starts today since we switched times last week and all."

"Oh," I grimaced. "It's at four, but I'm not coming today. Unfortunately, I'm moving to this house across town in the afternoon..." I trailed off.

His eyes widened as if realizing something. "Right! I read your tweet last week. Man, I feel sorry for you. I wouldn't want to move to a family I haven't met before either," Ed said sympathetically, patting my shoulder.

"Yeah, it kind of sucks. However, I'm eighteen in about a year, so I don't have to stay there for long before I can move to my own flat or attend University or whatever," I shrugged. Really, I was just trying to point out the 'not so bad' things about the move, but I doubted I sounded convincing. I literally hated it with every fiber of my body. I didn't want to live in a house full of people I didn't know. Why couldn't they move to our apartment instead? I mean, then I wouldn't have to leave everything behind. Though, I didn't really like the thought of having a new step brother and sister, nor a mother for that matter. I liked it the way it was right now, with only me and my dad.

Ed gave me a small smile. "Well, I hope it turns out well for ya, mate," he said before walking back to his other friends. "And thanks for telling me what time practice is."

I just gave him a nod in return and let out a sigh. Running a hand through my fringe, I looked up to see the bus turning the corner at the end of the street, moving in our direction. The moment it stopped in front of us, I hopped on and started walking along the bus, fist bumping with the people I recognized from school before sitting down next to my girlfriend in the back. "Hi, love," I greeted, leaning in to kiss her on the cheek.

Eleanor beamed at my touch, leaning her head against my shoulder as she took my hand in hers, threading our fingers together. "Hey. So, you're moving today, huh?" She hummed, her smile turning into a pout instead.

"Unfortunately, yeah. This will be the last time we're riding the same bus together, except for the times we're sleeping over at each other's places, that is," I told her, not wanting to meet her gaze. It was actually really sad because I enjoyed meeting Eleanor in the mornings and just have a long talk with her until we hopped off the bus at school. It was our daily routine, something I had grown used to, so it was nothing but sad to see it coming to an end.

"I'm going to miss it," she mumbled, as though she had read my mind.

"Me too."

For the rest of the ride, we stayed silent, enjoying our last bus ride together and just each other's presence, something we seemed to do quite often. Niall and Zayn had even pointed it out a few times, telling us how weird it was that we could sit in silence without it being awkward. The thing was, things were never awkward with Eleanor.

We departed with a kiss once we arrived at school, and I went to my locker to get rid of my jacket. On my way there, I stopped to have small conversations with students who claimed they knew me, although I probably only knew who half of them were. That was just typical for me, though. People always wanted to go around and brag about the fact that I knew them. Not that I complained. I liked the attention quite a lot actually. There were definitely no bad things about having people appreciating you like that.

I was just about to reach my hand out to put in my combination when I heard a familiar voice across the hallway, speaking to whom I presumed was his friend, Liam. "Yeah, they're coming today at four. Really looking forward to it actually, although the guy seems like an asshole."

Raising an eyebrow at his words, I shoved my jacket into my locker before slamming it shut. I started making my way through the hallway, purposefully bumping my shoulder into Harry's when I passed him. "Watch where you're going, loser," I muttered under my breath, sending him a glare.

He stumbled a little by the push but managed to catch himself before falling. "Speak for yourself," he snapped back once he noticed who it was.

Without thinking twice, I pushed him against the wall of lockers, trapping his body between it and myself. "Maybe you should shut that pretty little mouth of yours, huh?" I taunted, raising my eyebrows as if waiting for an answer.

He merely narrowed his eyes, clenching his jaw together. "Maybe you should just stop picking on me, seeing as it's to no avail anyway?" He tried to push me off of him, but I tightened the grip on the lockers behind his head so he couldn't move me anywhere.

"How about no?"

"How about you let me go so I can get to first class?" He fumed, pressing his books tighter against his chest as if to refrain some of his anger.

Rolling my eyes, I leaned in so close that my lips were brushing against the curls by his ear. "That won't be necessary because I'm out of here anyway," I whispered in his ear before departing from him, turning on my heel to walk away without looking back at him.

That annoying son of a bitch. I fucking hated him. He was the only one at our school who even dared stand up to me. Not that I usually picked on people, but if it were to happen, I was sure no one would have the guts to defend themselves, which was probably because most of the people here looked up to me and kind of feared me, in a good way.

Harry was an exception though, and I guess that was because of our past or whatever. However, he was still annoying, and I hated him for trying to look cool and impress people by defending himself. Of course I hated him for other stuff too, but that wasn't very important. Him trying to act cool was what bugged me the most nowadays.

The minute I stepped into Math class, the bell rang. I walked over to Niall who was sitting alone at a desk, his attention focused on his phone in his hands. Plopping down in the seat next to him, I put my hands over my face, already wanting the lesson to be over. "Hey, mate," I mumbled, slowly but surely getting his attention.

"Louis," he smiled before turning his eyes back to the screen.

Raising an eyebrow, I leaned over to get a view of what he was doing. Apparently, he was texting someone, and I assumed this someone was a hot girl, otherwise he wouldn't have ignored me like he just did. "Getting some, eh?" I asked, nudging him in the side teasingly.

"Shut up, Lou. And I don't know, to be honest. I've been texting this girl for a while now, but every time I try to hint at something, she acts like nothing. She's so oblivious it's freaking creepy, I swear," he said, shaking his head with a dry laughter.

"Don't worry about that, mate. Before you know it, she'll be on her knees, begging for you to fuck her."

Niall rolled his eyes. "We'll see," he chuckled.

Before I could open my mouth to say something else, Mr. Storm opened his annoying mouth and cut everyone off. Just his voice made my eyelids go heavy, so it didn't take more than a few minutes until I could feel myself zoning out, thinking about other things like football and girls or whatever was more interesting than Maths, which were quite a few stuff, to be honest.

"Mr. Tomlinson?"

Feeling someone wave a hand in front of my eyes, I snapped my head up to meet Mr. Storm's brown, stern eyes. "Excuse me, what?"

"I see you weren't listening like usual, Mr. Tomlinson," he hissed, glaring at me.

"Of course not. Why should I listen to something I know won't be useful in the future anyways? You know people don't need Maths once they've graduated, right? I mean, not all of us are going to become successful scientists, doctors, architects or whatever, you know? And I certainly won't, if you haven't figured that out yet," I winked, earning a few 'ooh's from students in the classroom.

Mr. Storm's face went pale as he gritted his teeth together. "I don't want to hear a single word from you throughout the rest of the lesson, is that understood?" He snapped, pointing a finger in my direction.

Raising my hands, I sent him a smile. "Believe me, that won't be a problem."

Zayn, who was sitting at the desk in front of me and Niall turned around to give me a high five. Feeling rather proud of myself, I gazed around the classroom to see the other people's reactions to what I had just said. Most of them were smiling encouragingly, but one of them stood out from the rest, and of course that someone was Harry Styles. Instead of smiling, he was glaring at me as if what I had just said pissed him off.

Well, too bad I didn't care about his stupid opinion anyway.

I was standing in the doorway of my room, looking at the emptiness that remained of it. There were no furniture left, just a shell with the same dark blue walls I'd had since I was five. My bed was in the moving truck that dad had driven to Anne's place in the morning to get everything fixed until we arrived in the afternoon, along with all my other stuff.

It was a rather emotional moment for me because this was the room my mum would always wish me goodnight in at nights when she was still around, and also the room she had once organized along with my dad.

Taking a deep breath, I forced the tears back and smiled weakly at the sight of my empty room. This was probably for the best though. Dad was happy, and that was all that mattered, right? What I felt about all this didn't really matter to anyone. I was just the son that dad would bring along, who didn't really have a say in anything.

I observed the room one last time before walking to the hallway where dad was waiting for me with his suitcase in hand. "You ready, son?" He asked sweetly, knowing this was hard for me, but he didn't know just how hard it really was. I had always been pretty good at hiding my true feelings, and I assumed this was no exception.

"Yeah, I guess," I muttered, walking past him, out of the apartment that I would never see again, ever. "I'll be in the car."

Dad nodded and walked into the flat to check so everything was as it was supposed to one last time, while I walked down to the vehicle and slammed the car door shut behind me before fastening my seatbelt. I then plugged my earbuds into my iPhone and turned on my Spotify list to block the world out.

A few minutes later, dad joined me in the car and put the key in the ignition. "Lou?" I could see him say by the way his lips were moving.

I pulled out a bud of my ear and turned to him. "Yeah?"

"Everything will be alright, okay? I'm sure you're going to feel at home at Anne's place in no time. The house is really great, and I know you'll get on with her kids. Obviously it's going to be tough at first, but I'm sure you're going to make it, right?" He smiled encouragingly.

Despite the fact that I didn't agree with any of that, I nodded my head. I didn't want to disappoint him or make him feel bad for doing this. He was my dad after all, and although I didn't always agree with his decisions and could snap at him at times, I felt like it would really break him if I didn't even try my best to make all this work. Presumably, he deserved this chance with Anne after everything that had happened in our family.

"Thank you, Louis." He placed his hand on my thigh, giving it a few taps before retrieving it again.

During the rest of the car ride, I listened to music without uttering a single word to him. I mean, even though I wanted him to be happy, I still wanted him to know that I wasn't very fond of this decision. I didn't want to move in with this family, and I wanted to show him that somehow.

"Lou, we're here. You coming inside to meet your new family?" He asked once he'd parked the car in what I assumed was the driveway of Anne's house.

The place was quite huge, to be honest. It was bigger than my dad and I's old apartment, probably multiplied by at least five. The house was white with grey frames and doors, and you could see from even in here that the place had two floors and a large garden. "Yeah, I'm just going to have a quick smoke, alright?"

Dad scowled at my words, but in the end just clenched his jaw together and gave me a curt nod. "Make it real quick if it's so necessary. They have all been dying to meet you," he muttered, opening his door to get out of the car.

Once he shut it behind him, I was left in silent, something I had longed for ever since he joined me in here. Pulling my earbuds out of my ears, I exited the car as well and walked over to the porch before pulling out my cigarette packet from my jacket pocket along with my lighter.

I had been a smoker for about a year now, something I wasn't exactly proud of. I always told myself I would never try it out seeing as it was really bad for your body and you could die from it. Yet here I was, seventeen years old and addicted. If it weren't for Zayn though, I probably wouldn't have even tried it out. He was the one who had urged me to do it at one of the many parties we'd been to, and eventually I couldn't refrain myself. However, I knew it was wrong to blame it all on him because it was my own decision after all. He had just been there to push me to do it.

Taking one last drag of the cigarette, I dropped it to the ground and stomped on it before opening the front door and stepping into the foreign house. The first thing I was met with was the smell of a freshly cleaned home. It was so strong it almost made my nostrils tingling. The next thing I was met with was a rather high-pitched voice I had been getting quite used to hearing lately.

"Louis, I'm so happy you are finally here!" My so-called step mum entered the entryway where I was standing, my hands stuffed in my jeans pockets. Before I could process what was happening, I was engulfed in a tight hug, her arms wrapped around my torso. "Oh, don't tell me you just had a smoke, young man. That kind of stuff is bad for you. Haven't your dad taught you better?" She scolded as she pulled away, scrunching her nose up a little at the smell.

I bit the inside of my cheek. "Uh, no? He doesn't really mind," I muttered awkwardly. Maybe having a smoke before entering my new home wasn't the best idea I had ever come up with...

"Oh well, we'll talk about this later. Now, my two kids are so excited to meet you. They're waiting in the kitchen along with your father," she told me, giving me a small smile.

Nodding, I took my jacket off and slipped off my shoes. Then, against my will, I followed Anne to the kitchen only to be met with a sight I could never have guessed I would see. There, at the kitchen table, my dad was sitting opposite a brown haired girl who looked just like the woman behind me but a few years younger, and beside her was none other than the person I hated most in the entire world sitting.

    I let out a loud gasp, and he did too once he caught sight of me standing in the doorframe.

    "Louis?"

    "Harry?"

Chapter 4

[Harry]

I couldn't believe my eyes. There was no way Louis Tomlinson out of all people was standing in the doorframe of my own kitchen right in front of my mother, his hands stuffed in his pockets. It didn't even look right. He was just not supposed to be there.

So this meant he was my new stepbrother? Seriously, what had I ever done to deserve this? All I wanted was someone I would get along with, not the one person who hated me the most in this entire world.

"What the hell?" Louis hissed, and I could see from the corner of my eye how he clenched his jaw together in anger.

"You guys know each other?" My mum asked in confusion, glancing back and forth between me and Louis.

I didn't even spare him another glance when I mocked. "Well, if you count him picking on me and making my life a living hell, then sure, we definitely know each other." I rolled my eyes, looking anywhere but him.

"Is this true, Louis?" Troy asked disappointedly.

Louis was biting his bottom lip, looking as innocent as ever even though we both knew he was as far from innocent as one could possibly come. He was acting like he hadn't just shouldered me this morning in the hallway and then pushed me against the wall of lockers. What a fucking pussy. "No. I don't know what he's talking about. I have never laid a finger on him. The only reason we know each other is because we were paired up for a project once. Other than that, I have never interacted with him."

Yeah, right, as if they were going to believe that. Why would we have greeted each other the way we did if we had only hung out for a project before? And with such anger? Not to be mean, but they would be idiots if they believed him.

"I'm sorry, my son, but I can't see a reason for Harry to lie about something this serious. Besides, it doesn't really make sense because you practically just hissed out his name," Troy said slowly, probably not wanting to upset Louis since he obviously knew about his temper.

"So you believe him and not me? Wow, thanks a lot, dad. I will remember that for sure. Good to know I have you on my side," he said sarcastically, rolling his eyes.

My mum stepped out from the spot behind Louis and walked over to place her hands on Troy's shoulders from behind, making Louis grimace for a second. "Come on, guys. This was supposed to be a fun meeting, not an opportunity for you all to start arguments. So, how about we stop fighting and make dinner instead?" She suggested, raising an eyebrow.

I glanced at Gemma who seemed deep in thought where she was sitting on her chair, a frown evident on her face. I had no idea what she was thinking about, but it wouldn't surprise me if it was about me and Louis and everything I had ever told her about him. She didn't even seem to notice that mum had suggested something.

Louis, on the other hand, seemed to think that mum's idea was not a very good one, more like the worst he'd ever heard. And, to be honest, I actually agreed with him on this. We would surely not be able to cook dinner together. That would definitely not end well. "No fucking way, I'm out of here. Where's my new room, anyways?"

Mum pouted, obviously not pleased with Louis' answer nor the tone he was using. She was that kind of mother who wanted her kids to have great manners, and not ones who had a terrible vocabulary and bad behavior. It wasn't hard to tell Louis wasn't quite keeping up to her desires by the looks of it. "First door on the right on the second floor," she mumbled, and Louis was out like a light, sending me a cold look on his way.

Troy let out a sigh, putting his hand over his face. "I'm so sorry about him, that's just his way of handling things. He'd rather run away from his problems than have to face them for too long. Hopefully, he'll warm up to all this new stuff soon, though."

Mum patted his shoulder reassuringly. "Don't worry about it, darling. I'm sure he's going to be okay."

"Yeah, right," I muttered under my breath, causing her to send me a warning look, which I just brushed off.

Troy and mum started making dinner together after that while Gemma stood up and grabbed my arm, pulling me aside. "Can I have a word with you?" She asked, looking at me expectantly.

"Sure," I said, taking her with me to the living room so we could be alone and not bothered by the two adults. "What did you want to talk about?" I asked, sitting down on the beige leather couch.

She sat down beside me, letting out a deep breath. "The Louis you were friends with two years ago is the same Louis as this one, right?"

I nodded slowly. "Yeah," I said as if this was the first time it really dawned on me that Louis Tomlinson was actually my stepbrother now. We would have to live under the same roof for at least a few months, until I turned eighteen. But I knew myself, and I was quite sure I wouldn't be too willing to leave my mother that soon. It wouldn't surprise me if I stayed another year or so even if Louis still lived here.

"How do you feel about that? I mean, you aren't on such good terms now, right?" She grimaced, remembering what I said just last week when I had come home from school and complained about him picking on me all the time, and also just a few minutes ago when she witnessed it in real life.

Shaking my head, I let out a sigh. "I haven't even processed it fully yet. It's quite hard to get your head around the fact that he's going to live here since I pictured my new stepbrother being a completely different person. I definitely don't like it, that's for sure. I'm not even sure how I'm going to be able to live with it. What if it'll get even worse now?"

She gave me a small smile. "Don't think like that, H. Besides, I'm going to be around here all the time, yeah? If you can't handle it, I'm going to make sure he doesn't do anything, alright?"

Flashing her an appreciating smile, I shook my head. "I'm sure I'll be fine. I haven't had any trouble with it before. It still just pains me sometimes that he could turn his back on me like that when we were such good friends. I don't even know what happened. All of a sudden he just downright hated me," I sighed, running a hand through my curls.

"Maybe he had a reason, though? I don't know, I'm just trying to see it out of his perspective. I mean, people usually do have a reason for their actions," she suggested, shrugging her shoulders.

I hated it when she had a point in what she said. What if Louis actually did have a reason for doing what he did to me? But if so, what had I done? I couldn't remember anything I did wrong. He was the one who had stopped attending our meetings, not the other way around. "I don't know, Gem. It will forever be a mystery to me," I sighed, giving up on ever finding out the real reason already. It wasn't like Louis would start talking to me and explaining things even if we were somewhat stepbrothers now. I was sure it wouldn't change a thing.

"I have said it before, and I'm going to say it again. Whenever you find the right opportunity, just take the chance and talk to him, okay? I know he might not want to, but we both know that's the only way you guys are ever going to get on good terms again."

"But that's the thing, Gemma! I don't even want to be on good terms with him. I hate him just as much as he hates me, and I'm fine with that. Sure, we might have to live under the same roof for a couple of months, but then I will be gone and we hopefully won't ever have to face each other again," I said, raising my voice an octave.

"Well," she muttered, rolling her eyes. "Then I don't know what to say. I wish you luck, though, brother, because you'll certainly need it. Just remember that you can always come to me if you ever want to talk about it, okay? I know pretty much everything that's happened between the two of you, so I'm sure I could help you out with whatever is bothering you."

A smile broke out on my face as I leaned in to give her a quick hug. "Thank you, Gem."

Right then, mum's voice was heard throughout the entire house. "Dinner's ready, guys!"

Not even thinking twice, Gemma and I got up and walked into the kitchen where Troy was sitting at the kitchen table while mum was just about to place a pot of spaghetti on it. Everything was set, so it was just for the two of us to sit down in two empty seats, waiting for everyone to join. Or, more like one particular person.

Louis hadn't arrived yet, which wasn't a surprise considering the way he left earlier. However, I was sure my mum wouldn't let any of us start eating without everybody being here, which unfortunately included him. "Try getting along with him, Harry, please?" Mum pleaded when she sat down in front of me, pouting her lips a little.

I furrowed my eyebrows together. "Why do I have to do anything? He's always the one to make the first move. If anything, tell him to try getting along with me."

She was just about to open her mouth when a brown-haired boy appeared in the doorway, looking rather sleepy if you asked me. His hair stood in all directions and his eyes were droopy, looking as though they would close any second. The fact that he just rubbed them only added to my assumptions. "How nice of you to join us, Louis," mum smiled, probably happy that she didn't have to call twice to get him to come down.

He merely nodded and walked over to sit down in the seat next to his dad, rolling his eyes when he caught me following his movements. "Can't take your eyes off of me, eh?"

I glared at him as I gave him the middle finger. "Stop flattering yourself, Tomlinson. You're not as hot as you think you are."

He raised his eyebrows. "Oh really? Because last time I checked the majority of high school thought otherwise. I don't think they would agree with you," he winked, smiling smugly.

I flashed him a death glare, causing mum to give me a warning look. "Harry, what did I just tell you?" she scolded, smacking me on the arm lightly.

Rolling my eyes, I watched Troy scold Louis as well, telling him to calm down and not to mind me. Louis' reaction was to mutter something inaudible, and really, the whole situation was just weird. The two parents were acting like we were two three-year-olds who couldn't take care of ourselves, which we definitely did, for your information. Well, at least I did. We just didn't enjoy each other's presence, that was all.

Dinner was uncomfortably silent that afternoon. Mum and Troy were the only ones who were talking, but even they seemed affected by the silence between us children. Gemma tried to make a conversation with me and bring Louis into it, but he was being annoying and didn't even lift his gaze to lock eyes with any of us. In the end, she just gave up and tried to join mum and Troy's conversation instead, leaving me and Louis to stare at our plates.

When we were finished, mum pointed out something that I hadn't thought of yet, and the realization hit me straight in the face. "Guys, you're sharing the top floor together, and therefore you also have the same bathroom. If I hear you arguing, I will not hesitate to ground you for the rest of the month. Both of you. No friends or parties. Is that understood?"

Louis went to disagree, but Troy stomped him on the foot under the table, causing him to shut up. I, on the other hand, nodded quietly even though I wanted to disagree as badly as he did. Why did we have to share the same freaking bathroom? Wasn't it enough that we lived in the same house?!

"Great. You're free to go now. See you all in the morning."

Gemma, Louis and I stood up, dropping our plates and glasses off in the sink on our way out of the kitchen. While Gemma and I said goodnight to each other, Louis went up to his room, slamming the door shut behind him.

"This was definitely not what I expected to happen today," Gemma said, nodding in the direction of Louis' bedroom.

"Me neither, even though Troy kind of described him as an asshole. I never expected it to be Louis out of all people. That definitely came as a shock to me," I sighed, running a hand through my messy hair.

She shrugged. "Well, we'll just have to accept it, I guess. It's not like there's anything we can do about it. Though, I gotta admit that he isn't my favorite person in the world judging by what I've witnessed today. He's quite grumpy, isn't he?" She chuckled, trying to lighten the mood a little.

I laughed, shaking my head. "Tell me about it."

Eventually, we departed to get to our separate rooms. It was only about eight in the evening, but I was feeling tired after everything that had taken place today. Besides, I needed to study for a test that was due Thursday, so going up to my room this early felt like a good idea. Or so I thought.

The first thing I was met with when I entered my room was the obnoxious noise of what some people called music roaring through the walls. Quickly losing my temper, I made my way into the bathroom, thanking whoever constructed it for not putting any locks on the doors when I turned the handle and poked my head into Louis' room. "What the hell?!" I shouted.

He was lying on his bed, phone in hand as he bobbed his head to the loud music. He didn't even acknowledge my presence, he was so caught up in his own business. "Louis!" I barked, stomping my foot angrily to gain his attention.

When he finally looked up to meet my gaze, his face darkened immediately. He picked up a small remote from the nightstand and turned the volume down on his speaker. "What the hell are you doing here?" He snapped. "This is my room, you have your own. Get the fuck out of here."

"Some people care about school and need to study, so would you kindly just turn the fucking volume down? What kind of music is even that? It's burning holes in my ears!"

Rolling his eyes, he sat up on the bed. "It's called rock. Haven't you heard of it before? It's like the oldest genre of all time," he said sarcastically, making me want to go over there and hit him.

"Of course I know what it is, idiot. I'm not stupid, unlike someone else," I said monotonously, and I could see him clench his fists together where they were placed on his lap.

"Whatever," he sneered. "I'll turn the volume down if you promise not to take a step into my room ever again. Deal?"

I nodded, flashing him a fake smile. "Deal."

With that, I retrieved to my room and sat down at my desk, instantly opening my Maths books to start studying. The funny thing (which really wasn't that funny) was that Louis also had a test on Thursday since we had all our classes together. Yet he acted as though he couldn't care less about it. I guess my tutoring sessions with him two years ago didn't help one bit. He didn't give two shits about school. To be honest, it had even gotten worse. At least he cared back then and wanted to bring his grades up, unlike now when he didn't even try to pass his classes for some reason I didn't know. Something definitely must've happened, and I would kill to know what.

That night I fell asleep with a frown on my face, thinking of what had happened during the day. It turned out that my anonymous stepbrother was none other than Louis, my enemy at school, which was really hard to believe. I would have to live with him until one of us moved out, and who knew how long that would be? But the worst thing was that I would never get away from it. Whenever we were going to have family meetings in the future, we would have to see each other, and my children would even be able to call him their uncle.

It was then I realized that I was stuck with Louis Tomlinson for the rest of my life.

Chapter 5

[Harry]

"That was all for today, class. See you again tomorrow."

I shut my books and got up from my chair to make my way out of the classroom quickly, wanting to get home as soon as possible. Before I had even turned the first corner to my locker, I felt someone tug at my arm from behind, pulling me back. I turned around to face the person, furrowing my eyebrows because who in the world would want to talk to me?

My eyes widened at the sight of Louis Tomlinson, the most popular guy at school, standing there, his hands in his pockets, and a sheepish smile on his lips. He was looking at his surroundings every now and then as if he was worried someone might catch sight of him. "Come on," he said, pulling me by the arm into the janitor's closet across the hallway before anyone could see us together.

Once he had closed the door behind us, he turned to me again, giving me a small smile. "Hi."

"Uh, hi?" I said, feeling confused as to why he out of all people would want to talk to me. None of the popular kids had ever even acknowledged me before. I bet they didn't even know who I was... or maybe they did, considering Louis was standing in front of me right now?

"Harry, isn't it?"

I nodded slowly. "Yeah. Why are you talking to me? Or more specifically, why did you just pull me into the janitor's closet? Have I done something to you?"

He shook his head. "No, of course not. I wanted to talk to you about uh..." He trailed off, biting his bottom lip hesitantly.

"About what?"

He took a deep breath. "You're smart, right?"

Shrugging, I sent him a confused look. "I've got straight A's, if that answers your question. However, it doesn't answer mine. Why are you talking to me? How do you even know who I am?"

It didn't make sense to me at all. Louis was that kind of guy who would rather die than talk to a nerd like me, so how come he was standing right in front of me and actually being nice? Sure, no one could see us, but that was only expected. The fact that he was nice, however, was what really caught me off guard. Louis Tomlinson kind to a nerd? No, I don't think so.

"Harry, we have all our classes together if you didn't already know that. That's how I know who you are. Anyway, I wanted to ask you if you could maybe help me out with something, please?" He said, pouting his lips in an adorable way. He looked like an innocent puppy, and I could tell people had a hard time saying no to that face.

"What do you want my help for? If you're here to ask me if I can do your homework, then the answer is no. I don't do anyone's homework but my own. It doesn't matter who it is, a friend or a popular guy like you. I never accept those kinds of offers," I said firmly, crossing my arms over my chest.

He let out a chuckle, leaning back a little. "You've got an attitude, I like it. But no, I don't want you to do my homework for me. Actually, I would like you to tutor me. I am failing in almost all of my classes and I could really use some help seeing as the teachers don't have time to help all of us. Would you please do that for me?"

Raising my eyebrows in shock, I opened my mouth, but nothing seemed to come out. He wanted my help to tutor him? But why me out of all people? I was sure he had some smart friends who he would rather choose to ask than a loser like myself. There had to be some kind of catch, or maybe it was all simply a dare or something. "If this is a dare, I swear I--"

"No, Harry. No dares or bets, I promise. This is all coming from me. I want to improve in school because my parents have started noticing how low my grades are and they want me to do well and I just can't disappoint them. So please, help me out?" He pleaded, sticking out his bottom lip for more effect.

I rolled my eyes and let out a sigh. "Sure, fine. Is there a catch though? I would like to know that before I agree with anything else. Furthermore, I would like to get some kind of reward for this."

He grimaced as he nodded his head. "Yes, of course. Whatever makes you do it is fine by me. We'll negotiate about the reward after our first meeting. And yeah, there kind of is a catch actually. You can't tell anyone about this because I wouldn't want anyone to know--" He started saying, but I cut him off.

"To know that you're spending time with me, I get it. You also don't want anyone to know that you need help with your

schoolwork. Don't worry, I won't tell anyone," I said, giving him a small smile.

He breathed out a sigh of relief. "Really? You would actually do that for me? I mean, we would have to hide from the other kids and probably have to have our meetings in the library or something, after school."

I shrugged. "Nothing I haven't done before. I usually spend time in the library after school, you know?" I chuckled, making him grimace.

"Yeah, forgot you are..." he trailed off, furrowing his eyebrows.

"That I am what?"

"Nothing. I gotta go. See you tomorrow after school?"

I nodded slowly. "Yeah, sure."

"Goodbye, Harry."

"Bye, Louis."

I woke up by the sound of my alarm clock going off, making me let out a loud groan. The dream was still very clear in my mind, and I was aware that it wasn't just a simple dream, but a memory. A memory of the first conversation Louis and I had.

You might think that he actually wasn't that bad back then, and the truth was, he *wasn't* that bad either. Sure, I didn't like him, but that was because he acted like a whole other person around his friends than it turned out he did when it was only the two of us. Before that meeting, I had never witnessed the nice side of Louis, so what else could I think of him?

Once I had talked to him for the first time, I thought I had got the opportunity to get to know the real him, but after he stopped showing up at our meetings, I started doubting myself. It felt like that Louis was only a stupid act to get me to help him out or something. No matter what, it didn't feel like that side of him was the real him anymore, and now I was almost sure that assumption was correct.

For some reason, though, I couldn't shake the memory of him being so kind to me out of my mind. There was something about the way he had acted back then that made me think that it was actually real, that it wasn't some stupid act he had come up with. Maybe it was because of the way his eyes would crinkle when I used to pull my stupid jokes or the way his high-pitched laughter would make my stomach do somersaults. Either way, it had actually felt real, and no matter how much I wanted to forget about it, I couldn't. It was like an annoying, nagging headache that you couldn't get rid of.

Letting out another groan (this time not from tiredness), I sat up and tried rubbing the sleep out of my eyes. It was only seven in the morning, yet my brain was working at high speed. It was definitely not smart to start the day by thinking about Louis. He was like a puzzle that was impossible to solve, and just the thought of him made my head hurt. The fact that I would have to face him in mere minutes didn't exactly make matters better.

Finally crawling out of bed, I made my way over to my mirror to take a quick look at myself. My curly hair was standing in all directions, looking as though it hadn't been washed in weeks, and my eyes were still half-open after my sleep. Sighing heavily, I decided I would have to take a quick shower before going down to join the rest of the family in the kitchen.

I walked over to the bathroom door and opened it. My gaze was turned to the floor and I had no perception of my surroundings, so when I looked up and saw a bare back in front of me, I almost fell backwards to the floor in shock. "What the fuck?" I gasped, staring at the boy who was standing at the toilet in only his boxers, taking a piss.

Louis turned his head to me, his mouth hanging open due to shock as well, I presumed. "I should be the one saying that. What the hell are you doing here? Are you seriously that desperate to see my flawless body?" He scoffed, flushing the toilet and adjusting his boxers a little.

Rolling my eyes, I leaned against the door frame. "You wish, Tomlinson. Now, would you *please* get out of here so I can have my well-needed shower?" I urged, putting emphasis on the word 'please'.

"Whatever," he muttered before exiting the bathroom to go into his bedroom.

The first thing I did once I was sure he wouldn't return was to strip out of my pajama pants and t-shirt along with my boxers. I then turned on the water, waiting a little while to get in since the hot water didn't come on right away.

A few minutes later, I finished and got out before hurriedly wrapping a towel around my waist. If Louis decided to come in here again, I didn't want to take any risks by standing here stark naked. Therefore, I also grabbed another towel to dry my hair quickly before returning to my bedroom. At least I felt safer in there since I knew he wouldn't come into my room willingly.

I dropped the towel to the floor and walked over to my closet completely naked. After a short while of contemplating, I decided to put on a pair of black, skinny jeans and a white, plain t-shirt. I wasn't much for dressing up myself (I liked to keep it simple), so I usually wore a pair of jeans and a simple t-shirt to school, or just daily. It wasn't like anybody cared anyway.

Once I was dressed and had run a hand through my wet curls to not make them stand in different directions, I went downstairs to where my family was sitting at the kitchen table. Even Louis had decided to get there on time, unlike yesterday when he had arrived at least five minutes late.

"Good morning, honey," mum greeted when I sat down in the seat next to Gemma.

"Morning," I smiled, avoiding the glare Louis was giving me from across the table. No one else seemed to notice it, which even I was happy about since I didn't want a replay of what happened yesterday. Therefore, I decided not to care about him at all.

Pouring cereal and some milk in my bowl, I picked up my spoon and started chewing on the food. "Harry, could you show Louis where the bus stop is today since he doesn't know that yet?" Mum asked, looking at me expectantly.

I furrowed my eyebrows. "Why can't Gemma do it? She knows where it is too," I muttered, staring at the surface of the table.

"Because I asked you to do it. Besides, a bird told me the two of you have all your classes together, so you even start school at the same time," she said firmly, clearly not pleased with my behavior.

Looking over at Louis, I saw him staring at the milk package before himself, trying his best to stay out of the conversation we were having even though what we were talking about concerned him. Troy, who was sitting beside him, had a proud smile on his face because of this, most likely not wanting a fight to unfold like it did yesterday.

I then flicked my gaze to Gemma whose face showed guilt. I knew she was this 'bird' mum was talking about because I was sure neither of Troy or Louis had told her that. To say I was mad at her would be an understatement. I thought I could trust her with these kinds of things, but no, she had gone to mum and immediately told her stuff about me and Louis. I just hoped she hadn't told her anything else.

"Fine," I muttered under my breath. "I'll show him the damn bus stop if it's so fucking necessary."

Mum slammed her fist in the kitchen table, startling all of us except for me. "Harry Edward Styles, I do not accept you using that tone on me, let alone your swearing. If you don't start behaving right now, I'll suggest you go up to your room and stay there until you have to leave for school. Is that understood?" She snapped, making me flinch.

I nodded my head slowly, not making eye contact with her. "Good."

From the other side of the table, I could hear Louis sniggering quietly, and I swear, I had never wanted to hit him as much as I wanted right then. Anger boiled up inside me, and I had to clench my hands around the side of the table to restrain myself from lunging at him. "Shut. Up," I seethed, staring at him.

He looked up at me and noticed that I was fuming, which of course only made him laugh even harder. Troy shot him a warning look, which eventually caused his laughter to slowly die down. "If the two of you are going to continue acting like this towards each other, I'm going to make you sit down and talk whatever your issue is out. And if that doesn't work, I will get both of you a job or something so you have no other choice but communicate with each other," Troy hissed, flicking his gaze between me and Louis.

Mum nodded in agreement, crossing her arms over her chest. Neither of Louis and I responded to Troy's threat, but I was sure the both of us got the point. Though, I knew it would be hard to follow his orders because Louis and I couldn't act otherwise towards each other, but I guess we just had to tone it down a little bit.

Once all of us were finished eating breakfast, we separated from each other. I went up to my room, followed by a silent Louis while Gemma went into her own bedroom and the adults to work. I was quite aware of his closeness, but I didn't say anything about it. Instead, I wordlessly made my way into the room and sat down on my bed, running my hands over my face.

Not even two minutes later, I could hear a knock on the door. At first, I thought it was Louis who was here to say something bitchy to me, so when the door opened and Gemma's head was revealed, I let out a sigh of relief. "Can I exchange a word with you before you leave?" She asked sheepishly, entering my room before I had even replied to her question.

She sat down beside me on the bed, giving me a guilty smile. "I'm sorry I told mum that you and Louis share all your classes. I mean, maybe it wasn't something huge, but I told her something I'm sure you didn't appreciate, and I apologize for that. It's just... I want the two of you to get along as much as mum and Troy do. It's hard to witness your hate for each other when I know you could be the best of friends if it weren't for your 'issue'." She ran a hand through her hair in slight frustration. "I mean, you even were kind of best friends once."

Furrowing my eyebrows, I shook my head. "I'm not happy about what you did, but I guess they were bound to find out about it eventually anyway. As long as you promise not to tell her or Troy something else, I'll let it slip. But, you can't just tell them things just because you want them to help me and Louis get along, it doesn't work that way. Neither mum nor Troy can fix mine and Louis' relationship," I told her, leaning back against the headboard with my arms crossed over my chest.

She sighed as she nodded her head. "I know, but I feel as though you need something or someone to push you to get on the right track. That's why I told mum about you two sharing classes, so she could tell you to show Louis the bus stop... I'm sorry," she added when she saw my angry expression.

"Honestly, I can't believe you actually wanted to put me in that situation. Do you know how fucking awkward it's going to be, walking with him for at least ten minutes? And if it won't be awkward, it will surely be unpleasant, and you know it. A single walk is not going to fix our stupid relationship, Gemma."

She pulled at her lip with her thumb and index finger, a crease evident between her eyebrows. "Well, maybe it wasn't the greatest idea I've come up with, but it was at least something. We all really want the two of you to get along, so when I told mum and Troy about the idea, they instantly agreed. Troy was the one who came up with the work thing, though," she muttered, glancing at me from the corner of her eye.

"I don't care about who came up with what, okay? I know mum and Troy are on your side, but it's not going to change anything. Louis and I still won't get along, alright?" I tried to convince her, raising my hands for more effect.

Letting out another sigh, she nodded her head in defeat. "Alright. I'm sorry for caring, Harry. I just want what I think would be the best for you," she mumbled.

"I know," I said, giving her a sad smile. "But I don't think Louis and I going back to being friends would be the best for me."

"And why not?"

"Because we're too different. We don't belong in the same surroundings. I'm sure this was bound to happen to our friendship sometime."

Chapter 6

[Harry]

Gemma left my room only a few minutes later, when both of us could hear Louis trudging down the stairs. She told me to follow her, implying that he shouldn't have to wait for me just because he didn't know where the bus stop was located. I let out a sigh, but reluctantly did what she said.

When I came downstairs, I was met with the sight of Louis standing in the entryway, slipping on his black Vans. Wordlessly, I walked over to him to do the same thing and shrugged on my jacket. "Bye, Gemma. See you after school," I called once Louis and I were ready to go.

"Bye, H!" She called back from her bedroom.

From the corner of my eye, I could see Louis roll his eyes, making me turn to him. "What?"

"Oh, nothing," he said, a smirk playing on his lips. "Just funny how you can't leave without having to say goodbye to your sister."

I shot him a glare, turning the doorknob to exit the house. "Shut up. You don't even know the feeling of having a sibling, so how about you just keep quiet, huh?" I hissed.

He did go silent after that, and a frown slowly made its way to his face. We started walking to the bus stop in uncomfortable silence, and the more time that passed by, the more concerned I got that I had hit a soft spot. Not that I actually cared about him, but it was odd to witness him being so quiet around me. He usually didn't hesitate to make a move to insult me whenever he got the chance to.

After a few minutes, Louis began searching his pockets for something, and the next second he was holding a cigarette between two of his fingers and a lighter in the other hand. I scrunched my nose up as he brought it to his mouth and reached up to light it. "Gross," I muttered under my breath, turning my gaze away from him.

"Huh?" He wondered, his eyes trying to meet mine. "You were saying?"

"I said..." I snatched the cigarette from his lips and held it up so he could clearly see what I was referring to. "That this is disgusting and bad for you for that matter."

He took it back from me immediately and placed it between his lips again. "Since when did you fucking care that I expose myself to bad stuff? It's my own decision anyway," he snarled, taking a drag from the cancer stick.

Grey smoke started spreading around us in thick circles, and I had to pinch my nose not to gag at the awful smell. "Whatever, it's still disgusting, and I'd rather you not do it in my proximity, alright?"

Rolling his eyes, he nodded his head. "I'll keep that in mind, wimp."

I didn't even bother giving him a comeback, knowing it would only make matters worse. Sure, I usually told him something in return when he would insult me even if it didn't make things better, but I was too tired of arguing with him at this point to do so now. Instead, I watched him from the corner of my eye, smoking the cigarette until it was only the butt left, and he had to drop it to the ground and stomp on it.

Only a few minutes later, we finally arrived at the bus stop, where several students were already gathered. Louis didn't hesitate to walk away from me and join some other guys who I knew played on the football team with him. It wasn't like I expected him to stay with me anyway, and it wasn't like I wanted him to either.

Letting out a sigh, I leaned against a pole nearby, and pulled out my phone of my jeans pocket, checking my social media. By the time I had checked my Twitter and Facebook, the bus pulled up in front of us, so I could finally get on. Louis was nowhere in sight at this point, but I assumed the command mum had given me was done with now, so I didn't even bother checking on him.

I started walking along the bus aisle to find an empty seat, but to my dismay, all of them were already taken unless you wanted to sit beside a jock. I found Louis sitting beside Zayn but didn't even look at him as I sat down in front of the two of them, next to their friend, Niall, against my will.

"Um, excuse me? What do you think you're doing?" He asked rudely, raising an eyebrow at me as his eyes flicked to see if Louis and Zayn were watching us; they weren't.

"All seats are taken, so just shut up, will you? You're not the only one who doesn't want me to sit here," I grumbled, placing my backpack on my lap.

Niall stared at the side of my face with a clenched jaw but didn't bother saying anything else. I wondered if he simply sucked at comebacks or if he was just not used to people defending themselves against him. I found it a bit suspicious because as far as I could remember, Niall had never given me a rude comeback, only nasty remarks and insults.

During the rest of the ride, I could see him texting someone on his phone with a frown on his face, but I knew better than to ask him about it. It wasn't like I cared anyway. I was just curious as to what brought the crease between his eyebrows. That was totally normal, right?

Once the bus came to a halt outside the school, I made a move to get up and get out of the vehicle but was suddenly tripped from behind, the impact sending me flying forward. Fortunately, a hand grabbed a hold on my wrist before I could hit the floor and injure myself badly.

"Thank y--" I cut myself off when I turned around to notice that Niall was in fact the one who had saved me from the fall, and by the looks of it, he was just as surprised by this himself.

"I, uh..." he trailed off and quickly let go of my hand before rushing past me and out of the bus that was now almost empty with students. I didn't miss the blush that coated his cheeks, though, and to say I was surprised would be an understatement. What just happened?

There was no way Niall Horan had just saved me from embarrassing myself and getting injured. He was one of the most popular students at school and Louis' best friend. He knew how much Louis hated me, and I was sure he found me annoying as well, especially since I didn't give two shits about the jocks. The idea of saving me clearly must've been on instinct because there was no way he had done it intentionally.

Still rather astonished by the scene that had just taken place, I got off the bus and made my way into school. People were rushing through the hallways even though the bell wouldn't ring yet in another fifteen minutes. I had never really understood why they did that, but it was nothing new to me, so

I silently made my way to my locker, where - as usual - my best friend was standing, leaning against it.

A smile crept to Liam's face when he caught sight of me. "Haz, you have to tell me everything! Who was it? Was he good looking? Do I know him? Was he nice?" He rambled, making me roll my eyes. He was most definitely referring to my stepbrother since I hadn't spoken to him about that topic yet.

I put the combination in my lock and opened my locker to get rid of my backpack and jacket. I then pulled out my Math books before shutting the locker again and facing the excited look on my best friend's face. "You don't even want to know who it is, believe me."

"What do you mean? It can't be that bad, can it? I'm sure you're just exaggerating," Liam objected, but you could see the excitement slowly disappearing from his eyes, as if he didn't believe his own words.

"Oh, it definitely is. In fact, it couldn't be any worse."

He was about to open his mouth when I suddenly felt myself being pulled away from him by a strong grip on my arm. I turned to see who'd grabbed me and was surprised that my eyes fell on a boy with feathery brown hair, his back facing me as he pulled me to the nearest room. It ended up being an empty classroom that for some reason wasn't locked. When he shut the door behind us, I tugged myself out of his hold with force. "What the hell do you think you're doing?" I spat, rubbing the now slightly red spot on my arm where his hand had just been.

He turned to face me, his eyes flicking down to my arm for a second before moving up to my face. "I didn't grip it that hard, stop weeping about it. Anyway, I pulled you in here because I wanted to let you know that you can't tell anyone that we're stepbrothers, alright?" He commanded, trying to sound and be intimidating by pressing his frame against mine so I was forced to back into the wall.

I grimaced at the pain that shot down my spine by the harsh impact and furrowed my eyebrows together. "And why is that so important? It's not like it actually matters."

He looked at me a bit surprised, but quickly recovered, and the next second the surprise was replaced by fury. "You think it doesn't matter? Well, maybe it doesn't to you, but it sure as hell does to me. My friends are literally going to kill me. Or even worse, make fun of me if they find out I live under the same roof as you."

My cheeks turned a dark red and I found myself clenching my hands into tight fists at my sides. "Wow, is that it? Didn't know you were such a pussy, Tomlinson. I thought you could handle something as small as that," I said, rolling my eyes, even though I was boiling with anger on the inside.

His face approached mine until we were mere inches apart. If it weren't for the hatred that glinted in his eyes, I would've thought he was going to kiss me. "If you so much as dare say that word about me again, I swear, I'm not going to hesitant to rip your head off, are we clear?" He threatened, raising his eyebrows while waiting for a response.

There was no doubt he wanted me to give in to him, but he could kiss that thought goodbye because he should know me by now that I didn't find him intimidating at all. I pushed at his chest hard enough for him to stumble backwards and for his body to separate from mine.

"Next time, attempt something better than trying to be intimidating, alright? Well, that is if you want to win an argument against me," I said before exiting the room without looking back at him.

At lunch that day, I was furiously picking off pieces of my tuna sandwich and stuffing them into my mouth. Liam was staring at me from across the table weirdly, clearly thinking that I must've gone crazy. "What's up with you today? You seem way different than you did just the other day," he frowned, bringing his can of mineral water to his mouth to take a sip of it.

"It's Louis. He stays making me so damn frustrated all the fucking time," I muttered.

Liam tilted his head and glanced over to the table across the room where Louis along with Zayn, the blondie, Niall and Eleanor were sitting, laughing about God knows what. "What has he done now?"

Louis suddenly looked up to shoot me a pointed look towards Liam, and I knew exactly what he meant by it. I hadn't told Liam that my stepbrother was in fact Louis yet, and I knew the jock was warning me not to do it anytime soon either. Sure, I wasn't affected by his attempts at making me give in, but I still knew better than to not agree with his commands. I mean, we lived under the same roof now. He could do practically anything to me with no problem at all.

Liam had been asking me all day who the mysterious brother was, but I had avoided the topic thanks to this. There was just something about Louis that always made me agree with whatever he told me to do, especially commands that consisted of not telling people a secret apparently, for some unknown reason.

"The usual, I guess. He's just been threatening me about this stupid thing all day, and it's really taking a toll on me. Sometimes I wish I could just tape his mouth shut so he would just keep that damn thing closed sometime," I said, rolling my eyes at the image of Louis' mouth being covered by masking tape. That would definitely be a sight.

"I see," Liam smiled timidly, glancing over towards their table again. He had this longing look in his eyes that I couldn't quite put my finger on what it meant. I had seen it a few times before, but I never caught the reason behind it.

Deciding to drop it, I looked over there as well to see Louis feeding Eleanor a cherry with a bright smile on his face. He was always happy around her, and that was most likely because they were in a relationship and he loved her. It was just so odd to see him smile like that, the way he had once smiled at me...

I felt a knot form in my stomach all of a sudden, and I had to look away from the couple to make it go away, even though it didn't completely. It was a strange feeling, something I had never felt before. It was almost like jealousy... but that couldn't be it, right? No, of course not.

My wandering gaze found Niall who looked rather left out, to be honest. He was looking down at his lap every now and then as if he didn't really want to be there. It all confused me because I had never seen him like that before. He usually seemed to be at home with them, but something obviously must have changed. What it was, I didn't know.

I was so lost in my thoughts that I almost let out a squeal when I felt someone sit down in the seat next to mine, the person throwing an arm around my shoulder. "Styles!" A familiar voice exclaimed in my ear, and I turned to see Ed smiling brightly at me.

Even though Ed played on the football team and was great friends with Louis and the other jocks, the two of us had always gotten along. We had known each other since kindergarten when we both had been in desperate need of a friend. From then on, we had always been close, and I was lucky to have him. It didn't matter that he and Louis were buddies, I knew Ed would never tell him anything that I said about him.

"Hi, mate," I smiled, and Liam nodded towards the ginger boy in acknowledgment.

"I was wondering if you wanted to come watch the game next Friday? We are playing against the team that's number one in the series, and I would love to have one of my best friends there to support me... please?" He pouted, his bottom lip sticking out adorably.

Rolling my eyes, I turned to Liam to see his reaction. He nodded his head with a smile on his face, and I let out a sigh. "I don't know, Ed. I don't really like watching football, you know? I've never really been a fan of it."

To be honest, the only game I had ever been to was when Louis had begged me to come watch him play once when we were still friends. He had literally pulled me to the field when there were no people around and placed me in a seat on the bleachers where I sat throughout the whole thing before he came back from the shower after the game and drove me home. Sure, it hadn't been that bad, but that was when Louis and I had still been friends. After our friendship, it had never really crossed my mind to go to another game. But like I said before, I wasn't a big fan of football, so that was probably the reason why.

Ed fluttered his eyelashes in an attempt to look cute, which made me smack him on the arm. "Don't pull anything on me, you know I can't resist your adorable faces," I chuckled, causing Liam to snort across the table.

I raised an eyebrow at him, and he reached his hands up in defense. "You guys are just so weird."

Ed looked confused. "What do you mean 'weird'?" He asked, trailing his hand up my arm until it was resting on my shoulder.

"That, for example," Liam said, motioning to Ed's hand. "I know you guys have kissed, yet you say you're nothing more than friends. Are you really sure about that? Because to me, you're not acting like just two buddies."

Rolling my eyes, I unwrapped Ed's hand from my shoulder, which made him pout a little, but I decided to ignore it. "No, we're definitely just friends. And that was one time, Liam. We were just experiencing whether we liked guys or not, okay? Nothing more, nothing less. We're just two close friends, right Ed?" I glanced at him from the corner of my eye to see him nod his head enthusiastically with a smile on his face.

"Yep, only friends. If we were more, I would've forced Harry to a football game a long time ago since boyfriends should support each other on those kinds of things, right?" He said, giving me a pointed look.

I nodded. "Yeah."

Even though we weren't together, he succeeded in making me feel guilty about not showing up at any of his games. And maybe that was why I decided to agree to attend the one he was talking about next week. Liam instantly jumped at the idea, implying he had nothing better to do. Somehow, I felt as though he was hiding something, though, but I didn't question him further about it. He would tell me eventually if something was on his mind.

Soon enough, the lunch hour ended and we had to get to our next lessons. I was just about to exit the room with Liam by my side when I felt someone bash into my shoulder. When I turned to see who it was, I was met with a pair of ocean blue eyes that looked into my own. However, it wasn't as pleasing as I made it out to be.

Louis gave me the classic 'I-am-keeping-my-eyes-on-you' sign with his fingers, and I just shot him the middle finger in return.

Seriously, he could go fuck himself.

Chapter 7

[Louis]

Every time I saw Harry that day, I sent him warning looks to make him understand that he couldn't tell anyone that we were stepbrothers. Actually, the fact that my friends wouldn't like the idea of us being siblings was just one of the reasons why I didn't want anyone to find out about it. Another was that I didn't quite like the idea myself. And, I didn't want people to go around reminding me of it. It was already bad enough that I had to face it every time I was at 'home'.

The main reason, however, was that I simply didn't want anyone to know. It was none of their business whether we lived in the same house or not. I didn't even care if it was just Harry's best friend he told, it could still spread around, and I didn't want that. At least not yet for a while.

Of course this involved me as well. I hadn't even told my girlfriend that the only person I really couldn't get along with was my stepbrother now. She would probably only try to interfere in everything, and I didn't want that either. The longer I could keep it from her, the better. There was only one problem, though, and it was that she had literally been begging me to bring her to my place so she could see how I lived now. The fact that I didn't want to tell her about my two new siblings didn't matter too much to her. She was mostly curious about my home, which I found a little weird but I didn't question it.

Anyway, I promised her that I would invite her over some time, but that it would probably be a while considering I would have to make sure Harry wasn't home at the time. Or better, that the fact that we were stepbrothers had dawned on me then, so I was somewhat fine with him being there if I brought her over. Though, I doubted that would happen anytime soon. For now, I just wouldn't bring anyone to Harry's house.

Considering Harry and I had all our classes together, we rode the same bus on our way home from school as well, which I secretly found great since I had forgotten the way to the house. Now I would only have to follow him there to take the right turns and whatnot. So, that was how I found myself hopping off the bus and looking around for the curly-haired boy.

There were quite a few people who jumped off here, so it was pretty difficult to find him in the crowd, but after a minute I could see him walking in the direction we had come from this morning. I shoved my way past the students and started following Harry at a pretty great distance. My intention was obviously not to get caught, but being the clumsy person that I could be sometimes, I just had to stumble on a pebble and let out a very manly squeal.

Harry instantly turned around to face me with wide eyes, probably startled by the sudden noise. "Louis? What the hell are you doing?" He asked, raising his eyebrows in confusion.

I scratched the back of my neck awkwardly as I sheepishly walked over to him. "I was just walking to the house, you know? We live in the same place now."

He rolled his eyes. "Were you following me? Because knowing you, you wouldn't have kept that short of a distance between us if you weren't," he said knowingly, crossing his arms over his chest.

Narrowing my eyes, I snorted. "Of course I wasn't, and stop looking so damn full of yourself. It doesn't suit you at all." I motioned to his crossed arms and the smug look on his face. No, it definitely did not suit him.

"Ha, no. I enjoy this way too much. So, why were you stalking me?" He asked, making me roll my eyes because he was so extra.

"Stop flattering yourself, Styles. I was not stalking you. If you so desperately want to know why I was walking so 'close' to you, it was because I forgot the way back home, alright? You're so full of yourself it's embarrassing, really," I said, and started walking in the direction I was positive the house was.

Harry quickly caught up and fell into step with me. "You forgot the way back home? Are you kidding me? We just walked here this morning and you can't remember?" He laughed, making me want to beat the shit out of him. I hated it when he tried to make me feel embarrassed. I was supposed to be the one to try and make *him* feel embarrassed, not the other way around.

"Listen here, Styles. I know my sense of locality isn't the best, but guess what? I don't give a flying fuck about that, so don't try to make me feel insecure about it, nor make fun of me for that matter. Are we clear?" I asked with a firm voice while he tried to stop laughing by covering his mouth with his fist.

After half a few seconds, he finally calmed down enough to be able to answer. "Whatever. I don't really care, to be honest."

Gritting my teeth together, I clenched my fists and started walking at a faster pace to hopefully get away from him. I didn't get very far before I could hear him calling my name, though. "Louis, it's this way."

I turned around to see him pointing in the opposite direction of where I was heading. Frustratingly, I made my way over and shouldered him once I passed him. He didn't say anything, just chuckled quietly under his breath, which didn't exactly make me like him more, rather the opposite.

Five minutes later, I was finally walking towards the front door of my new 'home' with Harry just a few yards behind me. He knew better than to walk with me, and I was thankful for that. God knows what I would've done if he had actually done so. Probably punched his pretty little face in or something similar to it.

Fortunately, the front door was unlocked. I hadn't been handed a house key yet, and I didn't want to stand there and wait for Harry to come and unlock it for me. So, I entered the freshly smelled house and slipped off my black Vans and shrugged off my jean jacket. "Hello?" I called out, knowing someone must be home since the door was unlocked and since the sound of the fan in the kitchen could be heard.

"Louis?" A female voice replied, and I recognized it as Anne's. She turned to me when I walked into the kitchen, giving me a small smile. "Where's Ha--" She started, but was interrupted by the sound of the front door opening.

"Mum?"

Anne's lips pulled up into an even wider smile at the sound of her son's voice, and something about it made my heart ache. Maybe it was because I didn't have a mum who could be as happy at my arrival when I got home, but I would surely not admit that to anyone.

"In here, honey," she called and turned to me again. "I'm making eggs and bacon, which will be done in just a few minutes. You can wait in here if you want."

I nodded as I quietly walked over to sit down at the kitchen table, fishing out my phone from my jean pocket to look busy. Not even a minute later, Harry stepped into the room and sat down across from me, his body turned to his mother who was standing at the stove. "How come you're home already?" He asked her, shrinking back in his seat.

"My boss decided to let me get off early since I have been working overtime two weekends in a row lately," she explained, flipping the eggs as she did so.

Even though I had my phone out, I wasn't looking at it, as you might have noticed by now. Instead, I was discreetly following all of their movements. "Oh, I see. Do you know when Gemma finishes school? I need to talk to her about something," he continued.

Anne shook her head, a cheeky smile forming on her lips. "Something you can't talk to your mother about?"

Harry's eyes flicked to me for a second before he pulled on a thoughtful face. "I'm afraid not."

The room fell silent after that and I decided to shove my phone back in my pocket after a minute, seeing as I wasn't using it anyway. I looked up to see Harry watching me with narrowed eyes, as if he was thinking deeply about something. "What?"

He merely shrugged as he turned his gaze to his mother who was now placing the eggs and bacon on a plate. "Mum, I'm going to the football game next Friday if that's okay?" He announced when she put down the food on the table. He wasted no time stabbing his fork in it to place it on his plate.

I choked at his words, my eyes widening. What was that? He was going to the football game? The football game I was going to participate in tomorrow? What? But he never attended any of our games, so why now?

Anne either decided to ignore the fact that I just choked, or she didn't notice it. "Of course, Harry. You don't even need to ask. What time do you think you'll be home?"

Harry's eyes met mine for a split second before they set on his mother. "Why don't you ask Louis? He's one of the players."

I was caught off guard by the fact that he had referred to me, but I quickly composed myself and cleared my throat. "Eh, well, since the game starts at five in the afternoon, I would say it should be finished at around seven. It depends, though," I told Anne who gave me an appreciating nod.

"Oh, okay. Well, then we'll eat dinner once the two of you get home." She brought her glass of milk to her mouth to take a sip of it. "What makes you want to go to this game, though, Harry? I didn't think you were interested in football," she asked, her eyes narrowing in slight suspicion.

Exactly what I was wondering. The only time he had watched a game that I recalled was when I had practically forced him there, and that, might I add, had not been easy at all. He was stubborn when it came to those kinds of things.

"You know Ed, right? One of my closest friends."

Anne nodded. "Yeah?"

"Well, he made me realize that I have never gone to watch him play before, so I decided it was time for me to do so now. I mean, you gotta support your friends even though you don't like the sport, right?" He said, taking a forkful of bacon and bringing it to his mouth so he could start chewing on it.

The fact that he was going because of Ed and not me this time made my heart hurt for some reason. I knew it wasn't supposed to, that I should've been over this a long time ago, but I couldn't help but feel disappointed. I wanted to punch myself for it.

Looking down at my empty plate, I bit my bottom lip, feeling Harry's eyes on me. I ignored him, though, and let out a deep sigh. "Um, I'm not very hungry. I'll just wait to eat dinner later instead if that's okay?" I asked Anne, my eyes focusing on only her and not the person to her right.

"Yes, of course. You're free to go whenever you want," she smiled warmly and I didn't even hesitate to exit the kitchen and walk up to my room.

The moment I fell on my bed, I clenched my fists and hit my pillow angrily. "Stupid, stupid, stupid," I repeated to myself, hating that I couldn't control my feelings better. Why did I still feel this way? Harry and I hadn't been friends in two years, so why hadn't these feelings disappeared yet? This was so damn frustrating.

I laid there for a few minutes before pulling out my phone of my jeans pocket and opening my message conversation with my girlfriend. We hadn't talked since lunch, seeing as we didn't have many lessons together nor hadn't had time to meet in between them. I texted her a quick 'how're you doing?' before putting the phone aside while waiting for an answer.

It came only a minute later, and from then on, we texted until it was time for me to go down and eat dinner. I didn't say very much during the rest of that evening, not even sending Harry cold stares like I usually did. Instead, I kept my mouth shut and listened to everybody else talking about how work and school had been. Sometime during the dinner, I could feel my dad eye me in concern, but I didn't care too much about it. There was nothing to be concerned about anyway.

At around ten in the evening when everyone was getting ready to go to bed, I decided to go out to the porch and have a quick smoke. I was stressing on the inside over everything that was going on at the moment; Harry going to the game because of Ed, him being my stepbrother and the sudden move, and more. So, a cigarette would definitely do me well at the moment.

I was leaning on the railing in the chilly November night, smoking the cancer stick when I could hear the sound of the front door shut behind me. Confused as to who could have possibly joined me, I turned around to see my dad walking in my direction until he was standing right beside me and leaning his forearms against the railing just like I was doing.

"It's quite chilly out here, isn't it?" He stated casually, looking out in the dark night that surrounded us.

I shrugged, taking a drag of the cigarette. "Not really. I like the cold," I replied, blowing out the smoke through my nostrils.

Dad let out a sigh, and I could see through the corner of my eye how he closed his eyes briefly. "I know this is hard for you, Louis, especially since you and Harry apparently already know each other from before and aren't exactly on good terms. Maybe all of this is selfish of me, moving in with Anne all, but you have to realize that I'm in love with this woman. I'm sure you would've done the same thing to your son if you were in love with someone, right?"

My eyes drifted to him and stayed focused on his face for a long time before they turned back to staring out in the night. "Probably," I muttered after a while of thinking. Because, if I really was in love with let's say Eleanor, and we were ready to move in together, my son probably wouldn't have stopped me from doing so. Unless he had a very good reason for me not to, that was. "The thing is, I just don't think I want you to move on, you know? From mum."

He placed a hand on my shoulder and squeezed it gently as he shot me a weak smile that looked more like a grimace. "I know what you're talking about, Louis, and part of me doesn't want to move on either. But I realized when I met Anne that all people deserve love even when you think you've lost it. I thought I lost it but look at me now. Here I am, finding love again. And just like I said before, I know this is hard for you, Louis, but could you please do me the honor of being happy for me? I would really appreciate my only son to feel like I've finally done something good in life when I've practically been a walking corpse for the past few years."

Breathing out a shaky breath, I nodded my head slowly. I dropped my cigarette to the ground and stomped on it before looking up at him. "I guess since you've moved on, I should probably do so as well. But it's... it's hard. I miss them, both of them," I couldn't help but sniffle.

Dad was there to comfort me right away, wrapping his welcoming arms around my body and pulling me into his chest. He leaned down so his chin was resting on the top of my head as he whispered 'I know, I know' repeatedly. The tears that had been threatening to fall throughout our entire conversation finally decided to let go and roll down my cheeks, dampening my skin.

I didn't know how long we stood there, enjoying the feeling of each other's arms wrapped around each other and just drowning in the pain that we both felt until we let go and dried our tears. I let out a dry chuckle as I stared at his tear-stained face. "Man, when did we become such cry-babies?"

He joined my laughter and shook his head. "Don't ask me, son. I'd say we don't speak to anyone about this, deal?"

A smile formed on my thin lips. "Deal."

Before he could step into the house again, I stopped him when he was about to turn the handle. "Dad?" I asked, gaining his attention right away.

"Yes, son?"

"I just want you to know that I am happy for you, even if it doesn't always seem that way."

Chapter 8

[Harry]

The days slowly passed by after that with nothing new happening. Louis and I still couldn't sit at the kitchen table together without throwing each other dirty looks, and mum and Troy were obviously growing tired of it. Especially mum since she desperately wanted all of us family members to get along.

Gemma and Louis hadn't talked very much to each other either that I knew of, and I guess that was because Gemma was aware of everything Louis had done to me, so she was a little cautious when it came to him. And Louis probably saw Gemma as someone that was related to me and therefore, decided he couldn't get along with her or something. Not that he absolutely despised my mother, though, but you could clearly see that he wasn't very fond of her either by the look he had in his eyes whenever she spoke to him. I didn't know if that was because of me, though, because it seemed to have more meaning to it, a meaning that was deeper than the hatred he had for me.

On another note, Louis had slowly started accepting the fact that we were now stepbrothers. Well, at least he had told me it was okay for me to tell Liam about it, which was a relief. My best friend had practically been nagging holes in my head, asking me who my stepbrother was and why I refused to tell him. I would usually only try to change the topic, but it was hard to do so because Liam and I told each other almost everything, and keeping this kind of a secret from him was not an easy thing to do.

His reaction had been something I wouldn't forget anytime soon. It was priceless, the way his mouth had formed an 'o', and his eyes widened in utter shock. He'd repeated the words 'you can't be serious' probably at least ten times before I had slapped my hand over his mouth to make him shut up. He had been speechless all day after that, only telling me for the first time when school was finished how bad he felt for me because of it. His sympathy was really appreciated, even though I told him it was okay. At least Louis hadn't done anything worse than normal yet.

I also made Liam promise not to tell anyone else about it because Louis and I wanted to keep it a secret since everyone would most likely freak out if they found out that the school's most popular guy lived with me, a boy who was classed as a nerd in some people's eyes, or just a 'normal' boy in others'. It was only partly a lie considering I knew that would most definitely happen, but Louis and I hadn't made an *agreement* not to tell anyone. He was the one who had told me to say this, and I didn't want to explain to Liam how I sometimes had a hard time disobeying his orders when it came to certain things. It was just too complicated.

I knew for a fact Louis hadn't told anyone that we were stepbrothers, though. I didn't know if it was because of what he told me about him being afraid of his friends finding out, or if it was something else. Something told me there was more to it, like for instance what I just mentioned about everyone freaking out over it. I was positive that was one of the reasons he wouldn't tell anyone. After all, he had a reputation to keep up, just like he did two years ago when we were friends.

At the moment, I was changing into my sports gear, getting ready to attend my last lesson of the day, P.E. It was the Friday I had promised Ed I would go to the football game he had later in the afternoon. To be honest, he hadn't shut up about it all week, reminding me every day how happy he was that I had finally agreed on attending one. If I remembered correctly, though, he hadn't asked me that many times before, but I decided not to bring it up. The main thing was that he was happy I was going to be there, and that was all that mattered.

Through the corner of my eye, I could see Louis pulling off his black shirt while talking to one of his friends. His six-pack was a sight I had been getting quite used to witnessing lately since he rarely bothered putting on a t-shirt in the mornings when he came down to eat breakfast. It wasn't like I enjoyed it, but I couldn't deny the fact that six-packs on guys were very attractive.

Mentally smacking myself in the forehead, I turned back to my locker and put on a pair of joggers before slamming it shut and going into the gym. A few people were already there, conversing with each other about God knows what. The only thing I managed to pick up was something about a celebration party, and I assumed it had to do with the game that was later this evening. I just hoped Ed wouldn't bring it up and take me and Liam to it. Parties and I weren't a great combo. I didn't like them, to be frank.

It turned out Mr. Wilson wanted us to play volleyball that day. My volleyball skills probably weren't the best, but I wouldn't say I was the worst one at it either. Louis and his friends liked to think they aced the whole thing since they were so-called 'sportspeople', but the girls and guys who played volleyball in their free time wouldn't agree with them. According to them, Louis and his gang just bantered around and thought they were great when in reality, they weren't. Not that I cared, it was just fun to witness the scene play out.

What wasn't so funny, though, was that I was on the same team as Louis. He made fun of me whenever I missed the ball and even once when I managed to get hit on the head. In return, I flipped him the bird and laughed under my breath whenever he made mistakes himself. Unfortunately, though, he had better ball control than me since he played football, so he had the great advantage that he could just kick or nod the ball over the net. Stupid volleyball rules that allowed football moves...

Once the lecture ended, I made my way into the locker room, feeling slightly lonely since I had no friends in this class. I tried not to be fazed by it as I stripped off my clothes, grabbed my towel, and headed for the showers. Luckily, not that many people were in here yet. I didn't quite like to shower around people because I would always receive these judging looks that said I shouldn't be there because I was bisexual and, therefore, found guys attractive. Usually, I would ignore them, but whether I wanted it to or not, it still hurt. Why would I be treated differently because of a small thing like my sexuality? I was just like any other guy.

I hung my towel on a hanger before getting under a showerhead and turning on the water. Just as I was about to open the shampoo bottle, though, I felt a tap on my shoulder. At first, I contemplated whether to turn around or not, afraid that it would be someone who was going to spat in my face that I didn't belong in here with the straight guys, but in the end, I decided I wouldn't care, and finally spun on my heel to face the person.

My breath got caught in my throat at the sight of an almost naked Louis standing in front of me, a towel lazily wrapped around his waist, hanging a little too low if you asked me. I turned my gaze up to his face and was surprised to see that he didn't look angry for once, which was definitely unusual. He never pulled on anything close to a happy face around me. "Louis, wha--" I started, but he cut me off.

"Are you going home after this or are you waiting here until the game starts?" He asked, his eyes flicking around to see if anybody was listening to our conversation or even paying attention to us. When he realized everyone in here had their backs turned to us, he looked back at me, raising an eyebrow expectantly.

The fact that he was talking to me in a somewhat normal tone of voice wouldn't really register in my head, so when I opened my mouth to reply, nothing came out. I had to close my eyes and inhale a large breath of air to get anything past my lips. "H-home, why?" I wondered, mentally hitting myself for stuttering. I never stuttered in Louis' proximity. That was something I had promised myself never to do. What even was this?

A small smile formed on his lips, and I had to blink my eyes a few times to know if it was actually real. Was Louis Tomlinson actually smiling at me? Impossible. "Great. I forgot my cleats at home and I haven't been handed a key yet, so I would've had to call dad otherwise," he said, biting his bottom lip.

"Oh." I didn't know what else to say, so I awkwardly looked down at my feet and fiddled with my fingers, feeling embarrassed that I was standing in front of Louis completely naked now that he was my stepbrother. That was just weird on so many levels.

Louis' smile turned into a smirk as he leaned closer to me, his hand grasping my shoulder lightly. "Just to give you some advice... If I were you, I would practice my subtle staring skills because it was obvious that you were checking me out just a second ago, but don't worry, I would check myself out too if I could," he sniggered in my ear before pulling away with a wink.

I didn't even have time to open my mouth before he had walked away from me to get into a shower himself. When what he had just told me registered in my head, I could feel anger boil up within me. The somewhat friendly thoughts I'd had about him just a second ago disappeared as fast as they had erupted. He was just so damn full of himself, always thinking about his stupid looks and whatnot. I hadn't even been checking him out, that lying son of bitch.

Frustratingly, I turned around to finish my shower, refusing to think about the feathery haired boy who was just a few showers away, now talking to one of his friends happily.

The moment I hopped off the bus, I didn't hesitate to start jogging to my house. I didn't want to have Louis walking right behind me like he'd done the last few days since he still had a problem finding his way back home. It had been a week, yet he still hadn't learned it. I wouldn't call that a bad sense of locality, that was just downright stupidity, but Louis was kind of stupid, so I shouldn't even be surprised.

The reason I particularly didn't want him to follow me today was because of what happened in the locker room earlier. He could find his way back home however he wanted, but he wouldn't get my help this time. He could use the map on his phone or whatever, I didn't care.

When I got home, I wasn't surprised to find the front door locked. Even Louis was aware that no one would be home, so it really didn't shock me at all. Gemma didn't finish school yet in another hour or so and mum and Troy worked late every weekday, besides when mum got off early every once in a while, like one day last week.

I unlocked the house and dumped my backpack on the floor in the hallway the first thing I did before I shrugged off my jacket and slipped off my shoes. I then made my way into the kitchen to grab a quick snack and pull out a glass from one of the cupboards, so I could drink some well-needed water. An hour of working out was quite exhausting when you usually didn't practice any sport.

Just when I was about to put the glass down on the counter, I could hear the front door opening. I didn't have to check to know it was Louis, although I was a little surprised that he had found his way back home that quickly. I thought he was going to take another ten minutes at least.

"Harry?" He called out, and I rolled my eyes at the harsh tone he was using. I guess we were back to normal.

A second later, he joined me in the kitchen and flashed me a cold look. "Why would you fucking run away from me like that? I could've gotten lost, for fuck's sake, and your mum would've been so disappointed in you if that was to happen, don't you think?"

I had to bring my fist to my mouth to quiet my laughter. "It's not my problem you still have trouble finding your way back here," I chuckled, feeling his intense glare at the side of my head, but decided to ignore it.

"Shut up," he muttered and walked out of the room, probably to get his cleats that he had forgotten this morning.

When he came back down from the second floor, he didn't even so much as say goodbye before he exited the house again. Raising an eyebrow at his sudden hurry, I walked over to the kitchen window just in time to see him hop into a car I didn't recognize. However, I did recognize the raven-haired guy who was sitting in the seat next to his, so I assumed one of his older friends was the one who drove the car.

Feeling pretty ridiculous for being so nosy, I walked to the entryway to fish my phone out of my jacket. I had two missed calls, and both of them were from Liam. We had planned to meet up outside school so we could walk to the football field that was on the other side of the building together.

After giving Liam a quick call, informing him that I would be there in twenty minutes, I put on my outdoor clothing once again and exited the house, locking the door behind me. I sighed when I realized it had started raining, and didn't hesitate to hug my arms around my body, hating that it was November and not February, which, in that case, would have meant that the summer was on its way. But no, of course not.

My hair was damp when I arrived at the bus stop, but at least I was lucky enough to get there at the same time as the bus, meaning that I could get on it immediately instead of having to wait in the pouring rain and get even wetter than I already was.

Since it was afternoon, there weren't many people on the bus considering no students needed to get to school. There were merely adults who didn't have a driver's license or a car that rode the bus at this time, and I found that great because it meant I didn't have to look for an empty seat to sit in. Most of them were unoccupied anyway.

Fifteen minutes later, the bus came to a halt outside school and I jumped off to make my way to the benches near the entrance. Liam and I had decided to meet up there, a usual place for us to meet up whenever we weren't going into school.

The rain had thankfully stopped falling from the sky by now, so I didn't have to shield my face as I walked to the destination only to find Liam already sitting there, waiting for me. "Hi, mate," I greeted, waving my hand a little when he turned to look at me.

"Harry," he smiled, standing up from the bench to join me. "You're right on time. The game starts in fifteen minutes, but we don't want to get the worst seats, so I'd say we go there right away, yeah?"

I nodded in agreement, and together we headed for the football field on the other side of the building. It turned out we actually were right on time because so far, only about twenty people were sitting on the bleachers, and I knew for a fact that the football team usually had at least a hundred people watching their games. Not only the students at school enjoyed watching them, but also family and people who just enjoyed football in general, which were more people than you would think.

Liam pulled me down to the seats closest to the field, much to my dismay. I didn't want Louis to catch sight of me, even though he already knew I was going to be here. I had no idea why I felt that way, I just did. Liam, however, seemed to want to be noticed by everyone on the field, and sadly, I had no say in this, because that boy had a strong will. I would never be able to pull myself out of his grip, nor win an argument against him. Once he was determined of something, no one could change his mind.

So, against my will, we sat down in the seats and waited for the game to begin. When there were only five minutes to go, the bleachers were crowded with people. They were already shouting at the top of their lungs, cheering like there was no tomorrow. I knew that if they were going to continue like that throughout the entire game, I was surely going to become deaf.

All the players were now out on the pitch, and the referee suddenly blew his whistle, signaling the captains of the two teams to go over to him. Louis didn't waste a second to jog up to the man, shaking his and the opponent's hands before they drew to decide what team was going to kick off.

Louis won, and just a minute later the game finally began.

Chapter 9

[Harry]

One thing I noticed when it was only a few minutes into the game was that Louis was really damn amazing at football. I didn't want to admit it, but there was literally no denying it. He played like a god, dribbling past player after player until he was close enough to the goal to kick a perfect score. Well, at least it looked pretty great to me.

He wasn't always that selfish, though. Usually (more times than I expected), he passed the ball to his teammates so they could take shots as well. The players that stood out from the rest were Louis, Niall and some blonde guy I had never acknowledged before. Ed was great too, but since he was the goalie it was hard to compare him to the others.

To my surprise, I was quite into the game, which I had not expected I was going to be at all. In all honesty, though, that was most likely because it was so even. The score was 3-2 after halftime, and it honestly couldn't be more nerve-wracking. I was biting my fingernails, and it wasn't even nearing the end yet.

Liam seemed to be as into the game as I was, staring at what was unfolding in front of him with wide, concentrated eyes, following the ball's every movement. I never thought he liked football since he had never told me he did, but apparently, I was wrong about that. I had never seen him this focused on anything that didn't have to do with school before.

I wanted to question him about it but decided I was going to wait until after the game. Right now, I was more interested in watching what was unfolding in front of me. The players were currently jogging out onto the field again after a fifteen minutes break. Ed positioned himself in front of the net while the other players took their own positions.

The referee blew his whistle to signal the opponents to kick off. The first thing that happened was that Louis stole the ball from one of the other team's players and started heading towards the net with Niall running right beside him. I couldn't help but notice the way Louis' flexible legs moved when he ran, so the muscles in them popped out in the sexiest way possible, and the way he so skillfully skipped towards the other side of the field. Woah, I did not just think that, okay?

Louis dribbled past one- two defenders and was just about to aim at the net when he changed his mind and passed the ball to Niall instead, who was already swinging his leg back to kick the ball towards the net. Unfortunately, though, the goalie seemed to be able to read their minds and blocked the ball with his fist at the last second. Many people in the audience who had been ready to celebrate a score, quieted down in disappointment as Louis and Niall jogged back to their half of the field, Niall with a sad expression on his face.

Before I could acknowledge anything else, Niall flicked his gaze in the direction of the bleachers and met my eyes. My first thought was that he was going to glare at me since that was what he always did, so when a weak smile formed on his lips, I was utterly shocked. It was gone within a second, though, so when I blinked to ensure myself that I was seeing what I thought I was, it wasn't there any longer, and he had gone back to focus on the game.

Weird, I thought to myself as I continued following the ball's movements.

The second half of the game was almost as eventful as the first one. The other team was the first to score, so it was 3-3, but Louis was quick to change that when he scored a goal just a minute later. Now, the score was 4-3 with our team winning, and only two minutes remained of the game. The audience was cheering like crazy already even though nothing was set in stone yet. Anything could still happen.

As if reading my mind, a brown-haired player from the other team stole the ball from one of ours and started heading towards Ed at an incredible speed. He dribbled past the defenders and got himself ready to shoot the ball by looking up towards the net. Everyone was holding their breaths, hoping for the best but expecting the worst.

Mere seconds were remaining of the game when the guy kicked the ball, sending it flying towards Ed who had to dive to the side to block the ball with his hands. It only brushed his fingertips, but thankfully it was enough to make it go outside the net instead of into it.

The audience erupted with cheers, practically burning holes in my poor ears, but right then I didn't mind it one bit. It was all just so amazing. Happiness and joy literally exploded in my body as a wide smile formed on my lips. I couldn't believe that I was here, at a football game, and actually enjoying myself this much. I never thought this was going to happen, ever.

To my great surprise, Liam turned to me and wrapped his arms around my frame, pulling me into a tight hug. "They made it!" He exclaimed, tensing up a second later when he realized what he was doing. He pulled away with a blush on his face as he scratched the back of his neck awkwardly. "I mean, they made it," he repeated, his voice sounding not even half as excited this time.

Rolling my eyes, I let out a chuckle. "You don't have to hide your happiness, I'm just as happy as you are," I reassured him, earning a smile from him.

"Well then," he said, pulling me into his arms again and giving me another tight hug. "I can't believe they actually made it! And they were so great, weren't they? Oh my God, we have to go down there and congratulate Ed on that awesome save he did!" He unwrapped his arms from me again to nod towards the field that many people from the audience were now heading for to congratulate the players.

I made a face, hesitating a little. Going down there meant being even closer to Louis and even risking to make eye contact with him. Eh, what the hell. We were stepbrothers, I was most likely going to make eye contact with him before this day was over anyway.

With that thought in my head, I followed Liam down the bleachers and onto the pitch where Ed was standing by one of the goalposts, talking to what looked to be some guy our age. He had brown hair and was rather short, but nonetheless, I didn't recognize him.

"Ed!" I yelled when he was within hearing distance.

He looked over the guy's shoulder at the sound of my voice, a wide smile forming on his lips as he caught sight of me and Liam. The guy seemed to understand the situation and walked off to congratulate the other players.

"I can't believe you guys are actually here! I never thought you would show up," Ed grinned, embracing me in a tight and sweaty hug. I scrunched my nose at the smell but reciprocated the hug anyway because I was so proud to be his friend and also so happy for him at this second.

"Of course we are! I would never let you down like that," I said, pulling out of the embrace. "Oh, and by the way, you were absolutely amazing out there. Why have you never told me to come watch you play before? It was awesome!"

Ed laughed, shrugging his shoulders. He went to hug Liam as well, who congratulated him as well. "I guess I didn't want to bother you since I knew you don't like football and all. But, judging by the look in your eye right now, I would say this game changed your mind."

I rolled my eyes. "Whatever."

Ed sent me a teasing look while Liam glanced over to the other people on the field, seeming to search for someone special. I followed his gaze only for my eyes to land on Zayn. He had an arm wrapped around the same blonde girl he'd been with the other week, a smile playing on his lips.

My eyebrows pulled together because this was not the first time I had caught Liam looking at Zayn. It had been going on for at least three weeks now, and I was starting to get really curious as to what the reason behind it was. Maybe Liam fancied Zayn? But, Liam would've told me so if that was the case, right?

"...what do you say?"

I snapped my head to Ed, who apparently had been talking to me - or us, and looked at him confused. "Huh?"

Ed rolled his eyes, running a hand through his sweaty, ginger hair. "I was asking if you wanted to come to the celebration party tonight. Niall is arranging it, so you're most definitely going to have a blast. He always throws the best parties."

Liam reacted at the mention of a party and turned to Ed with lightning speed. "You're inviting us to the party? Man, everyone's been talking about it all day. Harry, please tell me we're going," he pleaded, turning to give me a puppy face.

Since when had Liam been into parties? I mean, as far as I could remember, he had never even been to one before, so where did this come from all of a sudden? "Liam, I thought you didn't like parties," I said suspiciously, guessing that this must have something to do with a certain raven-haired guy.

"What are you talking about? I have never said that. I've just never been to one, is all. Though, I've always wanted to," he said, smiling at Ed, who looked a little suspicious himself.

"Well, okay. So, what do you say?" Ed asked, looking at me hopefully.

Scratching the back of my neck, I turned to give Liam a pointed look, but he just ignored it as if he hadn't even seen it. "Come on, Liam. Please don't do this to me. You know I don't mix well with parties. Besides, Louis is going to be there and I don't want him to humiliate me in front of all those people," I pleaded to the brown-haired boy, jutting out my bottom lip for more effect.

I was quite sure he wasn't even fazed by my attempt at winning him over because the next second, he told Ed we were going to be there. "When does it begin?" He asked excitedly, rolling back and forth on his heels.

Ed seemed just as happy as he did that we were going. "As soon as we have all showered. We're heading there right after." He turned to me with a concerned look on his face. "You don't seem very excited about this, Harry. I promise you're going to enjoy yourself although I know parties are not exactly your thing. Besides, if you don't like it, you can always go home, you know?"

I gave him a timid smile. "I guess," I muttered.

"Is that a yes then?" Liam questioned, almost jumping up and down from how excited he was.

Letting out a sigh, I nodded my head. "Yeah, but if it all goes to hell, I'm never going to forgive you, alright?"

Liam smiled wide. "Alright."

What the hell had I gotten myself into?

When Ed disappeared into the locker room, I pulled out my phone to send mum a text, telling her I wouldn't show up for dinner that night. I then figured Louis probably hadn't informed her or Troy that he wasn't going to be there either, so I sent her another text to tell her that as well. Even if I didn't care about Louis, I thought it was unfair for them if they cooked too much food when he wasn't going to show up anyway.

Liam and I were still standing by the goalpost, waiting for Ed to come back from the locker room so he could show us the way to Niall's house. Neither I nor Liam had been there before, so we needed his help to get to the place.

My back was resting against the pole as I observed my surroundings, noticing that Louis was still out here and not in the showers like almost everybody else on the team was. He was standing a few yards away with his arm wrapped around Eleanor's waist protectively as he talked to his coach. The sight made a large knot form in my stomach, and I had to look away not to throw up for some reason.

I never reacted this way when I saw Louis and Eleanor together, so what was different about this time? The only thing I could come up with was that Louis was my stepbrother now, but that wasn't even relevant for this situation. I had no idea what the reason for it was.

"Harry, Ed's coming," Liam suddenly spoke up, snapping me out of my thoughts.

I looked up to see Ed indeed walking in our direction, a sports bag thrown over his shoulder and his wet, ginger hair standing in all directions after the shower he had taken. "You guys ready to party?" He asked, winking at me since he knew I wasn't really into this.

"Of course," Liam answered while I just hummed a reply.

Together, we walked to the bus stop on the other side of the school and waited for the next bus to show up. To kill time, we talked about everything and nothing, really. It was everything from school to memories the three of us shared, and it wasn't actually boring at all. To be honest, it was probably the most fun I'd ever had while waiting for a bus to show up.

Fifteen minutes later, the vehicle pulled over in front of us and its doors opened to let us all in. Since the entire team and many more people were going to the same place, it didn't take long until the bus was filled. Luckily, Ed, Liam and I managed to get seats even if Ed had to sit beside some old lady who whined about it being too noisy in the small space.

Eventually, we finally got to Niall's place, and to my surprise, it was located just a few blocks away from my own. I recognized the area, but I had never really acknowledged his house before. Not that it was bad-looking (it was really beautiful) but because all of the houses in this area looked pretty much the same. It was one of those luxurious homes where the walls were covered in white and the rooms decorated with expensive furniture, which made me wonder if Niall had asked his parents for permission to arrange this party, or if they simply were out and he took the opportunity.

Nonetheless, the party was on full blast within just a few minutes since Niall had apparently prepared everything before he went to the game earlier today. All of the people helped him getting the alcohol out and turning on the music. Liam, Ed and I settled down on a couch in the living room, observing the people who were now dancing with each other like maniacs. Well, as I said before; parties and I didn't mix well together, at all.

Letting out a sigh, I turned to Liam and Ed and raised an eyebrow. "Is this the reason you wanted to go here? So we could sit on a couch and stare at everybody else in here letting loose? If so, I'm out of here. I don't want to spend my Friday night in a house I've never been before to look at people getting drunk off their asses."

Ed rolled his eyes, hooking one of his legs over the other. "Chill, Harry. The party is just getting started. Before you know it, you'll be out there dancing along to the music too," he joked, earning a glare from me.

"That's not what I meant. I couldn't care less about dancing. I just don't want to sit here all night long and stare at people. I've got better things to do than that."

"Like what?" Liam asked, turning to me.

"Look who finally figured out how to use their mouth."

He rolled his eyes, nudging me in the side gently. "Come on, mate, don't be so grumpy. We'll find something better to do. Just like Ed here said; the party is just getting started. It's not like we're going to sit here all night."

I muttered something inaudible as I crossed my arms over my chest, staring ahead of me. Something better to do? Like what? The best thing I could think of was to go home, but I doubted that was what he was getting at. What he meant probably involved a lot more dancing and alcohol than walking.

"Come on," Ed said after five minutes, standing up from the couch. "I'll show you something."

Suspicious, I slowly got up and followed him and Liam through the crowd of people, bumping into people I was sure I had never seen before and also some students I recognized from school. It was not the most pleasant sight I had seen, if I may say so. The party had only been going on for about half an hour, yet some of them were already drunk, and if there was one thing I found uncomfortable, it was being around intoxicated people.

"Here, have a beer," Ed said, handing me and Liam each a can of the brownish liquid.

Scrunching my nose up, I gave it back to him. "I think I'll stay away from alcohol tonight. One of us has to stay sober if we want to get home safely."

Liam shrugged his shoulders, taking a sip of his beer. "Since this is my first party ever, I might as well enjoy it," he reasoned, downing the whole thing.

Ed chuckled and drank from his can as well, making me roll my eyes. Three beers and four shots later, we were seated at a table in the kitchen, talking and laughing with each other. Ed and Liam were slowly losing control of their bodies by the alcohol that was now running through their systems, but for some reason, I didn't have anything against it. I usually disliked being around drunk people, but the two of them were actually quite funny when they were intoxicated. They were laughing and enjoying themselves more than I had ever seen them do before, which was definitely a sight.

"...and then I told him no way! You can't possibly have three feet, that is just impossible," Ed laughed, slamming his hand against the table, Liam joining him right away.

I smiled at my two friends, finding their jokes so bad that I couldn't help but laugh at them. Actually, I had never seen the two of them get along this well before. Ed was more a friend of mine than Liam's, but I guess with a little alcohol, a lot of things could change.

On another note, the need for leaving was slowly fading away from my body. Witnessing my friends having fun with each other and finally warming up to the party myself, I had actually started enjoying myself a little. Sure, I wasn't drinking nor dancing, but who says you can't have fun anyway?

"Hey, Harry. Co-ould you please go get me-e and Ed another dri-ink?" Liam giggled, and I just nodded with a smile on my face, happy that I finally had something to do. Even if they were a lot of fun, it was always nice to take a break and stretch your bones after sitting on a chair for so long. Besides, I was a little curious as to what was happening in the living room, where the party was on full blast.

So, I made my way into the living room and over to the table where the alcohol was being served and grabbed two glasses of some drink I didn't know the name of. I was just about to turn around and go back to Liam and Ed when I felt myself being splashed with some sort of liquid.

"Oh my God, I'm so sorry!" A male voice spoke from beside me, sounding truly apologetic.

I opened my mouth to say that it was no big deal when I saw who the guy was. It was Niall. He was dressed in a black t-shirt with a pair of black, skinny jeans. His hair looked a little messy, which I assumed was due to the party, and his eyes were a little unfocused, a sign that he was drunk. Nonetheless, they were still an ocean blue color, sparkling from the little light in the room.

"Harry?" He said in shock, his eyes widening at the sight of me.

I furrowed my eyebrows in confusion. Why in the world would he greet me like that? He hated me, just like all of his friends did, which included Louis. There was just no way he was in his right mind right now.

Speaking of the feathery-haired boy, by the way, I hadn't seen him here all night. Though, I was almost sure he was busy making out with his girlfriend in the bathroom or something similar to it. I didn't want to think it could be worse than that since it only gave me uncomfortable chills.

"Yeah?"

Niall scratched the back of his neck, wobbling a little but managing to catch himself on the table before falling. "Oh, nothing. J-just didn't expect you to be here, i-is all."

"Um, no. I usually don't go to parties," I said, finding it weird that he for the first time wasn't rudely talking to me. Maybe it was because of the alcohol, but right now, I didn't care. This Niall was much better than the other one, even if he was drunk off his ass at the moment.

"Well, that's too ba-ad. You should come mo-ore often, yeah? Think about it," he slurred, and I just inwardly chuckled at his behavior. This was so far from the Niall I usually witnessed that I almost didn't believe my eyes. Was he actually the same person? I doubted it.

When I didn't reply, he went to open his mouth again. "Look, I'm sorry I spilled my dri-ink on you. Maybe I could make up for it so-omehow?" He smiled suggestively, leaning forward a little to run his hand along my arm.

My eyes widened at his touch, and I instantly pulled away, suddenly feeling really uncomfortable. "Um, no, that won't be necessary. I... I have to go. See you later," I said hurriedly, quickly walking away from him.

I didn't look back when I began making my way back to Liam and Ed, who were probably getting impatient that I hadn't come back with their drinks yet, I was too afraid to see if Niall was following me. This was exactly what I meant when I said I didn't like being around drunk people. Things could get really damn uncomfortable if you weren't intoxicated yourself.

To get to the kitchen, I had to walk by the bathroom, and what I heard on the other side of the door made me furrow my eyebrows together. Was that the sound of someone throwing up?

Contemplating whether to do something about the situation or not, I bit my bottom lip. It could be anybody in there, but what were the odds that it was someone who wouldn't like my help? Probably zero, so I sat the two drinks on a table nearby before walking over to the door and knocking on it gently. "Hello? Are you okay?" I asked hesitantly, waiting for some kind of answer.

It took at least half a minute until I could hear a familiar voice on the other side of the door, and the sound of it made the muscles in my body freeze to ice. "Harry?" Louis whispered in reply, and a second later the door opened in front of me.

The sight of the feathery-haired boy made my eyes widen. His hair looked disheveled, as if he had run his hands through it several times, and his eyes were bloodshot. But it wasn't any of those things that told me he wasn't feeling well. It was the fact that his face was as pale as snow. How much had he had to drink tonight? He literally looked ready to pass out any second.

"Oh my God," I gasped, reaching up to cover my wide-opened mouth.

He checked our surroundings before pulling me into the bathroom and locking the door behind us. "Harry, what are you doing here?" He asked, sitting down on the toilet seat while running a hand over his face.

"I'm here with Liam and Ed, but that doesn't matter right now. What the hell? How much have you had tonight?" I walked over to him, bending down in front of him to get a better view of his pale face.

Don't ask me why I suddenly cared, I just didn't like the sight of anyone looking like this. It had nothing to do with the fact that this was Louis out of all people. It could've been anyone and I would've cared just as much about them.

When I reached up to pull his hand away from his face, he snatched it away, sending me an angry look. "What do you think you're doing?" He snapped, suddenly sounding a lot more sober.

I gulped, looking away from his intense glare. "Nothing. I-I was just making sure... Eh, whatever. You don't want my help anyway," I said, feeling dumb for even thinking he would accept my help. He hated me, just like he had always done. It didn't matter that he was pissed off drunk, his anger towards me would always be there.

Straightening myself up, I turned around to exit the room, but before I had even taken a step towards the door, a hand grabbed my arm. Confused, I turned to see Louis looking at me sheepishly, his bottom lip caught between his teeth. "Please, don't go. I just... fuck," he cut himself off, shaking his head in what looked like disbelief. "I can't believe I'm saying this, but I possibly... kind of... want your help?"

My lips turned into a small smile. "Well then, how about I take you back home? By the looks of it, you have partied enough for tonight, so I would say we go home and go to bed, yeah?"

He gave me a weak smile in return, nodding his head. "Sure."

Chapter 10

[Harry]

It turned out it was easier said than done to get Louis home. He was drunker than what he seemed to be. He couldn't even walk straight *with* my help. The only thing he kept doing was whine about how his head was starting to spin and how he wanted to say goodbye to all his friends before he went home.

After a lot of convincing, I finally managed to get him to shut up and go to the hall to get ready to go home while I made my way to the kitchen to give Liam and Ed their drinks and say goodbye to them. It turned out the two guys had gotten company by other people. They were still sitting around the kitchen table, but now a few other guys from our school were sitting with them.

When they saw me, Liam got up from his seat to walk over and hug me while Ed just smiled wide. With the drinks still clutched in my hands, it was quite hard to reciprocate the hug, but I managed to at least get my forearms around his muscular body. He asked me what took so long, to which I replied with a simple 'too many people, couldn't get through the massive crowd', and since he was drunk, he didn't ask further about it.

I then told the two boys I was going home and that they would have to manage without me the rest of the night. Liam was sad at first but gave in just a minute later when I said my mum was starting to get worried about me. Which was a lie, but he didn't need to know that.

Once I finally got to the entryway, Louis was leaning against the front door, his arm over his face as he groaned. "Harry, is that you?" He grumbled when I grabbed a hold of his free hand, pulling him out of the door.

"Yes, and we're going home right now before you get even worse," I muttered, dropping his hand to wrap my arm around his waist so he could support his body on mine. He leaned his entire body weight on me immediately, causing me to almost fall in the process, but I luckily managed to stay with my feet on the ground.

He tucked his face in the crook of my neck as he wrapped an arm around my shoulders, his hand squeezing my bicep. It was then I noticed that he was past the irritable stage of his drunkenness. This was a softer side of Louis that I hadn't seen in years, and to be honest, I was quite scared of what would happen next.

We started walking home in silence like that until he decided to break it when we were halfway there. He was now looking at the side of my face as we stumbled along the street walk. "You're quite beautiful, you know that?" He giggled, smiling up at me.

My heart fluttered in my chest at his words, and I had to swallow at least three times to be able to answer him. But I wasn't dumb, I knew he had no idea what he was talking about. He was drunk, meaning that he wasn't in his right mind. What he was saying right now wouldn't mean anything when he woke up tomorrow morning. "Louis, you're drunk, stop talking bullshit. Besides, you hate me. There's no way you can find me beautiful," I said, rolling my eyes even though my heart was beating at an incredible speed in my chest.

He shrugged, giving me another toothy grin before laying his head on my shoulder. "Doesn't really matter, though, does it? I can still find you beautiful."

I just shook my head and tried to shake what he just said out of my head. Louis did not find me beautiful. He was just drunk, and he had no idea what he was saying... but weren't drunk words usually sober thoughts, though? Well, probably not in this case. I couldn't even picture him meaning those words. He hated me. Moreover, he was my stepbrother. It was just impossible.

"Harry?"

Biting my bottom lip, I turned my head to him again. "Yeah?"

His face was now mere inches away from mine, and he was staring at me with this intense glint in his eyes that made it impossible for me to focus on anything but him. "Why do you hate me? Remember when we used to be friends? What happened to u-us?" He hiccupped.

Exactly what I had been asking myself the last two years... As I'd mentioned before, the only thing I knew was that he had stopped attending our meetings. Therefore, I found it a bit weird that he asked me this question. He should already know the answer to it since it was he who had stopped wanting to hang out with me. "I don't know, Louis. Why don't you ask yourself?" I mumbled, giving him a forced smile.

He furrowed his eyebrows in confusion, but he didn't say anything. The two of us continued our wobbling walk to our home and stayed silent for the rest of it. It wasn't until I had unlocked the door and shut it behind us that Louis broke the silence by falling to the ground when trying to pull his shoes off.

I burst out laughing, covering my mouth with my palm, which made him glare at me. "Shut up and help me instead," he whined, sitting up in a crisscrossed position on the floor, making him look like a little child who had yet to learn how to tie his shoes.

Rolling my eyes at him, I bent down to pull his Vans off for him before doing the same with my Converse. I then shrugged off my jacket and extended a hand to him so he could give me his as well. When I had hung up the two jackets on the coat rack, I pulled Louis up from the floor and wrapped a hand around his waist to steady him.

"Come on, let's go upstairs," I whispered in case I would wake up mum, Troy or Gemma, although Louis' fall might have already woken them up. But since neither of them had come out of their rooms yet, I assumed we were safe so far.

He merely nodded, and together we trudged up the stairs, almost slipping on one of the steps since it was so dark in the house and since Louis was still wobbling in my hold, but I managed to catch the railing before we could do so.

Once we were finally outside Louis' room, I opened the door and supported him over to his bed before helping him lie down on it. I pulled the covers over his now almost lifeless body, not caring that he was still wearing clothes. That, he would have to take care of himself if he didn't want to sleep with them on.

Without really knowing why I was taking care of him like this, I tucked him under the covers and gave him a small smile, to which he actually reciprocated with a sleepy one. "Goodnight, Louis," I said, straightening myself up to go over to the bathroom door and open it.

Just as I was about to exit his room, I could hear his voice behind me. "Harry?"

I turned around to face him where he was lying on his bed, his messy brown hair sprawled on the pillow and his lips pulled into a lazy smile. "Thank you."

I couldn't help but let another smile form on my lips. "No problem, Louis." And with that, I finally closed the door behind me and entered my own bedroom, inhaling a deep breath as I felt the familiar scent of my room surround me. There was literally nothing better than your own room and bed when you'd experienced an eventful day like this.

I was very exhausted, that was for sure, so I flopped down on my bed and started undressing before crawling under the covers, not even bothering to roll down the blinds. Mum would probably wake me up at the same time the sun would set anyway, so it didn't really matter if they were rolled down or not.

I closed my eyelids in an attempt to fall asleep, but I soon figured it was impossible after everything that had happened the past hour. To be honest, I didn't even know why I had helped Louis get home safely. I tried telling myself that it was because my mother would be disappointed in me if she found out I hadn't been there for him when he needed me at the party, but something told me that wasn't the real reason.

All I could say was that something was changing within me, and that was fast, but I didn't want to know what because I was afraid of what the outcome of it might be.

"Harry and Louis, breakfast is ready!" Troy called from the bottom floor a few hours later, waking me up from my light sleep. To be honest, I had barely slept a second that night thanks to everything that happened the night before with Louis. Nobody confused me as much as he did, and surely, no one made me think as much as he did either. In a negative way, of course.

Groaning, I opened my eyes only to be blinded by the sun that was shining through the window, its beams hitting me straight in the face. "Fuck," I muttered under my breath, rubbing my eyes to get rid of the sleep and now pain in them.

As soon as I had dressed myself in a pair of black sweatpants and a green, oversized jumper, and fixed my hair so it wasn't looking too bad, I made my way downstairs and into the kitchen where Troy, mum and Gemma were already sitting, Gemma munching on a pancake while Troy and mum were waiting patiently for me and Louis to arrive.

Before I could open my mouth and say good morning, footsteps were heard behind me, and I instantly knew that the last member of our 'family' had joined us. A little afraid of what Louis' reaction would be when he found me standing here after what had happened last night, I hesitantly turned around to face him. His usually sparkly blue eyes looked dull, as if he hadn't got a good night's sleep in weeks. His feathery, brown hair was standing in every direction, literally, and if you looked closely, you could see little bags under his eyes, a sign that he was either extremely hungover or just tired as hell. Since I had witnessed his drunk self last night, I was quite sure it was the first option, though, or maybe both.

My gaze lowered to his body, noticing that he had changed into a pair of grey joggers and a black tank top instead of those black, skinny jeans and the t-shirt he had been wearing when I put him to bed. The curious part of me secretly wondered if he had actually managed to strip his clothes off before he went to sleep last night or if he had simply changed when he woke up. But, that was only the curious part of me thinking.

My mum let out a gasp at the sight of him, and the next thing I knew, she was walking over to one of the cabinets to pull out an Advil for him. She handed it over to a confused-looking Louis along with a glass of water. "Dear God, how much did you drink last night, son?"

Louis scrunched his nose up at the word 'son' but didn't make any comment about it. Instead, he turned his gaze to me for a second, taking in my appearance quickly before averting it again. He then put the little pill in his mouth and chugged down the glass of water. "I... Well, to be honest, I don't remember a thing from last night. The last thing I recall is dancing with friends. Thanks for the painkiller, by the way. My head hurts like a bitch if you couldn't tell already," he smiled weakly, earning a concerned look from my mother.

I, on the other hand, couldn't help but feel my heart drop in my chest by the realization that he didn't remember that I had taken care of him last night, nor that we had actually had our first conversation in two years that didn't consist of either of us making any rude remarks to the other. It had actually been quite nice, now that I thought about it. It was almost like the old days, except the fact that he had been pissed drunk, but drunk Louis was actually not as bad as I thought he would be, considering I had a dislike for intoxicated people. He had actually been kind of... sweet? Well, at least when he had been in the second stage of his drunkenness.

"You're welcome, dear. So, how did you get home last night? I mean, since you barely remember anything, how did you manage to get back here?" She asked, her gaze flicking to me for a second.

Gulping, I decided to sit down beside Gemma at the kitchen table, not wanting to be part of the conversation, even though I was the answer to mum's question. If Louis didn't remember anything, what was the point of letting him know I had brought him home? It would only be embarrassing since he would most likely laugh at me for helping him when he 'certainly didn't need my help', even if he was the one to ask for it in the first place.

He knitted his eyebrows together, looking utterly confused. "I... I don't know," was the only thing he said. After a short silence, he walked over to sit down beside his dad while my mum sat down beside me.

"Well, I'm happy you got home, at least. Otherwise, I'm sure all of us would be worried sick by now. From one thing to another, how was the game yesterday?" She asked curiously, spreading some butter on her sandwich.

Louis grabbed the package of cereal and poured some in the bowl in front of him. "Well, since Harry was there, why don't you ask him?" He said, giving mum an obvious fake smile as he avoided making eye contact with me.

I almost choked on the piece of pancake in my mouth, coughing a few times. Gemma even had to pat my back to help me recover. "The game, huh? Well, uh, Louis and his team won. Though, I gotta say it was a close one."

The feathery haired boy nodded in agreement. "Yep, but our *incredibly* talented goalie managed to save the last shot, right Harry?" He almost snarled, emphasizing the word 'incredibly' for some reason. It made me frown. Why being so harsh about that? It was only the truth, after all.

"Yeah..." I trailed off. It was almost like he wanted to prove a point, but what point was it exactly? "Ed was pretty amazing, indeed. Probably the best player out there," I said with a shrug after a few seconds, secretly wanting to see his reaction although I was already pretty sure what it was going to be.

So, it didn't really surprise me when he scoffed and angrily shoved a spoonful of cereal into his mouth, looking at the wall beside him to avoid me. I smiled at the sight, knowing I had managed to piss him off. Of course he wanted me to say that he was the best player (which he was), but I obviously wasn't going to admit that. And I was sure he knew this, which was why he was irritated... right?

"Nice to hear it all went great, boys," mum smiled although it was a little forced since she could most likely sense the tension between me and Louis.

Believe it or not, but breakfast continued peacefully after that. Mum talked a lot with Troy while Gemma and I started a conversation about what had happened in our lives since we last talked to each other yesterday morning. I mainly explained how I had been with Liam and Ed at the party, not bothering to include either Niall or Louis since one of them was sitting right across from us and the other was his best friend.

Louis was mostly silent, staring down at his lap where he probably had his phone in his hand. The only time he talked was when Troy included him in his and mum's conversation and he replied with simple 'yes's and 'no's.

When all of us were finished and ready to get up and clear the table, Troy spoke up. "Louis, Harry and Gemma, tomorrow Anne and I have planned for all of us to eat dinner at this fine restaurant downtown, so don't plan anything with friends or something, alright?"

I flicked my gaze to Gemma to see if she had something to do with this, but when she shrugged her shoulders, I assumed she didn't. So, this was something Troy and mum must've come up with by themselves. Well, it didn't exactly make things better. I would still have to sit at the same table as Louis at a restaurant.

Unlike usual, neither of Louis and I opened our mouths to disagree, which was probably because we both knew it would be for nothing. We would have to go to this restaurant no matter what, whether we wanted to or not.

It wasn't hard to tell it was all set up for the two of us to start getting along. What they didn't know, though, was that they couldn't do anything about it because the only time Louis and I actually weren't at each other's throats was when there were just the two of us.

"Yeah, whatever. I'll be up in my room." With that said, Louis exited the kitchen with his phone practically in his face, not even bothering to put away his dishes.

Chapter 11

[Louis]

Spending a Saturday in a house you didn't really like while being hungover was not exactly the greatest thing you could do. If I didn't have such a killing headache, I would probably be out with my friends and do something better than lying on my twin-sized bed all day long. Sure, it wasn't exactly boring to text with your girlfriend, but there were still better things you could do, like for example meet her in real life.

My speaker was on full blast, and to be honest, I was a little surprised Harry hadn't barged into my room yet and yelled at me to turn the volume down like he'd done a week ago. Either he simply wasn't in his own room, or he just didn't want to see me or something.

Strangely, there was something about the loud music that calmed me. Most people would find it weird how the type of music I listened to could be calming, but I preferred rock music over anything, and I'd always been able to relax to it, especially when it was on full blast. Maybe I got that from partying or something, who knows? Either way, I had always enjoyed it.

It wasn't until about three in the afternoon that day that I first decided to log onto Twitter and check my news feed. By now, my headache was finally starting to fade, so I could focus on other things than the pounding feeling in my temples. Surprisingly, a lot of tweets from the night before had been posted, which was actually a little unusual. Sure, pictures were always taken and posted on social media, but this was not just a few, this was *a lot*.

I started going through them, clicking on each one I found interesting. When I came across one specific tweet, I had to do a double-take, though. In the picture were none other than my best friend and Harry's closest mate kissing. My eyes went wide at what I was witnessing. Since when did Zayn even like guys? I'd never seen him with one ever before. I mean, wasn't he dating Perrie just yesterday? This just didn't make sense at all.

Shaking my head in confusion, I continued scrolling through my newsfeed in search of some other shocking news. It took a few minutes, but soon enough, I found a tweet that made my body go rigid. It couldn't be... but I wasn't... I was with Eleanor all night, wasn't I? But how come...?

In the picture was a really drunk-looking me leaning against none other than Harry Styles' shoulder. My step brother's shoulder. The one living in the room next to mine's *shoulder.* Our backs were the only things that could be seen in the picture, but there was no doubt the two guys were us. And as if that wasn't bad enough, I even had my head buried in his neck. His motherfucking *neck.* My God, Anne wasn't kidding when she said I must've been really drunk last night. I just hoped I hadn't done worse things than this.

So, when a shocking realization hit me just a few seconds after I had logged off Twitter, I literally dropped my phone in my face. Since Harry was the one with me in the picture, where we had been standing in Niall's entryway, he must've been the one who took me home last night. There was actually no other explanation because I was sure I wasn't able to find my way back here with my sense of locality. It was bad, and I was sure it didn't get any better with alcohol involved. Moreover, none of my friends knew where I lived now, so there really wasn't any other explanation.

Without thinking twice, I got up from the bed with lightning speed, which turned out to be a bad idea because my sight went blurry for a few seconds due to the sudden movement. When I had finally composed myself, I sprinted out of my room and went straight into the bathroom, not even bothering to knock before opening Harry's bedroom door in hopes of finding the curly-haired boy there. But of course luck wasn't on my side today.

"Harry!" I called, exiting his room to sprint down the stairs and into the living room where I thankfully found him sitting on the couch with Anne and dad, watching the television.

His head turned to me abruptly in what I assumed was shock both from my outburst and just the fact that I had actually called his name. A glint of fear flashed through his eyes for a second, but it was gone before I had blink twice. Instead, he was now staring at me curiously as I approached him where he was sitting with his knees pulled to his chest and his chin resting against them. If I hadn't been so blinded by frustration and anger at the moment, I would've thought it was kind of adorable, the way he was sitting there, looking like an innocent little kid... wait, what?

Ignoring my thoughts and the two parents beside the curly-haired boy, I pointed a finger at Harry, then turned it in the direction of the staircase. "Upstairs. Now," I said sharply, anger lacing my voice.

He flicked his eyes to Anne and dad briefly before swallowing hard. "Wha--" But he was cut off by my father.

"Louis," he said warningly, raising his eyebrows at me.

I turned my attention to him in an instant, furrowing my eyebrows together. "I'm not going to hurt him, dad, Jesus Christ. I just want to talk to him about something *very* important, alright?" I almost snapped, because I was so pissed right now. Why didn't Harry just tell me about this? And what even made him do it in the first place? I thought he didn't care two shits about me. There were so many questions circling in my head that I needed to get answers to, and that was now.

Dad sighed exasperatedly, shaking his head in disappointment. "I'm sure whatever happened, Harry does not deserve to be exposed to your yelling, which I am positive you're about to do. Remember what we talked about a few days ago?"

I rolled my eyes, nodding my head. "Yes, but can you just stop assuming that I am going to hurt him all the time? I may not like him, but have you ever witnessed me do anything physical to him?" When there was no answer, I continued. "Didn't think so. Now, may Harry and I please be excused? I want to exchange a few words with him in private."

Without waiting for an answer, I grabbed ahold of Harry's arm, pulled him out of the room, and up the staircase. It wasn't until we were on the second floor that Harry reacted and tried to snatch his arm out of my hold. "Louis, what have I done now? Can't you just stay away from me for one single day? I'm really not in the mood to--" He started, but I cut him off by pulling him into my room and slamming the door shut behind us.

"What the fuck is this shit?" I tossed him my phone that was lying on my bed. At first, I thought he was going to drop it by the looks of it, but he managed to catch it before it fell to the ground.

He brought the device closer so he could see the picture on the screen, and his eyes widened when it registered in his head what, or rather *who,* it was. "Shit," was the only thing he said, which made me even more frustrated than I already was.

"That's all you have to say? Not even an 'I was drunk, I had no idea what I was doing?'," I scoffed, walking over to snatch my phone from his hands. "Just fucking explain to me why on earth you out of all people decided to take me home because it doesn't make sense to me at all."

With a sigh, he motioned to my bed as if asking whether he could sit on it or not, to which I rolled my eyes at but eventually nodded my head curtly. He took a seat on my bed with caution, pulling his knees up to his chest in the exact same position he'd been sitting on the couch downstairs. "You may not believe a single word I'm going to say, but just remember that I was the sober one last night, alright?" He said, giving me a somewhat cheeky smile.

I scoffed as I sat down on the chair in front of my desk and turned it so I was facing him. "Just explain already."

The smile dropped from his face and was soon replaced by a frown. "Okay, so I was just walking through the hallway last night when I heard you throwing up in the bathroom. Obviously, I didn't know it was you until you opened the door and pulled me inside. However, when we were in there, I noticed that you looked pale so I offered you my help..." He trailed off, running his hands over his face.

"Don't ask me why I did that, it just didn't feel right to leave you when you obviously wasn't feeling well. You didn't let me help you at first, but then changed your mind and told me to bring you home. I guess that's it," he said, looking up at me with this glint in his eye that told me that wasn't it at all.

There was definitely something that he wouldn't tell me, but I assumed he had at least told me the most important parts of what happened the night before. So, I shouldn't have to worry about it, right? Wrong. I was aware of how my behavior was when being drunk, so this worried me a hell of a lot. What if I had told him something that I shouldn't have?

Mentally panicking on the inside, I swallowed hard. "That's really it, right? I didn't do anything stupid like talk a bunch of bullshit? I tend to do that a lot when I'm drunk."

For a second, I could almost swear I saw his face falling, but it happened so fast that my mind barely registered it. He shook his head, his face empty with emotions. "Nothing else happened." And with that said, he stood up and pushed past me on his way into his own room, almost knocking me to the ground in the process. "Sorry. I was probably too drunk to remember how to walk straight."

He slammed the bathroom door shut behind him, making me flinch a little. Okay, so something apart from what he just told me definitely happened. Though, I had no idea what, and to be honest, I didn't want to know either because I was too scared of what it could be.

"Louis, we're leaving in five!" Dad called from downstairs.

It was now Sunday, and I was getting ready to go to this restaurant with my 'family' members. I was currently standing in front of my closet, going through my clothes to find something suitable to wear for the evening. A tank top? Nah, too causal. A button-up? No, not really my style.

Eventually, I settled for a black t-shirt with the logo 'Love Will Tear Us Apart' on it and a pair of black, skinny jeans. It wasn't too formal, but it would do. I was sure neither of dad, Anne, Gemma or Harry would care anyway.

After that, I styled my hair, swiping my fringe to the side and ruffling the rest of it a little. Once I was finished, I walked downstairs to see my dad in the entryway, stamping his foot against the floor impatiently with a grim look on his face. "You're late, son. I told you fifteen minutes ago that we were leaving in five, yet you come down here ten minutes after said time. What's your excuse?" He asked, raising his eyebrows expectantly.

I bit my bottom lip as I made my way over to slip on my Vans. "Um, I wasn't done, I guess?" I said, giving him a small smile.

He rolled his eyes, grabbing the door handle to open the front door. "Anne and the others are waiting in the car. Hurry up so we won't have to wait for longer than we already have." With that said, he shut the door behind him and left me alone in the house. However, just a second later, it was opened again and I could hear dad's voice. "Oh, and by the way, the key's in the key cabinet. Don't forget to lock the door."

When the door slammed shut once again, I let out a deep sigh and shrugged on my jacket. Why didn't he just wait for me? I mean, the only thing I had left to do was put on my jacket.

After checking myself in the mirror one last time, I grabbed the key and exited the house, locking the front door behind me as told before jogging over to the driveway where the other guys were waiting in the car. I opened one of the backseat doors only to find Harry sitting in the middle seat. How great.

Slamming the door shut, I took in the silence that surrounded the car, searching each of their faces except for Anne's since I couldn't see hers in the passenger seat. "What?" I asked, noticing the tension in the air. "I'm not even that late."

Harry scoffed beside me while I could see Gemma roll her eyes. "I just hope the waiter is going to say the same thing. Otherwise, we've all dressed up for nothing," dad said, shaking his head in disappointment as he turned on the engine and pulled out of the driveway.

"Ten minutes is nothing. They can't deny us just because of that, can they? I really doubt it." I crossed my arms over my chest once I had fastened my seatbelt and looked out the window, staring at the passing trees and houses.

"I'm quite sure they do, though. I've seen it happen once," Gemma pointed out, making me grit my teeth together. Instead of giving her a rude comeback, though, I continued looking out the window even if it made me feel dizzy from how fast we were moving.

During the entire ride, I was aware of Harry's thigh pressing against my own due to the small space in the backseat, and even if I didn't want to admit it, I couldn't deny the tingles that were shooting through my leg. Those stupid feelings were definitely coming back, and I hated it. The few months I spent liking Harry two years ago was some of the worst months I had ever experienced, and I didn't want a repeat of that.

Therefore, I had done everything I could ever since to forget about them, and I thought I was doing great, getting together with Eleanor and all, but my dad just had to start dating his mother so I now had to face him every single day. The best fucking decision he had ever made. Please note the sarcasm.

Harry didn't seem fazed by the fact that our thighs were pressed together. To be honest, he even seemed quieter than he usually was. In fact, he had been quiet ever since we had that talk yesterday afternoon about him bringing me home after the party. Well, he had at least been quiet in my presence. I couldn't speak for when he was around dad, Anne and Gemma. Anyway, something told me it was because of our talk, and it really made me wonder what did happen on our way back home from the party that night.

About five minutes later, we finally came to a stop outside the restaurant, and the torture I felt by feeling Harry's leg pressed to mine could finally go away. We all hopped out of the car and made our way to the entrance on the other side of the building. The place looked rather fancy with spotlights directed to the white walls and high windows that made it possible to see the many tables scattered on the inside. Knowing my dad, though, he wouldn't just choose any kind of restaurant to eat dinner, so this didn't exactly surprise me.

We entered the place and walked over to the counter, where a brown-haired, good-looking, middle-aged woman was standing, fumbling with a bunch of papers while talking on the phone. When she caught sight of us, however, she dropped the device from her ear and put on a polite smile. "Good evening, how may I help you?"

Dad stepped forward and cleared his throat. "We've reserved a table for five at six o'clock..." He trailed off with an apologetic look on his face. "I know we're a little late, but would it be possible to still get a table? We're really sorry if we've caused you any trouble."

The woman behind the desk hummed as she pursed her lips. "That won't be a problem, sir. Now, what's your name? I still need to check so that you really have made a reservation here."

Dad seemed a little taken aback that it had been so easy to convince her to let us get a table even if we were late, while I just stood there, smiling smugly. "Oh, of course. It's under Mr. Tomlinson, ma'am."

A minute later, we sat down at a table by the high windows. Dad and I were on one side while Anne, Gemma and Harry were on the other, something I was quite happy about since I didn't want a replay of what happened in the car by having Harry sit beside me again. It was better to have him across from me.

Once we had ordered our food and our drinks had arrived, Anne cleared her throat and flicked her gaze between me and Harry. "So, I've noticed you guys have been awfully quiet lately. Did something happen between the two of you or is it just a coincidence?" She asked, trying to sound casual even if you could tell she was really curious about it.

I glanced up at Harry only to see him biting his lip while looking down at the surface of the table. I was just about to open my mouth to answer her when he beat me to it. "Nothing happened, mum. Gosh, why do you have to care so much about our relationship? Can't you just let us be?" He sighed in annoyance, scrunching his nose up so a crease between his eyebrows formed.

Anne looked at my dad for help, and he stepped in instantly. "Look, boys. We just want to make this family work, alright? We don't want any of you guys to dislike each other because you will, unfortunately, in this case, have to live together for a while now. Anne and I have no idea what happened that made you guys hate each other, but obviously, we want to help you get on better terms. You have to understand that," dad said sincerely, but I couldn't help but clench my fists at my sides.

They had nothing to do with Harry and I's relationship whatsoever. Harry was right. Why couldn't they just let us be? A dinner like this would not bring us closer together, nor would any of their ideas. Why couldn't they just accept that? "Dad, please. If Harry and I wanted to get along, we would, alright? Nothing you and Anne come up with to bring us closer can make us do so. It's our problem, and even if you want to, you can't do anything about it."

Anne and dad exchanged a sad look while Gemma shook her head as she looked between me and Harry disappointedly. "Now, I may not really like you very much, Louis, and yes, I do have my reasons. However, what I want to say is that I know you and Harry haven't always been like this, and it's pretty sad to see that the two of you threw away the friendship you once ha--" Gemma was cut off by the table jerking.

It didn't take more than a second for my brain to comprehend that it was Harry who had stomped her on the foot and somehow managed to have bumped his thighs against the edge of the table. I knew this because Harry sent her a glare and discreetly rubbed his thigh where he had hit the table. However, he was already too late because Gemma had already said enough. To think I had actually trusted him back then...

"I can't believe you actually told her," I said emotionlessly, staring blankly at Harry who was staring back at me with a snow-white face.

"I... I just..." He trailed off.

"You promised."

Something seemed to snap inside him at those words because a second later, he was fuming and yelling. "So what if I fucking promised? Gemma is my sister. It's not like she would ruin your stupid reputation anyway. Besides, whatever vows we made during that time were definitely no longer valid after you abandoned me and started treating me like shit. What did I ever do to you, Louis?"

My face hardened with anger. "What did you ever do to me, huh? If you actually had a brain or some shit in your head, you would know. You would know how fucking awful I felt at the time, how much I just needed someone, but of course you didn't. You were too busy with your own shit." With that said, I stormed out of the booth, leaving my so-called 'family' behind with shock written all over their faces.

If only they knew the whole story of what happened to my and Harry's friendship two years ago. If only they knew.

Chapter 12

[Harry]

After quite some time, Louis finally got out of the men's bathroom and ate his food, even if he stayed quiet the whole night with his phone in his hand. Well, I couldn't say anything about it, though, because I did the exact same thing, except that I didn't have my phone. Instead, I was staring down at my half-eaten chicken with rice, waiting for the time to pass quickly so we could go home.

There was no question that mum and Troy were concerned about the two of us, even more now after the scene they had witnessed. They kept sending worrying glances between the two of us but didn't say anything, something I was happy about. The evening had definitely not gone as they first planned, and it seemed like they had accepted that and dropped the mission of bringing me and Louis closer together. Well, at least for now.

As for Gemma, she had this guilty look on her face throughout the entire dinner. She was aware that she was the cause of the fight between me and Louis, something she probably wasn't very proud of. Obviously, she hadn't thought through what she was going to say before she did, and well, this was the outcome of it. Louis and I didn't so much as look at each other for the rest of the evening thanks to what happened.

Although I wanted to be mad at Gemma for revealing that she knew of Louis and I's friendship, I couldn't help but feel as if it had been a good thing in the end. Not that I liked the fight Louis and I had, but it at least got me thinking again. I was finally one step closer to finding out what made him abandon me two years ago.

And that was what kept me up that night. My mind was spinning with different scenarios of what possibly could've made Louis leave, or what I did to make him leave, more specifically. But I couldn't come up with anything. The only thing I could think of was that Liam and I had started becoming friends at the time and that he was jealous of him, but that couldn't be it, right? Why would he even be jealous of Liam? It wasn't like he actually enjoyed me as a friend so much that he would get jealous of me being friends with other people, would he?

With those thoughts on my mind, I eventually fell into a very light sleep. I woke up at least five times, Louis' words still repeating in my head.

"What did you ever do to me, huh? If you actually had a brain or some shit in your head, you would know. You would know how fucking awful I felt at the time, how much I just needed someone, but of course you didn't. You were too busy with your own shit."

When I walked into school the next day, I was feeling rather down. My head hung low as I dragged my feet against the floor, my backpack thrown over my shoulder lazily, as if I couldn't care less about anything. It was quite unusual for me not to be excited when I walked through these hallways in the morning. I was usually a person who enjoyed school and going to all of my lessons. Hell, I usually even liked the atmosphere in here.

However, that was not the case today. After everything that had taken place last evening, I couldn't even so much as bring a smile on my face. Louis hadn't even bothered to throw me his infamous glares at breakfast this morning. He had just sat there, staring at nothing, literally. His eyes were blank, no spark in them whatsoever.

To be honest, I didn't really know why I was feeling so down. I mean, why should the fight between me and Louis affect me this much? None of our previous ones had done before, so I didn't know what was so special about this one. Maybe it was because this fight had to do with our friendship two years ago? No matter what, this was not how I usually acted after a fight between the two of us, and that was a fact.

Eventually, I arrived at my locker to find my best friend standing there as usual, although he wasn't wearing that wide grin on his face today. Apparently, I wasn't the only one feeling down this morning. "Morning, Liam," I greeted with a grimace as I put in my combination and opened my locker to get rid of my backpack and jacket.

"Hey," was the only thing he said, which made me more curious about what had happened to make him this sad.

I sneaked a glance at him with a raised eyebrow. "You don't seem very happy. Did something happen?" I asked cautiously, not wanting to upset him in case someone near him had died or something. Who knows, it could be anything.

A small, weak smile formed on his lips as he shook his head. "Nothing important. I just woke up on the wrong side of the bed, you know?" He tried to joke, but not even a little kid would laugh at him, I was sure of it.

"Ha ha, very funny, Li. Now, tell me what really happened," I demanded, grabbing my Math books and closing my locker to face him.

Before he could open his mouth, though, a tap on my shoulder interrupted him. He stared at the person behind me weirdly, as if he had no idea why they would be there. Frowning, I turned around only to be met with a sight that made my eyes widen. No wonder Liam thought it was weird that *he* out of all people was here, trying to get my attention. "Niall?" I asked in confusion, raising my eyebrows at him. "What are you--"

The blonde-haired guy held up a hand with a grimace on his face, signaling me to keep my mouth shut. "Look, I just wanted to apologize for my behavior at the party Friday night. What I did was just uncalled for and I don't know what the hell I was thinking. I just... gosh, I'm so sorry," he said, running a hand through his blonde locks nervously with a pink blush tinting his cheeks.

I just shook my head, feeling a little awkward about the whole situation. I could still remember the way he had tried to make me dance with him and also the way he had tried to seduce me. It was uncomfortable, to say the least, but he had been drunk after all, so I shouldn't blame him. Many people did weird things when they were intoxicated.

Liam's eyes stared at the side of my face now, a curious glint glistening in them. "Eh..." I trailed off uncertainly. "Don't worry about it. I know you didn't mean anything, so relax. I'm not going to tell anyone, by the way," I promised, giving him a timid smile.

He furrowed his eyebrows together but didn't say anything, which I found a little weird. However, I didn't question it but just waited for him to finally open his mouth. "Cool. Thank you for understanding," he muttered before turning on his heel and walking away from us.

For a moment, I just stood there, following his figure until it disappeared around the corner. What the hell was that? And why would he even apologize in the first place? I mean, I thought it was obvious he didn't know what he was doing that night, and that he had just acted on the alcohol. It even surprised me that he remembered he had actually flirted with me, judging by his actions that evening. It all just really confused me, making me want to push it aside and think about something else instead. It was just too much for me to handle.

Thankfully, the bell snapped me out of my thoughts, and also saved me from being questioned by Liam about what had just happened. Though, I knew he would probably ask me about it as soon as he got the chance to, so it only helped me for the time being. But, at least that was something.

Together, Liam and I made our way to the Math classroom and joined the students who had already arrived there. The bell had rung, yes, but there were still quite a few people who weren't here yet, one of them being a certain feathery haired boy who lived in my house. I sat down in my seat, dropping my books on the desk in front of me as I waited for the class to start.

Liam surprisingly didn't interrogate me about the Niall thing the first thing he did. Instead, he kept his eyes on the door, as if he was waiting for someone to walk through it. I didn't say anything. I was just happy he didn't bring anything up because I didn't want to explain what had happened at the party with Niall. He was drunk anyway, so it didn't really matter, right?

Mr. Storm was just about to open his mouth and begin the lesson when the door was pushed open. My eyes snapped up at the sound, only to find Louis entering the room with his arm wrapped around Eleanor's waist. They seemed rather deep in conversation, something Mr. Storm found annoying since they had arrived after the bell had rung, and had interrupted him when he was about to start the class. He cleared his throat, making the couple turn to him once they had sat down at a desk in the back.

"Yes, Mr. Storm?" Louis asked with mock politeness.

The teacher opened his mouth again, but just like last time, he was interrupted by the classroom door slamming shut. In walked none other than Zayn and that blonde girl he had been hanging with lately. My gaze flicked to Liam who was now resting his chin against his forearms that were lazily placed on the desk in front of him. To say he looked happy would have been a definite lie. He looked about ready to start crying his eyes out.

"That's it!" Mr. Storm snapped, banging his fist against the surface of his desk. "I'm sick and tired of you four always arriving late to my classes. It doesn't even help that I give you detention every single day, you still refuse to listen to me. I mean, come on! How difficult can it be to just get here on time?"

The classroom fell dead silent after his mini-tantrum. Through the corner of my eye, I could even see Louis staring at the teacher with widened eyes, which was not likely at all. He usually played everything off as a joke and never took things seriously. Maybe this would finally make him realize that he did act like an asshole sometimes.

To everyone's surprise, Eleanor was the first one to speak up. "We're sorry, Mr. Storm. We'll start behaving, we promise," she apologized with a dark blush on her cheeks.

He wouldn't have any of it, though, and to be completely honest, I had never seen him more upset in my life. Sure, Mr. Storm was usually quite strict, but I had never seen him snap like this before. "I believe it when I see it," he snorted, flicking his gaze between the four students with a disapproving look. "For now, you'll get away with detention, but if this behavior of yours repeats again, I would suggest you not even attend my lessons. Are we clear?"

"Yes, sir," Eleanor and the blonde girl muttered while Zayn and Louis still just stared at the man blankly.

It wasn't until the end of the lesson that the two guys looked completely composed, and I had to say that was very unlike them. They usually brushed things like these off as if they couldn't care less about it. But then again, Mr. Storm had never snapped this way at them before, so hopefully, they had finally realized that they should actually start listening to him. Their behavior pissed me off sometimes too, and it disappointed me that I was one of very few people who could see it.

Once the bell rang, I gathered my stuff and exited the classroom with Liam in toe. I walked with rather quick strides, not wanting to risk bumping into Louis and Eleanor. After the way he had treated me this morning, I was quite sure he wouldn't confront me at least, but I just didn't want to see what he would do if it were to happen. I didn't know what would be the worst; him giving me a rude remark or him just ignoring me. Both of the options seemed just as bad.

Liam followed me all the way to my locker, where I stopped to exchange my Maths books with my English ones. He was still being quiet, which reminded me that he never explained the reason why he was acting weird this morning. "So, are you going to tell me why you're awfully quiet today?" I asked him, making him snap his head up.

His eyes narrowed. "If you tell me why Niall Horan walked up to you this morning and apologized for something that happened at the party," he said, and I gulped. Shit. I was going to have to tell him after all.

"Alright, fine. Let's take it on the way to your locker."

He nodded curtly, and with that, I slammed my locker shut, and we started walking in the direction of his locker. It was silent at first, none of us wanting to take the initiative and start explaining. Eventually, though, I gave in and let out a defeated sigh. "Okay, so at the party when I went to get you and Ed new drinks, Niall spilled his drink on me. There was nothing special about it. He just seemed unusually nice, you know? I thought it was because he was drunk, and I guess that turned out to be it since he then went a little over the limit by stroking my arm and whispering in my ear in an attempt to seduce me. That was pretty much it, and I guess he just wanted to apologize for his actions earlier," I shrugged, although it still didn't make sense to me. Why would he apologize when it didn't mean anything? It was all just a drunken mistake, something to just look past and forget about. Well, at least it was to me.

Liam seemed deep in thought, as if he was trying to put something together in his head. "Has he done anything else to you lately?" He asked thoughtfully.

I shook my head, but then remembered that he had saved me from getting injured on the bus a few days ago and also met my gaze at the football game. Furthermore, I had noticed that he wasn't being his usual self at lunch when he was with his friends, but I doubted that had anything to do with this. "Well, he kind of saved me from falling on the bus one day and also caught my gaze at the football game. I don't know if that counts as something, though. Why?"

Liam's lips formed a small smile. "I don't know about you, but to me it sounds like someone's got a crush, especially judging by the way he reacted earlier when you said you knew that he didn't mean anything when he touched you at the party. Niall definitely fancies you," he smirked.

My mouth turned into the shape of an 'o', and I started shaking my head vigorously. "No, no. There's no way. I.... He hates me, Liam. You know he does! Haven't you witnessed when he's made fun of me all those times? He doesn't like me, Liam. You've got it all wrong."

"Actually, now that I think about it. He's been quite distant lately, hasn't he? He's not even paying attention to what his friends talk about at lunch anymore, and that's definitely saying something. He's so got a crush on you, mate," he said smugly, probably proud that he had put the puzzle pieces together all by himself.

"Whatever," I said, shaking my head. "Even if he does, the feelings are not reciprocated. I mean, how am I supposed to like someone who's never done anything but give me rude remarks? If he actually wants my attention, he should at least try a little better. That's why I have a hard time believing you, Li. I still don't think you're right."

He rolled his eyes. "Believe me, I am right, and you should give him a chance. If he tries to get closer to you, that is. I mean, he's definitely far from the ugliest guy at this school," he joked, giving me a teasing nudge in the side.

"Shut up," I muttered, and for some reason, an image of a familiar feathery-haired guy popped into my head, making me want to slap myself. I did not just think of my stepbrother, okay?

By now, we had arrived at Liam's locker a long time ago, yet he hadn't moved to open it. "So, now on to you," I said, raising an eyebrow at him. "Why the sad look on your face today?"

He let out a sigh and shut his locker with a slam. Right at that moment, Zayn walked by with the blonde girl, smiling at something she had just said. However, when they passed us, he looked up and gave Liam a glare that seemed to hold feelings that without a doubt meant something had happened between the two of them.

My gaze turned back to see Liam's reaction, and it didn't surprise me when he looked down at his shoes with a sad expression on his face. Yeah, something had definitely happened between them.

When Zayn and the girl were out of sight, I looked at him expectantly. "It has to do with Zayn, doesn't it?"

He let out a defeated sigh and looked up at me with a weak smile. "Yeah..." He trailed off hesitantly. I had waited so long to know what his thoughts on Zayn were, ever since he had started throwing these glances his way a few weeks ago. It could be anything from lo-- "We kissed at the party," he admitted at last, making my eyes widen in surprise.

"What?!"

He chuckled dryly. "Yeah... and I kind of... possibly have feelings for him?" he continued, staring back down at his shoes again.

I looked at him in shock, not knowing why I didn't already know of this. We were best friends. I thought we told each other these sorts of things? "And you haven't told me before because...?"

"Because I was embarrassed, okay? I know he's already got a girlfriend and it's so weird to have a crush on someone who's obviously unavailable and to top that off, way out of your league. I mean, have you seen him? He looks like some sort of Greek god for goodness' sake!" He let out in frustration, his cheeks heating up by the second.

I chuckled, giving him a smile as he shook his head, running a hand through his brown hair. "He's not out of your league, mate. Believe me. You two would actually make a pretty hot couple," I admitted truthfully. I had never really thought about the two of them together before, but when I pictured them in my head now, I realized they would actually look great together.

"Ha, yeah, as if."

Rolling my eyes, I gave him a pat on the shoulder. "Well, you said you two kissed at the party, right? Tell me more about it. I want to know everything."

He glanced at me, nodding his head after a few seconds. "Okay, so I don't really remember much from that night seeing as it was my first time being drunk, but I would be a fool not to remember kissing Zayn. Anyway, it was after you had gone home, and Ed and I had gone to the living room to dance. He was there, on the dance floor, and I guess he was just as intoxicated as me because we started grinding on each other, and then one thing led to another, and yeah..." He trailed off, scratching the back of his neck.

I gave him a thoughtful look, tugging at my bottom lip with my thumb and forefinger. "So, you're telling me you and Zayn kissed when he is already in a relationship with someone else?"

He nodded slowly. "I guess?"

"Well, to me it seems like he doesn't like his girlfriend as much as he makes it look like he does. I mean, if I were in a relationship with someone, I would not go and grind on someone else just like that. Sure, he was drunk, but since he obviously remembers kissing you, judging by the look he just gave you, he can't have been that wasted. I think he knew what he was doing, but that he doesn't want to admit it to himself that he has feelings for you," I concluded. It wasn't until the words escaped my mouth that I realized how true they were. It actually sounded very realistic.

Liam had his eyebrows pulled in a frown. "So, what do you reckon I do? I can't just go up to him and tell him to dump his girlfriend and be with me instead, no matter how much I'd like to do that. He would never look my way again. Plus, I would embarrass the hell out of myself."

I rolled my eyes. "Obviously not. You should tease him, make him flustered, and frustrated that he doesn't have you. Make him realize that he's better off with you than with that girl he is with at the moment," I suggested.

He contemplated it for a second. "But, what if he doesn't have feelings for me? Then what? I go and humiliate myself in front of one of the most popular guys at this school? I don't know about you, but I want to be able to go to school in the future without having to hide from everyone."

"Don't be so dramatic. At least you'll know whether he reciprocates your feelings or not. Isn't that worth it?"

He bit his bottom lip, looking at me for a long time before he let out a groan. "Fine, I'll do it. But if it turns out I've done everything just to humiliate myself, I'm blaming you, okay? You'll probably have to bring me my homework home from school as well," he threatened, making me chuckle.

"Alright."

Chapter 13

[Harry]

A few weeks passed by, and it was now the middle of December. Even if it was very cold outside, the rain hadn't turned to snow yet, something that wasn't very surprising seeing as it usually didn't snow very much here in Holmes Chapel. But since it felt like you were in the middle of the Antarctic whenever you stepped out of the house, you thought it might as well start snowing any day. To be honest, it was colder than it usually was in December, and that was not a good thing whatsoever. It just meant that you had to wear more clothes and warmer jackets. Not to mention, it was suffocating to walk to the bus stop every morning, especially when you were freezing your hands off.

Louis and I hadn't really spoken to each other after the incident at the restaurant. I still didn't know whether that was better than fighting with him, but the more days that passed, the more I started to realize how much I missed talking to him somehow. It was stupid, really, because I shouldn't be thinking about him in this way. I should be happy that we hadn't interacted in more than two weeks, but sadly that wasn't the case, and that realization honestly scared me.

When it came to what he told me that day at the restaurant, I hadn't really gotten anywhere. I mean, during the last years, I had been sure that he was the reason why we had stopped being friends, and now he just came out of nowhere and told me I was the reason? I just couldn't figure out anything I had done wrong. If I did, shouldn't I have already figured that out a long time ago since I had basically asked myself what happened between the two of us every day ever since we fell apart? Well, I would think so at least.

As for Niall, he had actually taken matters into his hands and talked to me a few times during the last few weeks. He even sat with me and Liam at lunch sometimes, something I found quite entertaining. It was nice to have someone other than just Liam - and sometimes Ed - there all the time, and Niall was a great guy once you got to know him and when he didn't act like a stupid jerk who only made nasty remarks all the time. I was actually starting to grow fond of him, but not in a 'more than friendly' way. I just liked his funny and kind of awkward persona, that was all.

Unfortunately, things hadn't gone that well with Liam and Zayn, though. Liam was trying his best to make Zayn notice him and had even tried to make a move, but so far, Zayn had barely even thrown him a glance. It saddened me to see Liam so miserable day in and day out thanks to this. I just wished I could do something about it, like walk up to the raven-haired guy and demand him to tell me whether he had feelings for Liam or not, or at least ask him why he had decided to kiss him if he wasn't going to do anything about it, but Liam had told me not to interfere with anything, so I didn't.

It was now Saturday, and I was sitting at the kitchen table in a pair of black joggers and a grey jumper, eating breakfast with my family. After living with Louis and his father for more than a month, I had finally gotten used to it. It no longer felt weird to say the word 'family' when I spoke about them, although it should since I still had a hard time understanding that Louis was my stepbrother. But, at least I had gotten used to him wandering around my house constantly.

Since it was only nine in the morning, Louis was still asleep and also the only one who wasn't present in the kitchen. This was nothing new, so mum wouldn't even comment about it anymore, which she had actually done in the beginning since she thought it would be nice for all of us to eat breakfast together. That desire had been forced to disappear, though, because Louis was not a morning person whatsoever, especially not on the weekends. He thought nine o'clock was way too early to wake up when you didn't have school to attend and to be honest, I kind of agreed with him there, but I didn't want to make mum even more upset by telling her I wouldn't join them at breakfast on the weekends either.

So, that was the reason why I was now sitting here, munching on some cereal while spreading butter on a piece of toast. Gemma was sitting beside me, pouring milk into her bowl as mum and Troy prepared their own breakfast. There were cooked sausages and scrambled eggs on a plate in the middle, but I decided a bowl of cereal and a piece of toast would do just fine today. We were having tacos later on anyway, so I would spare for that.

Surprisingly, a feathery haired boy appeared in the doorway just a few minutes later, rubbing the sleep from his eyes as he yawned loudly. "You guys are way too noisy. Why can't you just let me sleep for once?" Louis whined as he took a seat beside his father who chuckled at him.

Believe it or not, but the atmosphere had started getting better and better between all five of us. Louis wasn't being his bitchy self who didn't care about anything anymore, which in effect caused my mum to not have to raise her voice at the kitchen table. Though, he still didn't utter a single word to me. He never even glanced my way, just simply acted as if I wasn't there.

"You sleep for too long anyway, my son. Now, eat your breakfast and enjoy," Troy said jokingly, gesturing to the food scattered on the table.

Mum watched the two newest family members' interaction with a smile on her face as she chewed on her scrambled egg. "So, what are your plans for the day?" She asked, looking between all three of us teens.

Bringing a spoonful of cereal to my mouth, I shrugged my shoulders. To be honest, I had nothing planned today whatsoever. Not that I usually did something special on the weekends, but today I had absolutely no idea what to do at all. I had already done my homework due for next week yesterday, and Liam was away with his family the whole weekend, so I would probably have to stay at home doing absolutely nothing.

"I'm actually going on a date," Gemma announced, smiling cautiously while fiddling with her fingers.

My eyes widened. "What?" I asked, shocked by her words. "With whom?"

She turned in her seat to face me. "You know that guy I've been crushing on for months, right?"

I nodded, my eyes only widening by the second.

"It's with him," she confessed, her lips forming into another smile.

"Gemma! Wow, this is great news! Why didn't you tell me? I didn't even know you'd mustered up enough courage to talk to him, and now you're going on a date? Jesus," I said, shaking my head in disbelief. I remembered her talking about the guy a few weeks ago when he had just gotten back from a trip to

Spain with a 'hot' tan. Actually, that was the last time she had mentioned him around me, and considering I knew they didn't talk back then, things definitely must've happened since that.

"I guess we just never came across the topic," she shrugged. "Anyway, we started talking about two weeks ago when we were partnered up for a project. Mr. Holmes will always be my favorite teacher thanks to that."

I laughed, taking a bite of my toast. "So, what's his name?" Mum asked, raising her eyebrows expectantly at Gemma who now had a small blush on her cheeks. She probably just remembered that Troy, mum and Louis were there as well, and could hear everything she said.

"Um, his name's Devon Oliver," she replied sheepishly. "He's the same age as me, and we share the same Math and English classes."

I nodded in agreement. "Yeah, and from what I've heard, he's amazing, so don't worry mum," I joked, making her roll her eyes.

"I'm not worried that my daughter will find a bad guy, Harry. I trust her, and if she really likes him and he reciprocates her feelings, I'm absolutely okay with it. But, I'd like to meet him sometime, yeah?" She said, turning her attention back to Gemma.

"Mum," she warned. "This is our first date, so no need to hurry. You'll get to meet him eventually, I promise. It's not that he's shy or anything, but I just think we should get to know each other better before we meet each other's parents," she explained.

Mum bit her bottom lip hesitantly. "Alright, but you know how curious I can get, so you'd better hurry. I'm not a patient woman," she joked, although we all knew it was true. I bet even Louis knew about it, and he was the one who knew mum the least in our family.

"Speaking of dates," Louis suddenly spoke up, gaining everyone's attention. "I'm planning on inviting my girlfriend over for dinner tonight if that's okay? She might come over earlier, though, just a warning."

Troy's lips formed into a smile. "Eleanor? Ah, I haven't met her since we moved, which was a long time ago. Why haven't you brought her over earlier? She's always welcome, Louis," he promised, giving his son a pat on the shoulder.

"You have a girlfriend? Why wasn't I informed of this? That's wonderful, Louis. Of course you can invite her over, and she's more than welcome to eat dinner with us," mum said excitedly, clapping her hands together with a bright smile on her face.

So, everyone was basically smiling except for me. They were all super happy that Eleanor was coming over later to join our dinner, but I just couldn't bring myself to be so. Not that I didn't like her or anything, she was a nice girl who had done me no wrong, but the image of her and Louis together just didn't sit well with me. There was just something about it that made my stomach churn uncomfortably.

Louis then glanced my way, but it was only briefly. It barely lasted for a second until he turned his attention back to his dad and my mum. "Eh... I wasn't sure whether I was allowed to bring her over or not, but I thought now that we've been living here for quite some time that it wouldn't hurt to ask at least," he shrugged.

I narrowed my eyes at him because I was sure that was not true whatsoever. He wouldn't have cared a damn in the world if mum or Troy had told him that he couldn't bring her over earlier. So, there obviously must've been another reason as to why he hadn't invited her over yet, and judging by the glance he just sent my way, I had a feeling I was part of that reason. Though, I had no idea what it was about.

Obviously, mum didn't notice, so she gasped at his words. "Of course we wouldn't mind! She's very welcome, Louis. Don't think otherwise, honey. All of you guys' girlfriends and boyfriends are welcome as long as you don't do anything I wouldn't want you to if you catch my drift," she joked, although you could hear the seriousness behind her words.

Covering my face with my hands, I let out an embarrassed groan. "Mum, shut up."

"I was just saying, dear. It's not very polite to do such things when--"

"Okay mum, I think we get it. Thank you," Gemma cut her off, giving her a forced smile.

Mum raised her hands in defense as Louis burst out laughing. Even Troy had a smile on his face. "Jesus, this is hilarious," Louis said, throwing his head back in laughter.

"Okay, okay, I'm sorry. I know you guys wouldn't do anything to be impolite, but you can't blame me for reminding you, can you?" Mum asked, raising her eyebrows at me and Gemma.

I let out a sigh, shaking my head. "Mum, please. Can't you just drop it?"

"Alright fine," she finally said. "I'll drop it, but only because Louis seems to be dying of laughter, and I wouldn't want my son to get hurt by something I said," she chuckled, glancing at Louis who had stopped laughing abruptly. Instead, a frown was now evident on his face.

Strangely, I seemed to be the only one noticing this because Troy, Gemma and mum continued talking about God knows what while Louis remained quiet and stared at the glass of milk in front of him. It wasn't hard to tell that something was bothering him. The question was; what did mum say that made him shut up so fast?

A few minutes later, we were all finished and stood up to bring the plates, glasses and utensils to the sink. Troy offered to wash the dishes, which none of us disagreed with, so the rest of us exited the kitchen except for mum who stayed back to help him even though he told her it wasn't necessary.

I followed Louis up the stairs and was just about to turn to my bedroom when he stopped me by spinning around on his heel. "Pay attention, Harry, and think," was the only thing he said before turning around again and entering his own bedroom. The door slammed shut, and I was left there to stare at the spot where he was just standing, suddenly feeling very confused.

What was he talking about? And what did he mean by those words? Well, hopefully, I would get an answer to that soon.

It was four in the afternoon when the doorbell rang that day. At first, I thought it was Gemma's date who had arrived, but when I heard the door next to my bedroom slam shut, I realized it must be Eleanor. With a heavy sigh, I got up from my bed and pulled my earphones out of my ears. It wasn't like I wanted to, but I knew my mum would want me to be downstairs to greet Eleanor.

After all, I had been brought up nicely, so whenever someone was invited to our house, my mum expected both me and Gemma to greet the person by the door no matter who it was. Well, excluding the plumber or chimney sweeper or something like that. Those people weren't that important if she was home.

With heavy strides, I trudged down the stairs and entered the hallway where mum, Gemma and Troy were watching Louis help Eleanor take off her jacket. I wanted to roll my eyes at the scene, but instead, I quietly made my way over to stand beside Gemma. Eleanor's eyes immediately found mine and widened. "Wait, don't you go to our school?"

Awkwardly, I scratched the back of my neck as I nodded my head slowly. "Yeah, I'm Harry. And for your information, we even share a few classes," I explained, giving her a timid smile.

She turned to Louis with a surprised look on her face. "You never told me you had a stepbrother our age, Louis."

The feathery haired boy gave me a brief look before directing his attention to Eleanor, a somewhat forced smile forming on his lips. "No, I didn't see the need to tell anyone." His voice sounded a little bit harsher than I think he wanted it to because the next second he wrapped an arm around her waist and squeezed her hip reassuringly.

Her eyebrows pulled together. "Oh, I see. Anyway, it's nice to meet you, Harry. I'm Eleanor, Louis' girlfriend," she smiled politely, extending her hand for me to shake.

As if I didn't already know that, I wanted to say, but kept quiet and stared at her hand for a few seconds before hesitantly taking it in mine. "Nice to meet you too, I guess," I said emotionlessly, earning a nudge in the side from Gemma, and when I looked at her, she gave me a warning stare.

Also catching the displeased look on mum's face, I turned back to the brunette girl who was glancing at Louis a little alarmed. "Um..." She trailed off hesitantly. "Louis, why don't you show me your room, yeah?"

"Gladly," he said, moving his hand to the small of her back to bring her further into the house. As they were about to go up the stairs, he looked back to give me a smirk.

"We'll be upstairs," he announced, and with that, they were gone, leaving the remaining four of us to stare at each other. Or well, they were staring at one another while I was stuck watching the spot where Louis and Eleanor were just standing. What the hell did that smirk mean? There was no doubt he had some kind of plan going on in his head that had to do with me. I just wondered what he was going to do and how it was going to affect me.

After exchanging a few words with Gemma, mum and Troy, I went back up to my room and flopped down on my bed where my earphones were still lying. I put them aside and pulled out my phone from my back pocket to send a text message to Liam, hoping that he would reply quickly because really, I was bored as hell and just wanted something to do.

It took a few minutes, but eventually, I finally received a text from him and we started talking about his trip and also about school work since that was a common subject we conversed about. It wasn't until about half an hour later that I could suddenly hear noises coming from the bathroom, or Louis' room to be more specific. Now, don't misunderstand me, it wasn't *those* kinds of noises, but more like obnoxious giggling.

At first, I wasn't fazed by it and just continued texting away with Liam, but when the laughter started getting louder and even more obnoxious, I started feeling anger boil up inside me. Not only were the giggling sounds annoying, but they were also coming from Eleanor and were probably caused by Louis.

Against my will, images of what they might be doing in there flashed through my mind, and I found myself cringing. It wasn't like I thought kissing, tickling, or what the hell they were doing was disgusting, but I just didn't like the idea of them doing it so loud that I could hear... Yeah, that must be it.

The giggling sounds eventually turned into moans, and that was when I had enough. Without thinking twice, I flew up from my bed and made my way into my and Louis' shared bathroom to bang on the door. "Shut the hell up, would you?" I yelled through the wall, not wanting to witness what I was almost certain was going on in there.

Only a second later, the moans quieted down, and I could swear I heard Louis let out a snicker. The door to his room suddenly flew open, and there he was standing, all of his clothes on (thankfully) but his hair looking a little disheveled as if someone had run their fingers through it carelessly. His lips pulled into a satisfied smile as he tilted his head to the side while leaning against the door frame. "You were saying?" He asked, raising his eyebrows expectantly.

It was right then it hit me. This had been his plan all along. Somehow, he knew this would be my reaction to whatever he and Eleanor were doing in there, and now he had that stupid smile on his face because he now knew he had succeeded. What he got out of it, though, I had no idea.

Feeling a bit insecure by my realization and the way he was looking at me, I took a step back, biting my bottom lip. "Um, nothing. Just... I'll leave you alone," I said, my cheeks heating up.

To my surprise, he stepped forward and closed the door behind him so we were alone in the bathroom. He gave me this intense look that held so many emotions, emotions I couldn't put my finger on what they meant. "Do you remember?" He asked slowly, now sounding more serious.

"Remember what?" I asked in confusion.

He sighed, shaking his head. "Fuck, you're so oblivious it's not even funny. I can't believe you haven't realized..." He trailed off, making a face as if he had just said too much.

"That I haven't realized what?"

He looked down, shaking his head once again. After a second of thinking, he turned his gaze back up and sent me a glare. "Forget it," he said coldly, spinning on his heel and opening the bedroom door before slamming it shut behind him, leaving me standing there alone and utterly confused.

Chapter 14

[Harry]

To say that day was fun would be a definite lie. I had honestly never felt so bored, yet riled up ever before. Eleanor stayed for the rest of the day, and Troy and mum even told Louis she could stay the night if she wanted to, which she did, of course. That left me locked up in my room the whole evening with my earbuds in to block out possible noises that could occur, even if mum had told us it was inappropriate to do such things when the rest of the family was home.

What made me angry about it all was that mum and Troy seemed to like Eleanor. I know, what a stupid thing to be angry about, right? Well, there was something inside me that just didn't want my mum and Troy to like her, and actually, that was something I kept thinking of that night.

I asked myself the same questions over and over again; Why didn't I like Eleanor when she was being nothing but nice to me? Why did I feel this burning feeling in my stomach whenever I caught sight of her and Louis together? And why did I no longer feel the same hatred for Louis as I had done a few weeks ago?

I also thought about how I had started noticing things about Louis that I had never done before. The way his ocean blue eyes would shine whenever he was happy, the way these adorable crinkles would appear by his eyes whenever he laughed, and the way his pink, thin lips would turn into a beautiful, wide smile whenever he found something funny. To sum it up, I had started noticing things about him that a stepbrother shouldn't notice about their other stepbrother because, well, he was my stepbrother, and that would be weird.

So, when the realization hit me that I might actually have feelings for him, I could feel my heart drop to the pit of my stomach. I shouldn't be feeling this way, and definitely not about Louis. He was the one who had asked for my help with his homework two years ago and broken my heart by leaving me a few months later. Also, he was the one who had been picking on me ever since, and sometimes even made me feel like shit, although I had never shown it to anyone.

I could not have feelings for him, it was just impossible. But then again, why did my heart start beating faster when he told me he found me beautiful that night a few weeks ago? And why had I started getting jealous of the fact that Eleanor had Louis and I didn't? Because, after thinking about it, there actually was no other explanation for my hatred towards her. I mean, how could you possibly dislike someone that had done you nothing wrong otherwise?

Having all those thoughts mingling in my head made it impossible for me to sleep that night. I really tried to, but with my head spinning like crazy, it was just not happening. It didn't even work when I put in my earbuds to listen to some relaxing music, so I gave up. I was going to be dead tired the next day, though, that was for sure.

And so I was. I didn't do much at all that Sunday. It started off bad too because Eleanor was there, and that made me start thinking about the frightening realization I had come to the night before. I didn't even dare glance at Louis, too afraid of how I was going to react now that I knew I had some kinds of feelings for him. The only thing I did was stare down at my plate and try to be as quiet as possible not to gain anyone's attention.

It actually worked quite well because when I exited the kitchen a while later, I hadn't looked at Louis once, nor had I opened my mouth too many times. So, I was feeling pretty happy with myself as I walked up the stairs to read a book I'd had for a long time but never gotten around to start reading. I figured now that I had nothing better to do, this was the perfect time to do so, though.

However, that was until I was about to close my bedroom door behind me. Louis and Eleanor were climbing the last few steps of the staircase in front of me, looking happy with Louis' arm resting around her petite waist. They had smiles on their faces, and they just seemed so in love that it made my heart clench in my chest. I had to swallow down the lump I suddenly felt in my throat. The sight was painful to say the least, especially now that I knew why it hurt so much.

Of course, Louis just had to catch me staring at them and also open his mouth to comment on it. "What are you staring at? Got nothing better to do than just stand there, huh?" He scoffed, rolling his eyes as he led Eleanor to his room, shutting the door behind them without bothering to wait for my answer. Not that I would've given him one anyway.

I shut my own bedroom door behind me and laid down on my bed with a deep sigh. What had I gotten myself into? How could I have let myself fall for the guy that hated me the most and most importantly the guy I absolutely couldn't be with? It was just so damn stupid that I wanted to hit myself for it. Why couldn't I have fallen for Niall instead? At least his goal of the day wasn't to make my life worse. Furthermore, we weren't stepbrothers, so it would have worked perfectly.

The following hours, I spent reading the story I had planned to. It wasn't very entertaining, though, and if I had come up with something better to do, I would have done it right away. But, since Liam was still away with his family until later this evening and I still didn't have any homework to do, it was pretty hard to come up with anything. I must have the most boring life out there.

Eventually, Eleanor went home. It was pretty late in the afternoon when she did, but as soon as she was out of the house, I breathed out a sigh of relief. At least I wouldn't have to hear or witness her and Louis' love for each other anymore.

However, my life was still boring and so was the entire Sunday. Not only did I ignore Louis, but it felt as though he did the same thing. He stayed in his room the entire evening and only exited it when mum called us down for dinner. Not that I was any better. I only exchanged a few words with my family members that day, being the unsocial person I was sometimes.

Sooner or later, Monday finally came around and I could go back to school to meet Liam. To say I had missed him would be an understatement. I had never missed him as much as I did that weekend. So, when I found him standing at my locker like he did every morning, I ran over to him and threw myself in his arms, catching him by surprise. "Jesus," he laughed as he tried to wrap his arms around my body in return. "Someone seems to have missed me."

"Are you kidding? I've never missed you more than I did in the last few days. Why did you decide to go out of town this weekend out of all of them?" I whined in his ear, refusing to pull out of the hug just yet even if my jacket was wet from the shitty weather outside and I was probably soaking him at this very moment.

He pulled back a little so he could look at my face. "I'm sure it wasn't that bad, but if you wouldn't mind telling me, what exactly happened that made you feel that way? Because knowing you, you're only that needy of me when something bad has happened."

I flicked my gaze down to his collarbones as I bit my bottom lip hesitantly, contemplating whether to tell him about the realization I had come to or not. Then I remembered he didn't know practically anything about my and Louis' current relationship, not even what happened at the party, so I decided I was not going to tell him about it yet. It wasn't that I didn't trust him or anything like that, I just felt as though it was better that I kept it a secret for a while, especially since it was practically illegal for me to have feelings for Louis.

"I just realized something, and it was bad. I didn't have anyone to talk to, and the only thing I had was this stupid book that sucked. Not even my homework could help me because it was already finished and I just... I just needed you, yeah?" I pouted, giving him a puppy face that made him smile.

"To me, it sounds like someone just had a boring weekend, but I don't know," he teased, making me hit him on the arm.

"Shut up, it wasn't funny. If you had been there, you would've witnessed what a mess I was, but since you weren't, I don't think you should open your mouth."

He raised his eyebrows fondly, loosening his grip on me. "Oh well. You could've always talked to Louis. I'm sure he would've wanted to hear about your miserable life," he tried to joke, but the mention of his name instantly made me tense. If only he knew how close he was to figure out the reason I had been feeling so shitty during the weekend in the first place.

"Yeah, right," I snorted, trying to act like I usually did at the mention of the feathery-haired boy's name, but Liam instantly noticed the change in my behavior and voice.

"Did I miss something?" He asked, narrowing his eyes in curiosity.

I shook my head quickly, too quickly. "No! Why would you think that? Everything is as it's supposed to, I promise." I tried to give him a convincing smile, but the corner of my lips wouldn't reach high enough, and judging by the suspicious look Liam sent me, he didn't believe a single one of my words either.

"You want me to believe that, mate? I know you, Harry, and I can see that something clearly happened between you and Louis," he said.

"Then why did you even ask?" I muttered under my breath, so low that I was positive he didn't hear me.

"What did you say?"

"Nothing."

Liam went to open his mouth again, but much to my delight, the bell rang right then, signaling the start of the first lesson. Mentally thanking God, I opened my locker to get rid of my jacket and backpack before grabbing my Math books and slamming it shut. In the meantime, Liam crossed the hallway to grab his own stuff, joining me halfway to the classroom again.

Thankfully, he didn't mention anything about what we had been talking about earlier when we met up, but even if that was so, I was sure he hadn't forgotten about it. He still had that look on his face that meant he was thinking deeply about something, and that made me scared, to say the least. I wanted him to drop it, but by the looks of it, it seemed like he would ask me about it again as soon as he got the chance to.

Mr. Storm wasn't happy when Liam and I showed up two minutes late, but since we usually weren't tardy, he didn't scold us too much. He only sent us these looks, saying that it shouldn't repeat itself. With obedient nods, we sat down at a desk in the back, and it wasn't until I looked up at Mr. Storm that I noticed it was the desk right behind Louis and Eleanor. Well, shit.

Closing my eyes in frustration, I grabbed my pencil and started writing down the right numbers and answers on my notepad harshly. It only made matters worse when I realized that Louis would occasionally lean in to whisper something in Eleanor's ear. To be honest, it only made me more frustrated. I was frustrated with myself for feeling the way I did for Louis, but also for the fact that I had been dumb enough to choose this desk to sit at. I could've chosen one in the front where I wouldn't be able to see him at all, but no, of course not.

When the lesson ended, I stood up and gathered my stuff, seeing through the corner of my eye how Louis put his arm around Eleanor's waist as they began walking towards the door. Just as they were about to exit, though, he turned his head back to send a cold glare in my direction.

I could literally feel goosebumps rise on my skin, and no, not the good ones. If there was something he hadn't stopped doing since he talked to me in the bathroom Saturday, it was glaring at me. He obviously wanted me to remember something because that was what he said. The problem was that I couldn't remember anything that would fit into what was happening, or what he was trying to show me.

"So, what did that look Louis just sent you mean?" Liam asked on our way back to my locker. The hallways were full of people, so I almost didn't hear his question. I wish I didn't.

"Huh?" I hummed, trying to play dumb.

He rolled his eyes, turning to meet my gaze. "You know exactly what I'm talking about, Harry. What is it that you refuse to tell me? I thought we could tell each other everything, especially when it comes to things like family and people we know... people like Louis."

I bit my bottom lip. "I know, it's just... It's complicated, and I really don't want to talk about it. I just want to forget it, forget that he even exists because he's just... he's so annoying," I grumbled, running a hand through my curls.

"Tell me something I don't know," he chuckled dryly.

"Hello, guys," a voice suddenly spoke behind us, and the next second I could feel an arm around my shoulders. My first thought was that it was Ed, so when I turned my head to see Niall smiling at me, I was rather shocked.

"Niall," I said, a small smile slowly starting to form on my lips. Although all three of us usually ate lunch together nowadays, it still surprised me every time Niall chose to hang out with me and Liam. I was still so used to see him sit with Louis, Zayn and the other guys. Not that I minded that he was with us, though. As said before, I enjoyed his company.

"I was thinking since we all three share the next class that I could join you two if you wouldn't mind, that is." He sent me a hesitant, yet questioning smile as if my answer would really have an impact on him.

"Of course we don't mind. You're our friend now," I said, but judging by the way his nose scrunched up when I said the word 'friend', it was obvious he wasn't very fond of that reference. It didn't really surprise me because I knew almost for sure now that he had feelings for me, but I still acted as though I wasn't aware of them because I didn't want to make things awkward between us.

It wasn't that I didn't like Niall, he was awesome and I would probably consider getting with him if it weren't for the fact that I didn't really like him like that and since I was now positive I had feelings for someone else. Sure, nothing would ever happen between me and Louis, but still. I wouldn't want Niall to be some kind of rebound because that wouldn't be fair to him.

All three of us walked to English class together after Liam and I had exchanged our books. Niall had already done so, so he just tagged along and talked about an incident at his football practice the other day. The entire time, he kept his arm around my shoulders, occasionally squeezing my upper arm in a sweet gesture. It wasn't uncomfortable, but I felt as though it meant something else to him than it did to me. However, I couldn't let him down like that, so I pushed it to the back of my head and let his arm stay there.

What surprised me, though, was that he actually wanted to have his arm around me. Sure, he might like me, but he still had a reputation that I was certain he didn't want to lose, and having his arm wrapped around my shoulders wouldn't exactly make said reputation shoot through the roof, rather the opposite. So, I found it a little weird but didn't question it because it was actually nice that he didn't seem to care about the looks that were thrown in our direction thanks to his hold on me.

We were just about to walk into the classroom when I caught sight of someone I hadn't talked to in over a year. Her long, curly brown hair and chocolate brown eyes hadn't changed through that time, and I still found her beautiful. It was pretty sad that we grew apart after only a couple of months of dating, and broke up because of that but also because we couldn't find any time to spend together. Sometimes I could still find myself missing her, but only as a friend. I missed her company.

The girl was Miranda, the one I had dated two years ago, during the time Louis and I had been friends. We did almost everything together back then, and she was even the first girl or boy I ever had a relationship with. So, she was still kind of important to me.

"Hi," I greeted, giving her a small smile. She was talking to one of her best friends by the wall of lockers but looked up when she heard me call her name.

Her lips pulled up into a smile of her own and she waved at me happily. "Hey, Harry. Wow, it's been so long since I last talked to you. What was it? A year and a half?"

I nodded, suddenly becoming aware that Liam and Niall were still with me and that Niall still had his arm around my shoulders. Subtly, I unwrapped it from me, but I could see through the corner of my eye how his face fell by the gesture. "Yeah," I said. "So, what have you been up to since we last saw each other?"

She shrugged. "Nothing, really. I still love to dance, so that's what I've spent most of my time doing. Also, I joined the drama club I always used to tell you I wanted to join. What about you? How have you been?" She asked, shutting what I assumed was her locker as her friend flicked her gaze between the two of us curiously.

I surely did remember that she wanted to join the drama club when we were together. She would always talk about it, how cool it would be to act, and just pretend to be someone you're not. So, hearing that she had finally taken the step and joined the club made me happy. "That's nice. To be honest, nothing has really changed since we broke up. It's been alright, though," I chuckled half-heartedly.

Except the fact that I might possibly have gained a crush on my stepbrother...

Giving me a sweet smile, she tilted her head to the side. "That's nice. I'm really sorry, but I have to go to class now. See you around, Harry, yeah?"

"Of course," I replied.

Before she turned around to walk away with her friend, though, she looked over at Liam. "It was nice meeting you again too, Liam. It's been a while, to say the least."

A little surprised, the brown-haired boy nodded in agreement. "Definitely. It was nice to see you too, Miranda. I kind of miss your awful jokes that only Harry laughs at because he makes jokes that are twice as bad."

"Hey," I whined, hitting him on the arm.

Miranda rolled her eyes, letting out a light chuckle. "Harry, we both know it's true, though. We suck at coming up with good jokes. It's a fact."

"Alright, alright, fine. I'll give you that one," I said, laughing because well. It was true. I was aware that my jokes weren't the best ones, but hey, that's what made them so funny, eh?

A few seconds later, we finally separated and Liam, Niall and I walked into the English classroom where students were already sitting at the desks, talking with each other. The class hadn't started yet, thankfully, because even if it didn't always seem like it, I hated arriving late to class both because it usually pissed off the teacher and because it was embarrassing to have all the students' attention set on you.

Niall sat down at the same desk as me while Liam took the seat in front of us. "So, you and that girl dated?" He asked, trying to sound casual although you could hear that he was somewhat bothered by this fact.

I furrowed my eyebrows together. "Yeah, why?"

He shrugged, facing the blackboard ahead of him. "Nothing. I was just curious," he mumbled. A short silence followed after that until he suddenly spoke up again. "Do you still like her?"

Letting out a dry laugh, I shook my head. "No, I don't. We broke up almost two years ago. It would be stupid of me to still like her like that."

He nodded his head thoughtfully, biting his bottom lip. "Alright, I was just wondering."

"Sure," I said, rolling my eyes.

Right then, I could hear my phone buzz in the back pocket of my jeans. Confused as to whom it could possibly be that had texted me since the only people I usually texted were sitting with me at this moment, I lifted my bum and pulled it out of my pocket. The screen was lit up by a new text message from none other than Louis.

My heart picked up its pace at record speed as I scanned what it said with wide eyes. If you're wondering why I still had his number saved in my phone, I didn't even know myself, but right now I was glad I did. Or well, that was until I read what the message said.

Louis: Not only do you play with more than one heart at the same time, but you also always manage to rip mine out. Well done, Harry. I hope you know what you're doing.

Chapter 15

[Harry]

    To say I was stunned by the words that were in the message would be an understatement. My mouth wouldn't close for at least one minute, and my eyes didn't leave the screen either. Where did it even come from? I hadn't uttered a single word to Louis since we talked in our bathroom two days ago, yet here he was, telling me that I was ripping his heart out by doing something of which I didn't know? What did I do?

    My heart kept pounding like crazy during that whole period, and I didn't even dare glance around the classroom, too afraid that I would catch the feathery-haired boy glaring at me or something. To be honest, I was scared for dear life during that whole day. I tried my best to ignore him, keeping close to both Niall and Liam, but mostly Niall since I didn't want Liam to start talking about Louis again.

    It went quite well up until I had to attend the last class of the day; P.E. I bit my fingernails nervously as I made my way to the locker rooms, my backpack slung over my shoulder carelessly. My legs were literally shaking, and if it weren't for the fact that I was taking big, deep breaths, I was sure I would've fallen to the ground a long time ago.

    I had said goodbye to Niall and Liam just a few minutes ago, both of them looking worried to leave me alone even though they had no idea why I was shaking like a leaf. They asked me about it, but being the stubborn person I was, I kept it to myself because I knew they wouldn't understand if they didn't know the whole story, and I definitely couldn't tell them about it because that would include admitting my feelings for Louis, and that couldn't happen.

Slowly, I opened the door to the locker room, and hesitantly walked over to an empty locker. Since I had made sure to be here earlier than usual today to avoid a certain lad who was always late, there weren't many people in here yet, only three guys who I was almost certain were in my History class, but since I never really talked to them, I didn't know for sure.

Once I had checked Louis wasn't there, I hurried to unzip my backpack and change out of my clothes to put on my sports gear instead. It took me only about three minutes until I was finished, which I was happy about because Louis hadn't arrived yet and I could go out to the gym without having to face him. The only problem was that I was first in there, and that wasn't very fun. But, if it meant I didn't have to encounter Louis, it was worth it.

About five minutes remained until the lesson started when all students began to fill up the gym. Some people started playing some football to kill time while others sat down to have small talk. I always felt so left out in this class because I literally didn't have anyone here, but at least it was only in this one class.

"Okay, so today we're playing double badminton, and before you say anything else - no, you do not get to pick your partner. I'm going to be doing it for you to mix it up a little," Mr. Wilson informed us when the bell had rung and everybody was sitting in a half-circle around him.

The sound of people disagreeing was instantly followed by his words, but I couldn't say I had any problem with him picking partners. That only meant there was more of a chance I would end up with someone decent, and that would make it more fun. Not that I was very good at sports, but I wasn't that bad... was I?

Mr. Wilson first explained the rules before giving each student a card that showed a number. The one who had the same number as you was going to be your partner. When he gave me my card, I flipped it over to see number ten. Curiously, I looked up to see who had gotten the same one as me. Everyone was trying to find their partner, though, so it wasn't exactly an easy task to find yours.

"Who has number ten?" A familiar voice suddenly asked, and my insides froze to ice. Oh, no. Please tell me this was a joke. What were the odds that *he* out of all people had to be partnered with me? What was this? Some kind of payback for whatever I had done to him in the past?

My eyes found the guy I had done my absolute best to avoid the entire day. He was scanning the crowd of students who had yet to find their partner in hopes of finding his own, his ocean blue eyes sparkling from the lights in the room. My heart skipped in my chest, and I had to look away to stop myself from smiling. God, why did he have to be so beautiful? That son of a bitch.

With incredibly slow strides, I walked over to Louis, keeping my gaze to the floor because I was too scared to make eye contact with him. That message he sent me earlier today was the cause of this. I had no idea what he was going to do when he met me and actually had to talk to me. Was he going to mention it, or was he going to keep the same poker face on like he had done the past few days?

Without saying anything, I stopped beside him, seeing from the corner of my eye how his eyes set on me. "What are you doing here?" He growled so low that only I could hear it.

I didn't even look up at him when I showed him my card. "Fuck," he muttered and walked away. My eyes then lifted so they could follow his figure to where he was now standing, talking to Mr. Wilson. By the looks of it, he didn't get his way because his eyebrows were creased together as if he were mad at something.

It didn't take more than a second for me to understand that he was trying to switch partners. Of course he didn't want to be with me. But, I didn't want to be with him either, not after that text he had sent me. I would rather be with the worst athlete in here right now.

"I'm sorry, Mr. Tomlinson, but you don't get to switch partners. No one else does, so you don't either. Now, go over to your teammate and discuss how you're going to play together. I'm sure one lesson with Mr. Styles won't hurt you," I could hear Mr. Wilson say, and I let out a deep sigh. So, I would have to play with Louis after all, huh? Please shoot me.

Louis reluctantly went back to me, but not before grabbing a badminton racket and a shuttlecock. He didn't say a single word when he passed me to go to the court where we were supposed to play, he just looked straight ahead and ignored me.

With another heavy sigh, I grabbed a racket myself and got rid of the card before following him to the court where another team had now joined him. I stopped beside Louis and looked up at the ceiling, praying to anyone out there that this wasn't going to end up in disaster. As long as he was quiet, things would at least be bearable. Hopefully.

But of course I wasn't that lucky. It didn't take more than a minute until he turned to me, his eyes as hard as stone. "You take the front while I'll be in the back," he said emotionlessly. It wasn't really a question, but I nodded my head anyway and walked over to stand right in front of the net.

The first ten minutes were probably the worst ones. We didn't utter a single word to each other. The only thing we did was hit the shuttlecock over the net whenever it came to us. It was only when I managed to hit the side of the racket so the shuttlecock dropped to the floor that I opened my mouth, and it was to mutter the word 'sorry'.

Unsurprisingly, Louis was good at badminton. Whenever I dodged the shuttlecock, he was there to hit it for me and he basically succeeded to get it over the net every time. Sometimes he missed it as well, but I certainly did so more times than him, which didn't exactly come as a big surprise to me.

After about half an hour, however, we warmed up more to each other and even started handing the shuttlecock over to one another when it was the other's turn to serve. Once, our hands even brushed together, making goosebumps rise on my skin. I quickly retreated my hand in fear that he had seen it, but judging by the way a frown formed on his face, I was afraid he did.

When Mr. Wilson signaled that the lesson was over, we exchanged a look. It was nothing special, but more like a 'thank God, we made it' one. What surprised me though, was that he didn't make any type of sign about what he had written in that text message earlier. I thought he would try to make some kind of point about what he meant by it like he had tried to all those other times, but I hadn't noticed anything special. Or, I was just too blind or stupid to see it.

It turned out I spoke too soon, though, because when I was just about to enter the locker room, he reached out to grab the door handle before I could do so. "Enjoying playing with Niall's heart, are you? I bet so because that's what you do best, right? I would be more careful if I were you, though, because it might get back at you eventually."

I flicked my gaze up to meet his, but he had already slipped past me and entered the locker room. Well, shit.

During the rest of that day, neither of us even so much as looked at each other. Sure, Louis had football practice until six in the afternoon so it wasn't like we could, but he got home right when dinner was ready at seven. Mum and Troy were still obviously concerned about the two of us, and it seemed like they were even more so now that we wouldn't even snap at one another. However, there was still nothing they could do about it, and it seemed like they had finally understood that.

The only problem now was that I had yet to figure everything out. Like, literally *everything*. Louis had left me so many hints lately that my head was going insane from how fast it was spinning. Well, at least I thought they were all hints. I mean, why else would he send me those looks and give me those mysterious comments as he had done? He was trying to show me something, something that had to do with our past and why we stopped being friends. I just had to remember, that was all.

But, it was harder than I could have ever imagined it to be because as far as I knew, I had done nothing wrong. He was the one to stop attending our meetings, after all. I had still been there every Monday and Wednesday just waiting for him to show up. Furthermore, he was the one to start acting rude to me, so why did he claim that us not being friends any longer was my fault?

It was with annoyance I fell asleep that night. I was annoyed at myself for not figuring it all out, but I was also annoyed at Louis for saying things to me that didn't make any sense. It would be a whole lot easier if he just told me what I had done wrong and why he hated me so much in the first place. Because right now, that was what I wanted to know most.

I was walking to the library a Monday afternoon after school like usual these days. Just a minute ago, I had said goodbye to both Liam and Miranda, the two people I hung out with at school during the day. Now, however, I was about to hang with whom I would like to call my closest friend, and hopefully, he was already waiting for me.

By now, the hallways were almost empty of students since the bell had rung about twenty minutes ago, so it didn't take long until I arrived at the library where Mrs. Rose was standing behind her desk, sipping on a cup of what I presumed was tea. She had pretty short, grey hair that barely reached her shoulders and a few wrinkles on her face from old age. However, I wouldn't say she was older than about 55.

Her eyes met mine when she saw me entering, and a smile broke out on her face. "Good afternoon, Harry. Louis' waiting for you and has been for a while," *she informed politely. She was used to seeing me and Louis spend time here together, so the fact that she just told me this didn't exactly surprise me.*

"Thank you," *I smiled back, immediately heading for the group room Louis and I usually studied and hung out in.*

Once I reached it, I didn't hesitate to turn the door handle and enter the room. Louis was sitting at the table, his eyes drawn to something in his lap while his books were scattered in front of him. He was wearing a black t-shirt along with the same jean jacket he usually wore to school and a pair of black, ripped skinny jeans that I could see beneath the table. The sound of me slamming the door shut made him look up and put his phone on the table. "Hey, Harry," *he greeted, slight annoyance lacing his voice.*

I walked over to him and placed my backpack on the table beside his books. "Did something happen? You don't seem like your usual self," *I frowned. The Louis I was used to witnessing always had a bright smile on his face and greeted me with a happier tone than that.*

He shrugged dismissively, averting his gaze. "It's nothing."

Sitting down beside him, I unzipped my backpack and took out my stuff before throwing the bag to the floor. "Well, it's clearly something, otherwise you wouldn't have snapped at me like that just now," *I concluded, raising my eyebrows at him. I knew that if I raised my voice and demanded an answer from him, he would never give me one, so I tried my best to stay calm.*

He glared at me through the corner of his eye as he picked up one of his books and started flicking through the pages carelessly. "Where were you?" He muttered barely audible, completely ignoring what I had just said.

"Why are you asking me that?"

His eyes met mine for a split second, and was that disappointment I could see in them? But what was there to be disappointed about? Sure, I was a little late, but not more than fifteen minutes. He couldn't be disappointed about that, right?

He shrugged, avoiding my gaze. "Just asking. You're never on time for our meetings anymore, so I was just wondering why that is. You know, if you don't want to hang out with me any longer, you just have to say so. Sure, I'll be a little sad about it because I really do like hanging out with you. But if that's what you feel, I can't stop you from--"

"Wait, hold on a second," I interrupted, my eyebrows knitting together. "What are you talking about? Of course I want to hang out with you. You're like my best friend, Louis. Why would you think that?"

Even though he rolled his eyes, I could see how a small, genuine smile formed on his lips. It was gone the next second, though. "Well, as said before, you're never on time for our meetings anymore, and every time we hang out together it seems like you're not present. Also, you're always on your phone. I get that you have other friends, Harry, I do, but can't you at least pay a little attention to me sometimes?" He looked down at his lap when he said the last part.

As if on cue, my phone vibrated in my back pocket right then, and without really thinking about it, I fished it up and looked at the screen. Miranda had sent me a text, asking me if

I wanted to eat dinner with her and her family later today. A small smile broke out on my face, and I was just about to unlock my phone and reply to her when I could suddenly hear the door slam shut.

Looking up, I noticed that Louis was gone, and so was all of his stuff.

Chapter 16

[Harry]

I woke up with a jerk, checking my surroundings to see where I was. Luckily, I was back in my bedroom, which meant it had all just been a dream. Except the fact that it hadn't. It was not a dream. It was a memory just like the last time I dreamed of Louis and I's past. Unlike that time, however, this was a memory I had totally forgotten about, and maybe that was because I barely paid attention to him when he talked to me that day. I had been too caught up with my own stuff to notice that he was hurting from my actions.

Why didn't I notice this two years ago when it actually took place? Was I really that blinded by my love for Miranda and the new friendship between me and Liam? It was all so stupid, and I was now certain that this was what Louis meant when he said it was my fault that we weren't friends any longer. It all made perfect sense now. Of course he was mad at me. I had been a real asshole to him. But then again, I never thought he appreciated me enough to care about the fact that I texted Liam and Miranda sometimes. I thought he mostly considered me a friend because I helped him with his schoolwork, but I guess not.

I laid there for a while, thinking about what Louis had done to me lately, and tried to put every single puzzle piece together. There was one thing I still couldn't figure out in the end, though, and that was why he said I had ripped his heart out. I mean, sure, I had hurt him, but ripping his heart out did sound a little exaggerated, didn't it? Well, that was if he possibly didn't feel more than friendly feelings for me. But, that would be stupid because he didn't like me like that. If anything was impossible, then that certainly was.

Right?

[Louis]

Not to be mean or anything, but Harry was really damn stupid and oblivious. I had literally done everything to make him realize what he did to me two years ago when we were friends. To be more specific, I had tried doing exactly the same things he had done to me, even if it was harder for me considering we weren't really friends anymore, so what I did now didn't have the same effect, unfortunately.

But, he should still catch the hang of it, especially since he was the one who did it to me the last time. Intentionally or not, I didn't really care. What he did to me was still disrespectful and rude. Sure, I was the one who left him and started picking on him, but I thought that was the least he deserved after treating me like that. I mean, I thought we were supposed to be friends, yet he never paid attention to me when we hung out together. It was always 'Liam did this, Miranda did that' and I just couldn't bring myself to continue listening to it any longer. It was hurting me, and not only because he had befriended new people and also started dating a girl, but mainly because he decided to just stop caring about me. That was definitely what hurt the most, even if it stung deep when he mentioned that he and Miranda had gotten together. It hurt like hell, but it couldn't compare to the pain I felt when he stopped paying attention to me altogether.

As if that wasn't enough, many other bad things happened to me at the same time. I even considered taking my own life once but knew I wouldn't have the guts to do it. I was too weak. Furthermore, I couldn't do it to my dad since he had just lost two other important people in his life. It would surely have broken him completely.

That left me to try getting better by myself. I stopped caring about school whatsoever because I literally couldn't care less about my future or what I turned out to be. It was only the present that counted and for me to get better somehow. Schoolwork definitely didn't make anything better, so I dropped it completely. That was also when I got addicted to cigarettes. It was the only thing that kept me relatively calm, and I needed that so badly back then. The only problem was that now that I didn't find it so necessary any longer since my life was getting better, it was impossible to stop. Not that I had really tried yet, though.

Now you're probably wondering where and how Eleanor came into the picture, and let's just say I wasn't really looking for her. It was more of a coincidence that we got along so well and hit it off. She was the most popular girl at school and I was among the most popular guys, so our friends pretty much put us together. They said we were 'meant' for each other, or something like that. To be honest, I didn't really care back then. I was still pissed and sad about mine and Harry's falling out since I had also managed to grow feelings for the boy during the time we were friends. So, I just went along with it and at least hoped she would be a good distraction from him.

Fortunately, she turned out to be even better than that. It didn't take more than a few weeks until I started falling for her, although the feelings I had for Harry were still there, and I knew now that they had never really disappeared, even if I would have liked them to do so. There was actually a time when I was certain my feelings for Harry were gone, but of course my dad had to get together with his mum and make all those feelings come flying back by making us move in with them. Of fucking course.

Now, I was back to hurting again thanks to all of it. Sure, I still had feelings for Eleanor, but if I were being honest with myself, I had never felt as much for her as I ever did for Harry. He was just... wow. There were no words to describe him. He was just so beautiful, and I absolutely hated it. It would be so much easier if he were ugly and his personality sucked because I wouldn't be hurting like this if so.

It hurt me to see him with Ed, and not to mention with one of my closest friends. Something weird had happened to Niall because all of a sudden, he was pining after Harry like a lost child. It was ridiculous, and the fact that Harry seemed to enjoy his company only made matters worse. Call it jealousy or whatever, I didn't care. It angered me that Niall had managed to get Harry's attention when they weren't even friends and I couldn't. Did that mean I never meant anything to Harry at all? Well, it wouldn't surprise me.

Currently, I was standing in the shower, shampooing my brown hair while humming along to Justin Bieber's new song. It was a Saturday afternoon and I was preparing myself for a party with my football team. It was being arranged at Ed's place this time, and since he lived on the other side of Holmes Chapel, there were hopefully going to be lots of people there. I loved parties with huge crowds. I mean, you couldn't even call it a party if there weren't a lot of people there.

Once I was finished, I turned off the water and reached for the towel I was sure I had placed on the toilet seat, but for some reason, it wasn't there. Sighing heavily, I ran a hand through my wet hair. There were only two things I could do. Either I go out of the shower butt naked, fetch the towel from the cabinet in my room, and risk tripping on my wet feet, or I call Harry to come and get it for me.

Although I would have preferred to go with the first option, I didn't want to risk getting hurt. Besides, I kind of wanted to see Harry's reaction when he handed me the towel. Speaking of which, that was another thing I had tried to do during the past few weeks. Not only had I tried showing him what he had done to me when we were friends, but I had also tried to discover what he felt for me, whether he might have caught feelings for me or not.

In the beginning, I was rather doubtful because I had never seen a sign that he liked me before, but when he knocked on the door that time when Eleanor was over and yelled at us to quiet down, I started thinking that maybe he did feel something for me after all. Moreover, he had been grumpy that whole weekend, and something told me it had to do with Eleanor. Well, at least that was what I hoped for.

"Harry!" I yelled, shuddering from the coldness that was spreading through my body by the second.

It took a while, but eventually, he replied with a hesitant 'yeah?'.

"Can you bring me my towel, please? It's in my cabinet by the bathroom door."

Again, it took a few seconds until I could so much as hear a movement coming from his room. So, when he opened the door and poked his head through the gap, I was shaking like a leaf in the shower. "Are you being serious?" He asked, looking confused and utterly shocked.

Rolling my eyes, I let out a dry chuckle. "No, I'm just standing here, freezing my fucking ass off just because I find it fun. Of course I'm being serious! Now, would you *please* go and fetch it for me?"

Dumfounded, he nodded his head curtly, instantly making his way to my room and closing the door behind him. I bit my lip, contemplating whether this was such a great idea after all. I was literally shaking from how cold I was, and I didn't like having people wandering around in my room when I wasn't there, but this was Harry we were talking about. If he didn't hate me too much, he wouldn't do anything. So, let's just hope for the best.

Thankfully, it only took a few seconds until the door opened again and he returned with a black towel in his hand. His face looked as pale as snow when he walked over to me with hesitant strides, gnawing on his bottom lip. "Why do you look like you've just seen a ghost? Come on Harry, it's not like this is the first time you've seen me naked," I taunted, making his face turn a light shade of red.

"Shut up," he grumbled under his breath, tossing me the towel when he was just a few feet away from me. I instantly wrapped it around my waist and stepped away from the curtain to reveal myself completely. By now, my hair was getting dry and the water droplets on my skin were gone, which made everything a little less exciting, but I still noticed the way Harry's green eyes widened when I got out of the shower with only the towel covering my tan body.

"Take a picture, it'll last longer," I winked, and if looks could kill, I would be dead right now.

With newfound confidence it seemed, Harry crossed his arms over his chest and tried to stare me down. "You can't go a day without complimenting yourself, can you?" He snorted, shaking his head in what seemed like disgust.

A low growl escaped my lips, and the next thing I knew, I had him pinned to the hard surface of the wall tiles, my almost naked body pressed against his. The little confidence he had just gained seemed to wash down the drain as I stared into his eyes with the hardest look I could manage. "You were saying?" I asked, raising an eyebrow tauntingly.

He gulped, averting his gaze from mine without answering the question. I could feel his body start to tremble under my own, and I wondered if it was because of the fact he found me intimidating or if it was because he felt the same electric feeling in his skin that I did when our bodies touched. Not that it really mattered because I liked feeling in charge, but I would be happy if it was the second option. However, if I remembered correctly, he did say that he didn't find me intimidating, so that couldn't be the case, right?

"W-what are you doing?"

Without realizing it, I had zoned out and subconsciously picked up a curly lock of his hair and pushed it behind his ear. It was nothing but embarrassing that I had managed to let my guard down so easily. I should definitely have way more self-control than this.

Instantly, I dropped my hand to my side and stared at him in shock. I refused to let the embarrassment take over me and color my cheeks a pink red. Instead, I bit the inside of my cheek and took a step back before practically sprinting into my bedroom, almost forgetting to shut the door behind me in my hurry.

With a frustrated sigh, I flopped down on my bed without even bothering to put any clothes on. I ran my hands over my face and bit back a loud scream. Honestly, I wanted nothing but scream right now, but, but I knew it would only worsen the situation with Harry. If I were to do that, he would most definitely think there was something wrong with me.

Once the embarrassment had disappeared and I had dropped what just happened in the bathroom a little, I got up from the bed and made my way over to my closet. I was still going to the party tonight, but I hadn't picked anything to wear yet. Usually, I just wore a plain black t-shirt with my jean jacket and a pair of black, skinny jeans, but today I felt like trying something new. Therefore, I reached out to grab a grey, knitted sweater. To be honest, I had never worn it before, so this was a great opportunity to do so.

After putting all my clothes on, I hesitantly made my way back into the bathroom, making sure that Harry wasn't in there when I turned the handle and walked over to the mirror. The last thing I needed right now was to face that boy and have a repeat of what happened earlier.

The following minutes were spent fixing my hair. I put some gel in my locks and ran my hands through them so that my fringe was nicely swept to the side. When I was finished, I exited the bathroom and went downstairs to the kitchen where my dad was sitting at the kitchen table, reading the newspaper. He looked up once he acknowledged my appearance and sent me a small smile before furrowing his eyebrows in confusion. "Are you going somewhere?"

I rolled my eyes as I nodded my head. "Yeah. I told you yesterday that there's a team party at Ed's place tonight."

His face turned into a look of realization. "Oh, I remember now. Well, have fun then, I guess, and don't be too long, alright? I'd like to wake up tomorrow knowing that you are sleeping in your own bed," he said, adding firmness to his voice.

"Since when does it matter to you whether I sleep at home or not? I never got back from a party the same day when only you and I lived together," I muttered bitterly.

"Ever since I realized what an awful father I was for not having any rules when it came to you. I basically let you do anything, which is not a responsible thing to do as a father, and I'm sorry for that. I should've been there for you more than I was," he apologized, sending me a weak smile.

I shrugged. "It's whatever."

Dad opened his mouth to say something else, but right then, footsteps could be heard from behind me, which made him close it again. The sound of the fridge opening eventually made me turn my head in curiosity to see who it was, but the sight disappointed me. Or well, that's what I tried telling myself it did because, in reality, the sight was not bad at all. It was actually pretty damn good.

Harry was holding the fridge door open while sipping on a package of milk. He was only wearing a pair of black joggers that were hanging dangerously low on his hips. Too bad he had his back turned to me, otherwise the sight would've been even better.

He seemed to sense that he had just interrupted mine and dad's conversation because he eventually turned around and sent us an apologetic smile. "Sorry if I interrupted anything. I didn't see you there at first."

Too busy staring at his half-naked body with wide eyes, I could hear dad reassure him, "No no, don't apologize, son. Louis and I were just discussing a few things... which had me wondering, aren't you friends with this Ed guy too?"

Harry looked a bit confused at the question but nodded his head slowly. "Yeah, I am. Why?"

Through the corner of my eye, I could see dad clapping his hands together excitedly. "That's great! Then you two can go to his party together, right Louis?"

I snapped out of my trance at the mention of my name and turned my attention to dad. "What?"

He rolled his eyes, now seeming very happy all of a sudden. "I just came up with the amazing idea that you and Harry can go to Ed's party together. Not only would it be great for you guys to hang out, but you can also make sure that the other gets home safely. So, what do you say?" He asked hopefully.

My gaze flicked to Harry for a split second to see his reaction to this bullshit. It didn't really surprise me that he was looking down at his feet while tugging on his bottom lip with his teeth. We both knew what happened last time we were at the same party... or, I didn't know the full story, but I knew enough for me not to want it to happen again. Being drunk in Harry's proximity could end extremely badly. "Absolutely n--" I started, but Harry cut me off.

"Sure. When do I have to be ready?"

If I had water in my mouth at the moment, I would have sputtered it out right now. What the fuck was wrong with him? What the hell was he thinking? Did he actually want a repeat of what happened last time? "No way," I said firmly, and I could see Harry letting out a deep sigh. "There's no way I'm bringing him with me. Besides, it's a team party. Since when is Harry a player on the team?"

Dad raised an eyebrow. "Are you saying that the only people who are going to be there are your teammates? I may be old, but even I can tell that there are going to be other people there as well."

I let out a frustrated grunt. "Fine, whatever! I don't fucking care anyway. I leave in ten minutes. If you're not ready by then, I'm going without you," I said, turning to the curly-haired boy who now had a small smile on his lips.

"I'll be here." And with that said, he sprinted out of the kitchen and up to his room so he could start getting ready for the party.

Chapter 17

[Louis]

Just as promised, Harry trudged down the stairs ten minutes later. Right on time, that fucker. I still had no idea why he was so excited about the idea of going to this party, though. As far as I knew, he usually didn't attend that many parties, so I wondered what made him want to go to this one so badly.

My guess was that it was because it was being arranged at Ed's place, so it wouldn't be weird for him to show up there since he knew him so well. Or, it was because he knew someone was going to be there and he wanted to meet that person. Even though I didn't want to admit it, I was afraid that it could be the second option and that the person was Niall. It could be Miranda too, but I doubted it since I had only seen them together once during the past one and a half years.

Considering I kind of wanted to know whether Harry had feelings for me or not, I should probably see this as a great opportunity to ask him questions about it, but after that little incident took place in the bathroom earlier, I wasn't very fond of doing so anymore. Well, at least not today. I would rather not see him for the rest of the day if I were honest, let alone walk with him to the bus stop.

Shouldn't he be more against it too, though? It wasn't like him to agree to hang out with me willingly. That was usually the only thing we managed to actually have the same thought about, yet now he seemed to have no care in the world that we were going to have to walk for about fifteen minutes after that embarrassing encounter in the bathroom. I could not see the logic at all.

Once we had shrugged on our jackets and slipped on our shoes, dad walked into the hallway, followed by Harry's mum. They were laughing at something, acting like every other loving couple. It made me uncomfortable. Not that I didn't like the idea of my dad finding love again (even if I wasn't too fond of that either), but I didn't like that he was together with the mother of the boy I had feelings for. It was uncomfortable, to say the least.

When they caught sight of the two of us, they quieted down but kept the smiles on their faces. "Have fun tonight, boys, but not too much fun, alright?" Anne warned, sending Harry a pointed look although you could tell she wasn't being too serious. She probably knew that he wasn't one to be irresponsible.

I rolled my eyes, zipping up my jacket. "Sure. Come on, Harry. Let's go," I said, opening the front door only to be met with a harsh gust of air. This bloody weather was getting on my nerves. Sure, the cold didn't bother me that much, but when it was raining or blowing like this, I did have a problem.

"Don't be home too late!" Was the last thing I heard dad say before Harry shut the door behind us, and we started walking towards the bus stop. I brushed what he said off, knowing I would be home later than he was referring to, and wrapped my arms around my body to keep as much body heat as possible.

It didn't surprise me when a silence fell between me and Harry. I had seen this coming ever since he told me he wanted to tag along to the party. What did surprise me, however, was that he didn't pull out his phone or walk a few feet behind or in front of me the first thing he did. Instead, he was walking right beside me, his eyes focused on the road ahead of us. To be honest, it even looked as though he was trying to make a conversation but that he was unsure of how to start.

I was quickly losing my patience, though, and was just about to snap at him to just get whatever he had on his mind out when he finally opened his mouth to speak. "About what happened in the bathroom earlier..." He trailed off, biting his bottom lip hesitantly.

My body went rigid at his words, and if it weren't for the fact that I wanted to get to the bus stop as soon as possible to get away from the shitty weather, I would've stopped dead in my tracks. That was what he wanted to talk about? Couldn't it have been about schoolwork or something instead? At least that would have been a lot easier and definitely more comfortable to talk about than this. "Don't mention it. It was a mistake," I muttered, reaching into my jacket pocket in search of the pack of cigarettes I knew should be there, which it was.

Swiftly, I brought one to my lips and pulled out the lighter that I kept in my other pocket before lightening the cigarette. Breathing out a puff of grey smoke, I could see Harry scrunching his nose up in disgust. Right, he didn't like it when I smoked... Oh well. "So, you didn't mean to touch my hair, is that what you're saying?" He mumbled, keeping his gaze on the road.

I glanced at the side of his face, noticing that he was frowning for some reason. "Jesus Christ, Harry! Why do you have to make such a big deal of it? Yes, I touched your hair, and no, I didn't mean to do it. End of story. Can we move past it now?" I snapped, making him flinch.

He breathed out a deep sigh. "Sure."

A silence fell between the two of us where I took a few drags of my cigarette while Harry still kept his gaze locked on anything that wasn't close to me. The silence was suffocating, like a thick fog you couldn't breathe through, and it didn't take more than a minute until I'd had enough of it. "Why does it bother you anyway?" I asked, even if I just told him I wanted to drop the subject. Well, I was curious, alright?

"No reason."

Raising my eyebrows, I let out a snort. "If you say so."

Right then, he finally decided to turn his attention to me. His usually green eyes were dull from what looked like... pain? No, that couldn't be it, could it? "Yes," he promised, but you could clearly hear that he was lying. I wasn't going to question him about it, though, because I was sure he wouldn't tell me anyway.

"You know, I kind of figured what you've been trying to tell me lately... I think," he said next, and again, my body tensed at his words. Did that mean what I thought it did? Well, I sure didn't hope so. Otherwise, he knew that I had feelings for him right now, and that could not happen. Well, at least not like this because that would be embarrassing.

"Yeah?" I said, trying to sound nonchalant although I was nervous as hell on the inside.

He nodded slowly, kicking a rock on the ground.

"Tell me," I demanded.

By now, we were almost at the bus stop, but by the looks of it, there was no bus in sight just yet. That meant Harry and I still had time to talk before we would separate, and I didn't know whether that was a good or a bad thing.

The hesitation was evident on his face, his dark eyebrows knitted together in either thoughtfulness or concentration about how he should tell me what he had come up with. "Well, it's pretty obvious that it has to do with what happened between us. Otherwise, you wouldn't have started giving me these hints after the incident at the restaurant, nor would you have told me what you did in the bathroom last weekend," he explained, glancing at me quickly to see my reaction.

"Go on," I said emotionlessly, staring at the destination in front of us.

"So, as embarrassing and stupid as it is, I had no idea what you were trying to get at until I started having these dreams that were also flashbacks from different situations of our past. But, it wasn't until last weekend that I finally realized what I did wrong. It's literally so stupid, and I can't believe I was so blind. I thought everything was working so well, you know? Having you as my... friend outside of school and Liam and Miranda during the day... but I guess it didn't. Somewhere along the way, I lost my mind and did things I had no idea I was doing. I started somewhat ignoring you, and that's something I never wanted to happen. So, what I'm trying to say is... I'm sorry. I'm sorry for the way I acted towards you two years ago, and I know now that what I did was absolutely shitty even if I didn't think you cared about me or my presence that much." He let out a deep puff of air once he was finished as if a weight had been lifted off his shoulders.

I let out a dry chuckle, shaking my head. Carelessly, I dropped my cigarette to the ground and stomped on it before turning to him. "You seriously think that's going to solve everything? Harry, you downright stopped paying attention to me. We were friends. We hung out almost every day after school, then you all of a sudden found Liam and started dating Miranda. Of course it didn't bother me at first because you were able to befriend whoever you wanted, but when you just stopped caring about me... it hurt," I admitted, a little surprised that I actually did. I just wanted him to realize the pain he had put me through, even if he wasn't the entire reason I felt like I did during that time.

It went quiet for a few seconds, Harry seeming lost in his thoughts as he gnawed on his bottom lip while I just stared at the dark night that surrounded us. "I know, and I'm sorry. I didn't realize I was losing you as my friend. I just thought everything was going great, you know?" He mumbled.

"That's actually kind of funny because that means you didn't care about me whatsoever. I mean, did you ever really enjoy me as your friend, or were you just there because I paid you for it? Sure, I stopped doing so after a while, but did you only agree to continue hanging out with me to seem nice and not like a jerk?"

He looked a little taken aback by my words until he finally found the ability to talk. "Of course I enjoyed you as a friend, what are you talking about? Everything that happened between us was real, I promise."

I simply nodded, even if I didn't really believe him. "Can we just drop this? What happened back then doesn't fucking matter anymore anyway. I don't want to remember some of the worst years of my life."

He sighed heavily. "Do you still hate me, though?"

I let out a loud laugh even if there was nothing funny. "Hate you?" I said, staring at him intently. "If only what I felt for you was hatred." Shaking my head bitterly, I walked away from him and quickened my strides to get to the bus stop that was only a few yards away now.

"What's that supposed to mean?" I could hear him call after me, but I didn't turn nor wait up for him.

When I arrived at the bus, I hopped on it and walked over to sit down in the back. In case Harry still wanted to talk to me, I sank down in my seat so my head wasn't visible to anyone and ran a hand through my brown fringe. Part of me regretted what I had just confessed to him because he didn't deserve to find out the truth and attempt to apologize for what he did, while another part of me was kind of relieved that he at least had figured out what he had put me through, even if he still didn't know just how much he actually meant to me.

Once the bus started moving forward, I sneaked a peek to see if Harry was still looking for me or if he had sat down in a seat. Huge mistake. He was turned my way, his eyes going through every person on the bus in search of what I assumed was me. Quickly ducking my head again, I let out a quiet 'shit' under my breath.

It didn't take more than a few seconds until I could hear footsteps stop beside me, and the next thing I knew, Harry was sitting in the seat right next to me. "You never answered my question," he said, staring ahead of him.

I glanced at the side of his face, causing him to turn his head and look into my eyes. The sight of his piercing, green irises made a lump form in my throat, and I had to gulp to make it go away. "It's nothing, Harry. Don't worry about it," I muttered, averting my gaze quickly not to get even more lost in those beautiful eyes.

A frown appeared between his eyebrows. "How am I supposed to know how you feel about me when you refuse to tell me? If it's not hatred, then what is it? Because to me, it's pretty obvious that it is, in fact, hatred."

If there was something I disliked, it was not having control of conversations when I talked to people. I always wanted to be the one in charge, the dominant one, to be more specific, and especially when the person I had a conversation with was Harry. He was supposed to be the one at a disadvantage, who didn't know what to say or do, not the other way around. "I don't hate you, okay? That's all I'm going to say. Now, would you please be quiet for the rest of the ride? I don't want to hear your annoying voice," I snarled, turning so I was facing the window.

Harry let out a deep sigh. "Fine," he muttered, and just like promised, he stayed quiet until we had to get off the bus ten minutes later, and so did I. It was a nice silence, though, something you probably wouldn't expect since I was sitting next to the person I had stopped being friends with two years ago, but it actually was. I was mostly turned towards the window, looking out at the trees and passing cars that flew by, so it wasn't like I was very aware of his presence anyway.

Once we got off the bus, we started walking towards Ed's house that was thankfully not that far from the bus stop. Actually, it was the same bus stop I used to go to every day when dad and I still lived alone. I hadn't been here since we moved, so it was a little strange, but surprisingly, it didn't bother me too much. Maybe that was because I had finally started feeling at home at Harry's house.

During the short walk, Harry and I didn't exchange so much as a word to each other, and I was thankful for that because I knew that whatever we would talk about would only end up becoming an argument. However, when we were just about to walk up to the front door, he suddenly opened his mouth.

"Louis?"

Shocked by the sound of his voice, I turned to him, indicating that I was listening to him without saying anything.

"Be careful tonight, okay?" He said, and was that concern in his eyes? No, that could not be it. Harry did not care about me, and that he had shown me so many times before that I had lost count of how many.

Rolling my eyes, I let out a snort. "Whatever."

With that said, I walked up the steps to Ed's front door where you could hear music blasting through the speakers on the other side of it. I didn't wait up for Harry but turned the door handle and walked into the house that was already crowded with people.

Some of them were dancing to the loud music while others were either chatting with each other or playing different party games like 'truth or dare' or 'never have I ever'. There were also those people who were making out with each other on the couch or in the corners, but that was only natural. Like, what would a party be without it?

I was disappointed because the party seemed to have been going on for quite a while and I just arrived here. I had probably missed at least an hour and a half, which meant people were starting to get wasted and I hadn't even started drinking yet. Not only that, but I hadn't even found my friends, nor my girlfriend who I should probably pay more attention to for that matter.

So, the first thing I did was to make my way through the crowd of people that was dancing to get to the kitchen that was located across the room in hopes of finding people I recognized. On my way there, I bumped into at least ten teenagers who either elbowed me or pressed their body against mine. Getting a little frustrated, I pushed them away and finally entered the kitchen.

Thankfully, the first person I laid eyes on was a raven-haired boy who I also liked to call my best friend. What he was doing, however, made me stop dead in my tracks, and the frustration I had just felt was instantly replaced by shock. "Zayn?" I gaped, not finding any other words to say.

He quickly detached himself from the boy he had been kissing, and oh God, wasn't that Liam? *Again*? I thought last time was just a drunken mistake, but you don't kiss the same person twice without having feelings for them, do you? Well, something told me this wasn't a mistake, at least. "I-I..." He trailed off, flicking his gaze to Liam who was sitting on the kitchen table, panting from their heated make-out session.

I shook my head, letting a smile form on my lips. "I don't need an explanation, mate. I saw the picture from Niall's party. Why didn't you say anything, though?" I asked, the shock leaving my body quickly. Sure, I was surprised that he all of a sudden seemed to find guys attractive, but since I was bisexual myself, I didn't find it strange or hard to believe. If he liked guys or Liam in this case, I was happy for him. Besides, it hopefully meant that he would be okay with me being bisexual if I ever were to come out.

He opened his mouth to answer, but nothing came out. His gaze kept flicking to Liam who looked a little embarrassed by the situation, his cheeks tinted light pink. After a few seconds, though, Liam decided to cover up for the boy who was at a loss for words. "I... we are not together. I just... we..." He trailed off, scratching the back of his neck awkwardly.

Zayn looked down at the floor, biting his bottom lip as he nodded in agreement. My mouth formed the shape of an 'o', and I instantly understood the situation. Their make out session was not planned, just like what I assumed the kiss they had shared at Niall's party hadn't been either. That explained why he hadn't told me about it earlier, although it did not explain why they had just kissed again. I mean, you only make that kind of a 'mistake' once, don't you? "Oh, I see," I said, sending them a knowing smile.

Zayn flashed me a weird look but still didn't say anything. I took the silence that followed as my cue to leave the two of them alone. They obviously had some things to work out alone and I would not be in the way for them to have that talk. Therefore, I backed out of the kitchen with the smile still evident on my face.

It didn't take long after that until I was one of the many wasted people on the dance floor who were jumping along and singing to the music. By then, I had downed at least three cans of beer and three shots. I wasn't too intoxicated, but I would be lying if I said I wasn't affected by the alcohol at all because I was starting to feel a little dizzy.

Sometime during the night, I found Eleanor hanging out with her friends. We exchanged a few words, but I didn't spend too much time with her seeing as she wasn't really into dancing, which I was.

Strangely, I didn't see Zayn for the rest of the night. Either, he was still with Liam, or the house was just too crowded with people for me to notice him, but it wouldn't surprise me if it was the first option. And, something told me it was because I was sure something was going on between the two of them. Even if Zayn was already in a relationship with someone else, there was no doubt about it.

At the moment, I was standing by a table that was scattered with different kinds of drinks. I had just been talking to some girl who had been way too wasted for her own good seeing as she wouldn't stop giggling, but thankfully she hadn't tried to jump me or something like that at least, so that was good.

After grabbing another drink, I went out on the dance floor again and started dancing along to the music. My ears almost hurt from how loud it was, but by now, I had gotten quite used to it. It was worse at the beginning of the night.

Unintentionally, I suddenly danced backward right into something, or someone to be more specific. "Oh God, I'm sorry, I didn't--" I cut myself off when I turned around and caught sight of something that had my stomach turning and my heart breaking into tiny pieces.

Right there, Harry and Niall were standing. And as if that wasn't enough, their lips were pressed together.

Chapter 18

[Harry]

I knew what I was doing was stupid and completely heartless, but I couldn't help myself. I was desperate, and Niall was the first person I could think of, even if I knew I would hurt his feelings deeply. Besides, it all would have a bigger effect if the person I did it with was Niall since he was one of Louis' closest friends.

Seeing as Louis refused to tell me what he felt about me and I just had to know, I decided to take matters into my own hands and find out myself. I was aware that the method I was using wasn't exactly the best one I could come up with, but it would hopefully give me an answer at least, and that was all that I could think of right now.

So, that was how I found myself pressing my lips to the blonde-haired guy's when I saw Louis was just about to accidentally dance into us. I could see it coming before anyone else did, so I instantly took the opportunity I was given and grabbed a hold of Niall's waist, sealing our lips together.

As expected, Louis did react to the action, but unfortunately not in the way I had hoped he would. Instead of getting angry or showing any kind of emotion, he stared at the two of us with an unreadable look on his face before he suddenly turned on his heel and stormed off. The action caught me so off guard that I found myself standing there for a few seconds, just staring at the spot where he had just been.

That was until I snapped back to reality and came to my senses.

I quickly departed from Niall and looked at his shocked face. "I'm so sorry," I said, and I did really mean it, even if it probably didn't seem like it. He didn't deserve this, at all.

Before he had time to even so much as say anything, I left him in search of the boy I was desperately trying to figure out. I made my way through the crowd of sweaty bodies and dancing people, seeing Louis' figure moving towards the front door. He was getting away, so I quickened my pace and practically pushed the people standing in my way off. I could not lose sight of him.

It took quite some time, but eventually, I finally managed to catch up with him, and by then we were out in the cold night, in the empty streets. "Louis, wait!" I called, reaching out to grab a hold of his forearm to make him stop. He stumbled a little by the harshness but didn't make any kind of face at the action whatsoever. He remained emotionless.

"What?!" He asked coldly. "What the fuck do you want, Harry?"

My eyes widened at the tone he was using, but I quickly composed myself and cleared my throat. "I, uhh... I was just--" I started, but he cut me off.

"You were just what? Sucking my best friend's face off just moments ago? Yeah, I noticed, but thanks for the information. Next time you should let me know before it happens so I don't miss a single second of it," he said sarcastically.

I closed my eyes, shaking my head in confusion. "Wait, what?"

When I opened them again, I could see him roll his eyes. "Oh, come on! Don't be so fucking stupid, Harry. Isn't it obvious? I thought I'd made it clear enough for you a long time ago, but apparently not. You're so fucking oblivious it's laughable, really."

I just stared at him, blinking my eyes. What was he talking about? Well, I did have an idea, but it couldn't be what I thought it was, right? No, I was pretty sure it wasn't. "I'm sorry, what?"

Something flashed in his eye as he gritted his teeth together. "You're unbelievable," he muttered, and the next thing I knew, he snatched his arm out of my hold and turned around to continue walking in the same direction he had been heading before.

My eyes followed his figure for a second until I finally managed to get control over my body and began moving my legs towards him. Instead of grabbing his forearm this time, I went for his hand, and damn, was that a mistake. Or well, that was if you counted getting goosebumps all over your body as a mistake because that was what happened to me. It wasn't necessarily a bad thing, but when Louis could easily see my reaction to our skin touching, it definitely was.

He was turned to me now, his eyes fixed on my hand that was still holding his in a firm grip. It was like some kind of tingly sensation went through my arm at the feeling of it in mine. It was weird, to say the least, but I couldn't help but like it. A lot. "Louis, I..." I trailed off, finding it hard to get any words past my lips.

His eyes traveled up to my face, searching for something I didn't know. He took a step forward, standing so close to me that my breath hitched in my throat. "Tell me, Harry, why do you think I just ran off when I saw you and Niall kissing?"

My mouth opened, but nothing came out, so I just stared at him with wide eyes. He let out a sigh, shaking his head in what seemed like disappointment. "Come on, it's not as hard as you think it is. Actually, I think you know what I'm talking about, you just refuse to believe it for some reason."

Hesitating, I bit down on my bottom lip. Was what I thought to be impossible actually true? Could it be that Louis had feelings for me just like I had come to the conclusion that I did for him? Even if I knew I could be completely wrong, I couldn't help but feel butterflies erupt in my stomach. I also knew that it was absolutely wrong of me to feel this way about my stepbrother, but I really couldn't help myself.

Without realizing it, we had moved closer to each other. Louis' hand was still clutched in mine, but our faces were only inches apart now. I could feel his breath on my lips as he lifted his other hand to place it on my cheek. He reeked of alcohol, and maybe that should have made me hesitant about what was about to happen. For all I knew, he could be drunk and would forget this in the morning, but I literally couldn't stop myself because I also knew that this was a once in a lifetime opportunity. I would probably never have the chance to kiss Louis again.

"Louis..." I whispered, glancing up into his eyes that were focusing on my parted lips.

"Tell me if you want me to stop," he breathed, getting closer to my face by the second.

When I didn't say anything, a small smile formed on his lips and he closed his eyes shut. I followed suit, wrapping my arms around his neck even if I was slightly taller than him. It just felt like I was supposed to, especially when I could feel his hand that was holding mine let go of it to place it on the small of my back. Tingles started making their way over my skin at the feeling of him touching me, and suddenly, I was so eager to just have his lips on mine that I almost leaned in all the way to just crash them together.

Our breaths mixed as we inhaled deeply. It was all so intense that I bet anyone would just stop and stare like shocked owls if they were to walk by us right now. I had never felt this way with anyone before, and it was so exciting that I didn't know whether to smile as bright as ever or freeze in my spot. However, I knew none of those options were convenient right now, so in the end, I just decided to wait and see what would happen.

Louis pushed his chin forward, letting his soft and warm lips touch mine, but only for a second before he pulled back again. He still kept close, though, as if he was just trying it out. When he had repeated the action at least three times, I started getting frustrated. "Just kiss me, you fool."

He let out a small chuckle against my lips, and I could practically see him roll his eyes behind my eyelids. However, the next second, he finally closed the distance between us and pressed his pink lips against mine in a proper kiss this time.

If you have never experienced fireworks or shivers running down your spine while kissing someone, then let me tell you, you have definitely missed out on something. Because that was exactly what I felt when Louis started moving his mouth against mine. It was all so overwhelming that I had to blink my eyes open to see if I was dreaming or not. When it turned out I wasn't, I let out a gasp against his lips and pulled myself even closer to him, just wanting to be as near him as possible.

His hold on my lower back tightened, and he let his other hand trail down my body until it was resting on my right hip.

Our lips moved in sync, exploring new angles and adding more pressure as time went on. It was probably the most heated and powerful kiss I'd ever had, and we weren't even using our tongues yet.

As if on cue, he let his tongue slide along my bottom lip in a teasing way, making me let out a soft whine. I even parted my lips to let him enter my mouth, but he wouldn't budge. Instead, he let out a laugh and pulled back a little so our lips were barely even touching. "Don't be greedy."

"Shut up," I muttered, grabbing the back of his neck to pull him back into another heated kiss.

It was so weird that it took me so long to figure out my feelings for him. I mean, judging by my response to his kisses, I would say that most people might probably think I had been in love with him for a long time. But no, I had only known that I liked him for a week, which was unbelievable.

When the need for air eventually became too much for us, we pulled apart and slowly opened our eyes to gaze at each other. "That..." I trailed off breathlessly, keeping my arms around his neck.

"Was absolutely amazing," he finished, and I couldn't do anything but agree. "You have no idea how long I've been wanting to do that."

His words made me smile, but they also made me wonder. For how long *had* Louis been wanting to do that? Because as far as I knew, he hadn't felt that way for long, right? "How long?" I whispered, our faces just a few inches apart.

He made a face, shaking his head slowly. "Too long," was the only thing he said, and something about the way he did it made me understand that it was for longer than I had first thought, which was shocking. How come he had been picking on me during the last two years if he had feelings for me? To me, that didn't make sense at all. But then again, when did Louis ever make sense? Practically everything he did confused me.

After just staring at each other for I didn't know how long, he grabbed my hand and started pulling me in the direction of the bus stop. "Come on, let's head home. That party sucks anyways," he muttered, and I could feel myself smiling.

"Does that maybe have anything to do with what happened just a couple of minutes ago?" I asked, nudging him in the side teasingly.

He sent me a glare, his eyes shooting daggers at me. "Watch it, Styles. If I ever see you kissing one of my best friends again, I might have to shoot you... or them. It depends."

Rolling my eyes, I let out a quiet laugh. Together, we walked to the bus stop hand in hand without saying very much to each other, but that wasn't necessary either. Just his presence made me all fuzzy inside and I knew that I could definitely get used to this.

When I woke up the next morning, a wide smile formed on my lips as I remembered what had happened the night before. Once Louis and I had gotten home, we departed to go into our separate rooms, but not before sharing another kiss. There was something with it that made me nervous, though. He had pressed his lips against mine as if it was the last kiss we would share for a while, and that scared me to no end. But, I also knew that I could have just imagined it. I really hoped so.

To say I was happy would be an understatement. I had never felt this happy my entire life, and that said a lot. There was no longer any doubt that I had some quite deep feelings for the boy that was sleeping in the room next to mine.

Rubbing my eyes, I sat up in bed and started searching the room for a pair of joggers that I could put on. I hadn't eaten in what felt like ages because my stomach was growling like never before and I was absolutely starving. Therefore, I hurriedly put on my grey joggers once I found them and pulled a white t-shirt from my closet over my head. After that, I didn't think twice before leaving my room and sprinting down the stairs to the kitchen where I could smell freshly made pancakes coming from.

The first thing I noticed when I stepped into the room was my mum's presence. She was standing in front of the stove, flipping a pancake with a hand on her hip and a spatula in the other. The next thing I noticed was Troy sitting at the kitchen table, reading the newspaper with a pair of glasses on his nose that were almost falling off. "Morning guys," I greeted, unable to get the smile off my face. After what happened yesterday, I couldn't seem to make it disappear.

"Good morning, Harry," they replied in unison, my mum spinning on her heel to return my smile. "How was the party yesterday?"

I shrugged even though I wanted to go on about how it was probably the best party of my life considering what happened afterward. "It was okay, I guess. Nothing new happened."

Troy raised a suspicious eyebrow. "Are you sure about that? You seem unusually happy today. Did you find a nice girl you--"

"Troy," mum cut him off, sending him a glare, which made him laugh and raise his hands in surrender. "I'm sorry, love. I was just curious," he said apologetically, sending her a kissy face, which had her blushing a light pink.

I scrunched my nose up in disgust, shaking my head. "Please don't do that in front of me. That's just disgusting."

Mum rolled her eyes, turning around to flip the pancake she was currently making over.

"So, where is Louis today? He came home with you last night, right?" Troy asked, looking at me questioningly.

I nodded, and just the mention of his name made my lips twitch up into a smile again. "Yeah, we got home around midnight I would say. We weren't out for long, but I'm pretty sure he had a bit more than I did," I explained, biting down on my bottom lip.

To be honest, I was a little nervous about that topic. Sure, Louis didn't seem very drunk yesterday, but I still didn't know whether he was conscious of what happened or not. What if he didn't remember our kiss? Or even worse, what if what he said about me wasn't true? That would surely break me.

Troy shook his head in what looked like disappointment. "That boy and his drinking habit. I thought he had gotten better with that, but I guess not."

I merely nodded my head, sitting down in the seat across from him. It didn't take more than a few minutes until the next person entered the kitchen, but to my disappointment, it was only Gemma. "Good morning, guys," she greeted, flashing all of us a bright smile. Ever since she went on that date with the guy she had been crushing on for ages, she seemed happier than ever before, which was nothing but a positive thing.

"Morning," I mumbled in reply, grabbing the fork that was placed on the table in front of me to start fiddling with it impatiently. I just couldn't wait to see what Louis' reaction would be today. Yet, I was scared shitless. It was a 50-50 situation.

"Sleep well?"

I nodded as she sat down in the seat beside me, instantly pouring herself a glass of milk.

"So, that's it. The pancakes are ready to be eaten," mum suddenly announced, placing the last pancake on the plate on the counter beside her. She turned the stove off before grabbing the plate of pancakes and walking over with it to put it on the kitchen table. "Harry, would you please fetch the maple syrup?"

"Sure," I said obediently, standing up to get the said item from the cabinet across the room. I was just about to open it when a new voice was heard, and it made my body go rigid because suddenly, I wasn't ready to face this person at all.

Louis greeted our family members while I just stood there for a few seconds, my back turned towards them. "Harry, are you alright?" Mum asked, slight concern lacing her voice.

I turned around slowly, avoiding Louis as I gave her a small smile. "Yeah, I'm just getting the syrup as you told me."

She didn't look convinced but decided to just shrug it off and nod her head curtly. Biting my bottom lip nervously, I made my way over to the table and sat back down in my seat, placing the maple syrup in the middle of the table.

While everyone dug into the breakfast, I glanced up at Louis to follow his movements. Much to my disappointment and fear, it seemed as though he was trying his best to... well, being his usual self because he wasn't paying attention to me whatsoever. He just quietly placed a pancake on his plate and spread some butter on it.

As if that wasn't enough, I could feel Gemma staring at me from the seat next to mine, and judging by the frown on her face, I could tell she knew something was up between the two of us. It only took about five minutes until she elbowed me in the side and sent Louis a pointed look, which he thankfully didn't notice. "What happened?" She hissed in my ear.

Unfortunately, I couldn't play it off like I didn't hear anything because it was definitely loud enough, so I just shook my head in dismissal. "I'll tell you later." Which I probably wouldn't, but it would at least make her shut up for now.

The rest of breakfast continued being pretty silent and uneventful. Louis didn't so much as look my way once during the entire time, and that had me both worried and scared at once. Either, he didn't remember what happened, or he regretted everything and ignored me just because of that. Neither of the options sounded good. Honestly, all I really wanted right now was to go up to my room and bury myself in my bed so I could cry my eyes out because this was what I had been fearing ever since I decided to go against my mind and let his lips touch mine yesterday.

When I exited the kitchen twenty minutes later, I was cussing and yelling at myself in my head because how stupid could I be? Of course things would turn out like this. What had I expected? That he would wake up and greet me with a kiss right in front of our family? Like that would ever happen. He probably didn't even like me in the slightest, and all he wanted yesterday was some action or some shit. I mean, he even had a girlfriend, so why would any of the things he told me be true anyway?

Sure, it did seem like he was jealous of Niall when I kissed him, and it did seem like he really meant it when he told me that he didn't hate me, but I could have just been mistaken, and right now that sounded most likely.

Once I entered my bedroom, I threw myself on my unmade bed and let out a loud scream into my pillow. I could already feel tears form in my eyes while my heart was breaking more and more with every second that went by. I couldn't hear any sound coming from the room next to mine, but I knew Louis was in there. The question was if he knew what I felt right now, if he knew how much pain he had caused me.

And it was right then a scary thought hit me.

What if this was his revenge for what I did to him two years ago?

Chapter 19

[Harry]

Louis didn't acknowledge my existence during that entire Sunday. He mostly stayed in his room doing God knows what, but he was probably texting his friends or his girlfriend, which in that case wouldn't surprise me at all.

However, I couldn't say that I was being more social than him. I stayed in bed, listening to music in my headphones to block the world out and try to drown myself in my own thoughts. Maybe thinking about what had happened wasn't the best idea, but I couldn't think of doing anything better. I either did that or went down to the living room where my family members were and talked about things I didn't have a care in the world about. Besides, I didn't want to see anyone in the state I was in, so lying in bed was probably the best option at the end of the day.

Now it was Monday, meaning that I had to get ready to go to school, which also meant I was going to have to see Niall. It would probably be one of the most difficult and awkward encounters I would ever experience. Difficult because I didn't want to hurt him, even if I knew there was no taking back what happened, and awkward because we kissed and then I just left him without saying more than the words 'I'm sorry' afterward.

Another reason why I wasn't too keen on leaving my room was that I knew Gemma would interrogate me about the incident in the kitchen the other day. She would definitely demand some answers, which I didn't want to give her. I didn't like sharing my feelings or thoughts with other people even if it was my own sister in this case. I liked to keep personal things to myself. Well, at least for now, when I didn't really know what was going on myself.

And last but not least, I didn't want to leave my bedroom because I obviously didn't want to face Louis. I was sure that would only break me even more, especially if he kept on ignoring me like he did yesterday. I mean, I would have been happy if he just met my eyes for one second because then it meant he wasn't ignoring me at least, but since that didn't happen yesterday, I wasn't expecting it to happen today either.

Therefore, I decided to take my time to change that morning. The longer I stayed in my room, the less chance it was that I would see Gemma or Louis. However, I knew Louis wasn't a morning person, so he probably wouldn't be gone by the time I went downstairs anyway, but hopefully, Gemma would be at least, and that counted as something.

Once I had pulled on a black knitted sweater, I got out of my bed and strode over to my closet to pull out a pair of clean, black, skinny jeans that were ripped at the knees. It was freezing outside, but I couldn't be bothered. It wasn't like it would matter whether there were holes in my jeans or not.

After that, I looked at myself in the mirror to fix my curls a little. They were a mess today for sure, but I couldn't care less about how they looked right now, so I just lazily ran a hand through them and swept my fringe backward. Some days you just couldn't be bothered at all.

Sadly, I was all finished in only ten minutes, but I made sure not to do any of my toilet chores yet since there was a possibility Louis would enter the bathroom while I was in there. I would save that for later when I was sure he wasn't around, or I would just use the bathroom on the other floor where you at least could lock around yourself.

    To my slight surprise, the kitchen was empty when I entered, which I found absolutely amazing. This meant I wouldn't have to worry about either Louis or Gemma unless they would show up during the time I made or ate breakfast, that was. For now, though, everything was great, so I strode over to the fridge to pull out the milk and the jelly, which I would use to spread on my slice of bread later on when it was toasted. I also grabbed the peanut butter and cereals from the cabinet we kept them in.

    Once my breakfast was ready, I sat down at the kitchen table and looked out the window, letting out a deep sigh as I chewed on my cereals. If only life was simple, then I wouldn't be in such a mess right now. Louis would still be my somewhat enemy and Niall would only be Louis' best friend. To think so much had changed in only a few weeks was unbelievable, and it all started when mum and Troy informed me and Gemma that they were moving in together. Even if I didn't like to fight with Louis, I was willing to say I would rather do that than living with this pain one more day.

    I was just about to take a bite of my toast when I could hear the sound of a door slamming shut on the top floor. My head instantly turned in the direction as a knot formed in my stomach. There was only one person other than me who had their bedroom on the second floor and that was the person I was fearing to face.

    The sound of footsteps was soon heard in the staircase and I took a deep breath to prepare myself for what was to come, even if it was close to impossible. Much to my surprise, however, no one entered the kitchen. Instead, the next thing I heard was the sound of the front door slamming shut with great force. My eyes instinctively closed for a second at the noise before they opened again.

What was that? He was acting as if I had done something wrong when he was the one who had ignored me for an entire day after we had kissed. If someone was doing anything wrong, it was him. Then why did he seem so mad? As far as I knew, I hadn't done anything but try catching his attention, but since he hadn't been responding to me, I assumed he either regretted it or that it was his revenge for what I did to him in the past.

I just couldn't put my finger on why he was mad at me because clearly, that was what he was, right? Why else would he slam the door like that?

Deep in my thoughts, I ate my breakfast and finished getting ready for school before leaving the now empty house. I made sure to lock the door behind me, knowing mum would scold me if she found out I had forgotten to do it. Then I walked to the bus stop with my earphones plugged into my phone, listening to some relaxing music to take my mind off of the things going on right now, and surprisingly it helped quite a lot.

Once I arrived at the bus stop, I was shocked to see a crowd of students waiting for the bus to come. I thought I was late and would have to take the next one, but I guess not. However, that also meant Louis was here and probably Niall too, so I didn't know if it was such a good thing after all.

I turned my volume down to low and leaned against a lamp pole a few yards away from the crowd in order to not be acknowledged by anyone. I could see Louis talking to a few guys from the football team, nodding his head to whatever they said even if he didn't seem very into it. Whenever he smiled, it wouldn't reach his eyes, and believe me, I knew when he cracked a real smile, and this was not it. His usually bright, blue eyes didn't have that spark in them that they would whenever he found something funny for real, nor were the crinkles by his eyes prominent.

"Who's the lucky one you're checking out?" I could hear someone speak in my ear, and I almost jumped in shock at the sudden sound.

Turning around, I was even more shocked to see Ed standing there, his hands in his pockets with a cheeky smile on his face. "What are you talking about? I'm not checking out anyone. On another note, you scared the hell out of me, so you should apologize," I said, pulling the earphones out of my ears.

He rolled his eyes, shifting on his feet. "I'm sorry, little Harry. Did I make you pee your pants?" He joked, earning a jab in the shoulder.

"Shut up," I muttered, although a slight smile formed on my face. "What are you even doing here? As far as I know, you live on the other side of town."

He nodded in agreement. "I do, but I was sleeping over at Niall's tonight, which is why I'm here right now. I saw you standing all by yourself so I decided to accompany my friend since kindergarten. Now, aren't I just the best friend out there?" He said, batting his eyelashes.

"Sure you are, Ed. Sure you are," I snorted sarcastically.

"Hey, I'm offended."

"You should be," I winked, making him glare at me.

"Okay, enough about this. I want to know who you were staring at when I spotted you here because surely, there was someone. I know when my little Harry has an eye for someone special."

I opened my mouth to reply with something along the lines that I wasn't actually looking at anyone special (even though I was), but before I could do so, he cut me off by pressing his index finger against my lips. "Wait, could it be Niall? I mean, he hasn't been able to shut up about you all weekend, and apparently, you two even kissed at my party," he said, wiggling his eyebrows at me.

Biting my bottom lip, I scratched the back of my neck. "He hasn't?" I grimaced, fearing even more now that he would be absolutely crushed when I told him that the kiss basically meant nothing to me and that it was all just part of a plan to see what Louis felt about me. Well, of course I would leave out the part about Louis, but he would surely be heartbroken anyway.

Ed shook his head, the smile never leaving his face. "Nope. He's been gushing about your kiss ever since he woke up on my couch yesterday morning. So, if the one you were staring at was Niall, you certainly don't have to hide your feelings anymore because damn, that boy certainly likes you. He will be yours in a second if you just ask him."

Why did everything seem so easy with Niall yet so fucking difficult with Louis? It was like the world wanted me to like Niall while my heart wanted me to go after Louis. As mentioned before, it would be a lot easier to be with Niall, but I also knew I couldn't force myself to feel something for someone I didn't like in that way. Sure, Niall was sweet and nice, but he was like a brother to me, just like Liam. I only wanted to be friends, nothing more. It was weird that I didn't feel the same way about Louis, since he actually was my stepbrother.

Letting out a deep sigh, I looked up to see that Niall had joined the group where Louis was and that his gaze kept flicking in my and Ed's direction. I turned back to Ed, closing my eyes briefly. "Is it bad that he wasn't the one I was looking at?"

He let out a chuckle as he shook his head. "No, but I know someone who's going to be heartbroken because of that. You know, if you ever change your mind, I'm sure he'll always be there for you."

My eyebrows knitted together at his words. "Don't tell me he told you to come over here just so you could talk well about him. If that's the case, you can go tell him that those stupid methods don't work on me. If he ever wants a chance, he should man up and talk to me himself," I said, crossing my arms over my chest.

Ed rolled his eyes, letting out another chuckle. "Oh, come on, Harry. He's just nervous, is all. You would be too if your crush kissed you then just left you like that. He just wants to know how you feel about him, if you possibly like him back. But since you don't, I'm just going to go back and tell him--"

"No! You can't just do that! He's going to be so heartbroken, especially if it's coming from someone else. I'll talk to him myself when the time is right. For now, just tell him I refused to say anything about it or whatever. I want to fix my own mistake because that would be the only right thing to do," I said, trying to convince myself too that it would be the best. I mean, it would be a lot easier if Ed just told Niall that I didn't reciprocate his feelings, but it wouldn't be fair to him if he heard it from someone else. Besides, I didn't want to feel like a wimp, which I knew I would if I went along with this.

"Alright, whatever you say," he shrugged. "Now, will you tell me who you really were checking out when I joined you? Even if I mostly came here for Niall, I am still curious to know who you've got an eye for."

Luckily for me, since I didn't want to answer that question, the bus arrived right then, which meant I could leave him with a great excuse. "I'll talk to you later Ed. See ya."

He opened his mouth to say something, but before he had gotten a word past his lips, I had already left him. I headed for the bus and got in line to hop on it. When it was finally my turn, I started walking down the aisle to find an empty seat, but just to my luck, all of the front spots were taken so I would have to pass by a whole lot of people to find a seat. Of course both Niall and Louis were two of them, and what made it even worse was that they were sitting very close to each other. The aisle was the only thing separating them.

As if that wasn't enough, the only empty seat I could spot was the one right behind Louis, next to some girl I didn't recognize. I tried not to make eye contact with any of them, but I could still see Niall sending me a small, nervous smile while Louis flashed me one of his famous glares. I was a little taken aback by the fact that my stepbrother seemed to acknowledge my existence for the first time in two days, but the look he gave me made my heart drop in my chest. Like seriously, what had I done to him?

Could it possibly be about what I had done to him in the past? But why did it seem like he was mad at me then? I mean, if he wanted revenge, shouldn't he just be ignoring me like he had done yesterday since that was basically what I had done to him? God, this was all such a huge mess, and it was making both my heart and head hurt.

Running my hands over my face, I sat down in the empty seat and pressed my earphones into my ears again. Maybe I was being disrespectful towards the girl beside me, but in my defense, she was wearing earphones as well, so I didn't really care.

Thankfully, the ride to school was quite uneventful. Sure, Niall sent me a couple of looks, and I could see him talking to other people excitedly about something I had no idea of, but other than that, nothing else happened, which in other words meant that Louis didn't do anything from the seat in front of mine that included me. Of course.

Once the bus finally came to a halt, I didn't hesitate to get up from my seat and leave as quickly as possible. I just wanted to meet up with Liam so I could finally talk to someone about what had happened. Obviously, I would leave out the parts about Louis, but I needed to tell him about what happened with Niall. Otherwise, I was going to explode from how fast my head was spinning at the moment.

Before I could do so, though, I felt someone tap me on the shoulder from behind. I had just hopped off the bus and was heading towards the entrance of the school when this happened. Confused as to who wanted to talk to me, I turned around and was surprised to see Niall standing there, biting his bottom lip. "Um, hey," he greeted, giving me a small smile.

"Hi," I replied uncertainly, looking at my surroundings kind of awkwardly. Now that I was facing the situation I had known would occur sometime during the day, I felt worse than I did this morning. I wasn't even sure if I could still do it, hurt him even more than I had already done, I mean.

He was just about to open his mouth and say something when I could feel someone bash into my shoulder roughly. Caught off guard, I looked up only to see Louis send a glare in my direction. "Oops, sorry," he mocked, turning around and continuing walking towards the entrance without another word.

I just stared at his figure for a few seconds, trying to register what had just happened until I blinked my eyes a few times and paid attention to Niall again. He had his eyebrows in a frown and was looking at where Louis had been just a few seconds ago. "What was that all about? I mean, sure, I know you guys don't get along, but that just came out of nowhere."

Biting my lip, I started moving towards the entrance as well because the bell would probably ring any minute and I didn't want to be late. Niall followed suit, falling into step with me. "Eh, don't worry about it. We usually pick on each other like that," I said, shrugging as if it was no big deal. "Now, about what happened at the party... because that's what you wanted to talk about right?"

He took a deep breath, closing his eyes briefly before opening them again. To say he looked nervous would be an understatement. I just wondered what made him feel that way. I mean, sure, we had kissed and it was a little awkward, but why the nervousness? "Look Harry, I know I could be making a huge mistake right now and that I could regret this later on, but I just can't hold it in any longer."

He took a break, looking up into my eyes. We had now stopped in the middle of the hallway, but there were surprisingly not that many people around, which made this conversation a whole lot more serious and intense.

"I like you, alright? Ever since you almost fell over on the school bus that time a few weeks ago and I caught you, I've felt this sort of attachment to you. I'm not saying you should feel the same or anything, but then you kissed me at that party and I just thought... that you might actually like me too."

Chapter 20

[Harry]

    I didn't say anything for a while, and neither did he. It wasn't that I was shocked by his words because I already knew he liked me, but it just became so much more real when he actually said the words out loud. Furthermore, it made it even more difficult for me to say what I had been planning on telling him ever since I woke up this morning. If I told him that the kiss meant nothing to me, he would be absolutely devastated. That was why I now couldn't bring myself to open my mouth.

    Unluckily for me, the bell didn't want to save me this time like it had done so many times before. Instead, I had to face the situation and man up, but maybe that wasn't so bad after all because at least that meant I would have this conversation over with soon.

    He looked at me while biting his lip, waiting for me to say something. When he realized I wasn't going to do so, he let out a sigh. "Harry, if you don't like me, just say so. This tension is killing me, and I'd rather you say it now so we can have all this over with."

    Closing my eyes, I swallowed hard. "Look, Niall. It's not that I don't like you. I just don't feel that way about you, alright? You're like a brother to me, and I'm sorry for giving you the wrong signals at the party. I don't know what came over me. I was just so out of it that night. I'm sorry for leading you on," I apologized, looking down at my feet in shame.

So, that was it. I said it, even if it wasn't entirely true, but he didn't need to know that.

He let out a dry laugh, shaking his head. "It's okay, Harry. I get it, don't worry about it. I totally understand that you don't feel the same. I just wish you did," he grimaced, turning around to start heading in the direction of his locker.

Before he could do so, though, I grabbed a hold of his shoulder and pulled him back. "Please Niall, can't we at least be friends? You're such a sweet guy, and I would like to keep you in my life somehow even if... things turned out the way they did. Maybe it's too much to ask for because I wouldn't want you to hurt because of me, but I just can't help it."

His lips twitched into a faded smile. "It gladdens me that you enjoy my company, it really does, but right now I'm not sure if I could handle being around you without... being with you, or at least knowing you could have feelings for me. I'm sorry," he apologized, making another attempt at leaving me, and this time, I didn't stop him.

I watched his fading figure turn the corner at the end of the hallway before I slapped a hand over my face. What had I done? I wasn't used to turning people down, especially not people as sweet and good-hearted as Niall. He definitely didn't deserve this, but I had no other choice. It would only hurt him more in the end if I had said yes since I didn't have the same feelings for him as he did for me. I just hated the fact that I hurt him because he had done nothing but been nice to me.

Just a few seconds later, the bell rang, and I had to hurry to get to class on time. Luckily, Liam wasn't waiting for me by my locker like he usually did because I didn't want him to be late because of me, so I just shoved my jacket and backpack into my locker and hurried to the classroom with my books in my hands.

By the time I arrived, the other students were already seated in their chairs, waiting for Mr. Storm to start the lesson. This fact made it more awkward when I walked by the desks to sit down in an empty seat in the back because I probably had every pair of eyes in the classroom following my movements. I kept my head low, though, so I wouldn't meet any of them. No matter what, I could tell my cheeks were a crimson red as I finally looked around the room once I was seated at the empty desk, observing who was sitting beside whom.

It didn't surprise me that Louis was seated beside Eleanor because well, they were together after all. What did surprise me, though, was the fact that he seemed too busy staring at me to respond to her when she tried getting his attention. She was poking at his arm repeatedly, yet he didn't seem to notice it whatsoever, which shouldn't make butterflies erupt in my stomach, but they did anyway.

Quickly looking away, my gaze wandered to the front of the classroom where I could find my best friend sitting next to... wait, was that Zayn? And weren't they sitting a little too close to just be friends or acquaintances? What had I missed?

Shocked and rather confused, I shook my head with a frown on my face, wondering why Liam hadn't told me about this yet. I mean, I already knew he had feelings for Zayn, so there was no reason why he shouldn't, right? Then why was I clueless about it?

It turned out that I had to sit alone at my desk because I was the last one to arrive. Not that I minded, but this class usually took up every seat, so there must be someone that was missing. I let my gaze wander again, trying to figure out who the missing person was, and it didn't take more than a few seconds until I realized it was Niall. It made my heart break a little in my chest because I knew I was most likely the reason why he was absent. I mean, why else would he skip class?

With a sigh, I turned my attention to Mr. Storm, listening to what he had to say, and taking notes whenever he told us to. While I did that, I could feel Louis' gaze on me. Even if I didn't turn to meet his eyes, something told me he wasn't looking at me with hatred this time, but with intensity, like he was thinking deeply about something. Considering he was looking my way, I assumed whatever he was thinking about had to do with me.

Trying my best to ignore him, I bit my lip and continued taking my notes while listening to the teacher. For some reason, this lasted throughout the entire lesson. It wasn't like it bothered me because I didn't mind the butterflies in my stomach. I just found it weird. Furthermore, his mood swings were making me quite frustrated. One minute he ignored me, the second he was pissed at me, and the third he was just staring at me with a thoughtful look on his face. What was even going on in his head?

When the bell rang, signaling the end of first period, I gathered my stuff and exited the classroom. I searched the crowd of people for a brown-haired boy I liked to call my best friend in hopes of finally speaking to him about what happened with Niall and also what happened between him and Zayn, but unfortunately, I couldn't find him.

With a heavy sigh, I hurried to my locker to put my books away before making my way to Liam's across the hallway, hoping he was there and that he hadn't gone to our English class yet. Thankfully, I spotted the brown-haired boy at his locker, but he wasn't alone like I expected him to be. Instead, he was pressed against the wall by Zayn, and much to my surprise, they were kissing.

My eyes widened at the sight, and if it weren't for the fact that I was clutching my books tightly to my chest, I would've dropped them right there. When did this even happen and how didn't I know about it? To be honest, I thought Liam would call me the first thing he did if Zayn were to even touch him, but apparently not because he hadn't said a thing, and now he was *kissing* him.

Once the shock had left my body, I started moving my legs in their direction. Their lips were still locked when I stopped right in front of them, clearing my throat awkwardly. "Liam, you've got anything to tell me?"

Within a second, they separated and turned to me in surprise. Or well, Liam was surprised while Zayn seemed rather annoyed to have been interrupted, I assumed. I brushed it off and focused my full attention on Liam who was shifting on his feet while biting his slightly swollen bottom lip. "Uh, maybe?"

Rolling my eyes, I crossed my arms over my chest the best I could with my books in my hands. "When were you going to tell me you're together with your crush? I thought you would run to me the first thing you did if it were to happen, but I guess not."

His cheeks turned a light pink as he looked up at Zayn who now had an amused look on his face. "We... We're not really together, Harry, but we are kind of dating. And I'm sorry I didn't tell you sooner. I was just too caught up with other stuff, I guess."

I gave him a soft smile. "It's alright, mate. I'm not mad at you or anything. Actually, I'm happy that you finally got the one you wanted," I smirked, making his cheeks turn even redder.

Zayn wrapped an arm around his waist and looked at him with a cheeky smile on his lips. "So, you've had a crush on me for ages, eh?" He joked, raising one of his eyebrows playfully while bumping Liam's hip with his own.

"Shut up," Liam muttered, looking down at the ground to hide his face.

"Maybe not for ages, but it's definitely been a few weeks. He thought he was way out of your league, that he would never have a chance with you and those kinds of stuff," I admitted, knowing very well that he would be pissed at me for saying this, but I did anyway because it was so funny to see him in this situation. He would probably get back at me in the future, though, but right now I couldn't care less about that.

Zayn cooed at the embarrassed boy and pressed a light kiss on his forehead. "Well, for your information, I don't think you're out of my league at all. You're absolutely perfect for me. Now, I have to get to my next class, see you later?"

Liam nodded as he reciprocated the kiss Zayn pressed against his lips before leaving the two of us alone. The brown-haired boy still looked embarrassed with his cheeks flaming a dark red, but I decided not to tease him about it even more. He had already had enough of that, which I noticed the next second when his gaze landed on me. I swear, if looks could kill, I would be dead right now. "Run," was the only thing he had to say to make my feet move as quickly as possible in the direction of the classroom.

I didn't even care that it was five minutes until the next class started. As long as I got out of this situation alive, I would be happy. Unfortunately, though, I didn't get very far until I could feel a tight grip on my forearm, pulling me aside and into the bathroom. What was even scarier was the fact that it wasn't a public bathroom, but one that only had one toilet in it.

When I turned around, I expected to see mad, chocolate brown eyes staring at me with hatred, but instead, I saw a pair of ocean blue ones looking at me with frustration. My heart skipped a beat in my chest as the realization that it was Louis who had pulled me in here hit me. What in the world did he want?

"You have to tell me why you did it."

I knitted my eyebrows together in confusion, having no idea what in the world he was talking about. "Did what?"

He let out a groan, looking away from me with a pissed look on his face. "Why you decided to turn Niall down, of course," he said emotionlessly, his voice unusually flat.

My back was pressed against the wall, his body being way too close to mine for my heart to beat at a normal pace. It wasn't like he was touching me, but just his proximity made me feel flustered. Swallowing hard, I took a deep breath in an attempt to steady my heartbeat. "How do you even know about that?" I let out breathlessly, trying to meet eyes with him, but he refused.

"It doesn't matter. I want to know why you did it."

I looked down at my feet, biting my bottom lip. Why did he even care? It wasn't like he had feelings for me or anything. That, he had made very obvious the past two days, so why was he acting like this?

When I didn't answer him, he finally turned his head so our eyes could meet. To my surprise, it wasn't hatred I saw in them, but more like pain. This made me even more confused, and suddenly I wanted to know what was going on inside his head more than ever. "Why are you acting like this?" I asked instead of answering his question.

He didn't say anything, just kept staring into my green eyes. After a while, though, he shook his head and muttered a quiet 'fuck' under his breath. A second later, he tried pulling away and making a beeline towards the door, but I grabbed his arm and pulled him back before he could do so. "For God's sake, stop running away from your problems all the time! Tell me the truth. Tell me why you decided to kiss me then ignore me like nothing happened, and tell me why you're acting so weird right now just because I turned Niall down. Because I think you owe me some answers after everything that has happened."

Suddenly, my body was pinned to the wall by a pair of strong arms, gripping my shoulders tightly. His usually ocean blue eyes were now ice cold, staring into mine with a look that almost made me cringe. "Will you shut the fuck up? I don't owe you anything, alright? If there's anyone who owes things here, it's you. You owe me a ton of stupid shit," he snapped, making me blink my eyes a few times.

Taking a deep breath, I tried getting out of his hold by pushing at his chest, but he wouldn't budge. Instead, he only tightened his hold on me. "Don't you try to escape now. Tell me why you hurt Niall's heart. Otherwise, I might keep you in here for the rest of the day."

I could feel anger building up inside me because this was just so stupid. Why was he even mad in the first place? I was just telling him the truth. No matter what I had done to him, he did owe me some answers after all the confusion he had put me through. "Why do you even care? It's not like it's your heart I broke, and you're not even hanging out with him as much anymore. Nothing of this makes any sense. Besides, you didn't answer my question. I won't answer you if you don't answer me," I said firmly, narrowing my eyes at him.

"Fine!" He groaned, taking a step back so he could cross his arms over his chest. "I want to know what made you turn Niall down because I saw him running through the hallway with tears in his eyes earlier, and he is one of my closest friends, so of course I care about him. Therefore, I ran after him and he explained to me that you had broken his heart. There. Are you happy now?"

Actually, I wasn't because there were still so many things that were left unanswered, like for instance why he had ignored me after our kiss and why he had been acting so strange lately. Besides, it didn't even sound like he was speaking the truth. "So, you're saying you wouldn't have been acting like this if I didn't turn him down?" I asked, raising a questioning eyebrow.

He pressed his lips into a thin line as he looked away from my gaze. "Exactly," he muttered, but there was definitely hesitation in his voice. This made a smile form on my lips because maybe I wasn't way off track here. The only thing I needed to know now was the real reason behind his behavior.

However, before I could ask him anything more, he composed himself and looked up at me. "Now, tell me why you don't want to be his boyfriend. He is a great guy, very social and friendly. Like, what is there not to like about him?"

The way Louis was speaking about him made me wonder if he was jealous of Niall. He had a frown on his face while talking and he looked a little sad, as if he wanted to be described the same way but knew that he couldn't. I actually found it quite funny because I couldn't see a reason for him to feel that way. Sure, Louis wasn't the definition of a sweet and good-hearted guy, but I still preferred him over Niall romantically.

"Isn't it obvious? I can't believe you're even asking me this," I mumbled. "It's the same reason why everybody else turns people down. I simply don't like him. There's nothing wrong with him or anything like that, but I'm just not attracted to him in that way. Besides, I have my eyes on someone else." The last part wasn't meant for him to hear, but when his head suddenly snapped up in curiosity, I realized that he did anyway.

"Really? Who?"

Fuck. What had I now gotten myself into? I was basically digging my own grave here. "Why do you care?" I asked to turn this on him instead of the other way around.

He looked shocked for a second until he pulled his eyebrows together again. "I don't. I was just curious to know who my stepbrother fancies, but since it seems like that would be such a huge problem, you don't have to tell me."

"It is a problem because why would I tell you? You won't even tell me why you have been ignoring me after our kiss on Saturday. Is it because you regret it? Or is it because of what I did to you in the past? I mean, sure, I was acting like a jerk to you, and yes, I was being a blind idiot, but I apologized! I wasn't even aware of what I was doing, and the last thing I wanted was for things to turn out the way they did. I don't know how many times I have to tell you that I'm so fucking sorry!" I let out in pure frustration, running my hands through my long curls.

The next second, I was pinned to the wall again, but unlike last time, it wasn't in a threatening way, but more like an intimidating one. Louis' fingers dug into my biceps, not too tightly but not too gently either. "Look at me," he demanded, and I could feel his blue eyes stare at me.

I did as told, meeting his gaze while biting my bottom lip. My heart was beating uncontrollably in my chest at his proximity, and my breathing was uneven. Our faces were so close to each other that a little nudge forward would make our lips meet, and that fact only had my heart beating even faster. "I don't regret it, alright? As I told you, I've been waiting for ages to do that with you," he explained, looking right into my soul.

"Then why did you ignore me? And why did you act so cold towards me this morning? I don't understand... did I do something?" I let out weakly, trying to search his face for some kind of answer, but he just looked bitter.

"It's not that, Harry. You didn't do anything."

"You don't like me. That's it, right? You don't have feelings for me. And here I thought the reason you were acting the way you did just a few minutes ago was due to jealousy. How could I even think you were jealous of Niall because of what happened? How stupid could I be? Stupid, stupid, stup--"

I was cut off by his hand covering my mouth. "Could you please shut up for a second? You're not stupid, Harry. Actually, you were more right with your guess than I'd like to admit myself. I... I kind of like you, alright? It's difficult, but I have always had feelings for you."

Chapter 21

[Louis]

I couldn't believe that I finally admitted my feelings to him. For about two years now, I had kept them deep within me, almost been afraid to confess them to myself, and now it was finally out there. However, I knew it probably wasn't such a good idea, but I couldn't hold it in any longer. Besides, he should already know about them after everything that had happened lately.

Why it wasn't a good idea for him to know was the same reason as to why I had acted as if our kiss never happened Saturday night. It was because I knew we would never be able to be together. Not only were we two entirely different people, but our parents were also dating. If they were to find out that their sons had a relationship, they would probably make sure that we never saw each other again, or even worse, send us away to separate mental hospitals or something. It sucked, even if I was still grateful that I got to see him every day from morning to night.

I was aware that what I did to find out whether he liked me or not was a bit cruel, though. Kissing him probably wasn't the best decision I could make, but I had been waiting to do that for so long, and I didn't regret it. The thing was that it was basically for nothing. Nothing could ever happen between us, and that was something I had realized during our ride back home Saturday night.

Harry stared at me with his mouth wide open. "You... You actually like me?" He stuttered, and I rolled my eyes at him.

"Well, if it isn't already obvious, then yes, I do. Ever since we were friends two years ago."

"B-but, you hated me... and Eleanor! What about her? Why are you dating her if you like me?" He shook his head in frustration, probably because he couldn't put the pieces together, and looked at me in confusion.

I let out a sigh, closing my eyes for a second before opening them again. "As I said before, it's not that easy. I... I've never wanted to admit my feelings, not even to myself. When I realized I liked you, I tried to ignore it, thinking that it must be some kind of phase or something. However, when you got together with Miranda and stopped paying attention to me, I realized that it wasn't. I hated myself for it, but I was also so mad at you for not realizing how much I enjoyed and needed your company. That was the reason I started picking on you," I muttered, looking down at my hands.

This was the most vulnerable situation I had ever been in, and I didn't like it at all, but I knew that it needed to be said. Harry and I couldn't keep living in this bubble where things only happened without the other one knowing why it did. We needed to come clean, and if showing my vulnerable side was what had to be done for us to do so, then so be it.

He took a deep breath, a frown forming between his eyebrows. "Well, it still doesn't explain the fact that you're dating Eleanor now and have been doing so basically since we fell apart."

"It doesn't even matter," I mumbled because even if I knew it was important to have this conversation with him, it was still hard for me to go through with it.

"Yes, it does! How else will I know if you're telling the truth about liking me? As far as I know, you could be talking bullshit right now, and then when we're out of here, you'll run straight off to her!" He let out, looking at me in desperation.

"Harry, you don't understand," I sighed. "Haven't you realized that you and I can't be anything closer than stepbrothers? Even if I told you about Eleanor, it wouldn't change a thing. I'm still going to date her. You're my first choice every day, but imagine what our parents would say if they caught us? They would flip shit and probably kick us out of the house. I'm sorry, but I can't risk that."

He looked rather hurt by my words, and I would too if it was the other way around, but my dad was the only one I had left of my family, and I couldn't risk losing him like I had lost everyone else. "So you're just going to ignore your feelings and be unhappy? Is that what you're telling me?" He mumbled, his eyes not meeting mine.

I let out a deep sigh. "It's not like I'm unhappy. I'm just not as happy as I would be if I were dating you," I explained slowly so he would understand what I meant by it.

It looked like he was trying to comprehend it but that he found it hard to do so. His eyebrows were knitted together as he stared at the floor behind me. "I just don't understand why you have been trying to show me your true feelings when it's not going to lead anywhere. Because, that's what you have, right?"

I nodded curtly.

"Was your plan to make me fall for you so both of us would suffer from this situation? I don't get it, do you still want me hurt after all this time?" He asked me weakly, now daring to lift his gaze so our eyes could meet. His usually beautiful, green irises were now sad and filled with hurt, and I had to gulp at the sight, not to mention at the words he just spoke.

"I-I... You fell for me?"

Sure, I was aware that he reciprocated my kiss and that he was basically speaking the words 'I fancy you', but hearing him say it out loud was a whole different thing. It was as if the fact finally dawned on me, and I realized that I wasn't in this alone anymore. Harry and I were in this situation together, as he just said.

He rolled his eyes, taking a step forward so our chests were almost touching. "Well, duh. Why else do you think I kissed Niall right in front of your eyes? Additionally, if I didn't like you, why would I kiss you back?" He raised a questioning eyebrow, coming closer and closer to my face by the second.

Swallowing thickly, I looked down at his appealing lips that were just screaming to be kissed right now, but I had to control myself. This couldn't lead to anything, and I had to accept that. "I can't believe you used Niall to make me jealous," I said, looking at the wall beside his head to distract myself from his beautiful appearance.

From the corner of my eye, I could see him biting his bottom lip. "I'm not very proud of it, to be honest. It was just kind of an 'in the heat of the moment' type of thing, which was really stupid, I know, but I sadly can't take it back now," he sighed.

I just nodded my head, still not looking at him. "I never talked to him, you know? I found out what happened between you two this morning by myself. I was right around the corner," I confessed emotionlessly, trying my best not to be affected by his proximity.

His eyes widened as his mouth fell open. "You bastard! Are you kidding me? You were actually there?"

I bit my lip. "Yeah, I... I needed to hear your response to what he was going to say. I mean, he wouldn't stop talking about your kiss during the entire weekend, and it made me so frustrated. Then he went on about how he was going to confess his feelings and ask you out, so I figured I just had to know whether you would turn him down or not. Therefore, I followed you guys this morning and overheard your conversation."

Suddenly, a smirk made its way to his pouty lips, and the next second our lips were so close that I had to inhale a shaky breath. "So you were jealous after all, eh?" He winked.

Not liking to be at a disadvantage, I pressed my hands against his chest to create some space between us. "Well, of course I was, but I was mostly curious about whether you liked him or not," I lied because I was very aware that jealousy was the main reason why I had followed them this morning.

Rolling his eyes, he let out a snort. "If you say so."

Right then, the bell rang, which surprised me. I thought it had rung ages ago because it sure didn't feel like Harry and I had only been in here for five minutes. What surprised me even more was that he didn't make any move to leave. Instead, he looked into my eyes in deep thought. I could tell he was thinking by the crinkle between his eyebrows, and honestly, I couldn't look away from him. God, why did he have to be so naturally beautiful?

"You never told me if you planned to make me fall for you and if you still want me hurt after everything that happened in the past," he mumbled, the playfulness in his voice now long gone.

I pulled my eyebrows together, shaking my head. "I never intended to make you fall for me. I just wanted you to realize the pain you caused me when you started ignoring me. It had nothing to do with feelings or anything like that. To be honest, I never even thought of the fact you might like me back until a few weeks ago."

He looked surprised by this, yet still very confused. "But I still don't get it. Why did you kiss me if you knew it couldn't lead to anything? That just gave me false hope, you know? Besides, would it actually hurt so bad if we just gave it a shot? I mean, what are the odds my mum and your dad will find out about it if we are being careful?" He tried to convince me, but I had already made my mind up a long time ago.

"Harry, you just don't get it," I sighed, running a hand through my soft, brown hair. "I know the odds might not be that high, but I can't risk it. They're still high enough, and if my dad found out... I wouldn't be able to live with myself if he wanted nothing to do with me."

"I don't think they would kick us out, Louis, but if it for some reason would happen, can't you just stay with your mum? I mean, she would probably be delighted that you decided to move in with her."

And just like that, I could feel my heart drop in my chest. All the pain and thoughts I had managed to keep as far back in my head as possible came flying back like a snap of the fingers as if they had been there all along. And suddenly, all I wanted was to leave, get away from this bathroom and away from him. My legs started shaking, and before I knew it, I was slamming the bathroom door shut behind me, leaving a shocked and confused Harry to stare at the plain, white door in front of him.

Since the bell had rung, the hallway was thankfully pretty much empty, so I didn't gain anyone's attention as I made my way towards my locker. Once there, I opened it and grabbed my jacket before making my way towards the closest exit. As soon as I inhaled fresh air through my nostrils, I let out a deep breath and leaned my body against a pole nearby.

With shaking hands, I searched my pockets for what had been my lifesaver ever since the accident took place two years ago. My cigarettes. I lit one up with the lighter I always brought with me and took a deep drag from the cancer stick.

Instantly, I could feel myself calming down on the inside. There was just something about the smoke that always relaxed me whenever I needed it the most, like now for example. Even though I was aware that it wasn't the best way to solve the problem, it worked fine, and I didn't really care that it was bad for me. As long as it helped, I was happy.

I stayed there for a couple of minutes, not caring that I missed my first class, or that my friends were probably worried about me. I didn't even care what Harry thought or did at the moment, whether he had joined class or not. The only thing I focused on was to keep the thoughts about my mother out of my head and instead pay attention to the cigarette between my fingers.

When it was only the butt left, I dropped it to the ground and stomped on it before turning around to walk into the building again. Maybe I wasn't entirely composed after everything that happened, but I also knew that I couldn't be a wimp and stay outside for the rest of the day. As long as I could keep myself away from Harry, I would be alright... I hoped.

It turned out it was easier said than done to stay away from Harry, which I had known deep down since we shared all of our classes. I could feel his gaze on me several times during the day, but I tried my best to ignore him. At least he didn't attempt to talk to me, which I was more than happy about because I wasn't sure whether I could take that right now.

It wasn't like he had done anything wrong, but I knew he would only question why I had run away like that if he tried to talk to me, and I didn't want to have that conversation with him. Therefore, I tried my best not to make eye contact with him whatsoever.

It was hardest during the last class of the day; P.E. since we (of course) were selected to the same team while playing basketball, but it actually turned out pretty okay in the end. Sure, we made eye contact sometimes, but I looked away as quickly as possible whenever it happened.

What I was happiest about was that neither of my friends or Eleanor seemed to notice that something was off with me. In between my lessons, they only went on like normal and talked like they usually did. It actually calmed me more than it probably should because then I didn't need to worry about them asking me what was wrong.

When the last bell of the day rang, I quickly showered and changed into my casual clothing before heading towards the bus stop where some students were already waiting for the bus to show up. I sat down on a bench nearby and fished my phone from my jeans pocket to distract myself from reality. Not more than two minutes later, the bus showed up at the end of the street and came to a stop right in front of me.

I hopped onto it and sat down in an empty seat, waiting for it to start moving so I could finally get home after this long school day, and hopefully without Harry noticing me.

Once we were at the right bus stop, I jumped off and started walking home, checking my surroundings to make sure there wasn't any curly-haired boy in sight. When the coast was clear, I started heading to the house with quick strides. It thankfully only took a few minutes until I got there and could step into the empty home. The first thing I did was to shrug off my backpack, slip off my shoes, and hang up my jacket on the hanger before making a beeline towards the stairs. I didn't even care about the fact that my stomach was growling for food. That would have to wait until later.

I slammed my bedroom door shut behind me and literally threw myself on the bed, face-first onto my pillow. Closing my eyes, I let out a deep sigh and reached my hands up to hug the pillow against myself. It wasn't until then I finally let the thoughts and memories about my mother enter my mind again, and this time, I couldn't control them. Flashbacks from the day everything happened started playing on my retina, making my body start shaking a bit.

It was on a cold Monday night. Snow was falling from the sky and my dad and I were waiting for my mum and sister to get home from the doctor. My sister was only a few months old at the time, and the reason they were at the doctor was that she had been screaming more than usual the last couple of days and both mum and dad were worried. We all knew that dad and I should have gone with them, especially since it was the middle of December and they were going to Manchester, but dad had been working late and I had stayed at school with Harry a bit too long. Therefore, neither of us was with them.

Dinner was served, and dad and I were sitting at the kitchen table when he suddenly got a call.

I remembered how he looked down at the screen, furrowing his eyebrows since he didn't recognize the number. At the time, I didn't think too much about it. It was probably just someone from his work who wanted to know something, but when his entire face turned emotionless, I knew something had happened. My heart stopped beating immediately, and I could feel my body start shaking because I knew that it was about mum and Lottie. I just knew.

A few seconds later, he hung up, still with that emotionless look on his face. He didn't even have to say anything, I was already certain that it was bad news, really bad news. His face changed then. Instead of being entirely emotionless, he broke down. It was so hard to witness it because I had never seen my dad this way before. He was always so strong, holding his feelings back because he didn't want anyone to worry about him, but this time he couldn't help himself, and I understood why. Not at the time, but subsequently.

The only words he spoke were; 'mum', 'Lottie', 'accident' and the worst of them all; 'dead'. I remembered feeling my whole world crumbling down, and the dinner that consisted of chicken stew and rice that had been waiting so long to be eaten was far gone in my mind.

The worst part wasn't the fact that they were dead, but the fact that I would never see them again. I would never see the woman who gave birth to me again, the one I had always looked up to, spent my childhood with when dad worked late, the woman I thought would see me grow old. I would never be able to hug her or tell her how much I loved her again.

That was what killed me. It was unfortunately also at that time Harry started getting distant, so I didn't have anyone to talk to because I didn't have that close of a relationship with either of Zayn or Niall. We were just buddies who hung out at school. Harry was the one I could really talk to, the one I had started trusting with my life, but he was drifting away. So instead of caring, I decided to just drop everything and change completely. I started picking on Harry. I was mad that he didn't care about me anymore, but also because he thought that stupid girl was more important than me. I stopped caring about school again. Only this time, I didn't even care that my grades were bad, which I had done when I asked Harry for help. It was also at that time I started smoking, as I mentioned before. The only thing that actually surprised me was that I never tried to kill myself because I did have thoughts about it, trust me. But as I also mentioned before, I would never be able to do that to my dad. He had already lost two of the most important people in his life. I would never make him lose a third just because I decided to be selfish.

    Therefore, I went on with my life and tried making the best out of it, even if I felt like shit for at least a year. It wasn't until a few months ago that I was finally able to start moving on from the accident, and my sister and mum's deaths. It was tough, but I knew that if I didn't try to let it go, I would never be able to move on, which I was glad about now. It helped a lot, but that didn't mean I was keen on the fact that dad had found someone new. Even if I had managed to start putting everything behind me, I didn't want him to move on although I knew it was for the best. I just missed my mum so much it hurt.

I didn't know how long I lied there, my face buried in my pillow while being deep in my thoughts, but I could suddenly hear footsteps on the stairs. To my fear, I could hear them stop outside my bedroom, and for a second, I thought the person would knock on the door. However, a second later, the footsteps continued down the hallway to Harry's bedroom.

That was certainly a close one.

Chapter 22

[Harry]

I did it again. Why was it always that I screwed things up and made Louis get angry with me? If I didn't make the wrong actions, I spoke the wrong words, and if it wasn't any of that, it was something else. I just couldn't keep Louis on my good side. The problem this time, though, was that I didn't know what I had done wrong. Surely, there must have been something I said because I didn't recall doing something at least. The question was; what did I say wrong? Had I been too pushy when I asked him if he could give us a try? Or was it that he wasn't completely sure about his feelings after all and didn't want to give us a try because of that? I had no idea. The only thing I knew was that I said something that made him hate me... again.

At the moment, I was lying on my bed, waiting for dinner to be ready downstairs. It was still the same day that everything took place and everything I had done since I came home was to lay here, thinking. I had gone through the scenario over and over again, trying to put my finger on what I did wrong, but it didn't matter how much I tried, I couldn't come up with an answer anyway.

Cutting me off from my thoughts, the bedroom door opened and stole my attention. My heart skipped a beat, my first thought being that it was Louis who for some reason was the person on the other side of it, but when a brown-haired girl

I recognized as my older sister poked her head through the gap, it dropped to my stomach in disappointment. How stupid could I be, though? Why would Louis come to me after everything that had happened?

"Hello, brother. Can I come in?" She asked, a smile forming on her pink lips.

I shrugged, scooting to one side of the bed to make some space, indicating for her to join me. She closed the door behind her before striding over to the bed. At first, I thought she would just sit down on the edge of it, so it surprised me when she laid down beside me. "So, what did you want?" I asked when she didn't say anything.

Gemma turned her face towards me, a frown forming between her eyebrows. "I wanted to talk about you and Louis."

Well, of course she did. Everything in this family revolved around our relationship nowadays. It was like they couldn't think of anything else but for us to start getting along. To be honest, it was getting rather annoying by now. Couldn't they just care about their own business instead?

When she saw me rolling my eyes, she let out a sigh. "I know you don't want to talk about it, and I know we all have been a pain in the ass to you guys, but you need to understand that it would only be for the best if you guys just got on with each other. I mean, what happened between you that is so hard to forget?"

I bit my bottom lip, ignoring her intense stare. Instead, I focused my attention on the wall opposite us. "Too much. You don't even want to know. All I can say is that there's probably no way you'll be seeing us getting along anytime soon because last time I was around him he literally stormed off," I mumbled, the scene from today playing on my retina once again.

How his ocean blue eyes had gone from shining to looking so dull in the blink of an eye, just because of something I had said. My heart had sunken to the pit of my stomach at the sight, and it didn't make matters better when he left just a second later. I hated the fact that I was the reason he broke down like that.

"What happened then? Come on, I'm your sister. You know you can tell me whatever you want. You know you can trust me."

Letting out a feign laugh that sounded more like a snort, I turned to her. "Trust you? Yeah, sure. Last time I decided to trust you, you went off and told the one person you definitely shouldn't have told anything to about our relationship. To be more specific, you told Louis himself. Remember that?" I asked, referring to that one time at the restaurant when she revealed that she knew of Louis and I's friendship two years ago although I had promised him I wouldn't tell a soul about it.

She looked down at her hands that were folded on her stomach in shame, biting her bottom lip softly. "Of course I do, but that it was a mistake. I never intended to say anything, it just came out of my mouth." She met my gaze with an apologetic look on her face.

"I know, but I also know that it can happen again. Therefore, I am trying to be careful when it comes to saying things to you nowadays," I said a little jokingly even if I was dead serious about it. I couldn't risk Louis having another reason for hating me. It was already bad enough.

"I understand... I just... if you ever want to talk, you know I'll be here, alright? I know I haven't been the best sister lately, and I'm sorry about that, but I want to make things better... if you will let me, of course."

Letting out a sigh, I closed my eyes in deep thought. Could I trust her? She already knew about my and Louis' friendship, which was already too much, especially since she had spoken openly about it even if I told her she couldn't. On the other hand, it would be a relief to tell someone about everything that was going on and about my feelings for him because right now, I had no one other than myself. Was she the right person to tell, though? How could I be sure she wouldn't tell mum and Troy about it? Louis would definitely kill me if that were to happen, especially after what he said earlier...

Wait a second.

That was when he had stormed off. I had tried to convince him that he should give us a try. At first, he just seemed very determined that he didn't want to, but when I brought it up a second time, something snapped inside him. What was different then?

"Oh, God."

Gemma looked at me in confusion. "What?"

I turned to her with wide eyes. "Do you know anything about Louis' mum?" I asked slowly, afraid of the answer.

She looked at me as if I had grown three eyes. "What does that have to do with anything? Harry, we're talking about you and Louis' relationship, not--"

"Gemma, just answer me for Christ's sake. Do you know anything about Louis' mum? This is important," I demanded, cutting her off mid-sentence because I had to know. By now, I was certain it all had *something* to do with his mum.

Otherwise, he wouldn't have reacted like that at the mention of her.

She knitted her eyebrows together. "Alright, yes I do. She... uh, she isn't with us anymore. Actually, she died in a car accident two years ago along with Lottie, Louis' younger sister."

I inhaled a deep breath at her words, reaching up to run my hands through my curls. "Oh, shit."

This couldn't be happening. It was all just a huge mistake and everything was fine. Louis was just mad at me for being too pushy, not because I had mentioned his dead mother right in front of his eyes. Not at fucking all. How stupid could I be?

I mean, sure, I couldn't know that she had passed away, but I even mentioned that he could move in with her if things wouldn't work out here. Of course he reacted that way, anyone with feelings would, especially since she died just two years ago...

Wait, two years ago? But, Louis and I were friends two years ago, how come I didn't-- Oh, God, this was worse than I could have ever imagined, and I was certainly the worst friend out there. All this time and I never knew that he didn't have his mother with him anymore. I was so fucking awful.

"Earth to Harry!" Gemma waved her hand in front of my face frantically, trying to catch my attention without success.

Trying to compose myself, I let out a deep breath and closed my eyes for a second before opening them again. "I can't believe I was so stupid," I muttered to myself, shaking my head in self-disappointment.

The sad part was that I couldn't change anything. The mistake was already made when I stopped paying attention to him back when we were still friends. If I had just been a little more attentive, I would have noticed that there was something wrong with him. It didn't matter if it happened after we departed, I should have still noticed that something wasn't right. But instead, I had assumed that he had just gone from being nice to a cold-hearted person just like that. Did I mention that I was stupid?

The next thing I knew, I felt my shoulders being shaken by a pair of feminine hands. "Harry, what the hell is going on?!" Gemma shouted worriedly.

Blinking my eyes, I focused on my sister who was now sitting beside me, her eyes filled with anxiety. "Answer me," she demanded.

"I... I just realized I've made a huge mistake that I am not sure I can ever make up for," was what finally came out of my mouth.

Relaxing a little, she said with a calmer voice, "What mistake?"

I shook my head, putting my hands on the bed on either side of my body to pull myself up in a sitting position. With almost no effort, I got up from the bed and started making my way towards the door. When I was at the door frame, though, I turned around to look at my confused sister who was still sitting on my bed. "I have to fix something," was all I said before leaving the room.

Without thinking twice, I strolled through the hallway to the only bedroom on the second floor apart from my own, not really knowing what I was doing. All I knew was that I had to talk to Louis as soon as possible, and yet again apologize for my actions. I didn't want to have to go through this apologizing-process with him again since I had already done it so many times before, but I needed to. I wanted him to know that I didn't know about his mother, that I had no intention to hurt him whatsoever. I just hoped he would understand and not be mad at me, or kick me out of his room or something like that.

I was just about to raise my hand and knock on his door when I heard my mum's voice calling, "Children, dinner's ready!"

Closing my eyes, I let out a sigh and dropped my hand again. Why did she have to call right at this moment? Couldn't she just have waited another half hour or so?

Since I knew Louis would probably exit his room any minute and I didn't want to be caught right outside his room, I turned on my heel and walked down the stairs instead. Mum and Troy were already sitting at the kitchen table, Troy plating some food while mum was pouring water into her glass. When I arrived, mum looked up to flash me a smile. "Harry, come join us."

Without interjecting, I sat down in the seat in front of her and waited patiently for my turn to dig into what seemed to be Pasta Carbonara. At the same time, I felt nervousness build up inside me. I was nervous about Louis' reaction upon seeing me and also whether he was still sad or not. Maybe he had talked to someone who had made him think of something else? For all I knew, maybe Eleanor could have cheered him up. Not that I hoped for the latter, though. I just hoped he at least felt better and that my words hadn't hurt him too much.

Before it was even my turn, the next person arrived in the kitchen, and it didn't surprise me that it was Gemma and not Louis. She looked thoughtful as she sat down next to me without saying anything, just waiting for her turn as well. No talking was made during the next three minutes when we just took turns to plate our food, but as we all started to dig in, Troy knitted his eyebrows and looked at the still empty chair in front of him. "Have any of you guys seen Louis? I haven't heard a word from him since I came home. Do you know if he's up in his room?"

Gemma looked at me and raised an eyebrow questioningly. She was aware that we usually came home approximately at the same time. However, her action caused all eyes to set on me, making me feel a bit vulnerable. Picking at my food, I shrugged. "I think he's in his room, but I haven't seen him since school," I admitted.

Mum muttered something under her breath and put on a scowl on her face. "Louis, dinner's ready. Could you please come join us?" She called again, this time a bit more sternly.

I cringed at her voice, knowing exactly why he wasn't here yet. It hurt knowing it was all my fault. Me and my big, stupid mouth. Meanwhile, I could feel Gemma looking at me through the corner of my eye, and for some reason, it felt like she was starting to realize that the mistake I was talking about earlier had to do with Louis. It was all slowly becoming too much for me, feeling all their gazes turned my way with all this guilt building up on my inside. It made my breathing go uneven.

Before anything else could happen, the sound of a door slamming shut was heard from the second floor, and just a few seconds later, Louis was standing in the door frame. His brown hair looked disheveled as if he hadn't brushed it for days, and his eyes were bloodshot as if he had been crying for hours. The sight made a large knot form in my chest, and I had to look away not to throw up.

I could see him walk over to the table to sit down beside Gemma, though. While he did this, he didn't so much as glance my way, and it wasn't like I expected him to either. If he had done so, he would have probably just glared at me anyway, and that would have been worse than being ignored.

"Son, has something happened? You look terrible. Was it something at school?" Troy asked, worry lacing his voice.

Louis looked up at his dad and shook his head. "No, I just don't feel too well, is all."

"Are you sick?" Mum questioned, the irritation long gone from her voice now. Instead, she sounded worried.

He shook his head slightly without looking at her. While he plated his food and started eating like the rest of us, mum and Troy kept observing him with concern written on their faces. Gemma and I stayed silent, but since my appetite had decreased since Louis entered the room, I wasn't too tempted to continue eating like Gemma was doing. Instead, I picked at the food with my fork like I had done when Troy asked me if I had seen Louis after school.

After about twenty minutes with almost no talking whatsoever, the food was gone from our plates... Well, gone from everyone's plates except for mine, but thankfully no one questioned my lack of appetite or weird mood. The only one paying attention to me was actually Gemma, who kept sending me glances. Mum and Troy, on the other hand, seemed more worried about Louis, which I totally understood because he wouldn't meet any of our gazes throughout the entire dinner.

When mum got up to put the dishes away, Troy motioned for Louis to stand up and follow him to the living room. I was more than tempted to follow them and eavesdrop on their conversation, but I knew that would be wrong in so many ways, so I stayed in my seat and watched mum pick up all the plates from the table.

To my surprise, Gemma stayed at the table as well. I thought she would leave as soon as she could and go up to her room to text her boyfriend Devon or something, but apparently not. She turned her body towards me and raised an expectant eyebrow. "Spit it out," was all she said, making my stomach turn uncomfortably.

Through the corner of my eye, I could see mum looking at us curiously as she walked back and forth between the table and the sink. "What do you mean?" I asked even though I knew exactly what she meant.

Gemma rolled her eyes. "You know exactly what I'm talking about. I know something happened between you and Louis, so you'd better spill the truth. Otherwise, I'm sure mum is going to force it out of you," she said, earning a glare from me.

I hated it when she pulled the 'mum card' because she always knew she would win whenever she did.

"I don't know what you're talking about. Nothing has happened between me and Louis. We haven't even seen each other since school."

Mum turned off the water and crossed her arms over her chest. "So, something happened between the two of you at school then," she stated with a serious tone.

I turned to her, knitting my eyebrows together. "No, I... Well, maybe it did, but that has nothing to do with any of you. That's between me and Louis."

"You mentioned his mum to him, didn't you?" Gemma guessed, and if looks could kill, she would be dead right now. Of course she would figure it out after what happened in my bedroom earlier, but did she seriously have to say it in front of our mum? Things just got much worse, and they were already bad enough.

"Oh, please tell me you didn't, son. Troy has told me how bad Louis is still handling what happened to her. He said that if someone so much as mentions her, he can get quite upset," mum said, sitting down on the chair in front of me again.

I ran my hands through my hair frustratingly. "Well, how the hell was I supposed to know that? For all I knew, she was still alive and lived somewhere else here in town. How could I know that she had passed away?" I let out, but not loud enough for Louis and Troy to hear in the living room.

Mum gave me a reassuring smile, leaning over to squeeze my hand. "Of course you couldn't know that. It's just sad that it all had to turn out this way. But you regret it, then? You don't feel like he deserved it or something?" She asked, which made me frown.

"Why would I think that?"

To my surprise, a wide smile broke out on her face as she shrugged. "Well, since you and Louis haven't exactly been on the best terms ever since he and Troy moved in here, I figured you wouldn't feel regretful about it, but that just means you two are starting to get along, now doesn't it?"

I swallowed hard, giving her a tight smile in return. "Well, maybe you could say that..."

Chapter 23

[Louis]

I followed dad to the living room and sat down on the edge of the couch. He took a seat right beside me, his body turned my way. "Alright, what's going on?" He asked, and judging by the tone he was using, I knew there was no idea to try escaping the situation. He knew something was up, and he was not going to let me get away without an explanation.

Looking down at my folded hands on my lap, I let out a deep sigh. "It's nothing, really. Nothing worth discussing, at least. Someone at school just told me something that I didn't want to hear, is all."

He leaned back against the backrest and crossed his arms over his chest. "Something about your mum, maybe?" He guessed, and I looked up at him with a frown on my face.

"How did you know?"

He gave me a small smile. "I know you Louis, and you never get this upset by something that a person has said unless it has to do with her."

I let his words sink in and thought about it. Was he right? I knew I got upset at the mention of her, which I was pretty sure was inevitable, but did I never get upset by anything else? I doubted that, but maybe he just knew when it had to do with mum because I was his son and he had known me my entire life. "Alright, yes, it has to do with her. I just can't handle it. It's as if there's a bomb within me that explodes whenever someone just mentions her in my presence, and so many feelings blow up inside me."

"And memories," he added, biting his bottom lip.

I nodded in agreement, turning my head to meet his gaze. "It's been more than two years, yet I still can't handle it. I mean, you have moved on just fine. Why can't I do the same thing?" I asked, running my hands over my face.

He gave my thigh a pat and flashed me a reassuring smile. "There's one thing you should know, Louis, and it is that it won't matter how many months or years that pass, I will never really move on from your mother. She is and will always be a part of my heart, Lottie too. Even if they aren't with us anymore, they're still here, inside us," he said, gesturing towards his heart. "And they will always be no matter what. We won't forget them, but we still need to continue with our lives, Louis. Our lives didn't end because theirs did. We still have so many things to experience before it is our turn, and I know it's hard, but we have to fight through it, alright?"

Taking a deep breath, I gave him another nod.

"Maybe you still have a hard time taking in the fact that they aren't here anymore, but no one expects you to handle it any better than you are. After all, it hasn't been a very long time since it happened, and I also have my moments when my feelings overwhelm me and I have to take a break for a couple of minutes. It's nothing out of the ordinary. You just have to think positively and remember the good things, and not the fact that you miss them. Think about the memories we have together with a smile on your face and be happy about that. That way, it's going to be easier for you to move on, Louis. Trust me," he promised.

I swallowed hard, looking away from him again. Why did it always sound so easy when dad explained things to me? He was always so rational and knew exactly what the best thing to do was. I really admired him for that. I wished I could think as positively as him so I could avoid being so down sometimes. "Yeah, you're probably right," I mumbled.

"I know I am." He gave my side a light nudge in an attempt to cheer me up, and a small smile actually crept to my lips.

"Thank you," I said. "For being here. I don't know what I would have done if I didn't have you either."

"Then we're two," he smiled. "And you're welcome, son. I'm here whenever you want to talk. You know you can come to me whenever you want, right?"

I nodded. "Yeah."

"Alright, I'm going to see if Anne has finished washing the dishes. You coming with me?" He asked, looking at me expectantly.

I bit my lip, contemplating it for a second. The odds were pretty high that Harry was still in there since I hadn't seen him walk through the living room to go upstairs, but did I even have a reason not to see him? He hadn't tried to interact with me, so there was no reason not to follow dad to the kitchen. "Sure."

When we entered the room, Harry and Gemma were still sitting in the same spots they did when dad and I left, and Anne was sitting in front of them, the dishes still in the sink. Judging by the looks of it, they must have started talking about something important. Otherwise, it was weird that Anne had just stopped washing the dishes just like that. It was not like her at all.

"Did we miss something?" Dad asked as he sat down beside Anne again, flickering his gaze between the three of them.

I sat down beside Gemma and watched the scene play out. Anne looked at Harry before shaking her head. "No, we just had a small talk, is all. Would you help me with the dishes, please?" She asked, turning her attention to dad.

He pressed his lips into a thin line before nodding and standing up. Gemma, Harry and I sat in silence for a couple of minutes until Anne turned around and flashed us a smile. "You don't have to wait here if you don't want to. You're free to go up to your rooms or do whatever you feel like doing."

Gemma was the first one to react by getting up from her seat. "Alright, thanks for dinner. See you later," was all she said before she exited the room just like that.

A little taken aback by her sudden actions, I blinked my eyes a couple of times before turning to Harry who was staring at the spot where Gemma just disappeared from. Dad and Anne were already engrossed in a deep conversation about God knows what, so it was basically just me and Harry in the room, which scared me.

When he turned around to face me, I could feel my heartbeat pick up in my chest. What was he going to do? Would he bring up what we talked about earlier, or would he avoid it?

It just felt so weird now, knowing that he had feelings for me and that he knew about my feelings for him. It was just surreal. Like, who would have thought that the two people who for a couple of weeks ago couldn't even stand to be in the same room without picking on the other, now had expressed their feelings for one another? That was just insane, and although I knew it wouldn't lead anywhere, I couldn't help but like the thought of it.

His eyes found mine, and for some reason, they looked sympathetic, as if he knew something about me that he felt bad about. I had a feeling what it was, but how did he find out about it? I mean, it didn't seem like he knew about it this morning at least.

"Can I speak with you?" He asked with a voice like an angel, making my heart beat even faster in my chest.

To be honest, talking to him was one of the last things I wanted to do right now. Not only was I scared about what he wanted to discuss, but I was also afraid of losing control when I was around him. The more time that passed, the harder it seemed for me to keep my feelings under control. What if I would do something like that time in the bathroom when I had pushed one of his curls behind his ear? Or even worse, when I had kissed him that time after Niall's party? That could not happen, not if I wanted to keep my dad in my life.

Despite thinking this way, the word 'sure' escaped my mouth, and I wanted to smack myself on the forehead because of it. Why did I have to be so stupid?

A smile broke out on his face, making my chest swell with warmth. He got up from his seat and went to exit the room, but stopped in the door frame when he noticed that I wasn't following him. "You coming?"

Throwing a glance in dad and Anne's direction, noticing that they were still deep in conversation, I nodded and got up to join him. To my surprise, he didn't stop in the living room but kept walking towards the stairs. Butterflies erupted in my stomach as I realized he was bringing me to his bedroom. Now

YOU THINK I HATE YOU?

that I thought about it, I hadn't really been in there. Or, at least not for more than a minute, which to me didn't count.

Harry opened the door to his room and motioned for me to sit down on his bed that was placed in the middle of it. Other than that, the room didn't look too special. There was a TV on the wall in front of the bed and a desk in the right corner. The door to the bathroom that we shared was beside the TV, and his closet was placed to the left. I would say it looked like my own but a little bigger with a bit more space. However, I didn't mind that. I actually quite liked my room the way it was.

He closed the door behind us and joined me on the bed. I studied his face and noted for the first time that he looked nervous. "Alright, I think you know what I want to talk about, right?"

Looking away, I bit my bottom lip. "Harry, just forget it, okay? There's nothing to discuss, I--"

He pinched the bridge of his nose and closed his eyes. "Enough," he said, cutting me off. "I'm tired of you saying that there's nothing to talk about. We've got *plenty* of stuff to discuss, but you never want to. You always try to avoid everything, and I've had enough of it. I know something happened earlier when you just stormed off like that, and I am pretty sure why you did now, but how come you never told me? I was your friend, Louis. Why didn't you just tell me? I would've been there for you."

I let out a dry laugh, rolling my eyes. "Yeah, sure. If I remember correctly, you were too busy sucking some girl's face off and hanging with Liam at the time to even notice that something was wrong with me. Why *would* I have wanted to tell you?"

He looked down at the floor in shame, and that was when I noticed that he was actually sorry for what he had done. Maybe he didn't intend to hurt me at the time after all? Maybe he just didn't realize what he was doing?

"That doesn't mean I wouldn't have been there for you. If you had told me that your mum was in an accident, I would've reassured you that everything would be fine and I would've been by your side, you know?"

"Well, then that would've meant you only paid attention to me because something tragic happened in my life. I wanted you to hang out with me because you wanted to, not because you felt the need to. You understand?"

Furrowing his eyebrows together, he nodded slowly. "I guess..."

A silence followed after that, where we just sat there, lost in our own separate thoughts. It wasn't awkward or anything, and I guess that was because we were so caught up in thinking about our situation. However, when the silence finally repealed, it was thanks to Harry.

"So, about what you said earlier..." He started off, glancing at me through the corner of his eye.

Catching his gaze, I bit my bottom lip. "About me not wanting to risk anything when it comes to us?" I asked, although I already knew that was what he was on about.

He gave me a nod, breaking our eye contact. "Yeah."

"I meant it," I finished monotonously.

Don't misunderstand me, I did mean it, but I didn't want to mean it. There was nothing I wanted more than to be in a relationship with Harry instead of Eleanor, but I couldn't. My dad still meant the most to me, and I was sure I could not live with the thought of him hating me for something like this.

What if he found out about us and he and Anne decided to kick us out? I would be devastated.

He took a deep breath. "That's what I thought," he breathed, refusing to meet my gaze.

I wanted to give him a hug or just a reassuring pat on the thigh, but I knew that would be the wrong thing to do at the moment. He would either be mad at me for touching him right after I had explained to him that we couldn't be together, or I would lose control altogether and kiss the life out of him because he just looked so sad and vulnerable at the moment. My heart was beating like crazy in my chest right now just by the looks of him.

When I didn't say anything, another silence fell between the two of us. However, this time it was awkward because we were in a different situation. This time we weren't deep in our thoughts, we just didn't know what to say.

"So, that really means you are going to stay with Eleanor?" He mumbled, still refusing to meet my gaze.

"Yeah.." I trailed off.

I figured that if it worked just fine to be with her last time I tried to get over Harry, it would work this time as well. Maybe it would be harder now, though, since I knew he felt the same way, but hopefully, it would work eventually. Otherwise, I had to try to find someone else who would make me forget about him.

He nodded curtly to himself and stood up. "Alright, I think this talk is over. You can go now," he said emotionlessly, motioning towards the bathroom door.

I swallowed hard before getting up. My feet took me to the said door, but when I put my hand on the handle, I turned around to face the curly-haired boy again. "Harry, I... I'm sorry."

He was staring at the floor, but when I uttered those words, he looked up to meet my eyes. The amount of hurt I saw in them made my heart twist uncomfortably, and a sudden wave of nausea came over me. I didn't want to do this, I really didn't. Yet, I still knew I had to.

"Just go," was all he said, and it didn't make things better. If anything, it only made me feel even worse.

Letting out a sigh, I finally turned the handle and exited Harry's room. I closed the door behind me with a soft thud and entered my own room. The first thing I did was the exact same thing I had done when I got home this afternoon; I threw myself on the bed, buried my face in my pillow and cried.

Why did life have to be so unfair?

Chapter 24

[Louis]

The next couple of weeks were pretty uneventful. Harry and I didn't talk to each other, only if it was really necessary. Like for example when I had forgotten to bring my key to the house one day and had to ask him for his since he was going over to Liam's after school and couldn't unlock the house for me. Or, when he woke me up one time by his annoying snoring and I had to bang on his door and shout at him to make him shut up. It took a few minutes until he finally woke up, but then he only told me to go away and let him be.

Other than that, we had pretty much not spoken a word to each other, which of course Anne and dad had snapped up on. Obviously, they weren't pleased with it, but something was telling me by the look in their eyes that they were starting to get tired of trying to make us get along. I couldn't blame them because I would be tired of it too, but what they didn't know was that we weren't enemies like they thought we were. We just weren't on speaking terms.

As for Niall, he had gone back to hanging out with me and Zayn. He had always been quite the quiet guy, but it couldn't even compare to how quiet he was now. I would see him look in Harry's direction longingly every now and then, especially in the cafeteria and in class, and every time I caught him doing so, a burning feeling erupted inside me. I just couldn't accept the fact that he was looking at him like that. If anyone was to do so, it would be me. I was the one who was really longing for him since I could have him at this very second but didn't allow myself to because of the circumstances. I was sure Niall couldn't compare to how I felt.

It wasn't only the way he looked at Harry that made me irritated, though. He made me want to punch him for the fact that he wouldn't stop talking about the boy. It was always 'Harry did this, Harry did that, but wait... did you see how beautiful Harry looked when he smiled in class today?' There was nothing that made me more aggravated than that. Well, if the fact that I couldn't do or say anything about it didn't count. That was what frustrated me the most. I could only sit there and nod my head because he couldn't know I had feelings for Harry as well.

Things were going well with Liam and Zayn, though, almost too well if you asked me. They were the new 'wow' couple at school. Everyone seemed to like their relationship, especially the girls who wouldn't stop asking them different questions in the hallway every day. I was actually a little surprised about that because I thought more people would be against their relationship than there turned out to be. However, that only showed that things were changing in life and people were starting to get more accepting of stuff like homosexuality, which was nothing but a good thing if you asked me.

By going 'too' well, I meant that they were showing their love for each other almost a little too much. Not that I minded that they were being affectionate with each other around people, but sometimes it would get a little out of hand. Or, it was just me being jealous that they had something I couldn't have with the one I fancied.

Well, I did fancy Eleanor, and I could be like Liam and Zayn with her if I wanted to, but the truth was that it didn't feel the same anymore. I didn't know how to explain it, but whenever I saw Zayn and Liam together, there was something in me that longed to have the same thing as them but with Harry. Eleanor was just not him, and I hated myself for thinking that way. If I ever wanted to get over him, those thoughts had to disappear from my head, and that was quick.

I was currently sitting in class, doodling in my notebook since I was too deep in my thoughts to hear what the teacher was talking about. The only thing I was aware of was that Harry was sitting right in front of me next to Liam, and that his shoulder blades flexed every time he moved. Other than that, I had no idea what was going on around me.

"Mr. Tomlinson, why aren't you listening?" Mrs. Oliver suddenly asked, making the room go dead silent.

Every pair of eyes in the classroom turned to me, and if it weren't for the fact that I didn't mind the attention, I would probably have blushed right now, but the only thing I did was to raise my eyebrows. "Oh, I wasn't? I'm so sorry, Mrs. Oliver. It won't happen again, I promise."

I could hear Harry snort from the seat in front of me, even though he was the only one not looking at me, but I ignored it. Mrs. Oliver, however, shot me a glare before she turned her attention back to the other students in class and continued where she left off.

Nothing else happened after that, and soon enough, the bell rang, signaling the end of the class. Everyone got up from their seats and exited the classroom, including me. As I stepped out into the hallway, I inhaled a deep breath and started making my way towards my locker.

It didn't surprise me when I caught Liam and Zayn smiling at each other when I arrived, knowing they were with each other twenty-four seven these days, but what caught me off guard was that Harry was with them, his eyes trained on the phone in his hand. Usually, Harry wouldn't hang around them since he knew he would only become the third wheel - something I had experienced as well. So, to see him standing next to them made me squint my eyes in wonder.

Taking my eyes off of the three guys, I turned to open my locker and shove my books into it. I scanned my messy locker for the material I needed for the next lesson, letting out a frustrated sigh because I couldn't find it. Sometimes I hated myself for being so messy.

Probably two minutes later, I finally found my books, and frustratedly slammed my locker shut. When I turned around to see if the three guys were gone, my muscles turned to ice as my gaze fell on the curly-haired guy I also liked to call my stepbrother. Instead of three guys standing there, there were now four because a blonde-haired boy had joined them. That was not the thing, though. The thing was that it was none other than Niall and he was standing with his arms wrapped around Harry's neck, smiling into his eyes as if he was the most good-looking guy he had ever seen.

The worst part, however, was that Harry was looking at him the same way, making my heart break in my chest. The view hurt so much that I had to bite my tongue and look away. My eyes watered slightly, making me feel even more frustrated than I had been at my stupid locker. Without thinking more about it, I turned on my heel and made my way to the nearest exit, just like I had done that time when Harry had mentioned my mother in the bathroom.

What I did then was also what I did last time; I fished my cigarette package from my pocket and lit one of them up, inhaling the poisoning smoke while knowing that this was one of the habits Harry hated most about me. I didn't care about that now, though. All I could think about was what I had witnessed just a few seconds ago.

Was it possible that Harry had already moved on from me? I mean, it had been a few weeks since we last talked now, but could feelings just disappear like that? I knew mine hadn't, but I had also had feelings for him longer than he did for me. Did that matter, though?

What confused me even more was that Niall was the stupid boy he had his arms around. I thought Harry said that he didn't have feelings for him? Did he lie to me about that, or what the hell was going on?

I stayed out there in the January cold until my cigarette was gone. I then headed towards my next lesson that had probably already started a long time ago. It was English class, and sadly that was one of the few classes Harry and I shared with Niall, which meant that I was going to witness a sight I didn't want to see in just a few seconds. However, I would at least be prepared for it this time.

Once I stepped into the classroom, I slammed the door shut behind me, not even bothering to look up to meet any of the people's gazes as I made my way to an empty seat in the back. From the corner of my eye, I could see Mrs. Oliver sending me a glare, obviously for arriving late as usual. She didn't open her mouth to scold me, though, which I was happy about because I was not really in the mood to defend myself right now.

During the entire period, I had my face buried in my arms that were resting on the desk in front of me. Surprisingly, Mrs. Oliver didn't say anything about the fact that I wasn't working, but maybe that was because she noticed that I wasn't feeling very well.

I didn't throw Harry and Niall any glances during that hour, but I could still hear them converse with each other. Unfortunately, they were sitting at the table next to mine, so it wasn't like I could block their voices out either.

What they talked about, however, I didn't know. I didn't want to know, more specifically. The only thing I could think of was how stupid I was for not bringing my earphones so I wouldn't be able to hear them talk at all.

When the bell finally rang, I got up from my seat and walked out of the classroom. I was just about to start heading in the direction of my locker when someone bumped into my shoulder. Instantly, anger boiled up within me because if there was something I disliked, it was when someone accidentally walked into me. It didn't make matters better that I was already worked up.

I turned around to snap at the person but stopped myself when I noticed it was none other than Harry. However, by the looks of it, it didn't seem like he had bumped into my shoulder by accident because he wasn't even looking at me. Instead, he was chatting with Niall who was standing beside him, laughing at something he had just said.

Without even thinking twice, I grabbed a hold of his arm and pulled him away from my friend. I didn't care that we were in a hallway full of people watching when I pushed him against the wall of lockers and leaned up to his ear so he and no one else could hear what I said. "What the fuck do you think you're doing?"

Much to my annoyance, he didn't look the least bit intimidated. He just raised his eyebrows and let out a sigh. "What are you talking about Louis? I'm sorry, but I have to go. My next class starts in five minutes and--"

"I don't care about your stupid class, and I have the same one as you anyway so that is not even an excuse. I want to know why the fuck you're hanging around with him," I cut him off, nodding towards the blonde-haired guy who was frowning in our direction.

Harry let out a dry laugh. "Why do you even care?"

I glared at him. "I care because you told me you didn't have feelings for him and now you're making it look like it's the exact opposite. He is my friend and I don't like you playing with his feelings."

He snorted. "I'm not playing with his feelings. Go back to your girlfriend instead of caring about my love life. You have nothing to do with it anyway," he snapped.

I tried to pretend that his words didn't hurt, but I was quite certain he could see my face fall because his eyes turned softer than they had been a few seconds ago. "Well, if you say so..." I trailed off, letting go of him.

I started walking away from him, but to my surprise, he stopped me when I had barely taken a step. "But that's because of you. It's your fault things are like this. I wasn't the one to make this decision, it was you," he reminded me, making me grimace.

Turning around, I ran a hand through my hair. "Well yeah, maybe it was. I know what I did, I'm not an idiot. No matter what, though, I didn't move on in only three weeks, nor did I start playing with someone else's feelings, as you did." With that said, I walked away from him, leaving him standing there.

The students who had been around when I first pulled him away from Niall were now gone, making it easy for me to make my way to my locker. Once I got there, I tossed my books into it, not caring that I made a mess and probably wouldn't find them next time I needed them.

Why did life have to be so complicated? I just wanted everything to work out the way I wanted it to, where everything that I wanted to happen happened. However, stupid rules and stupid people had to be in the way of that, so unfortunately, things couldn't end up the way I wanted.

The next lesson I had was Chemistry. Thankfully, Zayn and Eleanor took this class as well, which at least meant I wouldn't be alone during the next hour. I doubted that would make things any better, though. Harry would still be there, and so would Niall, and that fact itself made everything shitty.

I started walking towards the classroom, knowing Zayn was probably following Liam to his class and Eleanor probably hanging out with her own friends, so I didn't bother waiting for them. Along the way, I didn't even look up to greet my friends from the football team like I usually did, but I couldn't care less about that right now.

To my surprise, Eleanor met up with me right outside the classroom, catching me off guard when she threw her arms around my body from behind. "Hello there, handsome," she chuckled in my ear, taking a step back so I could turn around to face her.

I did my best to form a smile on my lips, but I was sure it looked more like an ugly grimace. "Hi, beautiful."

Thankfully, she didn't seem to notice the lack of excitement in my voice since she continued smiling at me like never before. "How has your day been? I haven't seen you since this morning." She jutted her bottom lip out in a pout.

As I opened my mouth to give her a reply, the bell rang, cutting me off. "Um, I think we should probably head inside," I said, taking her hand and pulling her into the classroom where the students were currently settling down in their seats.

The first thing I noticed was that Harry and Niall were sitting at a desk in the front. Niall had his phone out while Harry was observing his surroundings thoughtfully. When my gaze landed on him, he looked up to meet my eyes. For a second, they flickered to Eleanor before going back to mine again. His face showed no emotion whatsoever, and I could tell mine didn't either.

Nothing else happened, but Eleanor pulled me to a desk across the room where we settled down. The class started, and everyone began listening to what Mr. Fletcher had to say. Well, everyone except for me since I was too busy staring out the window to care about any word he said.

My head was spinning like crazy with thoughts of what had happened today so far. First of all, Harry and Niall had caught me by surprise at my locker this morning when they had been holding onto each other. To be honest, I never thought I would ever witness that sight in front of me. When Harry told me that he didn't have feelings for Niall, he had sounded so convincing, as if he genuinely meant it. However, when I talked to him after English class earlier, it felt as though those words had never even left his mouth.

Second of all, Harry had told me that I had nothing to do with his love life, even though we had confessed our feelings for each other only three weeks ago. I didn't know whether to take that as if he had already moved on, or if he was just mad at me for making the decision I did about us. Either way, it hurt, but if it was the second option, I assumed I did kind of deserve it, even if it was for the best.

I was still afraid that it could be the first option, though, and that scared me to no end. Even though I knew we couldn't be together, it was reassuring to know that I wasn't the only one suffering from the situation. Sure, I didn't want Harry to be hurt, but knowing he at least had feelings for me made me feel better. So now when it seemed as though I couldn't even reassure myself of that, everything felt even worse than it had done when I woke up this morning.

The remaining question was; was knowing for sure that dad wanted to keep me in his life worth not having Harry? Strangely enough, I didn't know the answer to that anymore.

Chapter 25

[Harry]

During that day, I couldn't stop thinking about the words Louis had spoken after English class that morning. They were replaying in my head over and over again, making me both frustrated and angry because I knew he was kind of right. Sure, the main reason why he had come up to me in the first place probably wasn't because he felt sorry for Niall since I knew how he acted when he was jealous, but he still had a point.

I was being selfish and mean by doing this. It was even worse than kissing Niall at the party in order to make Louis jealous. I was just so desperate to move on that I didn't know what else to do. All I wanted was to forget about Louis or perhaps make him realize that it was worth giving us a try, as selfish as that sounded. However, it was already obvious that I was a selfish person, so it couldn't get worse anyway.

There was no doubt Niall didn't deserve to be used like this, though. I mean, sure, he was a great guy and I did like him, but not as much as I liked Louis. So, basically playing with his heart like I was doing right now was probably the cruelest thing I had ever done, and I hated myself for it. But, at the same time, I knew that if there was anyone I was going to be able to move on with, it was Niall.

I was currently heading towards my last lesson of the day; P.E. Niall was walking right beside me, his hand in mine while a big smile was gracing his lips. To be honest, I had never seen him as happy as he had been today before, and that fact only made me feel even more guilty.

"Alright, so are you watching the game tomorrow? We are playing against the best team in the series, so it would mean a lot if you came watching," he asked, looking at me with a puppy face.

He knew that I wasn't very into football, so he was aware that he had to make an effort for me to come. However, what he didn't know was that I secretly wanted to be there since that meant I would also see Louis playing, which was a sight I had missed ever since I watched them play last time. The only reason I hadn't been to another game after that was because it would be weird for me to suddenly start showing up there. So, this was a great excuse for me to go there tomorrow.

I pretended to think about it, waiting a few seconds until I finally replied. "Alright, but just because you asked so nicely," I winked, making his lips form into an even wider smile if that was possible.

"Thank you, Harry."

I gave him a smile in return, realizing right then that we were now standing outside the locker room. "I'll see you later, yeah?"

He nodded, taking a step forward to give me a hug. "Yeah. Bye Harry."

"Bye."

With that, he left me as I turned the handle of the locker room door. To my surprise, there were already a few people there. I thought I had been unusually early to class, but I guess not since the other guys usually turned up at the very last second and changed in a hurry. One student that wasn't there, however, was Louis, which didn't exactly surprise me since he was never one to show up on time.

Making my way over to an empty locker, I unzipped my bag and started getting changed. Thankfully, there wasn't any rude guy in the room that made any comment about my presence. As mentioned before, some people didn't accept the fact that a bisexual guy changed in the same locker room as them, and sometimes they decided not to keep that opinion to themselves but had to mention it to me. I hated it whenever that happened.

Five minutes later, the door opened and none other than Louis stepped into the room. His gaze scanned the area until it landed on me for a couple of seconds. It didn't last long, but just the fact that he acknowledged me made my heart skip a beat in my chest. Unfortunately, though, he didn't glance my way another time, but instead, he walked over to the other side of the room where there was an empty locker.

Checking the clock on the wall, I noticed it was only a minute until class would start, so I didn't have time to check out Louis while he changed if I didn't want to be late. Mentally swearing, I followed a few other guys to the gym and made my way to the line where Mr. Wilson was waiting for us students to arrive.

Louis emerged from the locker room right when the bell rang, making Mr. Wilson throw him a warning glance, as if it was a close one and that it should not repeat itself. To the teacher's frustration, however, Louis didn't even look at him but joined a few of his friends instead. I rolled my eyes at the scene, not surprised at all that he acted the way he did. It was Louis after all, what else did anyone expect?

After that, the lesson started. We were playing dodgeball today, something I found quite fun even if I wasn't the best at it. Sure, I wasn't the worst, but definitely not as great as the students who played a sport consisting of a ball were. Thankfully, I wasn't on the same team as Louis this time. Though, I wasn't sure that was better because now he could make eye contact with me since we were opposite each other, and the glares he threw my way had me swallowing hard and averting my gaze.

He didn't even seem to hide the fact that he was out to hit me with the ball. Even if I wasn't the closest one to him, he still aimed my way and tried to hit my body. It was pretty ridiculous, but I did kind of understand that he was mad at me.

Once the lesson ended, I hurried to change into my regular clothing before walking to the bus stop. Thankfully, the bus was already there so I didn't have to wait for it. I made my way towards it and hopped on. As I walked through the aisle to find an empty seat, I wasn't surprised to see one beside Niall. He waved at me happily and gestured for me to sit down beside him.

Swallowing hard and giving him a tight smile, I hesitantly took a seat next to him, placing my backpack on my lap. "Hi," I greeted.

"Hi there, beautiful."

We started talking about how our day had been and what we had planned for the remaining part of it. It should've felt awkward judging by the circumstances, but it didn't, and I had a feeling that was because it was Niall I was talking to. No matter the situation, things were never awkward with him, and that was definitely a positive skill he had.

The bus was just about to start moving when a familiar person showed up right in front of me. Well, he was walking past me to get to the back, more specifically. Louis' eyes met mine for a second before darting to Niall who was too busy staring at his phone to notice him. His eyes found mine again, and he just shook his head in disappointment. With that, he continued his way towards the back of the bus.

I let my eyes fall shut as soon as he was out of sight, and let out a deep sigh. Niall seemed to notice this and looked up at me. "You okay?"

My eyebrows were furrowed as I nodded my head. "Yeah, it's nothing. Don't worry about it."

He looked at me suspiciously, probably knowing that it wasn't nothing and that something actually was up. However, he didn't seem to want to push it because a second later, he slowly let his eyes fall back to his phone, and that was also when the bus started moving.

Unfortunately, it didn't take very long until the bus came to a halt again. I wanted the ride to last just a little bit longer, but of course I wasn't that lucky. I got up from my seat, sensing Niall walk right behind me as I did so. While we made our way out, he placed a hand on my hip to keep me from stumbling, which he knew I tended to do a lot on the bus. I should've felt weird about it, but to my surprise, I actually found it kind of cute. It just showed that he cared about me.

Once we stepped out in the cold weather, I turned to look at him. He was biting his bottom lip, watching me with a nervous smile. "So, I guess I'll see you tomorrow?"

I started nodding my head, seeing Louis exiting the bust right behind Niall. "Unless you would let me walk you home, that is."

My eyes landed on him again. "I'm sorry, what?"

His cheeks reddened and he looked down at the ground. "I was just wondering if it was okay for me to walk you home, but I'm not forcing you. I just wanted to be nice, and--"

I had to let out a small chuckle because quite honestly, he was cute when he was nervous. "Of course you can walk me home, Niall. It would be a pleasure since I wouldn't need to walk alone then," I promised him, seeing him relax by the second.

"Oh, that's great," he breathed out, obviously relieved by my answer.

"Sure."

And with that, we started heading towards my home. Even though it was at the beginning of February now, snow and ice were still glistening the ground, making it difficult not to slip. Therefore, I was thankful that Niall grabbed my hand and held it tightly in his own. However, I was sure his purpose of holding it wasn't to support me but rather to show off that we had something going on to other people.

Either way, his intention didn't bother me. If he felt like holding my hand to 'show me off', then so be it. We did kind of have something going on anyway, so why should it?

During our walk, I couldn't help but feel as though someone was following us, and to be honest, it was quite creepy. I kept looking behind us to see if there was someone there, but each time I checked, there was no sign of another person. I pressed myself closer to Niall's side, feeling a little uneasy but didn't say anything to him in case he would find it weird that I was freaking out over something so lame and stupid.

He seemed to sense this, though, and I could see him furrowing his eyebrows out of the corner of my eye. "What's wrong?" He asked, and I shook my head.

"Is... is it just me or does it feel like someone is following us?" I asked unsurely.

He looked confused for a second but decided to turn his head to check for himself. To my surprise, his eyebrows shot up. "Louis, is that you?"

My heart literally stopped beating in my chest, and I abruptly came to a halt, causing Niall to do so as well. I turned around to see if Niall was right, and well, of course he was. Right there, a few yards behind us, Louis was standing, his gaze turned towards the ground. His jaw was clenched and I could see no trace of a smile on his face whatsoever.

"No, I think I'm a monster. Of course it's me, Niall," he said, rolling his eyes, but not seeming amused whatsoever.

To say Niall was confused would be an understatement. "You live in this area now? I mean, sure, I know you moved and rode the same bus as me, but I didn't think you lived... well, here," he said, scratching the back of his neck.

Louis' eyes met mine for a second before steadying on Niall's. "Well, I do. Actually, I live pretty close to your friend over there," he said, nodding in my direction.

I shot him a glare, having no idea what his intention with this was at all. I mean, sure, there was only a bathroom separating the two of us, so yeah, you could say we lived *pretty* close to each other, but what the hell was he doing?

Niall turned to me in surprise. "You do? How come I didn't know this? I mean, my best friend and crush are pretty much neighbors and I had no idea?"

I could see Louis roll his eyes at the word 'crush', but I didn't put too much attention to it. Instead, I focused on Niall and just shrugged my shoulders. "I don't know. It never really came up, I guess. Besides, Louis over there is not one I usually want to talk about," I muttered, shooting the brown-haired boy a pointed look.

That was when Niall seemed to remember that Louis and I were quite the enemies, or well, as far as he knew at least. His mouth formed the shape of an 'o', and all of a sudden he turned almost awkward. "I see..." He trailed off. "Well, we should probably get going then. It's freezing out here, and it's getting pretty dark."

I looked up to the sky and noticed that he was, in fact, speaking the truth. It was getting dark, and the fact that my fingers were starting to go numb didn't make matters better. "You're righ--" I started, but was cut off by none other than my stepbrother.

"Would you mind if I joined you guys? I don't live that far away and as you were saying, it's getting dark and I wouldn't want you guys to get lost," he spoke, and I had to let out a snort. We getting lost? If anyone would get lost here, it was him and his bad sense of locality.

Thankfully, Niall didn't seem to notice the sound I let out but just looked at me questioningly. He knew by now that I wasn't very fond of Louis, so he probably wanted to make sure that it was okay if he joined us the last bit. The worst part was that I didn't want to seem like a jerk to Niall, so I unwillingly nodded my head and let out a sigh. "Sure, why not?"

Louis' lips turned into a small smile then, and I wanted to punch myself for feeling my heart skip a beat at the sight. I hated the fact that I liked him. "Great."

During the rest of the walk to my house, Niall and Louis did the most talking while I was just there with them, still holding Niall's hand. Sometimes Niall would ask me things, but Louis would always cut him off by questioning him something else then. I knew he did it on purpose, and I also knew that this had been his intention when he asked to join us, but hey, he just couldn't help himself, could he?

Once we were outside my house, I stopped and turned to Niall. "Thank you for walking me home, it was very nice of you."

He flashed me a smile, missing the look Louis was giving him from behind. I could see it very well, though. "No problem, sunshine. I'll do it again, just ask me."

I gave him an appreciating nod, stepping forward to wrap my arms around him in a hug. He reciprocated it immediately, his arms going around my waist. When I made a move to pull away, he took his chance and placed a kiss on my cheek, causing my skin to turn a light pink. "See you tomorrow," he grinned and turned towards an angry-looking Louis who had his hands clenched in fists at his sides.

His reaction made me want to smirk, but since Niall was still here, that would be weird and rather cruel, so I composed myself. "You coming, Louis?" He asked, not quite noticing that Louis was not very happy at the moment.

Maybe I was being mean to him for doing this, but he said he would still be with Eleanor, so why couldn't I try to move on with Niall? Sure, I didn't need to stick it in his face, but he was the one who had asked to join us in the first place, so he could only blame himself... right?

And yes, I knew I was being mean to Niall too, seeing as I was trying to be with him while I still had strong feelings for

Louis, but if the feelings were ever going to go away, I had to at least try to move on, right?

Louis nodded his head curtly, turning around to follow Niall as I stayed there, wondering what lie he would make up about where he lived. I was thankful that it was his concern and not mine.

With that, I walked up to the front door and entered the house, welcoming the warmth with ease. By the sounds of it, no one seemed to be home, but since the front door wasn't locked, I knew better. "Gemma, you home?" I called out through the house, knowing she was probably in her room.

I could hear laughter coming from it, and assumed she had her boyfriend, Devon, over. Rolling my eyes, I shrugged off my backpack and put it to the side. I then took off my jacket and slipped off my shoes before walking to the kitchen where I hoped there was food waiting for me. Before I had even gotten to the room, though, the front door opened again, and I instantly knew it was Louis.

Well, this was not going to end well, I could definitely tell you that.

Chapter 26

[Harry]

I gulped as I heard his footsteps coming closer to the kitchen where I was standing, facing the fridge. He was not going to be happy, I was sure of it. That was why I didn't turn around when he entered the room but stood still with closed eyes, waiting for him to open his mouth.

"What's going on?"

To my surprise, he didn't sound angry at all, just bitter. This had me frowning, and I turned around so I could face him. He was standing in the door frame, leaning against it while pinching the bridge of his nose.

"What do you mean 'what's going on'?" I asked, closing the fridge to focus fully on him.

He looked at me as if I were dumb. "You know what I'm talking about, Harry. Don't be stupid."

"Well, if you're talking about the fact that I'm dating Niall, then there you go. That's what's going on."

He let out a frustrated sigh and walked over to me so we were standing face to face. His intention was obviously to intimidate me, like always, but he should know better by now that I did not find him intimidating... well, not usually at least.

"But, *why*?"

A frown was still visible on my face. "Well, why are you together with Eleanor?"

"Because I like her obviously..." He said but didn't sound too sure if you asked me. It was as if he was trying to understand what I was getting at.

"Well, then I am dating Niall because I *like* him."

His jaw clenched, and he looked away from me for a second. "Why are you doing this? And to him out of all people? He's done nothing to you, yet you go around making him think that you like him, when in reality--"

I took a step forward, staring him right in the eye. "Sure, I may not like him as much as he likes me, but I'm trying here, okay? I might be mean and stupidly selfish, but I can't go around pining after you when you don't want anything to do with me, now can I?"

It was the first time in my life I witnessed Louis being speechless and a bit taken aback. He opened his mouth to reply, but nothing came out. However, it didn't take too long until he had collected himself... unfortunately. "I haven't said I don't want anything to do with you."

Well, that was the stupidest answer I could have gotten.

I raised my eyebrows, looking at him incredulously. "Are you even serious right now? The last thing I remember is you telling me that you don't want to risk your father hating you if he found out you and I are a thing."

"Well, yeah. Sure, but can you hear anything about me not wanting to do anything with you in that sentence?" He was refusing to make eye contact with me, staring at something behind my back instead.

I could feel anger boiling up inside me. "Don't you dare go that way. We both know exactly what I'm talking about. We have barely even spoken to each other since that evening, so I'm pretty damn sure what you told me meant that you didn't want anything to do with me, now don't you think?" I asked, looking at him knowingly.

He bit his bottom lip, and I could practically see how he hated being in this situation. I knew him, and if there was something he despised, it was being at a disadvantage.

He let out a sigh and finally turned his head to lock gazes with me. "Look, Harry, I know what I said was stupid, especially after kissing you and all that. I also know that I can't go around thinking that you will like me forever, but fuck, I can't help but get jealous when I see you with Niall, especially since he can't shut the hell up about how absolutely perfect you are. You know I'm trying here as well, right?"

Now it was my time to be speechless. I did not expect that at all. "I... I didn't think..." I trailed off.

Well, I did know he had been jealous when he saw me and Niall, but I never expected him to confess it. This was so out of his character that I could barely understand that it was Louis standing in front of me right now.

He raised his eyebrows, taking another step forward so I had to take one back in case I didn't want to be too close to him. "You didn't think what? That I hate to hear my best friend gushing over you? That I hate the feeling of even seeing you, knowing you aren't mine? Well, I fucking do, if you wanted to know."

With newfound determination, I furrowed my eyebrows together. "Then why aren't you doing anything about it?"

He looked away for a second, only to look back at me with bitterness. "Because I know there's nothing to do."

Now that made me angry.

Without knowing really what I was doing, I grabbed his shoulders and backed him up against the wall across the room, pushing him against it. "How dare you even say that? You know you could've done things, but you refused to. I understand that you did it because you're scared that your father is going to hate you. That's totally fine, but then you shouldn't go around complaining about how things are now," I snapped.

Again, he looked taken aback. Not only by my sudden forwardness but also by my words. I guess he didn't know that I had it in me.

He didn't say anything for a couple of seconds. For a moment, I thought he wasn't even going to answer me, but then he looked me deep in the eye as if he was searching for something. It was also then he said something I never expected him to say at that moment. "Why do you have to be so fucking irresistible?"

And then he grabbed the collar of my shirt and pulled me forward so he could press his lips against mine. I was so shocked that my eyes widened in surprise and I felt numb in his embrace. My brain couldn't register what was happening, and that was also why my lips wouldn't move against his.

He let out a low grunt when he realized I wasn't returning the kiss and moved one of his hands to the back of my head to pull me even closer. It wasn't until I could feel the tip of his tongue against my bottom lip that it dawned on me what was happening, and to my great surprise, I accepted it with ease.

My arms went around his neck as I pressed my body against his so his back hit the wall behind him. You couldn't even fit a piece of paper between our chests, that was how close we were as our heavy breaths mixed. Louis seemed more than pleased with this and trailed the hand that wasn't on my neck to the small of my back. It went under my shirt to rest on my bare hip, and to say I got goosebumps by the touch would be an understatement. I felt shivers running through my entire body.

I had waited for this since the night of Ed's party. The last time we kissed, to be more specific. However, this was even better than the last time. It was hotter and if possible, even more passionate. His tongue eventually pried my mouth open to slip between my lips, and I let out a loud moan when it came in contact with my own, swirling around it.

My fingers gripped his hair, and I couldn't help but pull at it a bit. So many hormones ran through my body at the moment and I just wanted to be as close to him as humanly possible. Louis let out a grunt by the touch, moving his lips to press kisses to my jaw and down my neck, finding a spot there that made me feel limp in his arms. God, what this boy did to me.

He switched our positions so he was the one pressing me against the wall, for better access and more dominance, I assumed. Another loud moan escaped my lips as he let his teeth sink into my skin and create a hickey on my neck. Considering his harshness, I assumed it would definitely leave a mark.

After that, he pulled back for a second to gaze into my eyes. "You really are beautiful. You know that, right?"

His words made my cheeks go red, and my teeth sunk into my already puffy bottom lip. He let out a low chuckle at my reaction and leaned in to press another kiss to my lips, not caring about the fact that I was biting one of them. I instantly reacted and reciprocated it, feeling like a helpless little boy that obeyed his orders.

Before he or I could do anything else, though, a voice interrupted us and suddenly Gemma was in the kitchen. "What's happening boys?"

Luckily, Louis had quick reflexes, so he pulled away from me before she had entered the room together with Devon. He looked at me with wide eyes before turning to her with a blush on his cheeks. "Eh, nothing's happening. Harry and I were just about to make some food, right?"

I cleared my throat, still feeling flustered by what happened just a few seconds ago. "Yeah, right. We were about to make some toasts. You want some?" I asked, uncertainty lacing my voice.

Gemma looked at us suspiciously, probably assuming that was not what we had been about to do at all. "You sure about that? Harry, your hair is practically everywhere and your shirt is wrinkled."

I looked down at my shirt and noticed she was in fact right. It wasn't even falling down my hips but was kind of unfolded above them. "Well, I had P.E. as my last lesson, so that's why it's all wrinkly," I said but made sure to fix it and run my fingers through my hair so they weren't all over the place.

When I was sure Gemma wasn't looking, I sent Louis a glare, blaming him for making me look like this. If she assumed things had been going on, it would all be his fault. However, she seemed to drop the topic there because she walked over to one of the cabinets. "You were about to make some toasts, yeah?" She pulled out a bag of bread and opened the fridge to fetch the butter, ham and cheese.

When neither Louis nor I replied, she rolled her eyes. "Let's make them together."

To say I was confused would be an understatement. Gemma was not one to just drop something like that. She usually questioned you until she got the answer, but apparently not this time. Or, she was just waiting until it was just the two of us to interrogate me.

No matter what, I accepted it and was just about to walk over to her when Devon took a step forward and reached his hand out to Louis. "I believe we haven't met. I'm Devon and you must be Louis, right?"

Louis stared at his hand for a second with a frown on his face, probably contemplating how he should react to the gesture. Much to my relief, however, he eventually reached forward to shake it. "Yeah, that's right."

Devon's lips turned into a playful smile. "I've heard a lot about you."

I could see Louis' Adam's apple wobble as he swallowed hard. He glanced at Gemma who had her back turned to us while spreading butter on one of the toasts. "All good things, I hope," he replied in an attempt to sound cheeky.

Considering the situation, I would say he actually managed pretty well with it. Well, this was Louis after all, and the Louis we all knew could be very cheeky when he wanted to, so it shouldn't have surprised me.

Devon let out a laugh as he stepped over to put his hands on Gemma's shoulders. "To be honest, not quite."

Louis didn't seem surprised, and he shouldn't be considering he knew Gemma wasn't a very big fan of him, but I could still see he disliked the way Devon said it, as if he was trying to make fun of him. Devon now had his back turned to us as well, and I could see how Louis' fists clenched together while he took a threatening step forward.

The last thing I wanted right now was to see him fight my sister's boyfriend in our kitchen, so I reached forward to grab his wrist and pull him back. He turned to me, and I just shook my head with a warning look on my face, implying that it wasn't worth it.

He let out a defeated sigh and visibly relaxed. Inside, I was screaming because I couldn't believe I out of all people had made him get on better thoughts, but I hoped I didn't show it on the outside because that would be a bit embarrassing.

Without a word, he sat down at the kitchen table and pulled out his phone while I decided to walk over and help Gemma with the toasts. Devon stayed by her side the entire time but didn't help. I assumed it was because he wasn't the best cook and didn't want to join Louis. However, that made me at least get some time to talk to him.

I had only met him once and that was when Gemma first brought him home a week ago. Louis had been at football practice, which was the reason why he hadn't met him before. Though, I couldn't exactly say that I knew him more than Louis did because we hadn't really talked to each other. He and Gemma spent most of the time in her room that evening, so now was a great time to get to know my sister's boyfriend.

"So, I heard you and Gemma met when you were partnered to make a project, is that true?" I asked just to make conversation.

I could see Gemma hold in a laugh at my lame attempt, but I decided to not care about her. Devon who had now moved his arms to around Gemma's waist instead put on a smile on his lips. "Yeah, that's true, although I liked her long before that."

He explained how he had been keeping an eye on her for at least a year, but that he had been too shy to go up and talk to her before that project. It was kind of cute to hear his story, and judging by the blush on Gemma's cheeks, she enjoyed hearing it as well.

It turned out Devon and I had some things in common, like for instance, he enjoyed school and had good grades. He wasn't much of a party-guy even if he went to a few of them now and then, and he wasn't much of a drinker either. It made me happy that I got along so well with Gemma's boyfriend, and she seemed glad about it as well. One person who didn't, though, was Louis. Through the corner of my eye, I could see him glare at us every once in a while while he was typing on his phone.

I decided not to care, though, because it wasn't his business that I wanted to befriend my sister's boyfriend. Sure, Devon clearly didn't like him, but that didn't mean I couldn't like Devon because of that. I mean, considering what Gemma must have told him about Louis, I probably shouldn't have liked him either.

Once the toasts were done, we all settled down at the kitchen table to join Louis who put down his phone when the plate was set down. Devon sat down beside Gemma, which left me no other choice but to sit down beside Louis. Not that I didn't want to, but I could feel the tension after what happened earlier building up between us. We hadn't even talked about it yet.

We plated our food and for a second, silence occurred, but Gemma broke it in a matter of seconds. "So, how's dating going, Harry?"

My eyes widened by her straightforward question, and I could see Louis tense at her words. I took a bite of my toast, pretending to think for a long time. "It's going just fine," was the only thing I said.

She quirked an eyebrow as her eyes trailed down to my neck. "Yeah, I can see that."

My hand flew up to where her gaze was set and my eyes widened if possibly even more. The skin stung, and I knew it was right there Louis had made a hickey about half an hour ago. Well, shit. "Ehhh..."

"So, who is he or she? Is it someone I know?" She asked excitedly.

Louis was frozen in his seat with no emotion whatsoever written on his face. I bit my bottom lip, knowing I had to come up with something to make sure no suspicion was set on him. "I don't know if you know him, but his name's Niall. He's in some of my classes."

I didn't know if I was the only one who could see how Louis' knuckles were all white around his glass of milk, but when I looked up, I could see Devon glancing down at it and knew that I wasn't. He was sabotaging my attempt to cover it up.

"Oh, that's nice. When do I get to meet him?"

Thankfully, Gemma didn't seem to catch on to Louis' behavior. She seemed too interested to hear more about Niall to care about anything else. "I don't know... We aren't that serious yet, but soon, I hope," I replied, trying to keep a straight face.

She nodded, taking a bite of her own toast before turning to ask Devon something. The rest of the time we ate was pretty tense. I could tell it was because of Louis because he wouldn't say as much as a word. Not that I expected him to after his greeting with Devon and just the fact that he usually didn't get on with either Gemma or me, but maybe I had hoped he would at least try to be nice. It was as if I felt responsible for him for some weird reason. It was very odd.

When we were finished, I got up to put away the dishes while Gemma and Devon exited the kitchen. Not only a second later, I could feel a presence behind me where I was standing at the sink, and I was suddenly turned around to face my stepbrother.

He was looking at me with this intimidating glint in his eyes that I had seen so many times before. However, this time, I could feel how it was actually starting to get to me.

"So, Niall was the one marking you up, eh?"

Chapter 27

[Louis]

"So, Niall was the one marking you up, eh?"

Harry was surprised by my presence and had to take a step back in shock. It didn't take too long until he had collected himself, though, and let out a deep sigh. "You know I had to say that."

I quirked an eyebrow although I knew he was speaking the truth. It wasn't like he could tell Gemma that I had been the one creating the hickey on his neck, but that didn't change the fact that I didn't want her to think it was Niall who had done it... nor anyone else for that matter. "You could've said you were clumsy during P.E. class and managed to fall over and hurt yourself," I suggested.

He snorted. "Yeah, because this totally looks like a wound I made out of clumsiness," he said, rolling his eyes as he gestured towards the darkening mark on his neck.

I didn't even hesitate before reaching up to trace it with the tips of my fingers lightly. Harry seemed utterly surprised by my action and stared at me with his mouth wide open as if he couldn't believe his eyes. Well, I would probably not either if I were him considering our past. "Maybe not, but I really don't like the fact that Gemma is now going around thinking Niall did this."

He looked up into my eyes with a cheeky smile on his face. "Are you jealous?"

I raised my eyebrows, stopping my hand from tracing his mark."Of course not. Why would I be jealous of someone who can be seen together with the boy I have liked for two years? That's just ridiculous."

He let out a laugh, shaking his head. "Yeah, not jealous at all, right."

"Believe what you want," I said, shrugging my shoulders as if I didn't care, although I very well knew that I did. I was beyond jealous if you couldn't tell by my behavior earlier. I didn't want anyone to think that Harry belonged to anyone but me. I still knew that he was right, though. No one could know what was going on between the two of us, so what else could he do but say that Niall was the one who had made the hickey?

He took a step forward and leaned down to whisper in my ear. "Well, I believe you want to be the only one touching me, kissing me, and even fucking me." He leaned back and gave me a wink.

I had no idea where this side of him came from. He was so straightforward today that I had been taken aback more times than I had ever been in my life before. It was weird... but still pretty damn sexy.

Once I had recovered, I took a step forward so he was forced to take one back and be pressed against the cupboards. "You like playing with me, don't you?" I taunted.

His arms were at his sides and it wasn't hard to tell he didn't know what to do with them. It was like he wanted to touch me but was afraid to. He bit his bottom lip, something I found quite irresistible. Whenever he did, I wanted to kiss the shit out of him, but I always had to control myself. If only he knew, though. "It would be a lie to say I don't enjoy watching you get jealous, yeah, because it's so damn hot."

"Watch it," I warned him, holding up a finger.

He chuckled, making his dimples pop and I had to swallow hard to keep from doing something I shouldn't. God damn, why did he have to be so beautiful?

"Or else?" He teased.

I looked away from him and muttered; "You don't even want to know."

Rolling his eyes, he crossed his arms over his chest. "Well, as much as I am enjoying having this conversation with you, I think we both know that we need to talk about it."

My eyebrow shot up. "It?"

"Us," he clarified.

I bit my lip, knowing he was right even if I didn't want him to be. I hated having talks. They only meant serious stuff, and I couldn't handle serious very often. However, I still knew that it was important now. Harry and I couldn't go around like this, not knowing where we stood or what we were.

I slumped my shoulders, letting out a sigh. "Yeah, you're probably right."

"Of course I am," he grinned.

"Alright, but we can't do it here. It's too dangerous considering what happened a few minutes ago when Gemma and that guy Devon walked in."

He agreed, grabbing my hand to pull me out of the room and up the stairs. To say I wasn't affected by his touch would be a definite lie. Whenever Harry touched me, I got goosebumps all over my skin, and this time was not an exception.

He led me to his room and shut the door behind us before sitting down on the perfectly made bed. With a look on the spot beside him, he gestured for me to sit down and I obliged without hesitation. It wasn't uncomfortable being around Harry anymore. If anything, it almost felt like it did when we were friends two years ago. "So, where do we start?" He pondered, looking at me expectantly.

"Let's start with the fact that we kissed just an hour ago, how about that?" I suggested.

Even if it was pretty dark in the room since his lamp wasn't the best, I could still see his cheeks go a little red by my comment. "Eh, yeah, sure."

When neither of us said anything after that, he looked at me through the corner of my eye as he bit his bottom lip nervously. "You regret it, don't you? You're going to say that it was a mistake and that we should go back to how we were before, right?"

As soon as the words left his mouth, he looked away from me completely and refused to meet my gaze. He was being so cute that I didn't even know what to do with myself, and I wanted to punch myself for thinking that I could stay away from this boy. He was my dream, yet I didn't make him mine when he had his arms open for me. How stupid could I be? I was lucky that we were sitting here right now, having this conversation because, for all I knew, he could have already moved on from me by now.

Without saying anything, I reached up to place my finger under his chin so I could lift it to make him look at me. A small smile crept to my lips as I shook my head slowly. "No matter how much I want to, I can't resist you, Harry. Sure, my dad could hate me if he found out about us, but if we are careful enough, I don't think it would be a problem. What would be, though, is if I went another day knowing you could become someone else's in any minute," I confessed.

The corner of his lips curled up by my words, and the next second he was full-on smiling at me with his famous Harry-smile. How was it possible that this boy even liked me? It was surreal. "So, that means you want to give us a try?" He asked hopefully, his whole body turned to me now.

I still had my feet placed on the floor, but he was now sitting with his knees pressed to his chest beside me. "No, that means I want to throw you out of this bed right now because I can't stand to see you," I joked, rolling my eyes.

He let out a chuckle, shrugging his shoulders. "Well, last time you were in here, *I* couldn't stand to see *you*, so maybe it wouldn't be so weird."

Letting out a sigh, I looked up at the ceiling before looking back at him again. "Don't remind me of that, please. It's in the past."

He agreed with a nod, still smiling, though. Maybe he was just too overwhelmed by what was happening to recall just how terrible that encounter had been. I, on the other hand, had thought about it every day since it happened, and it was definitely one of the worst days of my life.

After a few silent seconds, his smile dropped in an instant, and I could instantly tell he had thought of something. "Does this still mean you're going to date Eleanor?" He asked hesitantly.

Gazing down at my fiddling fingers on my lap, I nodded slowly before meeting his eyes. "I think that's for the best. It's going to help us hide our relationship from people. Otherwise, they could get suspicious, you know?"

A frown made its way to his face as he nodded slowly. "Sure, but what about what you said to me earlier today about me being mean to Niall for playing with his feelings? Shouldn't that concern you as well? Or do you still have feelings for her, or what?"

It wasn't hard to tell he was upset now, and I understood him. "About that, I kind of just said that because I was jealous of Niall, but it is still true even if I don't care about it as much as it seemed then."

"So you don't care about Niall, is that what you're saying?"

"No, I do care about Niall. I just don't care that much about what Eleanor thinks, if you get what I mean. I don't think she even likes me as much as she used to either, but I'm doing this for us, okay? That's the thing. I want us to be together and she could sort of help us with that." I really tried to make him understand where I was getting at, and I hoped he got it.

"So, does that mean it'd be okay for me to 'date' Niall as well?" He wondered, still with a frown on his face.

That was the question I had been dreading for him to ask because I didn't have a good enough excuse for him not to be seen with Niall in public if I were going to be so with Eleanor. The only thing I had hoped for was that he had more of a heart than I did and wouldn't be able to do such a thing to Niall.

When he saw my hesitation, he let out a dry chuckle. "This doesn't seem very fair. Now, I'm not sure whether I could do something like that to Niall, but did you think I'd be willing to see you together with Eleanor when you don't want me to be seen with someone else?"

I averted my gaze, not meeting his eyes because I knew he was right. I just couldn't help but think he would fall for Niall since he was much easier to be with than me, and not to mention the jealousy I would feel. Today was only one example, and it could've gotten way worse than it did. "I know you're right. I just hate seeing you with other people," I admitted.

He raised his eyebrows. "And you don't think I do? I mean, you've been together with Eleanor for years. How will I know you're not going to leave me for her if you're still going to be with her in public? I mean, she's not even going to be aware that you're with someone else!"

Letting out a sigh, I shook my head. "I'm not saying this is going to be easy, Harry. A relationship between two stepbrothers can't possibly be unproblematic, but I know I'm tired of hiding my feelings, and I want to be with you in some way. It's bound to be complicated, though."

"Okay, fine," he finally said. "On one condition."

I swallowed hard, not liking the thought of conditions. "And that would be?"

He pressed his lips together in a tight line. "No kissing other people, and if you can pretend to like someone else in public, I can do so as well because I refuse to be the only one suffering from seeing you with another person."

I had to think about it for a second. Sure, I was totally fine with the kissing part because I didn't want to kiss anyone but Harry, and I sure as hell didn't want him to kiss anyone else either, but it would be hard seeing him with other people right in front of my eyes. Though, it was only fair after all, and there would be less of a chance that people would get suspicious about us. "Fine," I agreed after a minute, looking up to meet his eyes. "It's a deal."

A smile formed on his lips as he reached his hand out to me. I took it to shake it firmly. I just hoped I wouldn't regret this later on.

We were silent for a few seconds after that until a cheeky smile formed on Harry's face. "So, that means it's okay for me to do this now?" He asked, leaning forward to place his hand on my neck, letting his fingers run along my skin.

Instantly, shivers ran through my body and I had to clench my fists not to let out any type of sound. "If I were you, I wouldn't do that," I said with closed eyes.

"And why not?" He asked sweetly.

I grabbed his wrist and held it in my hand quite firmly. "Because I don't know if I could control myself if you do."

For some reason, this didn't make him stop at all, rather the opposite. He broke free from my grasp and sat down on his knees so he was basically leaning over me, and cradled my head in his hands. Our eyes locked, a smile still evident on his face. "Why control yourself when you don't have to?"

His words made a low growl escape my lips, and the next second, I had him pinned to the bed, my hands on his biceps as I held him down on the mattress. "Believe me, you want me to."

He shook his head, running his fingers through my brown fringe. "I've waited for this; you, since the night you kissed me the first time after Ed's party, and now here we are."

A small smile crept to my lips as flashbacks of that night played through my mind. God, those kisses we had shared were amazing. That *night* had been amazing from the moment he chased me from Ed's house. "That doesn't mean I shouldn't control myself around you. I've waited for you longer than that, and believe me, the things I want to do to you are probably not even legal."

He let out a small chuckle. "Well, how about we start with kissing then?" He suggested, wrapping his arms around my neck to pull me closer.

There was barely any space between the two of us. If we were to open our mouths, we would practically be inhaling each other's breaths. I leaned in a little closer, ghosting my lips over his, making him let out a whine. Chuckling, I pulled back slightly to look into his gorgeous green eyes. "Eager, are we?" I winked.

He shot me a glare. "Maybe you have better self-control than you think you do," he muttered. "But that doesn't mean I have your patience."

With that said, he pulled me down all the way so our lips could meet. The feeling of his soft ones against mine made me let out a deep moan. I loved this feeling. If I could experience it every second of every day, I would definitely do so. It was absolutely incredible.

His fingers moved up to curl around the hairs at the back of my head, pulling a little at them as he did so. Meanwhile, I let go of his biceps to cup one of his cheeks in my hand. His reaction was to swipe his tongue along my bottom lip, something that made me go even crazier. I went to straddle his waist so his thighs were trapped between my body. Just then, his tongue slipped between my lips and started roaming my mouth. He did it almost teasingly, and I wanted to slap him for that, but instead, I settled with reaching down to pinch his bum.

He squealed, pulling away from the kiss for a second. "Louis, *what*?" He breathed in my face, panting slightly from our heated kiss.

I laughed, leaning down to nuzzle my nose against the soft skin on his neck. After placing a few kisses there, I looked up at him. "You were being a tease, so that was my revenge," I winked.

Snorting, he went to slap my arm. It was so gentle that I almost laughed at him for even making the effort of doing it. "You're mean," he muttered, but you could clearly see a smile hinting at the corner of his lips.

"We'll see about that," I chuckled, leaning down to mold our lips together again.

This time I didn't even hesitate before slipping my tongue inside his mouth, licking at places I had never touched before. Harry moaned, one of his hands trailing down my back to fist my shirt. As he did so, his nails scraped my skin, making me press down on him even harder. This caused our groins to meet, making me accidentally bite down on his tongue.

"Ouch," he whined. "Why would you do that?"

"Oops," I winked, making him roll his eyes.

"It hurt."

"Want me to kiss it better?" I suggested, wiggling my eyebrows.

"Oh, shut the hell up."

"Only if that means I can continue kissing you."

He let out a chuckle, making his chest vibrate against mine. "You're unbelievable."

"Yeah? Well, you're unbelievably beautiful right now," I said truthfully.

His cheeks went a little red. "Just shut up and kiss me."

"Gladly," I smiled, dipping down to place a kiss on his now puffy lips.

It didn't take more than a few minutes until we could hear someone shouting from the kitchen downstairs, though.

"Harry, Louis. Dinner's ready!"

Chapter 28

[Harry]

Of course, mum had to interrupt us. If it wasn't Gemma, it was the other person in my family. Next time it wouldn't surprise me if it was Louis' dad who did it... even if I certainly did not hope so.

Louis pulled away and buried his face in my neck, letting out a groan. "How about some fucking privacy?" He muttered against my skin, making me let out a chuckle.

"Agreed."

He made a move to get off me, but I pulled him back down with my arms that were still wrapped around his neck to press our lips together just once more. "Sorry, I had to," I said innocently.

Rolling his eyes, he shook his head. "Maybe I should have a limit on how much you are allowed to kiss me in one sitting," he pondered jokingly.

I slapped his bicep, making him let out a laugh. "You wouldn't dare. Besides, I'm pretty certain you're not complaining about it."

He pretended to think about it for a second. "Yeah, you're probably right."

"Probably?" I snorted.

He ran one of his hands through my curls, giving my lips another chaste kiss before flashing me a wink. "Yep, probably."

With that said, he hoisted himself off me and reached his hand out for me to take once he was standing with his feet on the floor. Glaring at him, I took it almost unwillingly although I knew he was only playing with me. That didn't change the fact that I could be a little pissed at him... but only a little.

He wrapped his arm around my waist when we exited the room. The action caught me off guard because I thought he would act as if nothing just happened between the two of us and go back to how we used to be. It made me smile, but of course, it would turn out I spoke too soon.

Once we were at the bottom of the stairs, he dropped his arm and leaned in to whisper in my ear. "Remember, act like we always do around each other, alright?"

With a sigh, I nodded. I didn't want to, but I knew he was right and that we had no other choice. I just wished things weren't like this. I wanted to be able to show everyone that he now belonged to me, especially our parents, but unfortunately I couldn't, and I hated it.

When we entered the kitchen, I wasn't surprised to see mum and Troy already sitting at the table with the food in front of them. It did surprise me a little that Gemma wasn't there yet, though, but I assumed that had to do with the fact that she still had Devon over.

Troy smiled at our arrival, but the smile soon turned into confusion. "Am I seeing correctly? Did you two just arrive at the same time?"

I mentally slapped myself on the forehead for being so stupid, and through the corner of my eye, I could see that Louis was thinking something similar to it by the way he was biting his bottom lip. It was the first time meeting our parents after our talk and we had already fucked something up. Great.

"Yeah, I guess we just managed to leave our rooms at the same time," Louis shrugged, acting as if it was no big deal.

I had to say that he was actually pretty good at acting, and it became clear when both Troy and mum seemed to buy it. None of them pushed it any further, Troy merely nodded his head. Both Louis and I let out a sigh of relief before walking over to join our parents at the kitchen table.

"Gemma and Devon went over to spend the night at his place, so it'll only be the four of us tonight," mum informed as we were all seated.

So that was the reason she wasn't here yet...

"Perfect," Louis muttered, rolling his eyes.

Troy shot him a warning look, which Louis ignored as he plated his food. Yet again, I was impressed by his acting. If I hadn't known better, I would easily have believed him. But now I knew that he was just playing since he didn't have anything against the thought of it only being the four of us having dinner together.

Mum ignored his comment and moved her eyes to me instead. Her gaze wandered until it landed on my neck. Oh, for fuck's sake, why didn't I think of covering it up after what happened with Gemma?

I put my hand on the spot I knew was now turning purple. "It's not what it looks like..." I trailed off, keeping my eyes on her to keep myself from glancing at Louis. That would not be a good idea at all.

She raised her eyebrows. "It's not? Because a bird told me you have started dating a guy named... What was his name again?"

The smile on her face was never-ending, I swear. It was a long time ago I saw her smile so wide, and I wanted to slap

Gemma across the face for once again having a big mouth. She just couldn't keep things about me from mum, now could she?

I cleared my throat. "Eh, I assume you're talking about Niall, but we aren't really da--"

"So you're telling me he wasn't the one who did that to you?" She asked, nodding towards my neck.

I knew I shouldn't, but I couldn't help but turn my head slightly to see Louis' reaction. To say he was happy would be a lie. His lips were pressed in a tight line while his hands were clenched into tight fists. "Well, sure... but nothing is official, if you know what I mean," I said hesitantly.

She put a finger on her chin as if she was thinking deeply. "Alright, but if you get more serious, I want to meet him. I'm so happy you're seeing someone again." She reached over to pat my hand that was lying on the table.

With a stiff nod, I agreed. What even was this conversation? The only thing I knew was that I didn't like it one bit, and I could tell a certain someone didn't either. "Alright, so what have you been up to today?" Louis asked quickly to change the topic.

And I couldn't be more relieved.

The rest of that evening was thankfully pretty uneventful. Louis and I didn't make any more slip-ups, or at least not that I noticed. Sure, we exchanged a few glances every now and then, but nothing I thought either mum and Troy caught.

However, in the evening when I was lying in my bed and trying to sleep, I couldn't help but toss and turn. I had never felt this way before, but it felt strange knowing that Louis was sleeping in the room practically next to mine. I wanted him to be closer, but I didn't have the courage to go knock on his door, too afraid he would get mad at me since mum or Troy could catch us sharing the same bed.

Therefore, it took quite some time to fall asleep that night because the thought wouldn't leave my mind. Furthermore, I couldn't stop thinking about Louis in general, and everything that had happened that day. My brain was spinning like crazy, and there was literally nothing I could do to make it stop.

That was why I was pretty tired when I woke up the next day. Nonetheless, I got up from the bed and put on some clothes before trudging down the stairs to make some breakfast. I wasn't surprised that I was the only one there since mom and Troy had already gone to work, Gemma was at Devon's place and Louis was... well, a heavy sleeper.

Deciding to be nice, I grabbed two bowls from the cabinet and placed them on the kitchen table along with the box of cereal, a package of milk and two spoons. I then grabbed the loaf of bread we used yesterday to put two slices in the toaster.

I was just about to pull out a knife for the butter from one of the drawers when I suddenly felt two warm arms wrap around my waist from behind. The sudden contact made me so shocked that I almost jumped on the spot.

A mouth was pressed against the back of my neck, and the next second the person was laughing against my skin. "Good morning, scaredy-cat."

I turned around in Louis' hold to give him a glare. "You came out of nowhere, how could I possibly not get scared?"

He raised an eyebrow, pretending to think about it. I, on the other hand, lost all sense of reality when his appearance sunk into my brain. His feathery, brown hair was so messy that I doubted it had been fixed today yet. A white, plain t-shirt was hugging his upper-body, although it looked a little too big on him, and his thighs and bum were clad in a pair of black, skinny jeans. Don't even get me started on the slight stubble that was growing on his cheeks... I certainly did not hope he was planning on shaving today.

I got so lost in his beauty that I didn't notice that he was waving a hand in front of my eyes. "Hey, I know I'm hot, but I would very much appreciate it if you actually listened to me," he winked.

Biting my bottom lip, I mumbled; "I was listening to you..."

He rolled his eyes, reaching up to brush a stray curl from my eye. "Alright, so what did I just say?"

"That you are very pleased to see me making you breakfast?" I tried, making the corner of his lips twitch.

Taking a step forward so our chests were pressed together, he leaned in so close that our lips were almost touching, his eyes locked on mine. "Even if I am very thankful for that, it was not what I said."

"What did you say then?"

He shrugged, taking a step back from me but keeping his arms around my waist. "Nothing important," he smirked, making me frustrated.

However, before I could ask him any further about it, the toaster popped, making me actually jump this time, and of course, this had Louis laughing. He laughed so hard that he even had to cover his mouth to muffle it. "Yeah, not easily scared at all."

I unwrapped his other arm from me and turned around to grab the toasts that were perfectly golden-brown. After that, I finally grabbed the knife I had been about to pull out earlier and pulled out the butter from the fridge on my way to the kitchen table. "Have fun making your own toasts," I grumbled, which made his laughter die down.

"Don't be like that, Harry," he pouted, walking over to try and snatch one of them from my hand, but I didn't let him.

"Nah, you were being mean. Make your own," I said stubbornly.

He reached forward to place his finger under my chin, lifting it up to look me in the eye. Leaning in, he placed a soft kiss on my lips, making my cheeks go a light pink. "Please?" He begged, fluttering his eyelashes.

"I hate you," I grumbled, sliding one of the toasts across the table so it was lying beside his empty bowl.

Happily, he walked over to sit down opposite me, giving me a cheeky smile once he was seated, but I just glared at him in return. "I know you love me, by the way," he joked, spreading butter on his toast.

I said nothing in return, just threw him another glare as I poured some cereal in my bowl. Just to make a point, I didn't say anything during the entire time we ate our breakfast. Since he didn't either, I first thought he didn't mind the silence, but when a crease started forming between his eyebrows after a few minutes, I could tell that he was affected by it and knew that I was doing it intentionally.

He broke the silence once he had emptied his bowl of cereal. "Alright, I'm sorry for being rude earlier. I shouldn't have laughed at you," he apologized, looking at me from across the table.

A smile formed on my lips, the bowl of cereal now empty in front of me as well. "I knew you would apologize eventually," I smirked, getting up to put my dishes in the sink.

When I turned around, I could see him staring at me with his mouth wide open. "You bastard," he let out after a few seconds. "I can't believe you had me thinking you were actually mad at me."

I shrugged, sending him a smile. "Well, now you at least learned a lesson."

"Yeah, right," he snorted, getting up himself to put away his dishes. "We'll see about learning lessons later on."

With that said, he shouldered me on his way out of the kitchen, leaving me slightly shocked. I did not expect that, to be honest. However, that didn't mean I wasn't a bit turned on by his words. The question was; what did he mean by them?

If I thought it was weird sleeping so close to Louis without being even *closer* to him, it was even weirder being in the same class as him and having to see him all the time without being able to touch or hold him. I didn't even know if weird was the right word, but more like frustrating. My fingers literally twitched whenever I caught sight of him.

As if that wasn't enough, it seemed like he didn't even acknowledge my existence, and that was more than just a bit frustrating. I wanted him to look at me the same way he had done yesterday and this morning when he scared me in the kitchen. The only time I actually caught him glancing my way was when I was hanging with Niall. Other than that, he was too caught up in his own business, like for example Eleanor and his phone.

I had never hated an agreement as much as I did now.

When I agreed to the bullshit we talked about yesterday, I didn't think it would be this hard. I mean, I had witnessed him and Eleanor before, but I had never found it so difficult to watch them as I did now. They didn't even share a kiss, but just the sight of her being in his presence had me feeling sick. I was supposed to be the person being close to him, not her.

It didn't make matters better that I despised myself for going around making Niall think that I fancied him. I mean, sure, he was attractive and all that, but just as I had mentioned so many times before, he wasn't *Louis*. He wasn't that little extra. But just because he wasn't, it didn't mean he deserved to be used like this. I was playing with his feelings, and I hated myself for it. Yet, I didn't know how to end things because I couldn't hurt him. He would be devastated.

That was why I found myself walking down the bleachers later that evening. I was here to watch the football game just like Niall wanted me to. Sure, it wasn't exactly against my will since that meant I was going to see Louis as well, but I still felt bad for doing it since Niall expected me to want to watch him play and no one else.

It didn't surprise me when I caught sight of my best friend sitting a few rows down, waiting for the game to start. I was pretty sure Liam had been to every game since the last one we had watched together. Not that it surprised me since he was there to see Zayn, I just found it quite entertaining considering he had never done it before.

"Hey, mate," I greeted, sitting down beside him.

He turned to look at me when he heard my voice and a smile spread on his lips. "Hi, there. Here for Niall?" He guessed, flashing me a wink.

Running a hand through my hair, I laughed half-heartedly. "Yeah, something like that."

Thankfully, he didn't notice anything weird and just carried on. "You two are getting quite close, aren't you?"

"I guess," I shrugged. "We've been seeing each other for a little over a week."

He nodded. "And how're things going with Louis? Is he still being a pain in the ass?" He joked.

The muscles in my body froze to ice. I was not expecting him to mention Louis because he hadn't done so in weeks. I barely even remembered that he knew we were stepbrothers.

His question surprised me so much that I couldn't form any words. It was that, but also the fact that things were totally different between me and Louis now than the last time we talked about him that made me speechless.

"I'll take that as a yes," he laughed, still not noticing that something wasn't right. Sometimes Liam could be really oblivious...

Only a few minutes later, the players finally entered the field. Just like the last time, Louis jogged over to the referee to shake his hand and the opponents' team captain's. Just the sight of him had me gulping. He looked so good in those shorts. I mean, his thighs and legs were just to die for.

Not long after that, the referee blew his whistle to start the game. I knew I shouldn't, but I couldn't help myself from following Louis' running figure. The way he moved across the field was just fascinating in itself, but he looked even better when he was controlling the ball. It wouldn't surprise me if I was drooling. I couldn't know for certain though, because all I could focus on was... well, Louis.

"You really do like him, don't you?" Liam concluded after a while, interrupting my staring and thoughts.

I turned my head to look at him. "You mean Niall?"

He rolled his eyes and let out a chuckle as if I were stupid. "No. Louis, of course. You haven't taken your eyes off him since he stepped out on the field.

Well, oh fuck.

Chapter 29

[Harry]

I stared at him with wide eyes, my mouth hanging open. Did I just hear what I thought I heard? "I-- what?"

He let out another chuckle. "Well, I'm not blind. You aren't very subtle, you know?"

Placing my hands over my face, I shook my head in exasperation. "God, you weren't supposed to find out. Not you, not anyone," I sighed.

"Does he feel the same, though?"

I turned to look at him, dropping my hands to my lap. Since he already knew about my feelings for Louis, would it hurt if he knew about our relationship as well? I mean sure, Louis was probably going to be pissed if he found out, but I also knew Liam was someone I could really trust.

So, deciding that it wouldn't hurt and that this was the perfect opportunity for me to finally vent to someone about... well, everything, I admitted; "Yeah, you could say so, I guess."

He looked a bit surprised by this, and I would too if I were him because there was literally no evidence that we had something going on. We hadn't shown any signs of it at school. The only thing people knew about us was that we despised each other, so the fact that we had feelings for one another would probably shock everyone. Additionally, Louis had been dating Eleanor for about two years now, so that fact certainly made it even harder to believe. "Wow. That's... well, that's something," was the only thing he said.

I bit my bottom lip, hoping that he wouldn't be grossed out about it. I mean, it wasn't exactly a normal thing that stepbrothers dated. "Yeah. Do you... do you think it's disgusting?" I had to ask, not being able to stop myself.

He furrowed his eyebrows. "No, of course not. I mean, you aren't blood-related or anything, so why should I? Sure, it's a bit weird since your parents are dating, but you aren't real siblings, so it shouldn't matter. It's just... I didn't expect it, I guess. I always thought Louis was straight."

So did I until I found out he'd had feelings for me since we were best friends two years ago... "Yeah, me too. I'm glad you aren't grossed out about it, though. I wouldn't know what to do with myself if my best friend turned against me."

He gave me a small smile, nudging his shoulder against mine playfully. "I would never do that, Harry. Best friends forever, right?" He smirked, making me laugh.

"Definitely," I agreed.

We were quiet for a while after that, just watching the game in silence until Liam decided to break it. "So, if you're with Louis now, why are you dating Niall?" He wondered curiously.

Looking down at my fiddling hands on my lap, I let out a sigh. "I'm kind of asking myself the same thing."

From the corner of my eye, I could see him looking at me in confusion, clearly not getting it. "What do you mean?"

"Well, it hasn't exactly been easy between me and Louis, you can say. It took a while until we accepted the fact that we liked each other, and... I guess I tried to be with Niall to get over him, but that's when Louis decided he wanted to give us a try..." I trailed off.

"And now you don't want to hurt Niall's feelings?" Liam finished, slowly putting the puzzle pieces together.

I nodded in agreement, letting out another sigh. "I don't know what to do. I can't hurt him by telling him it's over, yet I'm hurting him even more by staying with him, making him think that I feel the same way."

Liam thought for a while until giving me a look of understanding. "I get what you mean. It's a difficult situation you've put yourself in. However, I think the best thing you can do is to tell him the truth. Sure, he might be hurt and feel like he's been used, but in the end, he's going to be happy you told him sooner rather than later."

I knew he was right, but it was a whole other thing to actually do it. Yes, I was a damn coward, I know. "Then there's also the fact that Louis wants to hide our relationship the best we can. Therefore, he's still going to date Eleanor, and seeing as he's going to be seen with someone else, I think it's only fair if I will too. Sure, it's not fair to the one I'm 'using', but I just can't see him together with someone else, knowing he doesn't have the same issue to struggle with as me if you get what I mean?"

He nodded. "Yeah, I get it, but you have to think about Niall here. He doesn't deserve to be used like that, and I know you ain't that kind of person, Harry. You wouldn't hurt anyone by playing with their feelings."

Yet again, he was right. I wasn't like Louis. I couldn't play with someone's feelings as he did without feeling guilty about it. Niall was too good for that, and so was my heart. "You're right, Liam. I have to call it quits with him as soon as possible, and explain how I feel. If I want Louis to feel the same way I do when he's with Eleanor, I'll just have to do it with someone else. Niall deserves better than this."

He gave my shoulder a pat, satisfied with my conclusion. "You're damn right about that. Now, let's watch this game. I think we've missed probably ten minutes by talking," he laughed.

I turned my head to the field, noticing on the scoreboard that we had scored a goal while we had been talking. So, we had definitely missed a couple of minutes. "Oh," I chuckled, glancing around until I found Louis out there.

My throat got all dry when I did, seeing that he had been starting to get sweaty now. His forehead was glistening with waterdrops and his brown fringe was damp, making goosebumps form on my skin. God, he was just so damn beautiful that I didn't even know what to do with myself.

"I can see you drooling, Harry," Liam pointed out, making me let out a groan.

"Shut up, Liam."

When the game was over and they had won two to zero, the people on the bleachers slowly started dispersing while Liam and I stayed seated. We looked at each other to see what the other was thinking, but no one said anything. I was just about to get up and walk off when someone shouted from the field; "Liam, come down here!"

My head turned to the sound, noticing that Zayn was looking at us, gesturing with his hand for Liam to come join him. "Come on, Harry. You're coming with me," Liam concluded, grabbing a hold of my arm and pulling me down towards the field.

I was about to protest but stopped myself when I caught sight of Louis standing nearby Zayn, talking to one of his teammates. Okay, I was definitely going down there.

As we started making our way to Zayn, I noticed that Niall was still out there as well, talking to Ed by the goal. I looked away instantly, hoping neither of them would catch sight of me. I was going to tell Niall, but not now. Not today.

"Hi there, love," Zayn greeted Liam once we had joined him, walking forward to give his boyfriend a kiss on the lips.

I bit my lip at the sight of them together. I would love to do the same thing with Louis, but no, we were stepbrothers, and it would be weird if we did such a thing in public. God, I hated it.

"Hi," Liam blushed, taking Zayn's hand in his. "You were great out there, as usual."

Zayn winked at him. "Of course, did you expect anything else?" He joked.

While they talked, I kept glancing over at Louis who was now done talking to that guy. Instead, he was looking at something on the bleachers. I turned my gaze to follow his, a lump forming in my throat as I realized it was Eleanor. She was making her way towards him with a smile on her face, brown curls bouncing from excitement to meet her boyfriend, and I wanted to throw up at the sight.

When she finally reached him, they put their arms around each other, hugging tightly even though he was all sweaty from the game. Would it be mean of me to go over there and pull them apart? Because I was so close to doing it, no kidding.

Instead, however, I looked back at Liam and Zayn. To my surprise, I found Liam giving me a sympathetic look, to which I just shook my head. I mean, there was nothing any of us could do about it anyway. This was his so-called 'plan', after all.

"You guys have to come celebrate with us in the locker room," Zayn said excitedly, a wide smile on his face.

Liam gave me a questioning look, and I nodded. Sure, Louis would probably bring Eleanor with him, but I didn't want to let any of them down. Zayn seemed excited, and I could tell Liam wanted me to come as well, seeing as he wasn't very comfortable with all the other guys on the team apart from Ed and Niall.

With an appreciating smile, Liam mouthed the words 'thank you'. With that, we started making our way towards the locker room across the field. I could see a few other players doing the same thing, and some were probably already in there. I didn't dare turn around to see if Louis was gone or if he was still standing there with Eleanor. Instead, I kept my eyes on the ground, dragging my feet behind me a little.

I just couldn't help but feel a bit down about seeing Louis with Eleanor. Part of the reason why it was so hard for me to watch them was that they kind of looked really good together. They were the school's most popular guy and girl, after all. People had even expected them to get together before they even knew each other. It made my heart drop, knowing people wouldn't think the same thing about me and Louis. They would probably think we looked ugly together.

Once we finally entered the locker room, we were met with loud screams and cheers. A party was practically being thrown in here. Someone had brought a music player, the loud sound blasting through the speakers while sweaty football jerseys were being thrown around by the players. To say it smelled nice would be a definite lie, but by the looks of it, no one seemed to care about it. Maybe because all of them smelled bad anyway.

"Oh my God," Liam gasped, but instantly, a smile formed on his lips. He certainly enjoyed this, and so did Zayn because the first thing he did was to take his own jersey off and throw it at some guy who didn't see it coming and got it right in his face.

I chuckled at that, but to be honest, I wasn't really in the mood for partying right now. Not that I usually was, but now really wasn't the right time. Therefore, I sat down by one of the lockers and fished my phone from my pocket while Liam joined Zayn and all the other guys. I questioned myself if Liam actually wanted me to come as badly as I first thought. He seemed to enjoy himself without me by his side.

Too busy being caught up in my phone, I almost missed Louis and Eleanor's entrance five minutes later. From the corner of my eye, I could see them holding hands, something that didn't really surprise me, but hurt nonetheless. He hadn't caught sight of me yet. The first thing he did when entering the room was to notice his teammates. Just like Zayn, he took off his jersey, throwing it away just like everyone else had done. The sight of his toned chest made my throat go dry. Sure, I had seen him like that a lot of times, but he usually wasn't sweaty then. This was almost too hard for my eyes to handle.

I mean, his six-pack was glimmering with sweat as his v-line was on full display. To be completely honest, I wanted to go over there and hit him for doing this to me. Not that he knew I was in the room, but anyway. It was practically suffocating.

As if that wasn't enough, it was right then his eyes caught mine. I could tell I was drooling by the cheeky smirk that formed on his beautiful lips, and also by the way he popped his hip out while giving me a subtle wink.

Murder him, that was what I wanted to do.

"Harry, I'm so glad you came!" A voice suddenly spoke up, interrupting my thoughts, and breaking my eye contact with my stepbrother.

Turning to the sound, my heart dropped in my chest by seeing Niall and Ed standing there, smiling at me. I swallowed loudly. "Well, of course," I replied, even though it was probably impossible to hear over the loud music.

Niall took a step forward and leaned down to wrap his arms around me. I scrunched my nose up at the smell of sweat. "Ew, you stink, Niall."

He chuckled in my ear before pulling away. "Sorry."

Ed's eyebrows pulled together slightly. "How come you're in here, though?" He asked in confusion.

I turned my head to where I last saw Liam and Zayn, only to notice that they weren't there anymore. They had got lost in the swarm of sweaty football players. "I came with Liam and Zayn," I explained truthfully. "For some reason, Liam wanted me to join them, but now it seems like he forgot about that."

Niall sat down on the bench beside me, wrapping an arm around my shoulders. "Naw, Harry. If it makes you feel better, Ed and I aren't going to leave you."

I gave him a small smile, appreciating his kindness. "Thank you. However, I didn't actually mind being on my own since I don't really feel like partying right now anyway."

"Then why didn't you just leave?" Ed chuckled.

Because I wanted to see my sexy, hot and very beautiful stepbrother strip...

"Good question." I prayed that he didn't hear the hesitation in my voice when I spoke those words. I was a horrible liar, and I was aware of it.

He narrowed his eyebrows, looking at me suspiciously but decided to drop it in the end. His eyes drifted to my neck, though, making my heart stop beating. I had covered the hickey Louis created yesterday with some of Gemma's concealer this morning. Since she wasn't home, she would never find out that I had gone through her stuff... hopefully. However, as far as I knew, I had covered it up pretty great, and when I asked Louis about it before leaving the house this morning, he gave me a thumbs up followed by a wink. So, if the make-up hadn't been removed somehow, I wondered why Ed was looking at my neck right now.

To my great relief, he didn't say anything about it even if the crease between his eyebrows never evened out. I turned to Niall to get both of them on other thoughts, asking them what they thought of the game. Thankfully, they found the topic interesting, and a new conversation was made.

During the following thirty minutes, I sat there, conversing with Niall and Ed about everything and nothing until it was time for them to enter the showers. The so-called 'party' had finally died down by now, the music turned off and the guys not screaming as loudly anymore.

I felt like it was my cue to leave, but when I stood up to head over to the door, my eyes found Louis' across the room. He still wasn't wearing a shirt, but what was even worse now was that he only had a towel wrapped around his waist. I gulped at the sight, my feet refusing to continue walking towards the door.

What made it *even* worse was that he noticed me staring. He enjoyed the attention, it wasn't hard to tell by the way a cheeky grin formed on his lips. However, it surprised me when he mouthed the words 'stay' a few seconds later. I found my mouth hanging open, not being able to even move a muscle.

I just wondered if he wanted me to stay to make fun of me for having stared at him like three times since he entered the room half an hour ago, or if he was sincere and wanted my company on his way home or something.

In the end, I decided that no matter what, I wouldn't pass up on this opportunity, even if it meant Louis would make fun of me in the end. If he wanted me to stay, then so I would.

That was how I found myself sitting down on the bench by another locker, my phone in my hand while waiting for whatever Louis had in thought. Boy after boy left the room when they were finished, along with some of them's girlfriends. When Liam and Zayn left, Liam looked at me before glancing at Louis, who was drying his hair with his towel while talking to one of the other guys. Liam shot me a knowing smirk, making me glare at him in return. He chuckled, giving me a cheeky smile before leaving together with his boyfriend.

When it was Niall's and Ed's turn to leave, Niall walked over to me. To my surprise, he shot Louis a look before stopping in front of me. "You aren't coming?"

I shook my head slowly. "Nah, mum's coming to pick me up, and I don't want to freeze outside in the cold," I lied, looking down at the floor so he wouldn't notice that I wasn't speaking the truth.

"Oh, I see," he smiled half-heartedly, clearly a little disappointed that I wasn't joining him.

"Yeah, see you tomorrow?"

He nodded.

Standing up, I wrapped my arms around him, deciding that he was totally worthy of a hug. He returned it, his arms going around my waist. "Bye, Harry," he whispered in my ear before pulling away.

"Bye," I replied, and then he was gone.

It didn't take more than five minutes until the entire room was empty of people... well, except for Louis and I, that was. As soon as the door closed after the last guy, I could feel a presence behind me, making my heart skip a beat in my chest. To be honest, I didn't even notice when Eleanor left. I must have been too caught up in my phone...

"Hi there, beautiful."

I got up and turned around to face him, breath catching in my throat at the sight of him. He was now dressed in a white tank top and a pair of black, skinny jeans, his hair still wet from the shower he had earlier although he had tried to dry it with the towel earlier. The muscles in his biceps were *so* prominent in that tank top, and the fact that his hair was still wet made him even sexier. Not to mention the fact that his eyes were sparkling like never before from the lights in the room.

"You really enjoy checking me out today, don't you?" He chuckled.

I wanted to hit him, hit him for being mean, but also for being so incredibly good-looking that I didn't even know what to do with myself. "Shut up," I muttered.

"Well, that's what you get for 'learning a lesson'." He imitated what I had said earlier this morning, making my eyes go wide.

"You mean you've been doing it on purpose?" I asked in shock.

He laughed, shaking his head slightly. "I didn't even have to try hard, you did it pretty well without my help."

This time, I didn't even hesitate before reaching out to hit him on the bicep. "Shut *up*."

He took a step forward, our chests practically pressed together now. "If you really want to hurt me, you have to start hitting a lot harder than that, pretty boy."

I raised my eyebrows, moving so close that our mouths were almost touching. "Okay, but what if I don't want to hurt you?" I asked, making him smile.

"Then I would call you a wimp."

If my heart wasn't racing right now, I would probably have pulled back and scolded him for saying such a thing, but I had been waiting too long for this moment and I couldn't wait any longer to feel the touch of his lips on mine again. "In any other situation, I would have done something to you for just saying that, but God, I can't wait to kiss you," I groaned.

"Impatient, are we?" He questioned, raising an eyebrow.

My eyes fell on his lips that looked as inviting as ever, slightly chapped from the cold outside but yet so kissable and pink. I moved closer to brush mine against them, happy that he didn't pull back as I did so.

"Very."

With that said, he closed the gap between us, molding our lips together in a passionate kiss. His arms went around my waist, pulling me if possible even closer to him. In return, I wrapped my hands around his neck, fingers curling in his feathery, brown hair that was still a little wet from earlier. My back was suddenly pressed against the wall of lockers, the impact surprising me a little but not enough for me to stop kissing him.

He pressed his entire body-weight against me as his lips moved feverishly against mine, his tongue sliding across my bottom lip. I let out a moan at the feeling, especially when his hands wandered up, under my shirt. God, I just loved this, the butterflies in my stomach, and the goosebumps on my skin.

After a good five minutes of making out, he took a step back, our eyes opening at the same time. "I've been wanting to do that ever since I woke up this morning," he admitted.

I was actually a little surprised by his words because he hadn't shown a lot of signs of missing me in school today. "Really? Because from what I have witnessed, you've barely even glanced my way the entire day."

He let out a sigh, pushing a loose curl behind my ear. "That's because nobody can find out about us, remember? We have to be careful with this."

I pulled my eyebrows together. "Yet, it still feels like you'd rather be with Eleanor sometimes," I muttered under my breath.

He lifted my chin with his fingers, making me look at him. "I want to be with you. Only you, okay? Don't think about Eleanor or anyone else because no one matters as much as you do to me."

My chest exploded with warmth and happiness by his words, even if I still wasn't convinced. "Everyone thinks you two look perfect together, though," I said.

Rolling his eyes, he let out a chuckle. "Well, I don't care what they think. All I care about is my feelings and what I think, and you wanna know something?" He leaned in close to my face again.

I nodded slowly.

"I think that I like you a little too much."

Chapter 30

[Harry]

An entire week went by, and I had still not found the guts to tell Niall that I couldn't keep dating him. Other than that, nothing new had really happened. Louis and Eleanor were still hanging out at school as expected, but as promised, no kissing occurred, just the occasional hand-holding and hugs.

At home, we had kept being careful too, only showing affection towards each other when we knew there was no one around. Those times unfortunately rarely occurred, though, because when we got home after school, Gemma was usually there, and then both mum and Troy got home later in the afternoon as well. Sure, we did spend some time in each other's rooms sometimes when we were certain no one would come and interrupt us, but Louis was usually afraid they would hear us or something, so we barely hung out with each other at all, which was really sad.

It was like he was so close, yet so far away. I mean, there was only a room separating us, but it felt like he lived across the town just because we couldn't be near each other even in our own house.

I enjoyed the mornings when Gemma started school early or slept over at Devon's, though. That was when Louis and I could really act on our feelings and enjoy each other's company. Sometimes I made breakfast for him (when I woke up early), and sometimes we made it together. It was so nice and everything just felt so perfect. I wished we could have more times like those, I really did.

I was currently lying in bed, staring up at the ceiling. It was bedtime and I should have fallen asleep a long time ago considering I had school tomorrow, but I just couldn't bring myself to relax. Thoughts were spinning like crazy in my head, which made it impossible for me to sleep.

I didn't know how long I had been lying there, doing practically nothing but toss and turn while trying to make myself comfortable with no success whatsoever. It was probably past midnight now, and that made me even more stressed about falling asleep. If I didn't sleep long enough, I knew I would be dead the day after.

I was suddenly pulled out of my thoughts when a knock was heard on my door. It made my heart skip a beat, and it wasn't because the knock scared me, but because it was coming from the bathroom door and not the regular one. That could only mean one thing.

It was Louis.

A second later, the door swung open, and through the darkness of the room, I could see how his head appeared in the gap. His eyes immediately found mine, and he looked a bit surprised. It was probably because he didn't expect me to be awake.

"Aren't you sleeping?"

I shook my head. "No, can't."

He let out a sigh, running a hand through his tousled, brown hair. "Me neither."

Biting my bottom lip, I looked at him expectantly, waiting for him to say or do something since he was the one who had come to me. When he didn't do anything, though, I furrowed my eyebrows in confusion. "Did you want anything specific?" I asked.

He looked down at his feet, shrugging his shoulders. "No, just... Well, since I can't sleep and you don't seem to either, maybe you want to come sleep with me?"

My eyes widened at his request, not expecting him to ask that. He was so careful around our family these days that I never thought those words would leave his mouth. It made me nothing but happy, though, because this was what I had been wanting to happen for a week now, so there was no way I was going to decline his offer.

However, the fact that he was so shy about it made me want to laugh. Louis was not the shy type of person, so it always amused me when he seemed so vulnerable, but it was nice to see this side of him too.

Without saying anything, I pulled the covers off my body and got up from the bed. Louis had already disappeared into his bedroom, but not before flashing me a small smile. I followed him, closing the doors behind me carefully not to wake up anyone.

When I entered his room, the first thing I saw was Louis' figure lying in his bed, tucked under the covers with his head on the pillow and his eyes closed. The sight made my lips twitch because I loved seeing him look so innocent. It wasn't exactly every day you got to see him like this.

Without thinking twice, I walked over to him and sat down on the edge of the bed, looking down at his face.

"Are you going to stare at me all night or are you actually getting under the covers today?" He muttered, still with his eyes closed.

"How did yo--"

"I can feel it when you stare at me, Harry."

His comment made my cheeks go a light pink, and I thanked the darkness in the room for making it impossible for him to notice it. I didn't answer him. Instead, I grabbed the end of the blanket and lifted it up to crawl under it so I was lying right beside him, feeling the warmth of his body against mine.

Just his presence made me relax. It was like he was some kind of medication to cure stress. Well, at least my medication.

Instantly, he wrapped his arms around my body and nuzzled his nose into the back of my neck. He pressed a small kiss there before resting his cheek against my warm skin.

"Why do you only have one pillow?" I asked sleepily, having no idea where the thought came from at all.

He chuckled, moving his hand up under my shirt so it was resting against my stomach. "Because then you have no other choice but to cuddle with me."

The corner of my lips turned upwards. "I see."

"Mhm," he hummed against my neck, making goosebumps form on my body. "Goodnight, Harry."

"Goodnight," I mumbled.

And that night, I probably had the best sleep of my life.

The next day, I woke up to the sound of my mum shouting from the other side of the door. "Louis, it's time to get up!"

I frowned in my sleep, wondering why she had called me Louis. I mean, didn't she even know the name of her own son?

In an attempt to roll around on the bed, I noticed that it was impossible due to a pair of arms that were wrapped around my body. That was also the moment I realized that I was hot, really hot.

"Mhm," a voice hummed beside me, and right then, I remembered what happened the night before. Flashbacks entered my mind in the blink of an eye, filling it with images of Louis knocking on my door and asking if I could sleep with him.

My body instantly went rigid when everything dawned on me. I was lying in Louis' bed together with him while mom was on the other side of the door, telling him to wake up. Oh, shit.

"Louis," I whispered, patting his arm.

He moved a little, letting out a few grunts but didn't unwrap his arms from my body. I was starting to panic a little because I knew that mum would go to my door next. She always went to Louis' room first, before mine, and sometimes she even opened the door to check on me. That could not happen this time.

"Louis," I whispered again, this time a little louder. It wasn't until I shook his arm rather forcefully that I finally managed to wake him up, though.

"Harry?" He asked in confusion.

I turned around in his hold so I was facing him. "Yes, it's me. You have to let me go. Mum is outside and she's about to go knock on my door. If I'm not there then, she's going to wonder where I am and start looking for me."

His eyes that were squinted just a few seconds ago due to the fact that he had just woken up were now wide open. "Oh, shit," was the only thing he said.

Yet, he still didn't let me go. Instead, he tightened his hold on me and pulled me even closer to him. He leaned in so close that our faces were mere inches apart, looking me deep in the eyes. "Is it bad that I still don't want to let go of you?"

I let out a chuckle, reaching up to play with his feathery, brown hair. "It's not bad," I said. "It's absolutely horrendous."

He smiled, leaning in to close the gap between our lips. Although he had just been sleeping, his lips were moist and soft, feeling nothing but amazing against my own. Every time Louis and I kissed, it felt like our first kiss. There were fireworks and goosebumps everywhere, and I absolutely loved it.

"Harry, it's time to get up, honey."

My eyes widened at the voice, and I immediately parted from Louis. In an instant, he let me go, patting my bum on my way up from the bed. "You'd better hurry, sweetheart," he said jokingly, and I turned around to give him a glare.

"It's your fault I'm still here, so don't blame me if we get caught."

He raised his hands in surrender, still smiling. "Alright, alright. Now, get out of here."

I shot him the middle finger before closing his door behind me. From the other side of it, I could hear him laugh, and all I wanted was to go back in there and hit him because he deserved it.

As I entered my bedroom, I noticed that I had been right when I said that mum usually entered my room to check on me in the mornings. She was standing beside my bed, looking as confused as ever. When she caught sight of me, though, the look was instantly replaced by relief.

"Where have you been?" She asked worriedly.

I bit my bottom lip, pointing my finger towards the bathroom where I came from. "I was just washing my face. I do that every morning, mum," I said matter-of-factly as if she was being ridiculous for thinking differently.

A frown fell on her face. "But you usually never wake up before I get here," she stated. "Well, if you haven't set an alarm, that is."

I shrugged, feeling heat making its way to my face. Why did I have to be such a bad liar? "I just haven't had a good night of sleep, is all. I couldn't fall asleep last night, and then I woke up early."

Suspiciously, she looked at me with narrowed eyes. Why, just why did she have to be my mum and know me so well? She could probably tell that I was lying right now, but I hoped to God that she wouldn't question me about it.

"Fine, I believe you, but that's because I don't know where else you could've been."

No, because why would I be in Louis' room when she knows that we hate each other?

Mentally, I let out a sigh of relief. "Exactly."

"Alright, I'm heading to work now. See you in the afternoon, yeah?" She smiled, walking over to press a kiss to my forehead.

"Yeah, see you then."

With that, she turned around and left the room. I, on the other hand, threw myself on my bed and let out a huge sigh of relief while running my hands over my face.

I wondered how many times Louis and I would almost slip up until we actually did.

Later that morning, I found myself sitting beside Niall on the school bus. Louis was in the back with some of the other players on the football team, and by the sounds of it, he was having fun because their laughter could be heard all the way to the front. For some reason, his laughter stood out the most, and I wondered if that was because he had a pretty high-pitched voice, or because it was saved in my mind so I could hear him better than the rest.

I leaned towards the former option, but it wouldn't surprise me if it was the latter because Louis' voice was something I was getting quite used to lately, in a good way.

"So, Harry, what are you doing after school today?" Niall asked, looking at the side of my face to gain my attention.

I turned to him, swallowing down a lump in my throat. I had to tell him. I couldn't wait any longer. A week was already long enough, and I could hear Liam's voice in my head every time I just thought about it.

It's better if you do it sooner rather than later.

I knew he was right. I mean, Liam was always right. Also, I knew that the longer I waited, the more it was going to hurt Niall in the end. So, I had to do it now.

"Eh, not very much, I guess. I've got some homework to do, though."

"Is it Maths? If so, maybe we could study together because I'm falling a little behind?" He asked hopefully, his eyes practically beaming.

I ran a hand through my hair. "I'd love to, Niall, but I can't. I can't do it."

For a second, his gaze turned towards the back of the bus, and the action had me frowning. Why did he just look back as if he was looking at something specific?

"Oh, why not?" He wondered, his face full of disappointment now.

"Look," I said, holding his eyes with mine. "I've been wanting to tell you this for a while now. It's something I should have done a long time ago, and I am so sorry that it's taken me so long to do it..." I trailed off, taking a deep breath.

"You don't really like me. That's it, right?" He sighed, finishing my sentence.

Pulling my eyebrows together, I looked at him in confusion. "It's not that I don-- Wait, how did you know I was going to talk about that?"

He shrugged, his face showing no emotion. "I just... I've been kind of getting the vibes, you know? I am always the one suggesting things we can do together, and uh... the fact that you turned me down the first time I admitted my feelings for you doesn't exactly make these thoughts disappear."

Biting my bottom lip, I nodded slowly and thoughtfully. "Yeah, I understand. I just... although I know this is for the best, I want you to know that you are an amazing guy, Niall. If my heart had only agreed with my brain, I would have loved to be with you without a doubt, I promise," I apologized.

He let out a laugh as he shook his head. "Well, that helps... a lot."

I nudged his shoulder with mine playfully. "It's a compliment, trust me," I smiled.

He shrugged. "Well, since it apparently isn't enough for you to stick with me, then I'm not so sure about that," he sighed, his laughter dying down in an instant.

I placed a hand on his shoulder, looking him in the eye. "You're going to find the one for you one day, Niall, someone who loves you equally as much as you do them. You deserve that, more than anyone I know because you are an amazing guy. I really do wish I felt more for you, I do."

He bit his bottom lip, nodding once. "I'm just wondering... Is there someone else out there that you like? I mean, since it seems like it's so impossible for you to ever catch feelings for me. I'm just curious if it is because you like someone else."

His question made my body go rigid. I wasn't expecting him to ask that, and I had certainly not hoped he would. "I uh... Well, yeah. There is someone I like, but I don't think they like me back. That's why I wanted to give you a try. I thought I would start liking you more, but the other person just won't leave my mind, if you get what I mean?" I lied.

Well, it was only partly a lie. It was true that I had wanted to give him a try, but that was before Louis decided he wanted to be with me. However, it was a lie that I didn't think the person liked me back because I was pretty sure Louis had feelings for me by now.

Since it only partly a lie, it made the situation a lot easier because then there was a higher chance that he would actually believe everything I said.

"I see..." He trailed off, breaking our eye contact to look down at his lap. "I guess I hope the other person opens their eyes and realizes that you like them then because they are very lucky to have you fancying them."

His words made my heart ache. Why was he being so nice? He should be mad at me. He should scream at me, yell at me for playing with his heart, but no. Here he was, trying to make me feel better when he was the one really hurting. He was too good to be true.

"Niall, please stop. You're making me feel awful about this, and I know I am supposed to because you don't deserve this, but you can't say that. Tell me how much you hate me for doing this to you instead. That would make me feel a lot better," I said desperately.

A faint smile formed on his lips, making me feel even worse. He was not meant to look sad and hurt. He was meant to be happy and have real, genuine smiles on his face. Why did I have to be so awful?

"I just want you to be happy, Harry. I know it didn't seem like it the last time you turned me down, but I really do want that. So, if it's not with me, then I hope you'll be happy with someone else. Or, to be more specific, the one you have your eyes on," he shrugged.

Without thinking twice, I gave him a side-hug. I didn't care that he would hate me for it, he was just so worthy of one right now. He deserved everything and more. The least I could do was to give him a hug. Thankfully, he didn't pull away or tense up by it, and that made me happy. "You're definitely something, Niall. The one you'll end up with is going to be so lucky, I can tell you that."

He gave me a weak smile. "Thank you, Harry."

A silence fell between us after that, and just a few minutes later, the bus came to a halt outside of school. Niall and I went our separate ways as soon as we hopped off, and I could feel my heart break a little because of it. I would miss him. Even if I didn't have feelings for him, he was an amazing guy and I would love to be friends with him. I wasn't so sure we would ever be that after this, though. I had probably ruined the chance to even talk to him again.

Still, I knew this was the right decision to make. Just like Liam said, it was better to do it sooner rather than later. I mean, Niall's reaction hadn't even been bad. It all went a lot better than I could have ever expected, and that was because Niall was Niall.

Who knew the person I first thought was a total jackass like all the other jocks at this school would turn out to be one of the sweetest people I had ever met? Well, I certainly didn't.

Chapter 31

[Louis]

Ever since this morning, I'd had a feeling that something had happened to Harry. He seemed sad for some reason, and during our first lesson, he wouldn't meet my gaze when I looked at him.

It was now lunchtime, and I still hadn't had any time to talk to him. Sure, we did share all of our classes, so I saw him all the time, but that didn't mean I could talk to him. Whenever he exited the classroom, he disappeared. I even tried following Liam and Zayn once to see if he was with them, but he wasn't.

I was currently sitting at a table in the cafeteria, nibbling on a cheese sandwich with Eleanor on my side. Across the room, I could see Harry sitting with Liam and Zayn while looking at his phone. For some reason, Niall wasn't sitting there today, but with Ed at another table.

Speaking of which, I hadn't seen Harry and Niall together since the morning on the bus, which was definitely unusual these days. Not that I wanted to see them together, but my curiosity was taking over my jealousy right now.

"Lou, are you watching my cheerleading practice today?" Eleanor asked, snapping me out of my thoughts.

I turned to look at her with a frown written on my face due to my previous thoughts. "Sorry, what?"

She rolled her eyes but smiled. "I was asking you if you're watching my cheerleading practice today? I know you don't have practice yourself, so I was hoping you would."

I bit my lip, looking down at my barely touched sandwich. "Actually, I'm going out with my family for dinner tonight, so I can't," I explained, running a hand through my hair.

She pulled her eyebrows together. "But my practice starts at four. I'm sure you'll have time for both," she said, disappointment lacing her voice.

Looking over at Harry who had now started eating his lunch, I let out a sigh. "Actually, we eat dinner pretty early, and my stepmom hates it if we're not out on time."

A look of disbelief fell on her face as she rested her elbows against the table. "Alright, whatever. I can't force you anyway," she muttered.

I looked at her hesitantly, reaching over to take her hand in mine. "Eleanor, I haven't said that I don't want to go. I'd love to, but today I just can't, alright?" I explained, trying to make her feel better, and judging by the small smile that formed on her lips, I got the feeling that I had succeeded.

To be honest, I didn't really care about it. It was a lie that we were going out for dinner. The real reason was just that Eleanor's cheerleading practices were probably the most boring thing you could watch. The only thing the girls did was to either bicker or throw each other in the air. I'd rather go home and spend time with Harry than anything else, especially when I didn't have practice myself. She couldn't know that, though.

"Alright, maybe next time?" She asked hopefully.

I nodded slowly. "Yeah, maybe."

During the rest of the lunch period, I kept throwing glances at Harry. The sad part was that he didn't even seem to acknowledge me. He talked to Liam and Zayn occasionally but mostly focused on his lunch and phone. Something must have happened. Otherwise, he wouldn't act like that. He was always so happy and usually had a smile on his face. I knew him better than most people did after years of knowing him... Well, perhaps not personally but from a distance, and this was not the Harry I had come to know.

When the bell finally rang, I got up from my seat and threw away the garbage that was left of my lunch. After that, I departed from Eleanor, seeing as we didn't share the next class. She gave me a kiss on the cheek as a goodbye, which she always did, and I just waved at her. To be honest, I hadn't even touched her with my lips ever since Harry and I started going out. It just didn't feel right, not even a kiss on the cheek. I only wanted to touch Harry, and that was it.

As soon as I was alone, I started searching for the curly-haired boy. It wasn't exactly the first time I did today, but that didn't mean I was giving up. I needed to find him, and that was now.

I made my way to his locker, hoping that he would be there this time. Thankfully, I was lucky because he was there. However, he wasn't alone. Liam was standing in front of him with a slightly concerned look on his face while talking to him. This made me even more worried about what possibly could have happened.

After checking my surroundings to see if anyone was paying attention to me, I walked over to them and stopped right behind Harry. Liam looked over his shoulder to make eye contact with me, and suddenly a small, knowing smile made its way to his face. The action had me frowning. Did he know something I didn't?

He cleared his throat and gestured for Harry to turn around. When he did, I could feel butterflies make their way to my stomach thanks to his beautiful features. I couldn't believe this boy was actually kind of mine.

"Louis," he breathed, and that was when I noticed that the smile that usually graced his beautiful, pink lips still wasn't prominent.

I glanced at Liam for a second before looking back at him. "Can we talk?" I asked urgently, almost in a whisper.

He turned around as if to ask Liam if it was okay, and when he got a reassuring nod from his friend, he turned back to me and gave me a weak smile. "Alright."

With that said, we made our way to the janitor's closet, me walking ahead of him while he kept a fair distance between us. The second he closed the door, I instantly turned to him, backing him up against it. With one hand, I reached up to run my fingers along his cheek as I looked deep into his eyes. "Are you okay?"

He looked at me strangely as if he wasn't expecting my question. "What do you mean?"

A frown was evident between my eyebrows. "I've been watching you all day and I haven't seen you smile once. I was just wondering what happened because if you're not smiling, then something most definitely did happen," I explained.

He let out a sigh, reaching up to run a hand through his curls. He then looked up to meet my eyes. "It's nothing. I just feel really bad, is all."

"What do you mean 'feel bad'? Are you feeling sick?" I wondered, concern lacing my voice.

Another faint smile made its way to his lips as he shook his head. "No, I'm not feeling sick. I just did something to someone that I feel bad about."

His words had me thinking. It took a while, probably an entire minute until the puzzle pieces finally fell into place in my head. "It's about Niall, isn't it? You two usually hang out together at school, but I haven't seen you with him since this morning."

He bit his bottom lip, nodding slowly. "Yeah, I told him that I couldn't be with him because I don't feel the same way about him that he does about me, and now I feel terrible because I hurt his feelings and I hate it. I didn't want this to happen, and I certainly didn't want to play with his heart, but I was desperate and I wanted you and now I--"

"Hey, hey, hey," I interrupted him, placing my hands on his shoulders to stop his rambling. "Calm down, love. What you did to Niall was nothing, alright? I mean, at least you told him, which he should appreciate. Sure, he might be hurt right now, but it would be even worse if you'd let it go even further, now wouldn't it?" I reassured him.

He was quiet for a while, thinking about it. "Yeah, you're probably right, but I just can't help but feel bad."

I shifted my feet, looking away from him for a second before locking my eyes with his again. "You don't... you don't regret telling him, do you?" I asked hesitantly, worried about the answer.

If he did regret it, that would mean he most definitely had some kind of feelings for him, and I knew I wouldn't be able to handle that. It didn't matter if he liked me more, I couldn't stand the thought of him having feelings for Niall as well.

He looked at me in confusion. "What do you mean 'regret telling him'?"

I let out a sigh, running a hand through my hair nervously. "What I'm trying to say is, you don't regret telling him that you didn't want to be with him, right?"

"Why would I do that?" He asked, still very confused.

I shrugged, breaking our eye contact once again. "I don't know. Maybe you realized you had feelings for him and that's why you're feeling so down," I explained even if I didn't want to. If he hadn't thought about it yet, I didn't want him to get any ideas.

To my surprise, though, he started laughing. "Are you kidding me? Of course I don't have feelings for him. And for your information, I don't really regret telling him. What I do regret, however, is that I tried to make things work with him in the first place because deep down, I always knew that it would never do so."

Mentally, I let out a sigh of relief. He didn't like Niall, and he didn't have feelings for him. The fact made me feel more relieved than it probably should have, but since I was aware that I was the jealous type of guy, I wasn't exactly surprised by this. "I understand," I said, trying to hide my smile because this wasn't the best occasion to show happiness.

He could see through me, though, and looked at me in confusion yet again. "Why are you smiling?"

Clearing my throat, I shrugged my shoulders. "I know I shouldn't be happy right now, but the fact that you just told me that you don't have feelings for Niall just made me smile," I explained.

The faint smile that had been gracing his lips earlier now turned into a genuine one and my heart swelled in my chest. I loved his true smile. It was probably the most beautiful thing about him. When his dimples were on full display and the small crinkles by his eyes showed. Just... God.

He took a step forward so his back wasn't pressed against the door anymore, and the gap between us was almost nonexistent. His arms went around my neck as his face moved closer to mine. "You were actually worried that I had feelings for Niall?" He chuckled, playing with the hairs at the back of my neck.

I shrugged my shoulders again. "I was positive you didn't, but you can never be too sure, now can you?"

He shook his head in amusement, leaning in to ghost his lips over mine. "Well, for your information, I like you and only you. You're the only one I have feelings for," he said, kissing me quickly before pulling away again.

My lips tingled by his touch, and the fact that he was being such a tease made me want to back him up against the door again and ravish him, but of course I didn't. That would be rather inappropriate.

Instead, I wrapped my arms around his waist, moving my hands under his shirt to rest them against his bare hips. "I hate it when you're trying to be a tease," I muttered, rubbing my nose against his in an Eskimo kiss.

A cheeky smile formed on his lips as he nudged his nose against mine. "Why don't you do something about it then?"

I decided to back him up against the wall anyway, this time with more force than the last time. "Maybe I should," I said, closing the distance between the two of us once again.

With determination, I moved my lips against his pink, plump ones. They were soft, yet a little chapped from the cold weather outside. I mean, there was snow outside, so whose lips were not chapped right now?

He responded by biting down on my bottom lip, making me let out a loud moan. I knew he was trying to enter my mouth with his tongue, but when he swiped it along my lip, I declined him. He seemed frustrated by this because he let out a low grunt, to which I chuckled.

"Two can play at this game, darling," I joked, making him pull back for a second to give me a glare.

"Have I ever told you that I hate you?"

I leaned in to press our lips together again. "Too bad I know you don't," I mumbled against his mouth, running my tongue along his bottom lip this time. It didn't even take a second until he granted me access, letting my tongue enter his mouth. I wanted to laugh at his eagerness but decided against it. I didn't want to ruin this moment.

Our tongues fought for dominance for a few seconds until I won and explored every inch of his mouth. He let out a deep moan as I dug my fingers into his skin, probably creating marks but I couldn't care at this point. It was getting really hot and I wondered for how long I could keep going until I would get a little too excited.

I could tell Harry was starting to think the same thing because his lips started moving a little slower against mine. However, it was still very hot, and I knew that if I didn't stop now, things would have to go further and that could not happen here. Not in the janitor's closet at school.

Pulling back only to the point where our faces were still very close but our lips not touching, I looked into his wonderful, green eyes. "We're probably very late for class," I mumbled, making him chuckle.

"Yeah, probably."

None of us moved, though, not for an entire minute. We rarely had time for these kinds of moments. Well, 'time' wasn't probably the best word to put it, but more like 'the opportunity'. This fact made neither of us want it to end. I could have been in here with him for the rest of the day if other things weren't waiting for us.

"Alright, we should probably go now," Harry finally said, and I nodded in agreement.

"You go first?" I asked.

"Sure." He was just about to turn around and leave when I put a hand on his shoulder.

"Are you feeling any better now?" My voice was filled with sincerity, and I hope he noticed that.

He grimaced but nodded his head nonetheless. "Yeah, you made me get on better thoughts." It was probably not meant to sound cheeky since he was being serious, but his words didn't exactly sound innocent, which was the reason for my smile.

"I'm glad to hear that," I said, leaning in to give him one last kiss on the lips before he left, closing the door behind him.

I ran my hand through my feathery hair and took a deep breath as I stared at the closed door. I was starting to think that I had more than just strong feelings for that guy. What I felt for Harry was a lot more special than I ever thought it would be. The way I cared about him and got worried about him... I had never felt that way about anyone before. People knew me as the bad guy, the one who was cold-hearted and mean to people, but I certainly did not act like that guy right now.

Harry did things to me, things I had never felt or experienced before. I mean, sure, I had never been rude to

Eleanor, but I had never really cared about her the way I cared about Harry. He was something else, something very special.

After a minute of thinking, I finally exited the janitor's closet and headed to my locker to grab my books.

I hadn't even taken ten steps until I could feel someone stare at me, though. I turned to my left, only to see... no one. There was barely anyone in the hallway, but the feeling of being observed was really strong. The weird thing was that I couldn't see that anyone was watching me no matter how many times I turned around.

Feeling a little uneasy, I put my hands in the pockets of my jean jacket and continued my way to my locker. The weird feeling of being watched wouldn't leave my mind, though. It felt like someone was following me, but whenever I checked, there was no one there. I tried to be quick, but despite that, the feeling didn't leave me until I stepped into the History classroom.

The question was; was I just being very stupid or was someone really observing me? And if it was the latter, what did they want?

Chapter 32

[Louis]

Throughout the rest of that week, there were many times I had the same strange feeling that someone was observing me. It only occurred when I was at school, though, and not when I was somewhere else. I knew it could be that I was just overreacting because many people were going to our school, so anyone could be watching me without there really being a reason behind it.

I couldn't help but feel like this situation was different, though. It was more like someone was creepily observing me, and that would not have been the case if it was just some random student who was watching me in the hallway.

Even though it bugged me quite a lot, I hadn't told anyone about it. Not that I felt ashamed of it... Okay, maybe a little, but mostly because I didn't feel the need to tell anyone. I mean, there was nothing there whenever I checked anyway, so why should I even go around and worry about it?

That was not the only thing I was getting worried about, though. It felt like Gemma had started getting more observant in the last couple of days as well. Whenever we all ate together, she would look between me and Harry suspiciously. And it wasn't just in the kitchen this would happen, but whenever Harry and I were in the same room as her. It was making me nervous, and it only added to the list of why Harry and I should be more careful about our relationship.

However, when I mentioned this to Harry, he didn't seem very pleased, and I understood him. We didn't have much of a love life as it was now, and I wanted us to spend even less time together? Well, I didn't want it, but you got my point. We had to be careful, and I had been very clear with that ever since the start.

It was now Friday afternoon, and today, we were actually going out for dinner. It was something we hadn't done ever since what happened the last time we did. I guess neither dad nor Anne wanted a repeat of the disaster that went down then, so that was probably why they hadn't bothered to plan another family dinner at a restaurant. Not until now, that was.

I was currently lying on my bed, going through my phone while waiting for us to leave. As far as I knew, Harry was in his own room across the hallway, doing God knows what, but I had a feeling he was on his phone as well.

To say I was excited about going out would be a lie because I wasn't exactly looking forward to pretending that I hated Harry. It was actually something that I had started finding more difficult to do around our family, and I honestly wasn't sure if I could last an entire evening without showing my feelings for him. It would definitely be a hard task, which I was not looking forward to.

What I was looking forward to, however, was the opportunity to be around Harry. Usually, we couldn't be too close to each other since we were considered enemies, and it would be weird if we were seen together by our parents, but now that we didn't have any other choice, it was very nice and appreciated, even if we couldn't show how much we actually liked each other.

I looked at the time on my phone, noticing that it was only five minutes until we were leaving. Knowing Anne, she would get mad if I didn't show up on time. A few weeks ago, I wouldn't have cared whatsoever about her opinion, but ever since things had started changing between me and Harry, I had begun accepting my new family more and more. I was starting to become happy for my dad that he had moved on from mom, but I hadn't fully accepted it yet, which I wasn't sure that I would ever do.

A minute later, I decided to get up from my bed to put on my jean jacket, which I wore almost every day. I then checked myself in the mirror, going over my outfit in the process; my skinny, black, ripped jeans and my black t-shirt. The ends of my pants were unfolded at the ends, just like I always had them, and my hair was a little disheveled thanks to the pillow. I ran my hands through it a few times in hopes of it getting better, which it did a little.

Once I decided I was finished, I exited my room. The second I closed the door behind me, Anne's voice could be heard from downstairs; "Harry, Louis, Gemma, we're leaving now!"

"Good thing I'm here then," I smirked as I entered the entryway, where both dad and Anne were shrugging on their jackets.

When Anne turned to meet my gaze, a wide smile formed on her lips. "Wow, I'm proud of you, son."

I chuckled at her words before walking over to slip on my Vans. The second I was finished, another voice could be heard, a voice that I had come to know very well these past few weeks, and also a voice that made butterflies erupt in my stomach. Looking up, I met Harry's eyes for a split second, and that was all that was needed for my heart to skip a beat. God, I hated what that boy did to me.

"I'm here too," he said, turning to dad and Anne.

They both looked a bit surprised. Not because Harry usually was late, but because Gemma was the last one to arrive. Usually, I was last if you couldn't tell that already. However, it didn't take more than half a minute until the brown-haired girl joined us in the entryway, a small smile playing on her lips.

"Alright, then we're all ready to go, and we're on time for once," Anne let out happily, clapping her hands together.

I wanted to laugh at her excitement but decided against it because I would usually not do it, and I couldn't act all too different from what I usually did.

We all exited the house and got into the car. Of course we were sitting exactly like we did the last time we went out together, meaning that Harry's thigh was pressed against mine again. Only this time, it was even more suffocating because if we had been alone, I could have easily touched it without any problem, but now that we weren't, it was forbidden.

I bit my lip, glancing at the side of his face to see if he was reacting to our bodies touching too. Considering he was clenching his defined jaw pretty tightly, I assumed he was, and maybe that shouldn't have made me happy, but it did because it relaxed me knowing I wasn't the only one suffering from the situation.

From the corner of my eye, I could see Gemma observing us, or that was what it felt like, at least. Not that she was staring at us openly, but she was glancing our way every so often as if she was expecting something to happen between us. It made me uncomfortable, but I tried not to be affected by it.

To get on better thoughts and stop thinking about Harry's damn thigh pressed against my own, I fished my phone from my pocket. I had received a text from Eleanor, one where she asking if I had any plans after school on Monday. I could feel Harry glancing at the screen, and judging by the way he tensed, I assumed he wasn't very pleased with what the text said.

I was glad that I actually had a good excuse this time. I had practice on Mondays, and I was surprised she didn't know about this. She usually knew when I had practice, but I guess she had forgotten about it or something this time.

As I typed out the text, I thought about the fact that I should just stop doing all this. It wasn't very fair to Harry that I had a 'girlfriend' when I was with him. He wasn't with anyone else. Or, at least not anymore, so I shouldn't be either, but I couldn't help but feel like we were being uncareful if one of us wasn't 'dating' someone else. It was a dilemma, and I didn't know what to do about it.

Once the car came to a halt, I breathed out a sigh of relief, knowing I had made the whole ride without touching Harry in a way I shouldn't. We walked into the restaurant and judging by the looks of it, it seemed to be an Italian one. I could feel my stomach grumble just at the thought of it. I loved Italian food.

We sat down at a table, waiting for the waiter to arrive and hand us the menu. Dad and Anne sat down beside each other while Gemma, Harry and I settled down opposite them. It was just my luck that I ended up next to Harry, wasn't it? Fuck.

A minute later, a girl dressed in a short, black dress showed up. Her brown hair was tied in a messy bun, and according to me, she was wearing a little too much makeup, but I wasn't surprised because it felt like a lot of girls in this business usually went a little over the top. Not that I was judging her because of that.

"Here's the menu. I'll be back in a minute when you've decided what you want to eat and drink," she informed politely, her gaze sticking to Harry for a second. He didn't notice it, though, because he was too busy looking over the menu.

I wanted to laugh at the scene but contained myself because I didn't want to gain anyone's attention. It was quite hilarious, though, how he didn't even notice her. With a pout, she left our table and disappeared into the kitchen.

"I can't believe you just did that," Gemma laughed, looking at her brother.

He tore his gaze from the menu to glance up at her. "What do you mean?" He asked in confusion.

She put on a 'duh' face. "That waitress totally just checked you out, but you had your eyes glued to the damn menu. Talk about dissing people."

He still looked confused, his gaze wandering to his mum, who nodded her head in confirmation. "Gem's right. She was totally checking you out, son," she chuckled, and I could feel myself starting to become a little uncomfortable about the situation.

He just shrugged, though, and didn't seem fazed by it at all. "She probably wasn't anything special."

When he said that, he subtly placed a hand on my thigh, giving it a light squeeze. The gesture made me smile, and it also prevented me from opening my mouth to say something I shouldn't. If that were to happen, things would probably not have ended well.

On the other side of Harry, I could see how Gemma had her eyes narrowed as she was glancing at me. It was as if she was expecting something. A reaction maybe? Either way, I didn't like it, and I found myself swallowing hard, hoping that I wasn't showing any emotion whatsoever on my face.

When the waitress returned to get our orders, she showed her liking for Harry even more, much to my dismay. She openly winked at him when he told her what he wanted to have, and fluttered her eyelashes. It was ridiculous if you asked me, yet I couldn't help but react to it. Not that I made a scene, but I could feel anger boil up within me. I was very aware that Harry was beautiful, but could she at least try to be a little less obvious about her infatuation?

It was a relief that Harry didn't seem to show any interest in her, though. He just smiled at her politely and treated her like he would treat any other waitress or waiter. It calmed me down quite a lot, to be honest.

When it was my turn to order, you could probably cut the tension with a knife. Not that she seemed to dislike me since she obviously didn't know that I had a thing going on with her new love interest, but because I was being so tense.

"I'd like a coke and the Pasta Carbonara," I said, not bothering to be polite by adding the word 'please' in the end.

From across the table, I could feel dad shoot me a look of disapproval. Now I was definitely happy that he was used to seeing me be quite rude around our family. Otherwise, he would have probably been just as suspicious as Gemma was opposite him.

"Eh, alright. I'll be right back with your orders in a short while," the waitress informed us a little uncomfortably.

Anne smiled at her, and so did my dad. Once she was gone, dad opened his mouth to speak, but Gemma beat him to it. "May Harry, Louis and I please be excused for a second?" She asked, getting up before either dad or Anne had even said anything.

Dad closed his mouth slowly, nodding his head while seeming a bit confused. "Sure."

Anne looked surprised as well but didn't comment on it. I got up from my seat stiffly, knowing that this would not end well. I could tell Harry was thinking the same thing judging by the emotionless look on his face. We both knew that Gemma wasn't about to ask us something as simple as what we had done at school today. This was about something more serious than that.

Harry and I followed her to a secluded area in the restaurant where nobody was sitting. Checking our surroundings to see if the coast was clear, Gemma crossed her arms over her chest. "Alright, it's time to come clean, boys. I already know that something is going on between the two of you, but I want to hear it coming from you guys," she said, raising an eyebrow she flicked her gaze between us.

I glanced at Harry, noticing that he was already looking at me nervously. I bit my lip, turning my gaze back to Gemma. "Fuck," was the only thing I said, letting out a sigh.

And 'fuck' was the perfect word for the situation. This was not supposed to happen. Not today, not ever. No one was supposed to find out. Harry and I's relationship was supposed to be a secret forever. If this happened, I could lose everything. I could lose my dad and hell, I could even lose Harry in the process. That was if Gemma didn't keep her mouth shut, and we all knew how good she was at doing that.

I could tell Harry waited for me to answer her. He knew that this bothered me more than it did him, so there was no question that he wanted me to handle the situation, maybe even for his own best, so he wouldn't say something I didn't want him to say.

"Fine," I finally admitted. "Harry and I do have something going on."

A cheeky grin formed on her pink lips. "That's what I wanted to hear."

Harry raised an eyebrow at her. "What do you mean by that?" He asked, and I was just as curious as him about it.

Putting a hand on her hip, she gave him a look. "I mean that it's been quite obvious that you're a lot more than 'enemies', but I thought you would deny it considering how hard you've been trying to hide it. But I mean, do you seriously think I didn't notice that you had just been making out that time when I walked in on the two of you in the kitchen? And it was pretty obvious that the hickey on your neck, Harry, was newly made and didn't come from some guy named Niall," she chuckled, rolling her eyes as if it had all been obvious from the start. "And don't even get me started on how tense Louis became when that waitress flirted with you just a minute ago."

The curly-haired boy seemed speechless beside me while I ran my hands over my face, feeling nothing but exposed. What if everyone could see through our facade? What if Gemma wasn't the only one knowing or being suspicious about us? This was not good. This was not good at all.

When she noticed that neither of me or Harry was saying anything, she put her hands up in surrender. "Oh, don't misunderstand me here. I'm happy for you guys. Actually, I'm more than happy. To be quite honest, you make a really hot couple. Sure, I haven't exactly shown that I like you, Louis, but that was because you treated my brother pretty badly back in the days. However, now that he doesn't seem to dislike you anymore, I don't see a reason for me to do so either."

Harry furrowed his eyebrows. "You mean that you don't think it's weird that we're dating?" He asked incredulously.

She shrugged, not seeming to be bothered by it whatsoever. "I mean, sure, you live under the same roof and are kind of stepbrothers, but no, I don't really find it weird. If anything is weird, it is that you two hated each other only a month ago, and now you are lovers," she laughed.

I swallowed hard, sneaking another glance at the curly-haired boy whose cheeks had now turned a light pink color. "Eh, okay..." He trailed off, scratching the back of his neck.

"Alright, we should probably head back to mom and Troy now. I'm pretty sure the food is arriving at any second," she said, turning around to go back to our table, but Harry grabbed her wrist before she could do so.

"Please, Gemma, don't tell anyone about this, alright? And definitely not mom and Troy. They would absolutely flip shit if they found out and probably tell us to break up or something even worse. Just promise me to keep quiet, can you do that?" Harry pleaded, looking at her with puppy eyes.

She seemed a bit confused but shrugged her shoulders nonetheless. "Sure, I don't see a reason for me to expose you to anyone anyway."

Harry nodded. "Just, please be careful about it because it could ruin quite a lot, alright?"

She rolled her eyes. "Alright, Harry. I promise to be careful. I won't make the same mistake I did last time, happy?" When he gave her another quick nod, she smiled at him before going over to where dad and Anne were sitting and discussing something.

When Harry was about to follow her, I grabbed a hold of his arm and pulled him into the toilets, making sure to lock the stall behind us so no one could interrupt us. His back was against the door while I was standing right in front of him, looking him in the eyes. Before I could open my mouth to start talking, though, he put a finger on my lips.

"Wait, let me speak first," he pleaded, and when I gave him a nod, he continued. "I know what you're going to say. You're going to say that we should be more careful, that we shouldn't even look at each other in public and even try not to be around one another in our house. Or even worse, you're going to say that we should call it quits and stop doing this. But you know what? I won't let you do that. I won't," he said determinedly, crossing his arms over his chest.

Letting out a sigh, I ran a hand through my feathery, brown hair. I then took a step forward, reaching up to push a stray curl behind his ear. "Maybe I was going to say that, but you have to understand, Harry. This is not good. It's not good at all. If your sister found out about it, it's just a matter of time until our parents will as well. I just can't see that this is going to end well, but I don't know what to do. I like you so much, more than you probably know, but I just... I just don't know," I said frustratingly.

He wrapped his arms around my neck, pulling me even closer to him. "Then don't think about it, and just let it all happen. You don't have to put so much thought into everything. If something that shouldn't happen happens, then we'll figure it out, alright? But don't leave me. Just please, whatever you do, don't leave me," he pleaded, his green eyes looking so soft and beautiful that I had to take a deep breath.

Leaning in, I pressed a light kiss on his lips, lingering for a few seconds before pulling away. "I promise I won't leave you. I'm not even sure I would be able to," I admitted.

He sent me a small smile. "That's what I wanted to hear."

"But, we still need to be more careful," I reminded him. "We're not safe out there, and for all we know, there could be more people that are suspicious about us. During the last couple of days, I've had a feeling that someone's been watching me, and I don't know what it is, but it's something. We are not safe anywhere."

Even if he sighed, he nodded. "Got it."

"Now, let's go eat some good ol' pasta, shall we?" I smiled, trying to lighten the mood a little.

And seeing as he chuckled, I assumed I had succeeded. "We shall," he agreed, and together, we exited the toilets and went back to our family.

What we didn't know, though, was that we hadn't been alone in there, but how were we supposed to know that? We were just discussing some things, things that no one else was supposed to hear.

Chapter 33

[Harry]

As expected, the food was already on the table when we returned to our seats. Judging by the steam that was coming from it, it couldn't have been too long since it arrived, though, but mum and Troy didn't seem very pleased with the fact that we had been gone for so long anyway.

"Where have you two been? I hope you didn't disappear just to bicker with one another. This was meant to be a nice and cozy dinner, and then you just walk off like that," mum said disappointingly, shaking her head.

I gave her an apologetic look. "We weren't bickering, mum. When Gemma was done talking to us, we just had to visit the bathroom," I lied, turning to Gemma to give her a pointed look.

She nodded her head frantically. "Yeah, didn't I say that when I came back? They just had to use the toilet quickly."

Troy furrowed his eyebrows. "I thought you said they were coming in a minute because they had something to discuss?" He asked in confusion.

Wow, great Gemma. You're already doing so great with not trying to expose us...

She scratched the back of her neck awkwardly. "Yeah, they were going to discuss something in the bathroom, that's what I meant," she tried to save herself, but Troy looked very skeptical, and I didn't blame him.

"Well, it's not like it matters anyway. We're here now and the food hasn't even gone cold, so let's dig in, shan't we?" Louis suggested, but you could hear the slight tone of panic in his voice.

Mum nodded her head in agreement. "Yeah, Louis' probably right. Let's put this behind us, but I don't want this to repeat itself, alright?"

Louis and I nodded our heads quickly. After that, we all dug into our food, which was nothing but delicious. I had ordered a pizza Margherita, and the Italian version of it was just the best. I absolutely loved it, and judging by the silence that stayed during the entire dinner, I was certain I wasn't the only one enjoying my food. There were a lot of 'mm's' coming from my family members' mouths, which only added to my assumptions.

When the food was gone, the same waitress that served our food returned to our table. This time, I was aware of the attention she was giving me, but I wasn't interested. I didn't want to seem rude about it, though, so I just smiled back at her and tried to act civil.

"Did you enjoy the food?" She asked hopefully, flicking her gaze between all five of us, but stopped at me.

We all nodded our heads. "Yeah, it was absolutely delicious. There's no question that we'll be coming back, right guys?" Troy said.

"Definitely, it was amazing," Mum agreed, giving the girl a wide smile.

"What about you?" She asked me, batting her eyelashes expectantly. "What did you think?"

I raised my eyebrows, slightly surprised that she had spoken to me, although I probably shouldn't be. "Uh, yeah, the pizza was very great. I'll definitely come back to this place sometime."

She let out a small chuckle. "I hope it's not just for the pizzas," she winked.

Laughing dryly, I shook my head. "Yeah, sure."

From the corner of my eye, I could see Louis roll his eyes. "We're ready to take the note, please," he said, not even looking at her as he did so. I may also add that his voice sounded a bit flat.

To be quite honest, I found it entertaining when Louis was jealous. I mean, that meant he really did have feelings for me. Not that I doubted it, but it was always nice to have it confirmed. Additionally, it was definitely a turn on that he acted all grumpy just because a girl was flirting with me.

"Oh, alright," she said apologetically, handing Troy the note, who had already fished his wallet from his pocket.

After that, we all got up to leave the restaurant and go home. During the entire ride, Louis stayed quiet, and I wondered if it was because he was still grumpy because of the waitress, or if it was because of something else. Maybe it was due to what happened earlier at the restaurant when Gemma had wanted to talk to us? No matter what, he didn't say anything to me throughout the rest of that day. When we got home, he went straight to his room and stayed there for the rest of the evening.

I tried not to care about it, but I couldn't deny the fact that I was disappointed. He was kind of my boyfriend after all. It wasn't weird that I wanted to see and talk to him, right?

However, when I went to bed, I checked my phone before turning off the lamp and noticed that I had received a text from him.

Sweet dreams, love. See you tomorrow x

During the entire weekend, Louis stayed rather quiet and mostly kept himself away from us. There was no longer any doubt that it had to do with the fact that Gemma had found out about us because I was sure he wouldn't still be grumpy about that waitress. I mean sure, he could get jealous, but not like this.

Additionally, he didn't speak very much to me either. As lame as he was, he sent me these stupid text messages instead, which I found nothing but stupid. We lived under the same roof for Goodness sake. Why couldn't he just talk to me if he wanted to tell me something? It wasn't like mum or Troy would find out he had come to my room just to talk anyway. I didn't mean to be annoyed by it, but I couldn't help it. His way of being careful was a step too far, and I hoped he would figure that out soon.

When Monday finally rolled around, I got ready for school like always. Today, I went for a dark grey long-sleeved shirt with a pair of black, skinny jeans that were ripped at the knees. The shirt was probably a little too big, but I felt comfortable in these clothes, which was the reason I wanted to wear them. Who cared what everyone else thought anyway?

Louis wasn't in the kitchen when I arrived, but Gemma was. She was sitting at the kitchen table, munching on some cereal while reading something on her phone. "Morning, Gem," I greeted, letting out a loud yawn.

She took her eyes off her phone to look at me. "Morning, bro. Where do you have your boyfriend, eh?" She joked, making me roll my eyes.

"First off, he isn't my boyfriend. Second off, I don't know. I have barely seen him during the entire weekend," I replied grumpily, walking over to sit down opposite her.

She tilted her head to the side, looking at me a bit sympathetically. "Don't worry about it, Haz. He'll come around. I think he's just trying to adapt to the fact that I know about the two of you, don't you think?"

I nodded my head curtly. "Yeah, I hope so. Not to sound lame or anything, but I kind of miss him," I muttered, reaching forward to snatch some cereal from the box.

An understanding smile formed on her pink lips. "I get it. I mean, look at me. I haven't seen Devon since Friday because he's been away with his family, and I miss him like crazy."

Rolling my eyes, I let out a chuckle. "Yeah, but I have *seen* Louis. It's just that he hasn't acknowledged me in the way he usually does if you know what I mean?"

She reached forward to place a hand over mine, just like my mother usually did. "I know what you mean, brother, I do," she promised, the smile still prominent on her lips.

Before I could open my mouth to reply, the third teenager in the family entered the kitchen. His brown fringe was brushed to the side, something I loved when it was, and his eyes looked unusually alert for being this early in the morning. He was wearing a white, almost see-through t-shirt and a pair of black, skinny jeans. They looked almost like my own apart from the holes in the knees.

Just like always, I found him breathtaking. He always made my stomach do summersaults and my heart skip a beat. I wondered if that feeling would ever disappear. I certainly hoped not because it was a wonderful feeling.

"Morning," he greeted, giving us a small smile. He strode over to the fridge to pull out the butter and some ham.

I, on the other hand, couldn't help but feel a little bit disappointed. Not that I had expected it, but it wouldn't have hurt if he at least greeted me a little more affectionately. I mean, Gemma already knew that we had something going on, so it wasn't like we had to hide from her anymore. But, this was Louis after all, I had to remind myself that.

When he turned his back to us to spread some butter on a slice of bread, Gemma dropped her spoon in her bowl. "Now, that is not the way you greet your boyfriend, brother from another mother," Gemma pointed out, getting up to put the empty bowl in the sink beside him. "Go give him some loving because he hasn't gotten much of that lately, now has he?"

If looks could kill, Gemma would be dead right now. I could take care of myself. I didn't need her to tell Louis how to treat me, thank you very much. "Gemma, go away," I grumbled, getting up to practically push her out of the room.

"Alright, I'll leave the two of you alone, but don't do anything I wouldn't, yeah?"

With a sigh, I ran my hand over my face. "Just go before I kick you out of the house."

She gave me a cheeky smile before turning around to walk to the entryway. "Sure, and you can thank me later."

I rolled my eyes, turning around to grab a bowl from one of the cabinets. That was when I noticed that Louis was looking at me with raised eyebrows, an almost cheeky grin playing on his lips. "You think I haven't shown affection towards you lately, yeah?" He asked.

Shrugging, I looked down at my feet. "It's just... You have barely acknowledged me since dinner Friday night. I just... I missed you, as stupid as that sounds," I admitted, looking up at him almost shamefully.

He took a step forward to wrap his arms around my waist, pulling me towards him. "Well, if you didn't notice by my texts, I missed you too," he said, leaning forward to give my lips a light, affectionate kiss.

It made butterflies erupt in my stomach, and I had to bite my tongue not to smile wide. "Yeah, definitely missed that," I whispered, almost inaudibly.

When I came back to my right senses, a frown appeared between my eyebrows. "Why did you send me those texts when you could've just come into my room and talked to me?"

He let out a sigh, looking away. "You already know why, Harry. I have to try and get used to not having to be around you. Otherwise, I'll soon go around and show my feelings for you in school, and that wouldn't be good. It wouldn't be good at all."

"So, what you're saying is that you did it because you're afraid you'll get too attached to me?" I laughed, reaching up to trace the crinkle by his eye with my thumb.

He nodded his head. "Pretty much, yeah. Remember what I told you? You have no idea how much I like you. My feelings for you are so fucking strong, which means I need to have control over myself. The thing is, when I'm with you, I lose it completely, and if that were to happen at the wrong time and place, bad things will happen. That's why I distanced myself from you a little," he confessed. "But you have no idea how much I missed you," he whispered, getting closer to my face again.

"So much that you'll take a break from it for a while?" I asked hopefully, looking deep into his eyes.

"Yeah, maybe for a short while."

And with that said, he closed the distance between us once again, and well, let's just say we almost missed the bus that morning, but it wasn't like anyone knew the reason why anyway.

It was lunchtime, and Liam and I were sitting at a table in the cafeteria, munching on our cheese and ham sandwiches. Across the room, Louis was sitting next to a laughing Eleanor and some of his teammates. Zayn was sitting with them today as well, and that was something I found quite fascinating about Liam and Zayn's relationship.

They didn't need to be around each other every second of the day to be happy and satisfied. They still had time to hang out with their separate friends when they wanted to, and that was something I appreciated. It wasn't like I disliked Zayn, but sometimes it was nice to only have Liam around, just like old times.

Today was a great example because we were currently talking about Niall and his reaction to what I had confessed a few days ago. That was something we couldn't have spoken about if Zayn had been with us since he was unaware of what had happened. Furthermore, we could talk about Louis, which was something I found relieving since I couldn't talk about him with anyone else... apart from Gemma now, that was.

Speaking of Niall, he was sitting at a table together with Ed and a few other guys. Lately, he and Ed seemed to have gotten quite close to each other. Not that they hadn't been close before, but ever since I called it off with Niall, they had hung out more than I'd ever seen them do before. I wondered why that was.

"So, he took it pretty well then?" Liam asked, gulping down some water from his bottle.

"Yeah, I mean sure, he was sad, which is nothing but understandable, but otherwise, I think he took it pretty well, yeah."

He supported his head with one of his hands under his chin. "Hm, I wonder why that is. I mean, there was no doubt he had quite deep feelings for you. You should've seen the way he looked at you, man," he said, looking a bit confused.

I shrugged. "I mean, he did ask me if I had feelings for someone else. Maybe he already suspected that I didn't like him back?" I wondered out loud.

"Yeah..." Liam trailed off, turning his gaze towards the table where the blonde-haired guy was sitting.

I hadn't really seen much of him since that day, but whenever we met eyes, he would give me a weak smile. It pained me to see that he was still hurt, but I also knew that it was for the best. He would find someone that liked him just as much as he liked me one day, I was sure of it.

Liam and I continued talking about everything and nothing and were so caught up in our conversation that neither of us noticed that Ed was standing next to us all of a sudden. His head was tilted to the side as he looked at us hopefully. "So, there's a party at my place on Friday. Are you coming?"

Liam and I exchanged a look, my mouth still open from talking to him. "Eh..." Liam trailed off.

"Friday?" I asked. "Uh, we'll think about it, right Liam?"

He nodded his head slowly, probably surprised by the sudden interruption. "Sure. I'm just gonna check with Zayn and--"

"Oh, Zayn is already coming, and so is probably the entire football team. I hope to see you there, guys," he winked before walking off again.

Liam turned to me with a raised eyebrow. "Well, that was..."

"Weird," I finished, letting out a laugh.

He joined me, nodding his head. "Yeah, definitely weird."

"Are you going, though?" I asked, taking the last bite of my sandwich.

He shrugged. "I guess so. I mean, Zayn is, so I'll probably go there with him. Are you?"

"I don't know. It depends..." I trailed off, biting my bottom lip.

A cheeky smile formed on my best friend's lips. "It depends whether Louis' going to be there or not, aren't I right?" He chuckled, making my cheeks turn pink.

"Maybe," I mumbled, making him laugh even harder.

"I don't blame you, mate. I don't blame you."

"This is getting ridiculous," I groaned loudly as I walked home from the bus stop that day. Louis had practically sprinted off the bus to create some distance between us on our way home. I hated it even if I respected his need of being careful.

When we were getting close to the house, I decided to quicken my steps, though, and catch up with him. It wasn't until then I noticed that he had a lit cigarette between his lips, making my eyebrows knit together. Without thinking twice, I pulled it out of his mouth and threw it on the ground. "I thought you had quit smoking," I muttered, making him roll his eyes.

"I never told you I had quit. I just told you I've stepped down on it," he replied, looking ahead of himself instead of meeting my gaze.

Letting out a sigh, I dropped the topic... for now. It wasn't necessary to argue about that at this second. "Are you going to Ed's party on Friday?" I asked instead to change the subject.

He shrugged. "I guess. Everyone else is going, so I might as well too. Why are you asking?"

"Well, Ed came over at lunch and asked me and Liam if we wanted to come, so I was just wondering if you were going," I explained crossing my arms over my chest in order to keep myself as warm as I could in this cold weather.

To my surprise, he turned to me abruptly, looking at me almost angrily. "You're not going to that party, Harry," he growled, making me confused.

"Why not?" I asked, not getting why he was angry at this fact.

"Because... because if you'll be there, I know I wouldn't be able to control myself, especially not with alcohol in my system. I'd expose us without a doubt, that's why."

This time it was my turn to pull my eyebrows together. "That's a bad excuse, Louis. Of course you'll be able to stay away from me. You're already pretty good at it," I muttered, walking ahead of him to unlock the front door. Maybe I did because I was a little upset too.

I could hear him coming up behind me as my hand was on the handle. "Harry, I mean it," he said, the coldness still evident in his voice. "You don't want to be there. And as far as I know, you don't even like parties."

Opening the door to step into the warmth of the house, I turned to him, waiting until he had closed the door to start talking. "It doesn't matter whether I like parties or not, I wanted to go there. Ed is my friend and it's been quite some time since I was at a party. Sure, maybe I don't like to get drunk off my ass, but I like to hang out with my friends and just have some fun. If you don't want me to be there, then fine. Stay away from me then. As I said before, you're already pretty good at it, so it's not like it's going to be a problem," I muttered, making a move to turn around and take off my jacket, but Louis stopped me by grabbing my arm and pulling me towards him.

His nose was almost touching mine all of a sudden while his eyes were looking deep into my own. "I don't like the tone you're using," he said, making me roll my eyes. "But fine, you win. Go to the party if that's what you want so badly, but don't expect to see me if that's what you had in mind. I'll stay away, and believe me, I'm doing it for both of us. You wouldn't want me to be near you when I'm drunk," he almost threatened.

I let out a dry chuckle. "What? You think you would rape me or something, is that what you're saying?"

He didn't join my laughter but looked at me severely. "This isn't funny, Harry. Of course I wouldn't rape you, but I wouldn't be able to stay away from you, that's what I'm saying. I'd expose us to the entire school and then it would be over. We would be over," he explained, looking me deep in the eyes.

I gulped, nodding my head slowly. "Alright, I understand. But I will be there no matter what. If I won't see you, then that's fine. I have other people I want to see at the party."

He raised his eyebrows, tightening the grip he had on my hips. "Like who?"

I got even closer to him, leaning in to whisper in his ear. "Well, I know for a fact that Miranda likes to party..." I trailed off, moving my lips along his neck.

I leaned back to see the look on his face and let out a laugh at the way he had his jaw clenched tightly. "I'm just kidding. I'll probably hang out with Liam and Zayn," I winked, kissing his chapped lips that didn't move against mine whatsoever.

"I hate you," he muttered under his breath, making me snort.

"I know you don't."

Chapter 34

[Harry]

The next two days were pretty uneventful. Louis stayed pretty distant, but he thankfully eased up more and more each day that went by. Monday evening, he even came into the bathroom when I was there to get ready for sleep. We brushed our teeth in silence, looking at each other through the mirror the entire time we did so. It wasn't until we had both put away the toothbrushes that he pushed me to the hard surface of the wall, his body flush against mine as he literally attacked my lips with his own.

It turned out to be one of the better make out sessions we'd shared due to the frustration and desperation in it. You could tell Louis was bothered by the distance between us as well, even if it was his idea in the first place. Yet, I understood him. I just didn't want to hide even if I knew it was necessary.

To say sexual tension was building up between us would be an understatement. We hadn't done anything. We had just had heated make out sessions and touched each other with clothes on, but we hadn't gone any further than that, which was pretty sad if you asked me. It was getting really frustrating, and I wondered if Louis felt the same way. I sure hoped he did because I didn't know how long I would be able to last without something more happening between us.

It was now Thursday morning, and we were all sitting at the kitchen table for once. All five of us rarely ate breakfast together on weekdays since mum and Troy usually went to work early and Louis was a heavy sleeper, but today, mum and Troy were going to some meeting, and Louis was up on time, which was the reason for the special occasion.

Louis was the last one to arrive, though, and judging by the fact that he was just wearing boxers and a wrinkly, white t-shirt, and that his hair was sticking out in every direction, I assumed he had gone straight down here when he had woken up. Although he looked extremely tired, he actually gave me a small smile when no one else was watching, making warmth spread in my chest. I loved it when he acknowledged me like that.

"Morning, Lou," Troy greeted, spreading butter on a slice of toast.

Louis nodded towards him and muttered out a 'morning' in reply. After that, he strode over to the table and sat down opposite me, beside Gemma. There was an empty bowl in front of him, which had been waiting for him to arrive, and if I was the one who had placed it there, no one had to know. He filled it with cereal and milk before bringing a spoonful of it to his mouth.

"Did you sleep well?" Mum asked, munching on her own cereal.

He turned to her. "Yeah, I slept pretty heavily if you couldn't tell already," he laughed, pointing towards his unruly hair.

This caused every one of us to burst into a small fit of laughter. "Yeah, you're right about that," mum replied, giving him a smile.

Troy took a sip of his tea. "Alright, so Anne and I are going out tonight. We're having dinner with the people present at the meeting. I expect you to behave even if I know that all of you don't get along too well," he informed, looking between me and Louis knowingly.

Gemma burst into laughter, covering her mouth to stop the food from slipping out of it. "We'll see about the 'behaving' part, but I'll be staying over at Devon's tonight, so you don't have to worry about me at least."

I wanted to hit her for pointing out that, but I was sure it would only make things more obvious, so instead, I chose to ignore it. However, I couldn't help but blush about it. I knew she wasn't talking about the fact that Louis and I didn't get along but about something completely different.

Louis, on the other hand, glared at her, but thankfully, neither mum nor Troy seemed to catch up on what was going on. "Well, then I expect the two of you not to trash this place, okay?" Troy continued while looking between me and Louis, making Gemma laugh even harder.

"Don't be so sure about that."

This time, I actually stomped her on the foot under the table. She wasn't being funny whatsoever. If anything, she was ruining the facade Louis and I had been trying to keep up. I was pretty sure I could beat her to a pulp at the moment, and judging by the looks of it, Louis was thinking something similar to it. He was angry, there was no doubt about it.

Troy raised an eyebrow, looking a little exasperated about everything. "Well, I want the two of you to behave tonight at least. That's the only thing both Anne and I ask of you today. Can you do that?" He wondered, flicking his gaze between the two of us.

Louis and I exchanged a glance before nodding our heads. "Of course, dad. We promise to behave and not bicker with each other. Who knows? I might even go out in the evening if that makes you feel better," Louis suggested.

I could feel my heart drop at his words. This was our first and probably only chance at being alone together. Why was he suggesting something as stupid as going out? What if Troy would like the idea and agree with it?

Mum waved her hand in dismissal. "You do as you want, son. As long as you two behave, neither of Troy and I care what you do," she said, giving him a smile.

Gemma suppressed another fit of laughter, this time making me glare at her. I hated her right now, I really did.

Louis ignored her and smiled back at mum instead. "We promise not to do anything stupid, right Harry?" He said, giving me a wink which no one but me noticed.

My heart literally stopped beating in my chest at his words. With the straightest look on my face that I could make, I nodded my head. "Of course." I didn't know if any of them noticed anything, but at least they didn't mention it.

"Alright, we believe in you, boys. On a completely different note, I've really got to go now. See you in the afternoon," Troy informed, getting up from his seat. He walked over to kiss mum on the forehead before placing his plate in the sink and leaving the room in a hurry.

Mum smiled to herself before bringing the last spoonful of cereal to her mouth. "I have to go as well, children. I don't want to be late for the meeting. Have a great day at school."

With that said, she got up and brought her bowl along with the butter and cheese to the sink and fridge. She left without another word, and only a minute later, you could hear the door slam shut behind the two parents of the family. The three of us who remained in the kitchen looked at each other, or two of us were glaring at the third, to be more specific.

Gemma gulped at our stares. "I'm out," she said hurriedly, almost knocking the chair to the floor as she got up to leave the room.

"You'd better fucking run!" Louis shouted after her.

And if he hadn't spoken those words, I definitely would have.

Later that day when school was over and mum and Troy were ready to go out to eat dinner, Louis and I were sitting on each end of the couch. The TV wasn't even on. We were just sitting there with our separate phones in our hands. Gemma had already gone to Devon's place while mum and Troy were in the entryway, shrugging on their jackets and slipping on their shoes.

"Louis, Harry, remember what we said earlier," Troy reminded us as he entered the living room. He stopped in the doorframe to lean against it.

Louis looked up from his phone. "Okay, you've got to chill, dad. No one's going to get hurt here, and we promise not to fight each other. I mean, sure, we don't really get along, but we can stay away from one another. It's not that hard, you know?"

Well, if you asked me, it *was* pretty hard to stay away from him.

Troy shot him a small, appreciating smile. "Alright, I should probably stop worrying so much. I trust you guys. I mean, you're even sitting on the same couch right now without bickering. There's probably no need to worry," he said, and you could tell he was trying to convince himself.

I gulped at his words, realizing now that it was quite weird for me and Louis to even be in the same room as each other. I hadn't really thought about it. I mean, we weren't touching, so it didn't seem weird to me.

Judging by the tight smile on Louis' face, he hadn't thought of it either. "Yeah, no need to worry, dad. We'll be alright," he promised.

Troy nodded his head, waving at us. "Well, have a good night then, boys. See you later, I guess."

"You have a good night too, dad," Louis said, smiling at him.

I nodded in agreement. "Yeah, see you later."

With that said, Troy disappeared from the room but was replaced by my mum before Louis and I even had a chance to even exchange a look. She was dressed in a black, sparkling dress that reached her knees. However, her black fur coat was covering the top of it. She looked really good, though, I could give her that.

"I guess Troy has already reminded you of what we talked about at breakfast this morning, so I won't be a bother and repeat it. I wanted to wish you guys a good night, though. See you later in the evening, yeah?" She said, smiling at us.

I nodded my head. "Yeah, yeah. Just go now, mum. Troy's probably waiting on you," I smiled, hearing the front door click shut in the entryway.

She laughed. "Yeah, you're right. Bye guys," she waved before leaving the house with her boyfriend.

When everything finally went silent, Louis and I turned to look at each other. After a second of staring, we burst out laughing, shaking our heads. "I can't believe they seriously think we're going to trash the place by fighting each other," I chuckled.

He wiggled his eyebrows seductively. "We might not trash it by fighting, but we might do it by doing something else."

I couldn't help but blush at his words and look away from his stare. "Shut up," I muttered, lifting my knees to the couch so I could rest my chin against them.

He raised his eyebrows, the smile still prominent on his lips as he crawled his way to my side of the couch. "What? You don't want to?" He questioned, placing his hands on my knees, or on either side of my face, to be more specific.

I lifted my head to get a better look at him, my cheeks still burning from his words. "I never said I didn't want to," I mumbled.

"What was that?" He joked, and by now, his cheeks must be hurting from how wide he was smiling.

I pushed him away from me, making him fall back on the couch. "Stop it," I whined, and he let out a loud laugh.

"I should be the one complaining here. I was just pushed to the couch," he said, trying to sound hurt but didn't manage to do so at all.

Rolling my eyes, I let out a snort. "Well, you deserved it, even though I barely touched you."

He scoffed, lifting himself up to grab a hold of my arms and pull me down so I was lying pretty much on top of him, my face practically pressed against his. I let out an 'uff' at the sudden impact of his chest against mine.

"Well, I think it was rather mean of you."

I let my eyes fall on his lips, and they just looked so appealing right now. I wanted to kiss them so badly, but I wouldn't give in to him that easily. "It wasn't mean. I'm never mean," I mumbled quietly, but since he was so close to me, I could tell he heard it.

His chest vibrated by his laughter, making my body move along with it. One of his hands reached out to tuck a stray curl behind my ear, and a sudden flashback of when he had done the same thing to me without intention in our bathroom a few weeks ago went through my mind, and I couldn't help but smile at the memory. I loved it when he touched my hair.

"I'm pretty sure you could be mean, sweetheart," he winked, leaning in to brush his lips against mine.

When he tried to kiss me for real, though, I pulled away teasingly. A whine that I didn't think even he expected left his mouth, making me laugh. "See, you're being mean," he grumbled.

I pulled back even more, crossing my arms over his chest so I could rest my chin against them as I looked down at him. Tilting my head to the side, I shook my head. "Nah, I'm just being fair. You were making fun of me, so you didn't deserve a kiss," I smiled toothily, making him pout.

"Meanie."

"I should be the one calling you mean, though," I reminded him, making him roll his eyes.

"Would you just shut up and kiss me?"

I squinted my eyes, pretending to think about it. "I don't know, maybe I'll--"

But I was caught off by his lips that closed the gap between our lips. He had pulled me down with the help of his hands that were now on either side of my face and connected our mouths. I let out a moan, instantly giving in to him and letting his scent fill my nostrils. The kiss started slow and rather passionate but turned more eager and desperate after some time.

Our lips moved in sync as if they were two puzzle pieces. His hands traveled down my back until they were playing with the end of my shirt. Not even a second later, his cold fingers were running against my warm skin across my back, his nails scraping it.

Deciding to turn the kiss even more heated, I swiped my tongue along his bottom lip, getting a taste of him. He moaned at the contact and instantly granted me access to his mouth. Our tongues fought for dominance. He didn't want to let me win by giving me the desire to feel like the dominant one, and sadly, he eventually won, exploring my mouth with his tongue.

I could feel my skin tingle where he was touching me, and it didn't make matters better that his hands weren't being still. It made goosebumps on my entire back appear. To get back at him, I reached my hands up to pull at the hairs at the back of his neck. Judging by the moan that escaped his lips, I assumed I had succeeded, which made me smile mentally.

It wasn't until I could feel something hard against my thigh that I realized where this was heading. I didn't know if it was supposed to make me hesitate, but it didn't. It only made me want it more than ever, and it didn't exactly help that I was lying between his legs. If it weren't for our clothes, I couldn't be closer to him.

He pulled away from my lips a little to open his eyes and look into my own. His were darkened with lust, and I could tell mine were as well. I mean, I had been waiting for this moment for so long, how could they not be? Additionally, it was Louis I was doing this with. It was just impossible not to be turned on by him.

"Let's go upstairs," he breathed against my lips, and I didn't trust my voice enough to answer him, so I just nodded in response.

I thought I was heavy, but when he got up from the couch with me clinging to his body like a koala bear, I started doubting it. Or, it could just be that Louis was strong. I leaned towards the latter because I had seen his biceps before.

Our mouths were connected again, and I had to give him credit for managing to bring us upstairs without falling. I mean, he had no idea where he was going or where he put his feet, but somehow, he managed to bring us to his room and kick the door shut behind us. He instantly pushed me against the door, my legs wrapped around his waist as our mouths moved almost desperately against each other.

Heavy pants were escaping us, but neither of us could be bothered with pulling away to breathe. Instead, I moved my hands to his hair and pulled at the roots of it, messing up his entire hairdo, but I was sure he didn't mind right now. In return, he gripped my waist, his nails digging into the skin of my hips as he pressed his hard-on against my own.

Letting out the loudest moan yet, I pressed myself even closer to him, but I couldn't help but think that it wasn't close enough. Louis seemed to think something along the same lines because in the next second, he was pulling at the end of my shirt. "Off," he panted against my lips, and I lifted my arms obediently as he pulled it over my head.

Before I knew it, I was pushed down on his soft bed, the mattress hitting my back. Good thing it was a mattress and not the floor. Otherwise, it would have hurt a lot.

He let his hands discover the skin that was now on full display, his fingers moving along my chest and down to my abdomen. The feeling almost had me squirming. I just loved having his hands on me.

"Fuck, just get out of your damn clothes," I grumbled, reaching down to pull at his own shirt.

He chuckled but did as told, instantly pulling the shirt over his head and kicking off his skinny jeans so he was left in only his boxers. Since he was already taking his clothes off, he took the opportunity to pull off my jeans as well. "Happy?" He asked, raising an eyebrow at me.

I rolled my eyes but let out a chuckle. "More than happy."

"Good," he mumbled before crashing his lips against mine again. They were puffy and wet from our heavy kiss just moments ago, and I loved every second of it, knowing that I was the one who had caused it.

He got in between my legs so my knees were on either side of his hips, our clothed bulges pressing against each other. I let out another moan as he rocked his hips down, my nails digging into the skin on his back. I was probably leaving marks, but I couldn't care less about that right now.

His mouth left mine to move down my jaw, his tongue poking out as he moved all the way down to my neck, leaving a wet trail behind. He started sucking on my skin, and I knew then that I wasn't the only one leaving marks here. The feeling made my toes curl, and my grip on his back only tightened. "God, you're so damn beautiful," he muttered against my neck, his teeth scraping the skin.

He moved down on my body then, leaving kisses on my chest and nipples. The sensation that went through my body by his touch was almost unbearable, that was how good it felt. It made goosebumps form on my exposed skin.

I moved one of my hands to his hair, fisting it as I pulled at the roots once again. Everything was so hot. From the way he was touching me to just the fact that our naked skin moved against each other. It didn't make matters better that we were breathing quite heavily as well. The room was basically a sauna.

Once he started nipping at my hips, I decided that it was enough. I couldn't take this anymore. "Louis, shit. Just get in me already," I moaned, making him chuckle at my words.

He looked up at me, a cheeky smile playing on his lips. "Eager, are we?"

Giving him a glare, I scoffed. "To be honest, I don't really care. I just can't stand you teasing me like this anymore."

He laughed, nodding towards his nightstand. "There's a condom and a bottle of lube in my drawer."

I knitted my eyebrows together at his words. "Why are you keeping that kind of stuff in there?" I asked suspiciously, making him wiggle his eyebrows.

"You never know when you will need it," he winked.

Still very suspicious, I reached for the drawer. "Are you implying that you were expecting this to happen between us soon or that you were planning on using it with someone else?"

I didn't look at him when I said those words, so to say I was taken aback when he was suddenly right in my face the second I turned back would be an understatement. His ocean blue eyes were staring deep into mine, making me gulp at the sincerity in them.

"You think I was planning on using it with someone else?"

I shrugged, feeling weak under his intense stare. "Who knows?"

To my slight surprise, he leaned down to press his lips against mine, but only briefly. "You wanna know something?" He asked, still holding my gaze with his.

I nodded slowly even if I wasn't so sure I wanted to listen to what he had to say.

"You're the only one I want and probably ever will want to do what we're doing right now with."

Even if I wanted to, I couldn't bring myself to form any words. I was speechless, either from his intense stare or his words. It could be both at the same time. One thing I was sure of, though, was that he was speaking the truth. There was no doubt about it.

When he noticed I wasn't going to say anything, he took it as if he had succeeded with his message. "So, now that we're on the same page, are you going to pull the condom and lube out of the drawer, or do you want me to do it?" He asked, raising a questioning eyebrow.

It wasn't until then I realized that I had only opened the drawer but not grabbed either of the said things. My eyes snapped to it, and the next second I pulled them out, handing them to him. I noticed that the mood had basically been killed, but I wasn't any less turned on, though.

"You killed the mood, Louis," I mumbled, making him let out a chuckle.

"You reckon that *I* killed it? I wasn't the one starting to doubt myself," he chuckled, leaning down to pepper kisses along my neck. "But I'm pretty sure we can build it up again, don't you?"

With that said, he rocked his hips down to meet mine. When I let out a deep moan by the friction, he wiggled his eyebrows at me knowingly.

"Have I ever told you I hate you?" I grumbled.

He pretended to think about it. "Only a couple of hundred times."

A smile crept to my lips and he reciprocated it, the crinkles by his eyes on full display. Only a second later, our mouths were connected again, and if any of the kisses we had shared before had been heated and passionate, they couldn't even begin to compare to this one. It didn't take more than a minute until we were at the point we had been before we had our little conversation.

Our lips worked eagerly, tongues swirling together fiercely and hands roaming each other desperately. There was nothing either of us wanted more than one another at this point, but even if we were close to each other, we were still not close enough.

In a matter of seconds, we were both completely naked and Louis was fumbling with the condom, almost shaking from how intense everything was. I nearly laughed at the way he was biting his lip while focusing on opening the foiler but decided against it. I didn't want to ruin the moment like it had almost been ruined before.

Once he finally managed to open it, he rolled the condom on his length. I was gripping his hips as he did this while he was straddling my naked waist. Once it was on, he looked up to meet my eyes, seeing the uncertainty in them.

"You haven't done this before, have you?" He asked.

I shook my head. "Not with a guy, no," I admitted, looking away from him shamefully.

He grabbed my chin so I was forced to stare into his beautiful, blue eyes. "Well, I haven't either, so no need to worry," he reassured me, making me visibly relax. Not that it would have mattered if he had done it with another guy, but it was reassuring to know that I wasn't the only one being new to this.

"I'm sure it's going to hurt like a bitch if we don't prep you, though," he smiled, and yeah, I was pretty aware of that too. I mean, I wasn't that oblivious to gay sex...

To make a point, he reached down to trace his index finger around my rim after coating it with some lube. I tensed a little at the unusual feeling but didn't say anything when his finger entered me. He was slow and sincere at first, which I appreciated. He knew I wasn't used to the feeling and wanted me to relax before doing something else.

It didn't take very long until I ordered him to add another finger, and soon, he was thrusting them into my hole. The pain that was first apparent when he had added the first finger was now gone and was replaced by pleasure and lust.

"Oh my God," I moaned when he hit a certain spot, and I instantly knew he had found my prostate.

"Feels good, yeah?"

I nodded frantically. "So good. God, I think I'm ready," I informed him.

"You sure?" He asked sincerity, wanting to be completely sure that I was speaking the truth.

"Yes, I'm sure," I panted, reaching up to wrap my arms around his neck so I could pull him down for a kiss.

"I want you, and I want you now," I breathed into his mouth, and he didn't need to be told twice.

So with that said, he pulled his fingers out of my bum and lined himself up with my hole after coating himself with some lube. His hands were gripping my biceps pretty firmly as his dick slowly entered me. I gasped at the stretch, reaching down to claw at his back at the feeling. He didn't mind, though, but tried to go even slower to make it more comfortable for me.

Once he had bottomed out, he inhaled a heavy breath and pulled away to look me in the eye. "You okay?"

I nodded reassuringly. "Yeah, I'm okay. You can start moving."

He did as told and pulled all the way out before thrusting back in again. The sensation that went through my body was amazing, the way his length stretched my walls and hit my prostate immediately. I let out a deep moan as he continued thrusting into me, his grip on my biceps becoming tighter by the second.

My legs were wrapped around his waist, my heels digging into his back. The only sounds that could be heard in the room were our heavy pants and our skin slapping as he kept going deeper and deeper inside me. I leaned up in an attempt to connect our lips, but considering our breaths weren't exactly even, it ended up with our lips only touching and our breaths mixing together instead.

As more pleasure entered my body, I could feel myself getting closer to the edge. Heat was building up in my stomach and I knew I wouldn't be able to last much longer. "I'm g-gonna come," I warned him, causing him to pick up an even faster pace.

It was all that was needed for me to spurt my liquids onto my stomach, reaching my high. Only a second later, Louis came into the condom, his body going lax on top of me. It took a few minutes until we could breathe normally again, and that was when he pulled himself up on his forearms that were on either side of my head.

A wide smile was playing at his lips, his eyes sparkling with love and admiration. "You're so beautiful, you know that?"

The way he said it made my cheeks turn pink. I didn't know if it was because it came from nowhere, or if it was just the fact that he said it after we had just had sex that made me react like this, but it warmed my heart to hear those words coming from him. "I don't know about me, but I know someone else who is quite beautiful," I smiled, making him laugh.

He pulled out of me, going slow so it wouldn't hurt me. However, I couldn't help the little whimper that slipped through my lips. Once he had gotten rid of the condom, he leaned down to kiss my mouth. "I'm sorry I hurt you," he apologized.

Rolling my eyes, I shook my head. "Even if it hurt a little, it was definitely worth it. It was the best sex I've ever had," I promised him.

He raised his eyebrows, giving me a cheeky smile. "Best sex with your stepbrother, eh? That's something," he joked, causing me to frown.

"You just ruined the moment, Louis. That sounded gross, ew," I said, scrunching my nose up.

He laughed, nuzzling his nose into my bare neck. "Well, too late to regret it now, isn't it?"

I hit him on the bicep playfully. "Sure, but instead of stepbrother, I'd like to call you my boyfriend..." I trailed off, waiting for his reaction nervously.

I knew that we had just been intimate with each other, but what if he didn't want to be together with me after all?

His body tensed on top of me, and for a second, I started regretting my words really badly. That was until he pulled back from my neck with the widest smile I had probably ever seen on his lips.

"Yeah, I'd like that very much."

Chapter 35

[Harry]

We stayed there on Louis' bed for a while, just tracing each other's bare bodies while talking and just enjoying each other's company. It was nice, really nice. It was something we had barely had time to do before since it felt like the only thing we did otherwise was to try staying away from each other.

However, when we heard the front door open on the bottom floor, we started panicking a little. And by a little, I meant a lot. Louis literally tossed me off his bed, making me hit the floor pretty hard. I looked up at him with a glare on my face, to which he shrugged his shoulders. After that, we hurried to dress ourselves and fix our hair the best we could. The most problematic thing was all the love bites that were covering our necks. Louis even had a red mark forming on his jaw.

While he tried to fix it up the best he could, I changed his covers and threw the dirty ones in the washing machine that we had in our bathroom. That was pretty much all we had time to do before there was a knock on Louis' door. I hurried into my own room while he threw himself on his bed, acting as if he had been lying there the whole time.

Through the walls, I could hear my mum's voice sounding unusually happy. Not that she never was otherwise, but the tone she was using had to be because of something specific. It didn't take more than a few seconds until she was knocking on my door as well. She poked her head inside, a wide smile playing on her lips. "Hi there, son," she greeted, opening the door a little wider so her entire body was visible. "Had a nice evening?"

I nodded my head. "Yeah, just been doing some homework and some other stuff," I replied, shrugging.

"Alright, would you mind coming downstairs for a second? Troy and I have something to tell you."

I visibly gulped at her words. What if Louis and I had left any evidence of what we had done down there? "Sure," I said, the uncertainty evident in my voice.

She looked a little confused about this but didn't say anything. Instead, she turned around and exited the room, closing the door silently behind her. I didn't even hesitate when I shot up from the bed and ran into Louis' room, wincing a little at the pain in my hum. It didn't surprise me that he was still lying on his bed, staring at the ceiling with wide eyes.

"Do they know?" I asked, panic lacing my voice.

His eyes wandered to mine, looking at me for a few seconds until he shrugged. "To be honest, I don't know, but judging by the look on your mum's face, she seemed quite happy at least. I don't think she would be happy if they had found out about us," he explained, and his words instantly calmed me down because he did have a point.

The question that remained then was why he was staring up at the ceiling like he was about to cry?

"Why are you acting so strange then?" I asked, sitting down beside him on the edge of his bed, reaching out to trace his cheek with my fingers.

A warm smile formed on his lips the moment my skin touched his. "It's nothing. I'm just worried about what our parents want to tell us. It seemed quite important since she came up here the first thing she did when they arrived."

Again, he had a point. Since when did he become so intelligent? "That's true. What do you think it is about then?" I asked, genuinely interested in what he was expecting them to announce.

He placed his hand over mine, lacing our fingers together. "No idea, but let's go down and find out," he said, hoisting himself up from the bed, taking me with him by our connected hands.

"You go first," he ordered as he closed the door behind us.

I just nodded, walking down the stairs the best I could after our intimate actions earlier and into the living room where mum and Troy were already sitting, watching TV. I sat down beside mum, bringing my knees to my chest. "So, what did you want to say?" I asked, looking at them expectantly.

Mum still had a wide smile on her lips while Troy looked rather proud. "We'll tell you in a second. We're just waiting for Louis to come down first," Troy informed, taking mum's hand in his own and squeezing it.

Only a second later, Louis arrived and sat down on the couch beside his dad so they wouldn't get suspicious. Otherwise, there was some empty space beside me as well. "Alright, what's going on?" He questioned, getting straight to the point.

His eyes wandered to their joined hands, and I could see that his jaw clenched slightly. I wanted to know what was happening in his head at the moment. Why did he react like that when he noticed they were holding hands? I thought he was getting used to the thought of them being together by now?

Troy looked at mum whose smile only widened if that was possible. "So, I know we should probably wait until Gemma is here as well, but we just couldn't... or I didn't, more specifically," mum said.

My eyebrows knitted together. Seeing as she was dragging out on it like this and that she had wanted Gemma to be here as well, it had to be something quite important.

"Okay, so you know that we were going out to eat dinner with the people who participated in the meeting this morning, right?" Mum began, and Louis and I nodded simultaneously. "Well, I found out that it wasn't exactly a dinner with other people when we left the house. Troy just wanted me to think it was."

When she didn't say anything else, Troy cleared his throat. "I proposed to her."

Mum squealed excitedly, reaching her left hand in the air to show us the ring. "And I said yes!"

Okay, that, I did not expect whatsoever and judging by the way Louis' jaw dropped, I assumed he was shocked as well. My heart wasn't even beating in my chest, that was how unprepared for this confession I was. I mean, they had been together for what? A little more than half a year and they were already engaged? How was that even possible?

And what would happen to me and Louis now? If they got married, we would be stepbrothers for real, like on fucking paper. Now we were just stepbrothers to be, and that didn't sound quite as bad in comparison. Things just got even more complicated than they had been before.

Thankfully, Troy and mum didn't seem surprised by our reactions, and that was probably because they thought we hated each other. If only they knew, though.

"I know you two probably aren't as happy about this as we are. That's why we thought we should tell you about it first. But guys, you have to realize that we want to live with each other. We are happy together, and hopefully, that's going to overpower your hate for one another someday. We want you to be happy for us as well, you know?" Mum explained, placing a hand on my own. I had it on the couch beside me, and it was frozen in place just like my entire body.

"I..." I trailed off, not knowing what to say.

What could I say? That I was ecstatic that they were engaged and that my boyfriend would be my stepbrother? Sure, I was happy for my mum, that she had finally met someone she really liked, but did he really have to be Louis' dad? It could be any other guy and I would have jumped with joy for her right now.

"We are happy for you guys. We're just... a little shocked since you haven't been dating for a very long time. Not that it should surprise us considering you moved in with each other rather quickly, but engagement and marriage are something different. That means you really want to spend the rest of your lives together, and yeah..." Louis said, biting his lip.

For a second, his eyes met mine, and the look he gave me was sad, so sad. The worst part was that I knew what he was thinking. He thought this was the end for us. There was nothing that could save us anymore because as long as our parents were together, they would find out about us at one point. Maybe not now or this year, but what about in five years? Or twenty?

When the realization hit me, everything became too much for me. I couldn't stay here, watching my mum be so happy when I couldn't be with the one I wanted, the one I loved.

That was why I got up from the couch and ran up to my room, slamming the door shut behind me. When mum came to knock on it about half an hour later, I didn't even open my mouth to give her an answer. I wanted to be alone because that was what I was going to end up being in the future anyway.

The next day, Louis and I didn't talk to each other throughout the entire morning. Sure, we didn't eat breakfast together, so it was impossible to talk to him then, but when we met eyes in the entryway when I was leaving the house to walk to the bus stop, he just averted his gaze while biting his lip.

If I slammed the door behind me a little too hard, no one had to know, but I was sure Louis noticed it. To think that we had sex not even twenty-four hours ago was pretty hard to believe. I could barely believe it myself.

Things weren't better in school either. If anything, they were even worse. He didn't look at me one single time, and it felt like he was trying to be closer to Eleanor than he had the last couple of weeks. It saddened me, that he was really trying to 'get over' me or whatever. It hurt so fucking bad, to be honest.

Liam instantly noticed that I was sad and questioned me about it at lunch. He knew it had something to do with Louis. I mean, when did my mood not have to do with him? Apart from that one time when I was feeling down about Niall, that was. I told him the truth, that our parents had gotten engaged and that Louis and I hadn't talked since their confession.

He went quiet then. He understood that it was difficult for us, but he also thought it was ridiculous of Louis to ignore me.

We were a couple, after all. We should be able to talk about everything no matter what it was about.

I agreed with him, but the question was; did I want to talk to him? Did I want to hear him pretty much break up with me? Maybe I was even the one who had stayed away from him in fear of what he was going to say if we were to have a conversation. I didn't know, but the idea of talking to Louis right now actually scared me. The look he gave me yesterday told me more than I wanted to know.

Later that day, I found myself standing in front of my and Louis' bathroom mirror, fixing my hair for the party. I wasn't nearly as excited about going to it as I had been a couple of days ago, but I had promised Liam that I was joining him and Zayn earlier this week, and I tried to convince myself that it would be good for me. Hopefully, it would get me on better thoughts, at least.

I didn't feel the slightest bit bad about it anymore, though, because it wasn't like Louis would have a hard time staying away from me, as he had pointed out he would. He had made that pretty damn obvious today.

Thankfully, Liam had promised that he and Zayn would come pick me up so I didn't have to take the bus. I didn't know how Louis was getting there, but the last time we had partied at Ed's place, we had taken the bus together... and it was also at that party we had shared our first kiss. Okay, I should stop thinking about that. What I meant was that it wouldn't surprise me if he took the bus this time as well, so riding with Liam meant it was less of a chance I would bump into Louis.

I checked the watch on my wrist, noticing they should be here any minute now. Hurriedly, I exited the bathroom and ran into my room to shrug on a white button-up, zipping the buttons on my way downstairs. I met Gemma when I was about to enter the entryway, and she sent me a smirk.

"Well, don't you look hot, brother?" She said, making me roll my eyes.

"Shut up, Gem."

She placed a hand over her heart dramatically. "Hey, I just complimented you. You should be a lot nicer than that," she whined.

Letting out a dry laugh, I slipped my shoes on. "Well, thank you so much then, my dear sister," I said, looking up to give her a smile.

"Much better," she smiled happily, clapping her hands together. "And oh, have fun tonight."

I nodded, standing up to shrug on my winter jacket. "I hope I will too."

She didn't question my lack of excitement, but a frown crept to her face. Before she had time to say anything, though, a honk was heard outside. "Alright, gotta go. Love you," I said, turning the door handle.

"Isn't Louis going with you?" I could hear her ask behind me, causing me to halt in my movements.

I turned around to look at her. "No. I don't know where he is," was the only thing I said before closing the front door behind me. Instantly, the cold air hit my face, making me wrap my arms around my body.

I ran to Zayn's car and got inside the warmth. I greeted them from the backseat before leaning my head against the backrest.

We didn't talk very much during the ride. The radio was on, though, so what we did was to sing along to the music blaring from the speakers. Zayn and Liam were more into it than I was, but neither of them noticed anything, and even if they did, they didn't say anything.

Once we arrived at Ed's house, I instantly noticed that the place was pretty packed. I thought we had been early, but seeing as the music was at a high volume and loud voices were coming from the house, there was no doubt that a party was going on in there.

We entered the place without even knocking on the door, walking straight into the crowd of people. Some people were mingling in the entryway and another room next to it, while some were dancing in the living room. Liam was quick to grab my arm and pull me into the kitchen where all the alcohol was being served. Zayn was right in front of us.

"Okay, so I think you should drink some tonight, Harry. You need to get your mind off stuff and alcohol is the perfect solution for that, I promise," he said to me, handing me a glass of what looked like beer.

At first, I shook my head, but when he gave me those famous puppy-eyes, I couldn't resist. With a sigh, I took the glass from his hand and looked at its content. "This is only because I don't want to think about a certain person, alright?" I told him, and he nodded, giving me a cheeky smile.

"That works for me."

With that said, I lifted the glass to my mouth and took a sip of the brownish liquid. I scrunched my nose at the taste. It tasted very bitter and it wasn't my thing whatsoever. If I were to like any type of alcohol, it would have to be something sweet.

"This is disgusting, Liam."

He laughed. "Well, if you want to get your mind off you-know-who, then chug," he chuckled, making me roll my eyes.

Giving it a second chance, I brought the glass to my lips again and let the horrible beer fill my mouth. Just to get it over with, I chugged down the whole thing in one go. Judging by the look on Liam's face, it must have looked pretty funny because he was trying hard not to laugh his ass off.

"Jesus, Harry. Well, we should definitely get you another drink," he laughed, patting me on the shoulder.

I wiped my mouth with the back of my hand, shaking my head. "I think I'll wait until I get something else. That was disgusting," I complained.

Within the next half an hour, I had tried at least three other drinks, and I must say that one of them wasn't all that bad. It was a sweet one and tasted of watermelon. It was quite strong, though, so it didn't take very long until I could feel myself getting a little tipsy.

Liam eventually joined Zayn on the dancefloor, which resulted in me sitting on the couch in the living room, watching everyone let loose. So far, I hadn't seen either of Ed, Niall or Louis. I hadn't even seen Eleanor, or the other guys I recognized from the football team. They were all just a bunch of strangers, and the thought made me feel a little uneasy. It was the same uneasiness I usually felt at parties when I was surrounded by drunk people. Only this time, I was a little drunk myself.

It didn't take very long until a familiar guy showed up on the couch beside me, though. With his red, unruly hair and blue sweater, he wasn't difficult to recognize. "Hi there, mate," Ed greeted, giving me a side-hug on the couch.

"Hey," I said, giving him a small smile.

"How come you're sitting here all alone?" He asked, raising his eyebrows questioningly.

By the looks of it, he didn't seem drunk whatsoever. Had he even had something to drink tonight?

I shrugged my shoulders. "Liam's dancing with Zayn and I didn't feel like it. I haven't seen anyone else I recognize but you, so I guess that's why."

He patted my shoulder. "Wanna come with me and play truth or dare with a couple of other people? It's not as noisy in there," he suggested, knowing that I didn't like this kind of atmosphere all that much.

Letting out a chuckle, I tilted my head to the side. "Sounds better than sitting here, at least."

"Great," he smiled, standing up from the couch.

He began walking through the crowd of people, probably expecting me to follow behind. It was quite difficult, though. Not only was I tipsy, but there were also *a lot* of people in here, making it hard to see him through the massive crowd. Moreover, the loud music was practically making my ears bleed. Maybe parties really weren't my thing, after all.

A few seconds later, I finally found myself standing in front of a wooden door. Ed turned the handle, showing five people sitting on the floor in what looked like his bedroom. What had me freeze in place was not because of his room, though, but the brown-haired boy sitting on the floor with his arm around a wavy, brown-haired girl. What was he doing here?

"Alright, people. I have found another player," Ed informed the teenagers, causing them all to look up at us.

Louis and I instantly met eyes, and his reaction was very similar to my own. The smile he'd had on his face instantly dropped and he visibly gulped. Niall was one of the other five people, and he was the second person I met eyes with. He gave me a weak smile, which I reciprocated stiffly.

The other two people were another couple from the football and cheerleading team. I didn't really recognize them but knew they were good friends with Louis, Eleanor, Niall and Ed.

"Hey, there," Eleanor greeted, giving me a warm smile.

"Eh, hi," I responded, walking into the room even if the only thing I wanted was to run back to the dancefloor. I didn't even care that I was surrounded by strangers there. It was better than being surrounded by these people.

Timidly, I sat down beside Niall, looking at Ed who gave me an appreciating smile as he plopped down next to me. I introduced myself to the two people who didn't recognize me and learned that their names were Dan and Angela. They seemed rather nice, so they would probably be my only hope here.

"So, whose turn is it?" Ed asked eventually, flicking his gaze between the five of them.

So far, Louis hadn't opened his mouth since my entrance. It didn't surprise me. He certainly wasn't expecting me out of all people to join them, and considering we hadn't talked to each other in almost twenty-four hours, it was predictable that he was going to be quiet.

"I think it's Eleanor's," Dan said.

Ed clapped his hands together. "Great, let's get back to this."

Eleanor cleared her throat, flicking her gaze between every player. "Alright, Ed, truth or dare?" She asked.

"Uhm, I think I'll go with truth."

"Pussy," Dan complained, causing Eleanor, Angela and Niall to laugh.

Ed just rolled his eyes. "Shut up, Dan. You chose truth before too," he reminded him.

Dan flipped him the middle finger as Angela leaned her head on his shoulder with a loving smile on her face.

"Okay, so what made you realize that you were bisexual?" Eleanor questioned Ed whose eyes lit up.

My eyebrows rose at the question, not expecting it at all. Judging by the way Louis tensed beside her, I assumed he wasn't prepared for it either. Ed seemed rather happy about it, though, for some reason.

"Actually, it was thanks to my dear friend Harry here," he said, ruffling my curls jokingly.

I tried to get his hand out of my hair, giving him a glare once he dropped it to his lap again. "Heey, don't touch my hair," I whined, trying to fix my curls again.

While doing this, I could feel eyes on me. It wasn't just one pair but two. From my left, I could see Niall biting his lip with a sad look on his face, and when I looked up to the person sitting in front of me, I could see that those ocean blue eyes that I had come to love weren't as blue as they usually were. Actually, they were pretty dark as they glared between me and Ed.

My heart skipped a beat in my chest because it was the first time during the entire day that he reacted to something that had to do with me, and I couldn't help but feel a little happy about it.

"Aw, don't be like that, Hazza. I know you love me," Ed winked, puckering his lips at me.

I scrunched my nose up. "Gross."

He laughed, something Eleanor, Dan and Angela did as well. "So, you've been a thing, eh?" Dan asked, raising his eyebrows.

Ed shook his head, a smile on his lips. "Nah, not really. We just made each other realize we were bisexual, is all," he said truthfully, and I was thankful he didn't continue joking around because Niall was squirming beside me and Louis was literally glaring daggers at the red-haired boy.

Ed noticed the look on Niall's face and gave him a reassuring smile before locking eyes with Louis. His eyes narrowed a little as he bit down on his bottom lip. "Alright, Ed. Your turn," Eleanor said, scooting closer to Louis.

Ed shook himself out of his thoughts. "Niall, truth or dare?" He asked, looking determined as he gave the blonde boy a knowing look.

I furrowed my eyebrows together. Something wasn't right. I couldn't put my finger on what it was, but something was off. Way off.

"Dare," he said, his voice shaking a little.

"I dare you to kiss Harry on the mouth."

Chapter 36

[Harry]

"I dare you to kiss Harry on the mouth."

The tension that filled the room after that sentence could literally be cut with a knife. Everything went silent, even Dan and Angela were surprised by the dare. They were probably aware that Niall and I'd had something going on but that it was over. Well, I was pretty damn sure Ed did at least, so the question was; why in the name of God did he dare him to kiss me? This was just not making sense. What was going on?

I looked at Ed with wide eyes before turning to meet Niall's gaze. To my surprise, he gave me a small smile and a shrug. I was sure he would be as shocked by this as everyone else was, or at least be against it, but it seemed like the opposite. It was as if he expected the dare, which only made me even more confused.

Slowly, Niall got on his knees and started leaning towards me. My eyes widened even more by his action, and I turned my gaze to Louis. The shock was now gone from his face, replaced by anger and jealousy instead. His hands were also clenched into fists. Well, at least the one that was at his side. I couldn't know about the one around Eleanor's waist. There was no doubt he didn't like what was about to happen, though, and again, it made me happy that he showed some sort of reaction. He still had trouble controlling himself around me after all.

Suddenly, I could feel a pair of hands on my shoulders, turning me to the left gently. I looked into a pair of blue eyes, but not the same blue ones I had started falling in love with, unfortunately. Niall's face was close, too close for it to be comfortable.

"I'm sorry," he whispered sincerely as he leaned in even more to close the gap between our mouths.

I could barely feel his lips ghost over mine when his entire presence suddenly disappeared altogether. Confused by the action, I opened my eyes that I had closed when his face got too close. Don't even ask me why I hadn't just pushed him away myself. It must be because of the alcohol because I was certain I didn't want him to kiss me. The only lips I wanted on mine belonged to the person who was sitting across from me.

However, when my eyes were open, I noticed that Louis wasn't sitting there anymore. Instead, he was hovering over Niall with a tight grip on his collar. "Don't you fucking dare," he snapped, glaring at the blonde-haired boy.

Niall's eyes widened as he shook his head frantically. He didn't say anything, though, and that was probably for the best because it looked like Louis would kill him if he just so much as dared open his mouth.

"And you," Louis hissed, turning his cold eyes to me. "I'd like to have a word with you, immediately."

With that said, he let go of Niall and grabbed my bicep. The grip was quite tight, tight enough for me to be afraid it would leave a mark. Without saying anything, I frowned at the feathery-haired boy. I hadn't even done anything, so why did he want to talk to me?

"Alright, calm down, Tomlinson," Ed chuckled, and when I turned to him, I noticed that he was trying his best not to laugh loudly.

Louis snapped his head to look at the red-haired boy, his face growing even angrier. "What the fuck do you have to do with this?"

Ed raised his eyebrows, raising his hands in surrender. "A better question would be what you have to do with all this, but alright," he shrugged, sending him a smirk.

Louis just growled at him before turning back to me. "Now," he urged, helping me up with the grip he had on my bicep.

He started pulling me towards the door, but before he closed it behind us, I could see that Eleanor looked as shocked as ever while Niall just looked really sad, and Ed was laughing.

I didn't have much time to think about them, though, because before I knew it, Louis was slamming the bathroom door shut behind us, pressing my back against it.

"Didn't I tell you it was a bad, fucking idea to come to this party?!" He shouted in my face.

I didn't know if it was because of the alcohol or if I just knew him too well now, but I wasn't intimidated by him whatsoever. I just crossed my arms over my chest and listened to him. "Well, sure, but considering you've been pretty good at ignoring me the last twenty-four hours, I reckoned it wouldn't be a big problem," I shrugged.

He narrowed his eyes at me. "Do you think this is funny? Do you know that I could've easily done something worse out there like exposed us to all of them? And do you want to know what would have happened then? We would be dead, Harry. Dead."

I stared him deep in the eyes, my own narrowing a little. It was a good thing that I wasn't more intoxicated than I was. Otherwise, I wouldn't be able to control myself to this extent. "As if we aren't already. I saw the look you gave me yesterday, Louis. You already see an end to all this, so why does it even matter? Besides, I didn't even do anything. We were just playing a game. How can you even blame me for this?"

He looked a little taken aback by my words, but it didn't take more than a few seconds until he was glaring at me again. "You could've made things easier by just staying home," he muttered.

I let out a dry laugh, shaking my head. "You don't own me, Louis. I can do whatever I want. You're supposed to be my boyfriend, not someone who thinks they can boss me around."

He took a deep breath, letting out a sigh. "I know I don't own you, Harry. I just... I can't fucking picture you with someone else, and especially not Niall's damn lips on yours. It was just too much to handle," he explained, shaking his head.

Reaching my hand up, I cupped his cheek, which made him look up at me. "I understand, but do you think it's easy for me to see you with Eleanor every single day? It kills me, Louis. Yet, I don't complain because I know it makes you feel safer in school."

A crease formed between his eyebrows. "But I don't kiss her, Harry. I barely even touch her. I just... ugh, why is this so fricking hard? I wish things would be easy, but they're not. They're so fucking complicated, and I hate it."

I let out a sigh, dropping my hand from his cheek. "I hate it too," I mumbled.

A silence fell between the two of us where we just looked into each other's eyes. Even if we were quiet, it was like we were talking to each other with our gazes. It wasn't until he leaned closer to me, getting so close to my face that I had to back up against the door behind me, that he broke the silence.

He placed his hands on my hips as he bumped his nose with mine gently. "Would you have kissed him?" He wondered, making me let out a chuckle.

I wrapped my arms around his neck, playing with the hairs at the back of it. "To be honest, I don't know why I didn't push him off. I didn't want to kiss him, but my brain wasn't really working properly, and I blame it on the alcohol I had earlier."

Louis raised his eyebrows, looking amused. "You had alcohol? I thought you were Mr. I-don't-do-any-bad-stuff," he chuckled.

Rolling my eyes, I tugged a little harder at his hair to make a point. "Hey, that's mean. I've done bad stuff..." I trailed off, biting my bottom lip.

Still looking amused, he said; "Like what? Handed in your homework too late? Oh, no wait. You and Liam arrived late to class once now, didn't you?" He joked, pinching my hip.

"Shut up," I muttered under my breath.

He moved his hand to lift my chin up. "What was that?" He asked, raising a questioning eyebrow.

"Shut up," I said a little louder, causing an amused smile to form on his thin, pink lips.

"I know something that will make both of us shut up."

And before I had even time to question him what that could possibly be, he pressed me to the door entirely and crashed our lips together. The kiss was heated as our breaths mixed together, lips never leaving each other. It turned more desperate when his mouth started moving more feverishly against my own. His hands trailed up my white button-up, tracing my naked back that had visible evidence of what we had done yesterday evening.

He swiped his tongue along my bottom lip, asking for entrance. I granted him access instantly because I had missed this. For a second, I even thought I would never experience his lips on mine again, and maybe that was why I was so desperate.

Our tongues swirled together as my hands wandered further up to pull at his smooth hair.

When we were nearly out of breath, Louis pulled back a little, taking my bottom lip between his teeth to suck on it gently. The feeling had my knees go weak, and if it weren't for his hands that were holding me, I would've fallen to the floor, no doubt about it.

He certainly felt it because he let out a light chuckle. "You alright there, eh?"

I pouted at him, our faces still very close. "I'm fine, thank you very much."

He winked at me before getting a little more serious again. "So, my lips or Niall's?" He asked, his eyebrows arched.

Pretending to think about it, I pursed my lips and narrowed my eyes a little. "Hmm... that's a hard one..."

"Oh, shut the hell up," he growled, leaning in to press his mouth against my jaw, trailing down to my neck. He left small kisses until he started sucking on the skin.

I couldn't help but let out a moan when he found my sweet spot, and that was apparently his cue to pull away. He gave me a cheeky smile, to which I glared. I wanted to hit him, but instead, I found myself muttering; "Well, of course I'd choose your lips over Niall's, you idiot."

He laughed. "That's what I wanted to hear."

A few minutes later, we exited the bathroom, and I decided that I didn't want to go back to the room we had been in before. If anything, this was a good excuse to leave even if they all would think I chickened out or something. I didn't care, though, and Louis was happy with my decision as well, so it was a win-win.

To be honest, I didn't think Louis wanted to go back there either, but one of us had to. Otherwise, suspicion would arise, and that was the last thing we wanted right now. Additionally, he was there first, so it would be best if he was the one to go back.

I, on the other hand, went to the living room to see if I could find Liam. I had pretty much lost all my interest in this party by now, but he was the one who had driven me here, so I had to tell him that I was going home. Since I also came here to be with him and Zayn, so it would be mean of me not to tell them that I was leaving.

Once I had reached the crowded room, I shouldered my way past the people in search of my best friend. Considering there were pretty much only strangers in here, it didn't take long until I found the brown-haired boy, dancing with his boyfriend. However, dancing probably wasn't the right word, though, because they were more jumping than dancing.

I tapped Liam's shoulder when I was just behind him, and he instantly turned around to face me. "Oh, hi there, Harry! Having fun?" He yelled over the loud music.

Grimacing, I shrugged my shoulders. "Actually, I'm here to tell you guys that I'm going home. I'm so thankful that you drove me here and all, but I'm getting tired, and I barely recognize any of the people in here," I explained, lying a little.

He nodded in understanding even though his face turned into a look of slight disappointment. "I get it. Is it okay if you take the bus, though? I'd rather stay for a little longer and I'm pretty sure I wouldn't be able to drive in this state either for that matter," he said apologetically.

I waved a hand dismissively. "Of course. I just came here to tell you that I was taking the bus. I wouldn't ask you to drive me home," I chuckled, making him smile.

"Alright, good night then, Haz."

"Night, Liam. Enjoy your time with Zayn," I smirked, and he rolled his eyes.

"Sure."

With that said, I walked away from the two and made my way out of the house. I didn't even look back as I started walking towards the bus stop. The sad part was that it took at least thirty minutes until I was hopping onto the warm bus that took me home.

Half an hour later, I was standing outside my house, shaking like a leaf from the cold outside. I could barely fit the key in the keyhole, that was how cold I was. Eventually, though, I managed to unlock the door, and I didn't hesitate to enter the warmth of my home. It didn't surprise me that it was dark inside. I mean, it was probably past one in the morning, so my family members probably went to sleep a long time ago.

I walked up the stairs as quietly as I could and went into my bedroom. The first thing I did was throw myself onto my bed, letting out a deep sigh as I ran a hand through my hair. To say this night had been eventful would be an understatement. I mean, Louis hadn't even talked to me during the entire day, and yet we were making out in one of Ed's bathrooms tonight. Not to mention the fact that he had gotten incredibly jealous of Niall.

Speaking of which, that whole scenario had been quite fishy. I mean, why would Ed even dare Niall to kiss me in the first place when he knew what had happened between us? It was like it was all a set-up, as if they had planned it all out, for some reason. I just wondered why. Why was it necessary to make a dare like that? Was it because Niall wanted to kiss me? Well, I couldn't think of something else.

I didn't know how long I kept thinking of it until my eyelids started getting heavy. Have you ever had that feeling of being so tired that you didn't even want to get up and get yourself ready for bed? Well, that was how tired I was right now. My clothes were still hugging my body and my bed was still made, yet I couldn't even bring myself to sit up.

My head was throbbing a little as well, probably due to the alcohol, and that fact didn't exactly make matters better. However, with all my will-power I eventually managed to get myself into a sitting position. I barely managed to, but I got out of my clothes and got under the covers as well. Just as I was about to close my eyes and fall into a heavy sleep, I could hear Louis' bedroom door shut from the other side of my room.

It made me relax a little, knowing that he had made it home safely at least. With that in mind, I could feel myself drift off to sleep as I hugged the sheets close to my body.

What I didn't know then, however, was that I would wake up to quite a disaster, but what I didn't know, I didn't need to worry about.

I was woken up by the sound of my bedroom door slamming against the wall. It made me sit up on my bed abruptly, and I opened my eyes to see Louis standing there, his face looking pale and upset at the same time. His jaw was clenched as he was gripping something in his hand tightly.

"What the fuck have you done?" He snapped, his eyes turning dark.

Furrowing my eyebrows, I looked at him in confusion. What was he talking about? I mean, I just woke up, so my brain wasn't working properly, but even if that was the case, I couldn't remember that I had done anything wrong. "What are you talking about?"

"This," he said, walking over to shove the thing he had in his hand in my face, which turned out to be his phone.

Squinting my eyes to see what the screen showed, they instantly widened at what they saw. I took his phone into my own hand to get a better look, and he let me. On the screen, there were plenty of them. Plenty of photos, and as I scrolled down, I noticed there were plenty of tweets and even some recordings as well.

All of them were proof that Louis and I were two stepbrothers who had feelings for each other.

Chapter 37

[Louis]

When I entered Ed's room after being away with Harry, I was met with a lot of different reactions. Eleanor looked at me with an unreadable expression on her face while Ed and Niall looked at me knowingly. Dan and Angela just seemed confused, and I didn't blame them. They probably had no idea of what was going on.

Ignoring Ed and Niall, I sat down beside Eleanor. "Where's Harry?" She asked in confusion.

I shrugged. "He didn't feel well, so he decided to go home," I replied, causing Ed to snort.

"Go home? Didn't feel well? What nonsense are you talking about, Tomlinson?" He asked, raising an eyebrow at me.

If I wasn't already fed up with his behavior before, I sure was now. It was as if he knew something that he kept to himself but at the same time tried to show everyone, which was nothing but weird. "Yes. He didn't even want to participate in this game to begin with. He just told me."

Ed chuckled dryly. "And why would he tell you, one of his worst enemies that? Why would he even want to talk to you in the first place, huh?" He questioned expectantly.

I swallowed hard, knowing that this was a very bad and risky situation. I mean, Eleanor even knew that Harry and I were stepbrothers, so she could expose us at any second. However, it seemed like I was lucky this time because she kept her mouth shut, and I was pretty sure that was because she was still rather shocked by everything.

Everyone was staring at me now, and their intense gazes made me look away. "Well, I don't know. You ask him," I said curtly, and with that, I ended the topic, which I was nothing but happy about. I wanted to talk about something else, anything else.

The following minutes were rather tense. Niall was as quiet as a little mouse. He didn't even dare look my way, which I appreciated. I didn't know what I would do if he did. I was still pretty angry that he had tried to kiss Harry. Not that he was the one to blame considering it was a dare, but something was fishy about it.

It didn't take long until we all felt pretty done with the night. Eleanor was leaning her head on my shoulder, but she seemed tenser now than she did at the beginning of the night. Angela was lying with her head on Dan's lap while Niall was constantly rubbing his eyes tiredly.

To be honest, I was getting pretty tired myself, and lying down on my bed was rather tempting right now. "Alright guys, I think we might as well head home. What do you say, Angela?" Dan asked, looking down at his almost sleeping girlfriend.

She yawned, sitting up while nodding. "I'm tired as hell."

"I agree. I'm getting rather sleepy myself. You joining me, Lou?" Eleanor asked, looking at me.

I nodded. "Sure. I'll walk you home," I offered, making her smile tiredly.

"Great."

With that said, we all got up from the floor and started heading towards the door. Once I got to the doorframe, I was stopped by a hand on my shoulder, though. "Sleep well, Louis," someone whispered in my ear, and I instantly recognized it as Ed's voice.

I got uncomfortable chills by it, but I didn't bother to answer him. Instead, I continued walking, my hand on Eleanor's lower back as I kept my head down. We went out of the house and started making our way towards her place.

"What was that all about before? And why did you get so worked up when Niall was dared to kiss Harry?" She asked after a while of silence.

I gulped at her words but decided to play it cool. "I'm just very protective, you know? Harry's kind of my brother and he has been together with Niall, but they broke up not too long ago. I didn't want Harry to feel sad all over again if they were to kiss just because of a dare, you get me?"

Wow, I was pretty good at lying, I had to give myself that one.

She nodded her head slowly as if she was trying to put the puzzle pieces together. "Why didn't you just tell Ed that then? He seemed rather suspicious for some reason. I'm sure he would have understood if you'd just told him the truth."

I hummed, looking ahead of me. "No one but you knows that Harry and I are stepbrothers, though, and I didn't really feel like spilling the beans right then. No one would have believed me anyway, considering they think Harry and I hate each other. I mean, sure, I don't really like him, but he is kind of my brother after all, and I do feel as if I have to protect him," I explained, biting the inside of my cheek.

I didn't like this conversation. I didn't like it at all. It felt like I was on the verge of telling her too much. Well, enough for her to figure everything out, or at least make someone else figure things out for her if she were to tell anyone.

"I guess I understand," she said after a short silence. "So you were telling the truth when you said that he went home because he wasn't feeling well?"

Grimacing, I nodded my head. "Yeah. He didn't know that we all were going to be in that room, especially not Niall. Moreover, he definitely wasn't expecting Niall to be dared to kiss him. He didn't want to go back to face them after that, so he decided to go home. He wasn't feeling very well about everything, so I was telling the truth, yes."

At this point, we were standing outside Eleanor's house. We had stopped by her gate and were now facing each other. She gave me a small smile as she took a step forward to wrap her arms around my neck. "You know, it wasn't like I didn't believe you. I just thought the entire situation was kind of messed up since Ed was acting so weird. I'm sorry if you thought I didn't trust you," she mumbled in my ear.

I pulled back to reciprocate her smile. "I never thought you didn't trust me, but I understand why you felt that way. To be honest, I'm surprised by Ed's behavior as well. I don't know why he got so curious or whatever that was. It was just weird."

She nodded in agreement and was just about to turn around and start walking towards her front door when I grabbed her forearm. "Wait," I ordered, making her turn around in confusion. "Would you please not tell anyone that Harry and I are stepbrothers? I kind of want to do it myself," I pleaded.

A light chuckle left her lips as she shrugged her shoulders. "That works for me. It's none of my business anyway."

Mentally letting out a sigh of relief, I gave her another smile. "Alright, thank you."

Waving a hand dismissively, she took a step forward to give me a kiss on the cheek. "No problem. Goodnight, Lou."

"Goodnight, Eleanor."

With that said, we separated. She walked into her house while I made my way to the bus stop. When I entered the dark home forty minutes later, I could really feel how tired I was.

Once I had gotten out of my outdoor clothing, I stumbled up to my bedroom and closed the door behind me, and it didn't take long after that until I was lying on my bed and drifting off to sleep.

Considering it was Saturday and the day after a party, I was surprised to find myself waking up at eight-thirty in the morning. I didn't do it on my own, though, but by my phone that kept beeping. With a groan, I reached my hand out towards my nightstand to grab the device.

Squinting my eyes, I tried to read what the screen said and was surprised to see that I had been tagged in not only one, but at least ten tweets. This fact made me feel more awake, and I unlocked my phone to see what the fuss was all about.

Oh, how I wished I hadn't. Because there it was, all over Twitter, plenty of proof that Harry and I were stepbrothers with feelings for each other. It made my heart stop beating.

The next second, I could feel anger boiling up inside me. It was an instinct, a bad reaction that I couldn't suppress. So without even thinking twice, I got out of my bed and practically sprinted to Harry's room, swinging his door open.

He woke up instantly, sitting up on the bed abruptly. "What the fuck have you done?" I snapped, gripping my phone tightly in my hand as I glared at him.

His eyebrows pulled together in confusion. "What are you talking about?" He asked, so without uttering a word, I shoved my phone in his face so he could see the tweets we had been tagged in.

"This."

He took the device from my hand to read what it said, his eyes widening as he scrolled through them. "What... who...?" He trailed off, not believing his eyes.

I snatched my phone back harshly. "Well, you fucking tell me. I haven't told anyone. This is all your damn fault. Who did you tell?" I growled, hovering over him.

He didn't cower, though. Instead, he glared back at me. "I haven't told anyone. How can you blame this on me? The only ones that I know of who are aware of it are Liam and Gemma. So you fucking tell me who did this because I have no idea at all!"

Breathing heavily, I shook my head. "You told Liam? How can you be sure he--"

"I trust him," he cut me off, his voice as cold as ice. "He's my best friend, and I know he would never do anything like this to me. Now, what about Eleanor, huh? Are you sure she--"

"I trust her too," I said, calming down a little, but just a little. "I can promise you it wasn't her."

He took a deep breath, running a nervous hand through his hair. "Well, then I don't know. I haven't told anyone. Come on, let me see," he said, nodding towards my phone that I was gripping so hard that my knuckles had turned white.

Sitting down on the edge of his bed, I handed him the device once again. This time, he crawled his way over to sit beside me so we could look at it together. He started scrolling through the tweets again to get a better view of what they said and what the pictures showed.

"Look, this one is of us at Ed's last party," he said, showing the picture of when my drunk self was leaning my head on Harry's shoulder while he was trying to support me with a hand around my waist. This was taken months ago.

With a frown on my face, I started thinking. Who could it be? I mean, as far as I knew, a stranger must have taken this photo, but how was I to know? I hadn't exactly been in my best condition that evening.

"Oh, shit," Harry gasped as he found a picture of our family eating dinner at the Italian restaurant not too long ago. "Someone was watching us."

Just like I had suspected. Well, maybe not necessarily that time, but during the last couple of weeks, I had felt as though someone had been watching me. This just proved that I was right.

"There's a recording here as well," Harry continued, clicking on the link.

It was of my and Harry's conversation in the bathroom of the restaurant. We were talking about being more careful since Gemma had just found out about our relationship. If this wasn't proof enough that we were together, then I didn't know what was.

Gulping, I covered my eyes with my hands. This couldn't possibly get any worse. Not only had dad just proposed to Anne the other day but now everyone knew that Harry and I were in a relationship too. Where was this going to end? Was it even going to end?

"Hey, isn't this of you when Niall was walking me home the other day?" Harry interrupted my thoughts.

I looked at the screen again, seeing myself in a picture where I was walking towards the front door of our house. I narrowed my eyes, remembering that afternoon very well. It was indeed that day when I had followed Harry and Niall home and had practically snuck up on them. I had walked Niall home before turning back to go to the house.

"It is..." I trailed off, my brain spinning like crazy.

Harry's head suddenly snapped up, his eyes meeting mine. "Do you think... You don't think Niall has something to do with this, do you?" He asked uncertainly, biting his bottom lip.

I shrugged because honestly, I had no idea. I didn't know anything anymore, and I hated it. I hated not having control over something this important. I just sat there, my mind going blank as Harry kept reading over the tweets. It wasn't until at least five minutes later that he noticed I wasn't saying anything and looked up at me.

When he saw my pale face, he took my hand and entwined our fingers. "Lou, it's gonna be alright," he promised me, making me smile even if it turned more into a grimace because it was pretty cute that he still had his hopes up.

I shook my head, meeting his gaze. "Don't you realize that this is the end, Harry? After this, people are going to look at us strangely and think we are disgusting. I mean, it's only a matter of time until dad and Anne will find out as well, and then we're going to be screwed. This," I said, lifting our intertwined hands. "Will have to stop if we want a somewhat normal life again with our parents and friends in it."

He swallowed hard, squeezing my hand tightly. His eyes turned so sad and hurt that my chest tightened. I hated seeing him like this, especially since my words were the cause of it. However, I knew it had to be said because it was the truth. It was our reality now, something we had no choice but to face.

"Please don't say that. I don't care if people are going to think differently of us now. I just care about being with you. I know we haven't been together for a long time, but these feelings I have for you are stronger than I've ever felt for someone in my life. If you break up with me... I don't know what to do. I understand that you want your father in your life and that you don't want to lose your reputation, but God, I don't know how to live with the fact of knowing you aren't mine anymore," he confessed, opening his entire heart for me.

I had to look away from him so the tears that had started building up in my eyes wouldn't fall. "Don't make this so hard, Harry. I wish things were different, that our parents weren't together. I really do. But now things are as they are and we can't do anything about it. When we agreed to start going out with each other, we knew that this could happen, that there was a huge risk that things could go wrong, and now here we are. Maybe it's already too late, but we can't keep it up no matter what. We gave it a try, and even though I might lose the only real family I have left, I'm happy that I experienced this time with you. It's been the best few weeks of my life."

He let out a sniffle, and when I turned to look at him again, I noticed that he had tears running down his cheeks. "Hey, don't cry," I pleaded, reaching up to wipe his tears away with my thumb.

His eyes met mine and he shook his head. "H-how can I not? You're basically breaking up with m-me, of course I'm sad. I... I love you, and you... Y-you are ready to let me go," he hiccupped.

I opened my mouth to give him a reply, but nothing came out. He loved me? I mean, I knew I loved him and had done so for quite some time now, but we had never uttered those three words to each other before, and hearing them escape his mouth made me speechless. It warmed my heart and broke it at the same time because even if I was happy, I was also sad since none of it mattered anymore.

"Harry, I... I don't know what to say. I... I love you too, so, so much. I've loved you for a long time, but you know just as well as I that it doesn't change anything. We have to do this, and you know it. I *know* you do. Please just... understand that I don't want to hurt you. I'm just doing what I know has to be done," I whispered, placing my hand that wasn't already holding his on top of ours and squeezed tightly.

His sniffles only increased, and soon, he was burying his face in my neck, his curls tickling my cheek. He pressed his wet lips against my skin and gave my neck a light kiss. "W-why do things have to be like this?"

I wrapped an arm around his body and started rubbing his arm soothingly. With a sigh, I shook my head. "I don't know, Harry. I guess God doesn't want us to be together," I muttered, making him look up at me with a frown on his face.

"That's just bullshit, Louis, and you know it. This doesn't have to do with God. It's just bad luck. Someone out there, the one who posted all those tweets, doesn't want us to be together. It's their fault, not what God decided. Someone wants to hurt us, that's it. Because, I know for sure that I'm destined to be with you, no matter what anyone else says."

He looked at me with so much love in his eyes that I couldn't help but smile. Why did he have to be so beautiful? The way his dimples showed whenever he was genuinely happy, the way a crease would form between his eyebrows when something concerned him or just his pink, plump lips that I could kiss forever if I had the opportunity to. I didn't even deserve his beauty, and I definitely didn't deserve to be together with such a good-hearted person in general. He was just flawless, and I absolutely hated the fact that I couldn't be with him even now when I knew he felt the same.

"God, why can't I just be with you?" I groaned, leaning in to rub my nose with his.

His lips twitched hesitantly, his cheeks still wet with tears. "I'm asking myself the same thing."

We didn't say anything for the next couple of minutes. We just looked into each other's eyes, and my heart was aching in my chest during the entire time. It was like I wanted to cry, but no tears fell. Harry didn't cry more either, and I assumed that was because he was numb, just like me.

Sadly, it was soon time for the two of us to go down and eat breakfast with our family. I didn't want to leave the room and go out and face reality. If I could, I would stay in here with Harry for the rest of my life and hide from everyone. Unfortunately, though, we couldn't. So, I reluctantly got up from the bed, taking Harry with me in my arms.

"Louis, how… how are we going to act?" Harry almost whispered when I was ready to move towards the door.

I turned around to look at him and shrugged my shoulders. "I guess we'll act like we always do, and if they find out about us, then we'll face the consequences then."

He nodded even though a crease formed between his eyebrows. "But what about at school tomorrow?"

I bit my bottom lip, letting out a sigh. "Act like you usually do, although I'm sure people are going to talk about us. Just... Just try your best to ignore it, okay? It's going to die out when they realize that nothing is going on between us anymore."

He nodded again, but slower and more hesitantly this time. His gaze was turned to the floor as he shifted his feet anxiously. I lifted his head up by the chin. "Hey, look at me," I ordered, but he still wouldn't meet my eyes.

"It's gonna be okay, alright? We're... we're gonna be okay," I said, even though I didn't even believe my own words.

That was when he finally decided to meet my gaze. He didn't say anything, though. He just threw his arms around my neck and buried his face in the crook of it. "I love you," he whispered against my skin, making me close my eyes.

I couldn't hear him say those words right now. It hurt more than it made me happy, and that spoke for itself. I had waited so long to hear those words coming from his mouth, but now it was just too late.

"I love you too, Harry."

Chapter 38

[Harry]

Sunday didn't turn out any different from how we usually acted at home. We never showed that we were in a relationship when we were around our family anyway, so it wasn't like we had to act differently than normal. However, we had stolen glances at each other when we knew no one was watching before, but after the party had taken place, we pretty much ignored each other like we were thin air. It hurt. It felt like there had never been something between us, and that was worse than knowing it had been something that had now ended.

Gemma was with Devon the entire weekend, so I hadn't had time to talk to her about it all. Hell, I didn't even know whether she had seen the tweets or not. I wanted to hear her opinion, what she thought about it. Not that it would change anything, but it was always better to talk to someone than keep things that hurt to yourself. I was aware that Louis didn't have anyone to talk to, but I couldn't exactly help him with that.

On Monday morning, I got ready for the day as usual before walking down to the kitchen. It was no surprise to see that it was empty. Whenever Louis didn't want to see me, he always made sure that we weren't in the kitchen in the morning at the same time. So, without caring too much about it, I made myself breakfast and sat down at the table, looking out the window as I ate.

My brain had been all over the place the last few days. It wouldn't just focus on one thing, but it kept going through the last conversation Louis and I had and also every memory we had shared.

I hadn't cried since it happened. I had wanted to more times than once, but it hadn't gone further than my eyes getting teary. I was sure that was because I felt so empty. Knowing the boy I loved would never be in my arms again made me feel so lost and helpless. It hurt so much that I couldn't think straight. As I said, I couldn't even focus on one thing at a time anymore. The worst part was that it had only been two days. I wondered how it would turn out in the long run.

To be honest, I was pretty happy that I didn't catch sight of his figure this morning because it would only hurt more to see him, knowing that I couldn't touch him or kiss him. I couldn't even tell him how much I felt for him because it didn't matter anymore. It was over.

With a heavy sigh, I brought the last spoonful of cereal to my mouth and swallowed it down. After that, I put the empty bowl in the sink before going upstairs to brush my teeth.

Five minutes later, I was standing in the entryway, tying my shoes. That was when I heard a pair of feet walking down the stairs. On instinct, my eyes looked up to see who it was, even though I should already know since there was only one person but me who was home and had their bedroom on the second floor.

My tongue got stuck in my throat when our gazes met. It was only briefly because the next second, Louis looked away from me. In the short amount of time that our eyes were connected, though, something burst inside me and I was pretty sure it was my heart. My breathing got heavier by the second but calmed down slightly when he disappeared into the kitchen quickly.

Damn, what was I going to do with my life? Why did we have to live in the same fricking house? It was just unbearable.

A few seconds later, I found myself slamming the door shut behind me, and I started making my way towards the bus stop. I walked with my head down, not wanting to see or be seen by anyone. Once there, I was disappointed to see that the bus hadn't arrived yet. There were a few people already waiting for it, and I didn't want to be near anyone, so I stopped a few yards away, leaning against a lamp post.

If it weren't for the fact that it was freezing outside, I would have fished my phone from my pocket, but since it was, I'd rather not get my hands out of my jeans pockets. Thankfully, it didn't take more than a few minutes until the bus finally showed up at the corner of the street.

The students started lining up to get on as quickly as possible, but I kept myself at a distance considering I didn't want to get anyone's attention. Unfortunately, that was inevitable since I had to get on the bus while the other people were already seated.

I could instantly feel gazes on me, even if I still had my hood on and kept my head down. They were staring at me as if I was some kind of monster, and I could feel myself squirm uncomfortably.

I sat down in the first empty place I could find, making sure not to choose the window seat so no one could sit beside me. I placed my backpack beside me and finally pulled out my phone from my back pocket.

It was only a few minutes later that I could hear a familiar voice on the bus. I was used to hearing it laugh whenever I was here, but this time, it sounded angry and snappy. Feeling confused, I looked up to see Louis glaring at a guy on the football team, his fist ready to swing at him. "What was that, Jimmy?" He threatened, raising his eyebrows expectantly.

It surprised me that this Jimmy guy didn't look scared at all. In fact, he was rolling his eyes at the feathery-haired boy. "Oh, come on. As if a gay boy who's fucking his nerdy stepbrother could hurt me? Please," he snorted, looking Louis in the eye.

The blue-eyed boy's face was red with anger. I swear, if looks could kill, Jimmy would be dead right now. "I'd absolutely love to see you lying bleeding on the ground right now, but I won't give you that pleasure. I'm not some loser who gives a fuck about another person's life, so therefore, I'm just going to leave you to hopefully start thinking about your own damn one instead."

With that said, Louis continued his way through the bus, sitting down in an empty seat himself and ignoring the stares he received from the other students. He had gained a lot of people's attention, so there wasn't exactly only *one* person looking at him. When he passed me, he didn't even blink an eye but just kept his gaze forward while walking along the aisle. I wasn't surprised.

I looked back down at my phone then, but not before glancing at that Jimmy boy once more. He was actually fuming, probably angry at the fact that he had practically lost the argument. A smile formed on my lips because Louis had actually stood up for us and not caved in like I thought he was going to. It warmed my heart whether I wanted it to or not.

A few minutes later, the bus came to a halt outside of school. I was quick to stand up and hop off since I didn't want all the students to walk past me only to throw more of those glances my way. I started making my way into the building, walking through the entrance and proceeding towards my locker. During the entire time, I made sure to hide myself the best I could under my hood, but despite that, I could still hear people whisper about me.

Even if I didn't see them, I could still feel them pointing at me as I walked through the hallway. They were saying words like 'disgusting' 'fag' and 'nerd'. I didn't want to take the words to heart, but it was almost impossible not to. I knew what Louis told me the other day about ignoring the people talking shit about me, but I just couldn't.

Just as I was about to stop at my locker, I was shouldered by someone, making my side slam into the wall of lockers. "Watch where you're going, you disgusting fag," the person snapped.

I just looked down at the floor and slumped my shoulders. The person walked away laughing, and I wanted nothing but to disappear into thin air. I mean, I knew people wouldn't exactly like the fact that Louis and I had been in a relationship, but I didn't expect them to be this hateful about it.

"Harry!"

Turning around abruptly, I was nothing but happy to see my best friend standing there, his arms open wide for me. Without even thinking twice, I took a step forward and wrapped my arms around him, burying my face into his neck. "You don't know how happy I am to see you, Liam," I whispered against his skin.

His arms tightened around my body as he let out a deep sigh. "I saw the tweets. Is everything okay?" He asked with concern in his voice, pulling back to get a look at my face.

Running my hands over it, I shook my head. "It's awful, Liam. Everything has been absolutely horrendous since the end of last week. Mum and Troy got engaged, Louis kind of broke up with me, and now on top of that, the entire school practically despises me."

He gave me a sad, sympathetic look. "I'm so sorry, Harry. I wouldn't even wish my worst enemy any of that. But did you just say that Louis broke up with you?" He questioned surprisingly.

Letting out a sigh, I nodded my head. "Yeah, I did. I mean, I do understand him. This is what couldn't happen if we were to get into a relationship, and since it now did, there's no other option but to end it. Mum and Troy would have probably found out about us eventually anyway, and not to mention what the people here would say. It's just impossible. We're just not bound to be in a relationship."

I knew what I said the other day about how Louis and I were made for each other, but now I had just lost all my hope. I loved him to bits, but did that even matter when no one else wanted us to be together?

"I understand..." He trailed off, biting his bottom lip. "It's just sad, you know? I know how much you like him. I mean, you would be blind not to see the admiration you have in your eyes whenever you look at him. I don't want my best friend to be heartbroken either, and you out of all people deserve to be with the one you love if they love you back."

I gave him a sad smile, wrapping my arms around his neck to give him another hug. "You don't know how happy I am that

I have you. I wouldn't know what to do without you right now. You're always there for me when I need you the most."

He laughed dryly, patting my back. When we separated again, he pulled his eyebrows together. "You don't know who posted all those tweets, do you?" He asked.

Shaking my head, I looked down at the floor. "No, but I wish I did. I want to know who it is that doesn't want me and Louis to be happy. I want to know who it is that hates us so much that they want to see us heartbroken," I sighed.

Liam nodded slowly, seeming to be thinking about something. "Well, as far as I know, I don't know anyone who hates you or would want to hurt you. It must be something Louis has done if that's the case. Not that I think he has enemies, but you're like the child of an angel. No one could possibly not like you."

Another sad smile spread on my lips. "I'm glad you think of me that way, but I don't know... I could have done something that I don't know of," I shrugged, but Liam just shook his head determinedly.

"No, I'm pretty certain this doesn't have to do with you. If you want to, I'll help you find out who did this and why they did it."

I nodded my head. "I'd like that very much. Thank you, Liam."

He flashed me a genuine smile. "Of course, Harry."

That morning was probably one of the worst mornings I'd had in my entire life. In class, people would toss crumpled paper at me while giving me rude remarks, and it was the same thing in the hallway. I felt so small, as if I was worth nothing. People treated me like I was some kind of rag doll they could say and do anything to. If it weren't for the fact that I felt so empty inside, I would have minded more than I did. Sure, I did mind that they treated me so badly, but I had no energy to do anything about it. I just felt like a walking shell.

It didn't make matters better that Louis didn't seem to be treated the same way. When we were in class, people just threw him nasty glances, but they didn't say anything to him. I didn't know whether it was because of his reputation and high status at this school or something else, but it hurt that I was treated differently than him.

Of course I didn't want him to be called different names and things like that, but I didn't want to be the only one suffering like this. To be more specific, I didn't want to be the only one feeling this bad.

He didn't seem to be his usual happy self today, though, and that was something new. On top of that, he was by himself and not with Eleanor, and it made me wonder if she had 'broken up' with him now that she knew the truth. I was pretty sure she couldn't have been happy about it, at least, and if I were her, I wouldn't stick with him either, so that was most likely the reason behind her absence.

When lunch rolled around, I found myself sitting at a table with Liam and Zayn, nibbling on a tuna sandwich. To be honest, I wasn't even hungry, but I knew better than not to eat. Food was important to survive. It didn't matter whether you felt down or not.

Across the room, Louis was sitting with some of his friends from the football team, but by the looks of it, they didn't seem to be acknowledging him. In fact, they seemed to be ignoring him, and I couldn't help but feel bad about it. All I wanted was to go over and give him a hug so I could feel his arms around me and just be in his presence because that was the only time I felt really content.

"Hey there, guys."

Looking up, I noticed that Niall and Ed had just made an appearance and were now sitting at our table. Liam and Zayn greeted them while I just nodded my head in acknowledgment. Niall flashed me a concerned look, but I decided not to care about it and just looked away from him.

I started fiddling with the plastic wrapper of my sandwich, ignoring the other four people and keeping their voices out. It wasn't until I heard someone call my name that I looked up at them questioningly. "What?"

"Are you okay, Harry?" Ed asked, raising an eyebrow at me.

Shrugging my shoulders, I looked down at the surface of the table. "Well, as okay as you can possibly be when you've just broken up with your boyfriend and have the entire school hating you."

"You and Louis broke up?" Niall exclaimed, making me look up at him with knitted eyebrows.

"Yeah? Well, kind of. We haven't really talked about it, but it doesn't even matter," I muttered.

"Why doesn't it matter?" Ed asked curiously, and I turned to look at him.

"Because he won't talk to me after all those tweets were posted. This is what he dreaded when we first got into a relationship. That was why he didn't want us to be together in the first place. He wanted us to be a secret since he knew how everyone would react if they knew the truth."

Both Ed and Niall exchanged a look that made me curious. What were they thinking? Niall eventually shook his head, giving me another look of sympathy. "I can't do this anymore," he said.

Liam and Zayn were also listening closely now, Liam seeming very curious all of a sudden. "What do you mean?" He asked, crossing his arms over his chest.

The blonde-haired boy gave Ed another look before turning to me. Ed looked nothing but scared. He knew what Niall was about to do and he wanted to stop it, but he knew he couldn't do anything because Niall had already made his mind up.

"Ed and I posted the tweets."

The silence that fell after that sentence could be cut with a knife. Everyone but Ed was staring at the blonde-haired guy with wide-open mouths. What did just escape his lips?

"What the fuck are you saying?" Liam burst out, and Zayn had to hold him down in order for him not to pounce on Niall.

Ed covered his face with his hands as he shook his head. Niall looked ready to cry and I was just speechless. I didn't know what to say or how to react. It just didn't make any sense. What was their reason?

"I said Ed and I--"

"I know what you said, dumbass. The question is; *why*? Why would you want to hurt them like this? Do you guys even know how much shit Harry has had to go through because of what you did? I can't believe how you as his friend would want to hurt him like this," Liam snapped, glaring daggers at the two boys.

Niall looked down at the table in shame. "We didn't want to hurt him..." He mumbled.

Ed shook his head in agreement. "No, that wasn't the reason why we did it."

"Then what was it? Why did you go through with this shit?" Liam wanted to know and raised his eyebrows.

Niall and Ed exchanged another look before looking down in defeat.

"We did it for Harry because we know the real Louis Tomlinson, and the real Louis Tomlinson is not worth someone like Harry Styles."

Chapter 39

[Harry]

"We did it for Harry because we know the real Louis Tomlinson, and the real Louis Tomlinson is not worth someone like Harry Styles."

Liam let out a loud snort. "Is that supposed to be some kind of excuse? I mean, come on guys. Don't you have anything better to come with?"

While he continued being upset about it, I studied Zayn. His eyebrows were pulled together and he seemed to be in deep thought. It was as if he knew something. That was why I was the only one who wasn't surprised when he eventually opened his mouth.

"I think I know what Niall means by that..." He trailed off, making Liam turn to him with wide eyes.

Niall turned to Zayn as well, the concerned look on his face turning into a small smile. Ed looked a little happier too while I just had the biggest lump in my throat. I mean, if Zayn - Louis' best friend - agreed with what Niall just said, then it had to be some truth to it. I wasn't sure I wanted to hear it, though.

"Zayn, babe, what are you saying?" Liam asked, taking his hand in his own.

The raven-haired boy ran a hand through his hair as he let out a sigh. "I'm guessing it has to do with the way Louis has treated and spoken about Harry, right?"

YOU THINK I HATE YOU?

Niall nodded sadly, turning to look at me. "I swear, Harry, I never wanted to hurt you, but when Ed noticed that Louis was the one you had fallen for, I couldn't help but do something about it. You don't know what he's said about you. He's called you the worst names you could possibly come up with. I mean, he would even go around in the locker room after practice and talk about how much of a 'stupid nerd' you were. Don't even mention how poorly he treated you. You don't deserve him, Harry. You're worth so much more than him," he almost pleaded.

Ed nodded in agreement, meaning that he had the same mindset as Niall. I wanted to say that I was happy they cared about me so much, but I couldn't. The anger I felt overpowered everything. I knew that Louis hadn't been exactly nice to me in the past, but I hadn't been to him either. Besides, I knew the reason why, and they didn't. They didn't know the truth. They didn't know that he had been mean to me just because I had ignored him when he needed me the most. They didn't know that he was mean to me because he was jealous of my girlfriend and friendship with Liam. They didn't know that he did it all just because he was in love with me.

My jaw was clenched and so were my fists. I glanced at Zayn one more time to see if he knew the truth, but when he seemed just as concerned as Niall and Ed, I decided I couldn't stay here. They had ruined my chance at being with Louis just because they didn't know the truth. I honestly couldn't even stand the thought of being around them right now.

With that in mind, I stood up abruptly, my chair hitting the floor in the process. The loud sound made everyone in the cafeteria look my way, but I couldn't care less. Without another glance at my so-called 'friends', I stormed out of the room and headed towards the only place I knew I could be by myself right now; the toilets.

On my way there, I could feel people throwing me confused and disgusted looks, but I was getting used to it by now, so I decided not to care about it. Instead, I focused on getting to my destination as quickly as possible so I could finally lock myself up in the toilets and be by myself. Once I was sitting on the toilet seat, I pulled my knees up to my chin and started crying. Everything that I had kept inside me during the last two days just came crashing down on me and I couldn't stop it anymore.

I didn't care that I was in a public bathroom and that there could be other people in here as well. Most of the people were in the cafeteria anyway so the possibility wasn't even that high. Hugging my knees even closer to my chest, I buried my face in the fabric of my black jeans, letting my tears fall on them. I was so caught up in my thoughts that I almost missed the sound of someone knocking on my stall.

"Go away, Liam. I'm not in the mood to talk," I sniffled, looking up at the green door.

"Harry, it's Louis."

The second I heard his voice, I stood up abruptly, unlocking the stall so quickly that I almost hit the door right in Louis' face. If he hadn't taken a step back, I would have.

Instantly, I flung myself forward and wrapped my arms around him. He had to grab my hips so we didn't fall to the ground by the harsh impact of our bodies crashing together. Once he had a hold on me, he backed me up so we were inside the stall again and locked the door behind us. I had my face buried in the crook of his neck, sobbing even harder now that he was here.

"Hey, what happened, love?" He asked worriedly, caressing my back.

My heart skipped a beat when he called me 'love', and I wondered if he had suddenly changed his mind about everything.

I pulled back a little so I could get a look at him. His eyebrows were pulled together in concern and his eyes looked a bit confused. I let out a sigh, shaking my head. "It was t-them, Louis. Ed and Niall were the ones who posted the tweets. They s-said they did because I didn't deserve you, that it was because they cared about me."

His hand on my back suddenly froze, and I could feel how it clenched in a fist. His face turned red with anger but I knew it wasn't directed at me. "I knew those two fuckers were up to some shit," he seethed, breathing heavily through his nose.

I tried to calm him by reaching up and caressing his cheek, but his jaw wouldn't unclench no matter how hard I tried.

His eyes eventually found mine. "What did they say then? That I'm not as nice as you and therefore don't deserve you? Too bad I already know that."

Letting out half a sniffle and half a laugh, I rolled my eyes. "That's just nonsense. I mean, you can be pretty genuine sometimes," I joked, making him glare at me.

"Seriously, Harry? This is not the best time to joke around. We just found out that two of our best friends have outed us to the entire school and therefore can't stay together. Not just that, but they did it for some lame reason too. It wouldn't surprise me if it turns out it was just because of jealousy. Niall probably still likes you and wanted to do all he could to tear us apart," he muttered, averting his gaze from mine again.

I let out a sigh, shaking my head. "You're right. This is not the best time to joke, but you should know that you are nice and caring when you want to be, and you do deserve me. As for Niall, I don't know, to be honest. I just think he thought he was doing me a favor, but he didn't know the truth. He just saw the bad you who had called me names and was mean to me. He didn't know the reason behind it, and the same goes for Ed."

He thought about it for a while, his eyebrows knitted together in concentration. "You might be right about that, but I can't help but feel slightly betrayed. I thought they were my friends, but if what they said is true, it means that they don't genuinely like me and that they have never really been my true friends."

Well, I couldn't argue with that. I mean, if Ed and Niall's intention was to do me a favor, they hadn't cared about Louis at all. Maybe they just thought he was playing with my feelings or something, but either way, that was no excuse. If they were his friend, they wouldn't have done that to him without knowing better. "You must be very disappointed," I said, biting my lip.

He shrugged as he started to move his hand along my back again. "Well, it just goes to show that you can't trust anyone, even if you think they are your friends."

I nodded curtly, letting out a sigh. The tears had stopped rolling down my cheeks now, but I still felt just as bad as before. However, it did help that Louis came here to comfort me. "What are we going to do now?" I asked, looking up at him.

His jaw was still clenched and his eyes hadn't turned back to their usual ocean blue color yet. "I don't know. Is there anything we can do? Everything is already too late. Shit has already happened. I mean, haven't you noticed the way people have treated us today?" He asked, raising his eyebrows questioningly.

Averting my gaze, I let out another sigh. "I know. I just... I just wish there was a way for us to still be together. You mean the world to me. I mean, just you showing up here made me feel so much better, and knowing I will have to live without your presence in the future literally kills me..." I trailed off.

He cradled my head, cupping my cheeks in his small hands. "I'll always be here, though. You'll always be my stepbrother, so we will never be too far from each other," he reminded me, looking me deep in the eyes.

I swallowed hard. "Maybe not technically, but it'll feel like you're miles away when I know I can't have you as close to me as I want to."

This time it was his turn to let out a sigh. He let the pad of his thumb run along my bottom lip as he looked at me thoughtfully. "It's not going to be easy, I know, but at least we will always be in each other's lives one way or another. That's better than nothing, right?"

I shifted my feet, looking down at my shoes the best I could when he held my head in his hands. "Right..." I muttered.

Right then, the bell rang, almost making me jump in surprise. Louis noticed how tense I suddenly got and let out a laugh. "Still easily scared, eh?" He winked, trying to lighten the mood.

I glared at him. "And you were the one who told me it was a bad time to joke around. Yeah, right," I said, rolling my eyes.

The smile dropped from his face. "Yeah, sorry."

Without thinking too much about it, I leaned in and kissed him quickly. I then slipped out of his hold and unlocked the stall. "It's okay. See you later."

Even if I didn't see his face, I could tell that he was shocked by my actions. He stayed in his place when I shut the door behind him and exited the bathroom to head to class. On my way there, I made sure to wipe the last tears off my cheeks and keep my head down so no one could see that I had been crying.

I tried not to think about Niall and Ed's confession during the next hour, but it was almost impossible not to. I just couldn't believe that they had been the ones sneaking on us and outing us like that. It was actually a little scary. It wasn't just that, though, but just like Louis, I also felt a bit betrayed. I thought they were my friends too, yet they kept this to themselves and didn't even think of talking to me about it personally before they decided to tell the entire school. It was just so unbelievable that I wanted to pull my hair out of my head. How could they have done such a stupid thing?

When the last bell of the day rang and I was ready to head to the bus stop outside school, I was interrupted by a female voice that I recognized very well. I was in the hallway, facing my locker when this happened, and to say that my body tensed at the voice would be an understatement. It literally froze to ice.

"Harry?"

I turned around to face the brown-haired girl I had dated about two years ago, swallowing hard at the sight of her. She was wearing a green bomber jacket and a pair of blue, ripped jeans. What surprised me was that her lips were twitched in a smile, considering the entire school had looked at me disgustingly the whole day.

"Miranda," I noted, my eyes wide open in shock because why was she out of all people here talking to me?

She put a hand on her hip and tilted her head to the side. "So, I heard you and Louis are dating. Is it true that you're stepbrothers as well?" She asked curiously.

I looked down at the floor in shame, thinking that she would run away in disgust when I replied to her. "Um, yeah, but we've kind of broken up now."

To my surprise, she stayed in her place, her eyebrows pulling together in confusion. "What? Why would you do that?"

Looking at her incredulously, I let out a snort. "Are you mental? People have been talking shit about us the entire day. We would be dead in a couple of weeks if we were to continue dating. At least, they would never stop harassing us," I confessed.

She still looked confused as she bit her bottom lip thoughtfully. "I get what you mean, but come on. You guys don't have more than a few months left here in this school. I'm sure you would be able to survive till then. Also, if you really like each other, I'm certain things will work out for you no matter what."

Now it was my turn to knit my eyebrows together in confusion. "Why are you taking this news so well? Why aren't you disgusted like everyone else? I mean, you if anyone should be considering you've been together with me. Aren't you like weirded out or something?" I questioned, slinging my backpack over my shoulder.

She shook her head slowly. "No, of course not. I mean, sure, I was a little surprised when I heard that you were stepbrothers, but come on. I've known ever since we dated that

Louis has feelings for you. He wasn't very subtle with the glares he shot me whenever you and I were together. Nor was he with the way he kept looking at you. You'd be blind not to see the heart eyes he had for you, you know?"

I could feel my cheeks heat up by her words. Was this true? How come I had never noticed it, though? Surely, it must've been because of how caught up I was with Miranda at the time. I was just too blind to notice that Louis even wanted to be with me.

Running a hand through my curls, I gave her a small smile. "Is that so?"

She let out a light chuckle, nodding her head. "Yeah, very much so. That's why I wasn't surprised when I heard that you were together. Did you seriously have to become stepbrothers for you to notice this?" She asked, looking at me playfully.

I nodded shamefully, letting out a chuckle myself. "I guess..."

"Well, what I was trying to say is that even if things are bad now, you shouldn't give up on what you have. Who cares if you live in the same house and that your parents are dating? In a couple of months, you'll be out of there anyway and no one will know that your parents live together. I know how much Louis likes you, and I can imagine how much you like him, so why give up on something like that? Also, don't care about what the pricks here say. They're just jealous because they can't have either of you," she smirked, making my heart swell with love for this girl.

Now I really understood why I had dated her back in the days. Not that I felt the same anymore, but she was so caring and sweet. I definitely wasn't ashamed of the fact that I had been together with her. I mean, who expected her out of all people to be accepting of my and Louis' relationship? Well, I sure didn't.

Without a second thought, I stepped forward and wrapped my arms around her petite body. When I felt her arms go around my figure as well, I let my eyes fall shut, enjoying the feeling of not being hated by someone that wasn't very close to me anymore. It felt nice, really nice actually.

Once I pulled away, I gave her an appreciating smile. "You don't know how happy you just made me. My day has been so shitty, but now you've definitely lightened it up. You're like the only one apart from Liam who hasn't been against me and Louis. If only you knew how much it means to me that one more person is accepting of us."

"Well, even if we aren't together anymore, I want you to be happy. I still care about you, and I know that Louis likes you, so why would I not be accepting of you? Love is love after all, and as long as you're happy, I am too, and so should everyone else be."

I sent her another wide smile, shaking my head incredulously. "Well, I can definitely see why I dated you," I laughed and she joined me.

With a flick of her hair, she said; "Of course. Aren't I just amazing?"

"Very much so," I chuckled.

It wasn't until then I remembered that I had a bus to catch, and I was sure it was not going to wait for me. Once I realized this, my eyes widened and I put my hand on Miranda's shoulder. "It was really nice talking to you, Miranda, and I appreciate your acceptance, but my bus is literally leaving at this second, so I've gotta go."

She rolled her eyes, waving a hand in dismissal. "Then what are you still doing here?" She asked, raising an eyebrow playfully.

With a grin on my face, I shrugged my shoulders. "See you later."

"Bye, Harry," she laughed.

I started walking towards the exit but made sure to turn around when I replied with a 'bye' to her.

"Oh, and don't forget to take your Louis back!" She reminded me.

"I won't!" I shouted back, the smile never leaving my face on my way to the bus that was just about to close its doors when I arrived.

Once I was seated, I couldn't help but shake my head in disbelief. How come one person's acceptance and words could make me feel so much better? At lunch, I was ready to give up on me and Louis altogether, but now after I had talked to Miranda, it was like I had suddenly gained hope again. It was an amazing feeling, and I just wanted things to turn around now and go my way instead of against me.

And hopefully, they would. But then again, when was luck ever on my side.

Chapter 40

[Harry]

It took me a few minutes until I could feel it. Someone was staring at me. It wasn't one of those stares filled with disgust that I had received the entire day, but more like an intense one. With a frown on my face, I turned to my left, noticing that Niall was sitting in the seat across from me. His eyes were stuck on my figure as his lips were pressed in a thin line.

The second I noticed that he was the one staring at me, I averted my gaze abruptly, looking out the bus window instead. I didn't want anything to do with him right now, not after this morning. I had been avoiding both him and Ed the entire day, and so far, it had worked just fine. Until now.

Thankfully, he didn't say anything. He just kept staring at me as if I was some kind of unsolved puzzle. I wanted nothing but to exit this bus as quickly as possible and get away from him, but unfortunately, there were still a few more minutes until the bus would come to a stop.

Doing my best to ignore him, I fished my phone from my jeans pocket and scrolled through my social media. It wasn't until the bus came to a halt and people started getting ready to stand up that he looked away from me. I mentally let out a sigh of relief and got up myself to exit the bus.

It turned out I wasn't that fortunate, though, and I probably shouldn't even be surprised about that. The second I was out in the cold, I could hear a familiar voice behind me, making my muscles freeze. Against my will, I turned around to face the blonde-haired boy I had once thought I could trust but didn't anymore.

"Niall, what do you want? Honestly, I'm not in the mood to--"

"Harry, please. Just listen to me," he pleaded, looking at me with puppy eyes.

I crossed my arms over my chest, looking at him skeptically. "What do you have to say that could possibly make things better? You and Ed, who I thought were two of my closest friends, have ruined my chance to be with the one I love. There's nothing you can do to make up for it."

He let out a sigh, running a hand through his hair. "Look, I'm sorry Ed and I outed you and Louis like that, but you have to realize that he is not a good guy, Harry. You're not like him whatsoever. I mean, he smokes and you hate people who smoke. He also acts like some kind of diva who thinks he rules the school. I just... I just don't understand how you can possibly want to be with him," he said helplessly.

A crease formed between my eyebrows. "How can you even say something like that? I thought you were his friend, yet here you are, talking shit about him. If you knew him, you would have known how caring and sweet he can be. He's nothing like you just described. Sure, he smokes, but that doesn't make me love him any less. He's wonderful when he wants to be, and the fact that you're here, talking about him like this makes me sick," I blurted.

He swallowed hard, looking at me nervously. "I didn't... I didn't mean to sound rude or anything. I was just trying to protect you. I care about you, Harry. I want what's best for you, and I know Louis isn't," he said, his eyes pleading.

"Did I hear someone say my name?"

My heart instantly skipped a beat in my chest at the sound of that angelic voice. I would recognize it anywhere, and it always made a smile form on my lips. Turning around, I noticed that Louis was walking up to us, his arms crossed over his chest with an eyebrow raised expectantly.

Niall's eyes widened at the sight of the feathery-haired boy. "I... Hey, Louis," he laughed nervously.

"Don't you dare 'hey' me, Niall. I know very well that it was you and that red-headed bastard who posted all those tweets," he snapped, glaring at the blue-eyed boy.

Niall didn't reply. He just looked down at his feet in shame, his cheeks flushed. Once he looked up again, Louis continued talking. "I can't believe I actually thought you two were my friends. Actually, I would even be ashamed of calling myself Harry's friend if I were you. Do you have any fucking idea of what mess you two have caused? Harry has been treated like shit today, he's been called names and I don't even know what just because you decided to tell the entire school that we had a thing for each other. I don't care about me, but he doesn't deserve any of it."

My heart swelled with love for this boy. I loved him so much it couldn't even be put into words. Just the fact that he was standing up for me at this second just showed how caring he actually was. Niall seemed shocked about it, and it didn't surprise me considering he thought Louis was nothing but a cold-hearted bad boy.

"I... I didn't think people would react that way. Is... is it true, Harry?" He asked, looking at me worriedly.

I just looked back at him with a blank expression on my face, and judging by the way his face fell, I assumed that he got my message. "It was not my intention whatsoever, and neither was it Ed's. We just thought we did what was best for you, Harry."

Louis let out a loud snort. "Best for him? I mean, come one, Niall. Don't we all know that all this doesn't just have to do with the fact that I'm the one he has feelings for? Just admit that you're sad and jealous of the fact that it's not you. You love him, don't you?" He stated flatly.

Niall's cheeks turned, if possible, even redder and he looked down at the ground again. "Of course I love him," he mumbled, almost too quietly to hear. "And of course I want him to be with me, but I want him to be happy more than anything, and I know that he could do so much better than you."

Louis' nostrils flared as he gave Niall a death stare. "Don't you think I already know that? I know I'm not good enough for him, that he deserves someone better, but I waited two fucking years for him. I was too selfish to let go of him. However, you should know that he's not as innocent as you might think he is."

My cheeks heated up as I remembered the way I had treated Louis back in the days. He was right. I wasn't exactly innocent either.

Letting out a sigh, I decided to join the conversation again. "He's right, Niall. I've done bad things to him too, and I did deserve the way he treated me. That's why I was so mad at you and Ed when you told me the reason you posted the tweets. Louis and I share quite an eventful past, but we've fixed it all now. We've put it behind us, okay?"

Niall bit his bottom lip, looking at me and Louis apologetically. "I guess neither of us should have interfered with your relationship like that. I mean, it's quite obvious that you know each other better than we thought you did. I'm uhh... I'm sorry for what we did. Neither of us meant to hurt you."

Louis just rolled his eyes, clearly getting sick of this conversation. "You do know that it's already too late though, right? You've already ruined everything."

With that said, he turned on his heel and walked away. When he did so, Niall shot me a confused look. My heart sank in my chest by his words and I looked down at my shoes sadly. "What did he mean by that?" Niall asked curiously.

Looking up at him, I shot him an emotionless look. "He meant that it's already too late. We can't be together any longer thanks to the way people treat us now that they know we have a thing for each other. He also thinks that his dad will disown him if he finds out about it," I muttered.

He let out a deep sigh. "Oh, I see..." He trailed off.

When neither of us said anything else, I decided that I was done with this conversation as well. But just as I was about to turn around, Niall grabbed my wrist to stop me. "I just want you to know that I really am sorry, Harry. I thought you were just too blind to notice who Louis really was. I didn't know you knew him on the level you did."

I feigned a smile, nodding my head. "You didn't know, and you were just trying to protect me, I get it. But, it would've been better if you had just come and talked to me about it personally instead of outing us to the entire school like that."

He nodded shamefully. "Yeah, I'm sorry about that."

"I gotta go now, Niall. I guess I'll see you around," I said, looking in the direction where Louis had walked off.

"Yeah. Bye, Harry," he muttered.

With that, I started walking home. I kept a rather fast pace considering I wanted to catch up with Louis. I wanted to talk to him about Miranda and how accepting she had been, how she thought we should give our relationship a try despite everything that had happened.

It wasn't very easy to walk fast, though, considering it was very slippery outside, so whenever I tried to quicken my pace, I always ended up stumbling. It was that, and Louis didn't walk very slowly himself, which didn't exactly make it easier for me.

Once I finally caught sight of him, I let out a sigh of relief. In a matter of seconds, I was right behind him, grabbing his wrist. Judging by the shocked look on his face when he turned around, he had not been expecting me. "Harry?" He asked confusedly.

I looked up at him, biting my bottom lip. "Can we talk?" I asked nervously, afraid that the answer would be a straight 'no'.

His eyebrows pulled together in a frown as he looked down at his left hand. My eyes followed his only to land on the lit cigarette between his fingers. I gulped visibly. I didn't actually like the fact that he smoked, but as I said to Niall, it didn't make me love him any less.

Before he could open his mouth, I reached my hand out, taking the cancer stick from his hold. "This isn't good for you, Louis."

To my surprise, he let me take it and didn't even complain when I stomped on it to put it out. He just let out a sigh and ran a hand through his hair. "I know, it's just a bad habit I have whenever I get stressed," he explained.

My lips pressed into a thin line. So, smoking was his rescue whenever he felt stressed about something? "So, it calms your nerves, or what?"

He shrugged. "Yeah, I guess you can put it that way."

Letting out another sigh, I started walking again, and Louis walked with me. "So, what did you want to talk about?" He asked, his words coming out in a mutter.

I looked at the side of his face, admiring his beauty. His jawline was so defined, and I loved the crinkles by his eyes that appeared whenever the corner of his cheeks twitched. He was just breathtaking.

Shaking myself out of my thoughts, I remembered why I had walked up to him in the first place. I wanted to talk to him about Miranda. "I talked to Miranda today..." I started, watching his face at the mention of my ex.

His jaw clenched and so did his hands. He didn't say anything for a couple of seconds, but I let him take his time. "Yeah, I saw you two hug when I was leaving," he muttered, looking into the distance.

Oh. I did not expect that, but it didn't matter. That hug was just friendly anyway. It wasn't like he needed to worry about it. "Okay, but that's not what I wanted to talk about. She..." I trailed off, not really knowing how to explain it.

Louis turned to me then, looking at me with his eyebrows pulled together. "What? Did she tell you just like everyone else that it's disgusting you're together with your stepbrother? Well, guess what? I've heard that too many times today, so I'd rather not hear it again."

"That's not what she said at all," I explained, looking back at him. "It was rather the opposite. She encouraged me to stay with you. She told me that she noticed the way you looked at me when she and I were together and that she was certain you have liked me since then. She also said that we shouldn't listen to the people talking shit about us because they're probably just jealous that they can't be with either of us now," I smiled, examining his features.

He swallowed hard and averted his gaze as he picked up his pace, leaving me a couple of yards behind him. He didn't say anything when I caught up with him, and that fact made my heart drop in my chest. He didn't feel as hopeful as I did about it. He probably just thought it was for nothing because the majority of the people hated us anyway. "You don't think what she said matters, do you?" I sighed.

When he didn't say anything and just kept his gaze forward, I bit my bottom lip anxiously. It took at least a minute until he ran a hand through his hair and let out a groan. "You're right. I don't think what she said makes any difference. Most of the people hate us and they will never stop if we don't do anything about it. Besides, our parents are bound to find out about us if we don't break up."

I could feel frustration build up inside me. "Sure, I do understand that you're afraid of our parents finding out, but why do you care so much about the people at school? It's not like you have received as much shit today as I have. The only thing they've basically done to you is ignoring you. Besides, we'll be out of there in a few months. We won't have to see any of those people again, so it doesn't matter what they think," I explained.

He went silent again, looking rather thoughtful. Was it possible that he was thinking through my words, that he was actually considering changing his mind? God, I really hoped so. It was getting difficult to be the only one having my hopes up about this relationship.

Unfortunately, we arrived at the house before he had opened his mouth. I didn't want to pressure him to talk, so I kept my mouth shut as we entered our home. It surprised me that the front door wasn't locked, and judging by the way shock flashed through Louis' eyes when I turned the door handle, he was as well.

Knitting my eyebrows together in confusion, I started untying my shoes once Louis had closed the door behind us. "Hello?" I shouted through the house.

Gemma showed up around the corner, looking at us with a serious expression on her face. A lump instantly formed in my throat, making me swallow hard. "Harry, Louis, I saw the tweets. Is everything okay?" She asked worriedly.

It surprised me that she was alone and didn't have Devon over. It was pretty rare that they weren't hanging out with each other these days. Not that I cared right now because I had more important stuff to think about.

Louis didn't say anything, and when I looked at him and noticed that he showed no sign of doing so either, I took it upon myself to answer her. "Could've been better," I breathed, hanging my jacket on the hanger.

She pursed her lips, her eyes landing on Louis. He didn't meet her gaze but focused on taking off his own jacket. Her eyes fell back on me, and she had a sympathetic look on her face. "Did you--" She started, but Louis cut her off, surprising us both.

"They hate us. Everybody thinks we're disgusting and everything is just shit, alright?" His voice sounded as cold as ice, almost making me cringe in uncomfortableness.

Gemma nodded slowly, biting her bottom lip. "Do you think mum and Troy are going to find out about it?"

I shrugged, and so did Louis. "We don't know, but we're afraid so, yes," I mumbled, looking down at the floor.

She shifted from one foot to the other, letting out a deep breath. "What are you going to do? Are you sticking together or?" She asked, flicking her gaze between me and Louis questioningly.

Looking down at the floor, I found myself unable to speak. I didn't know what to say because I wanted nothing but to keep being together with Louis. Judging by his behavior and words today and even yesterday, though, I wasn't very sure that he wanted the same thing. Maybe he thought I wasn't worth it, or it was just that he was too afraid.

"We think it's too risky, right Harry?" Louis said after almost half a minute, looking at me pointedly.

When I just watched him without saying anything, Gemma instantly realized that we didn't share that thought. She squinted her eyes, watching me curiously. Louis closed his eyes frustratingly, running a hand through his hair. Just as Gemma was about to open her mouth and say something, Louis grabbed his backpack from the floor and walked out of the entryway and up to his room, slamming the door shut behind him.

Letting out a sigh, I shook my head sadly. "I don't know what to do, Gemma. I just love him too much to break up with him like that. Sure, practically everyone at school hates us, but I don't care. Louis makes me happy, and to me, receiving hate is worth it if it means I can be with him," I explained.

Gemma walked up to me, embracing me in a warm and loving hug. It was so nice and soothing to hug her, someone I had known my entire life and someone who had always been on my side no matter what. There were so much love and emotions that built up in our hug that I could feel my eyes welling up with tears.

"Hey, it's okay, Harry. I understand. I would've thought the same if Devon and I had been in your situation. Louis is just scared. I don't know if it is because of his reputation or the fact that our parents may find out about you, but it's one of those two options. It's not that he thinks you aren't worth it. I'm sure that he loves you just as much as you love him. I can see it in his eyes when he looks at you. He's just frustrated that he can't be with you," Gemma reassured me, making me smile weakly.

"You really think so? Because I'm actually starting to doubt that he thinks I am worth it. I mean, it's not that I don't get that he's scared. I understand that, but if I can see through that, why can't he?" I mumbled against her shoulder.

She pulled back a little so she could look at my face. "I think it is because of his past. We haven't been through what he's been through. We never lost our dad, he just left us. Try putting yourself in his situation. If you didn't have anyone but mum, not even me, wouldn't you have been just as careful about having her love you as he is with Troy?" She raised her eyebrows, looking at me expectantly.

I bit my lip, realizing that she was right. If I had been Louis, I would have probably been just as scared as he was. I just... I just wanted him to be with me, and I wanted him to want to be with me too.

"I guess you're right..." I trailed off, meeting her gaze.

She flashed me a small smile. "I really hope things will work out for you because I want nothing but for you two to be happy, and I'm sure mum and Troy want that as well in the long run."

"I really hope so too."

Chapter 41

[Louis]

Once I had slammed my bedroom door shut behind me, I let myself fall on my bed, a frustrated grunt leaving my lips. Why couldn't Harry understand? I mean, I understood that he wanted us to be together. I wanted nothing else but to be with him too, but he knew how much my dad meant to me. He knew that I couldn't risk losing him. I also couldn't stand seeing Harry get so much hate.

All day, I had to watch how badly everyone treated him. If it wasn't in the hallway, it was in the classroom, and since we shared all of our classes, I witnessed it all. He had no idea how much it hurt me to see him get treated like that without being able to do anything about it, if I didn't want things to only get worse.

I listened to what Harry said about us soon leaving school, but it didn't matter. I wasn't sure if I could even last a week of seeing him get treated so badly. So, add these two factors together and you would understand why it was better if we weren't together. I mean, all odds were against us and they had always been. It was like we had started something we knew wouldn't work out in the end anyway.

It wasn't only Harry I was frustrated with. I was frustrated with myself for even thinking that we could be together in the first place. If I hadn't been so stupid to try showing him what he had done to me two years ago and also try finding out if he reciprocated my feelings, then none of this would have happened. Harry wouldn't have fallen for me and I would have just accepted that we would never be together.

Now things weren't like that, though, and I had done all these things I shouldn't have done, so basically, I was the only one to blame here. I shouldn't have made him fall for me in the first place because things would have been so much easier then.

The worst part - something I was ashamed to admit - was that I didn't regret the time Harry and I had spent together. To be honest, it had been some of the best weeks of my life. Maybe I should hit myself for even thinking that way, but I couldn't help it. I mean, sex with Harry was just... it was mind-blowing. It was definitely the best sex I'd ever had, and I'd had sex with a few people. Not to be mean, but Eleanor wasn't even half as good as Harry.

Speaking of the brown-haired girl, she had been another difficult matter today. She wasn't happy when she met me at my locker in the morning, she wasn't happy at all, but I didn't expect her to be either. I knew she had found out that I had basically been cheating on her, so I couldn't exactly expect something else. What did surprise me, however, was that she hadn't been as mad as I thought she would be. She was sad if anything, and to be honest, that was even worse than having her be upset with me.

I just didn't like feeling guilty. Usually, I was good at not feeling that way, but with Eleanor, it was just inevitable. We had known each other for more than two years and we had practically been together ever since then. We knew everything about each other, so how could I not feel guilty? Apart from my dad and Harry, she was the one who knew me best, so it hurt seeing her being sad by something I had caused and done. It was stupid of me to fake date her when I knew that I would feel guilty about it afterward.

What Harry had been right about was that I hadn't received nearly half as much hate as he had. Sure, my friends had pretty much ignored me during the entire day and shot me a few disgusted looks, but that was only predictable. Jimmy had made a snide remark on the bus too, but I had expected more. Maybe it was due to my reputation, that I was known for being a 'bad boy', and that people were afraid of treating me the way they treated Harry because of that, but that was a bad excuse if so. It wasn't like I was riskier to bully than Harry.

Something that surprised me was the way I had reacted to everything. A few months ago when I was afraid of just being seen together with the curly-haired lad, I would have probably played along with his bullies and even laughed and made fun of him myself, but that wasn't the case anymore. I didn't know if it was because of the fact that I was more grown-up and mature now or if it was because I knew how much I loved him. I leaned towards the latter because I couldn't even picture myself hurting Harry that way any longer. I loved him way too much to even think about it.

I never thought I would say this, but the cold-hearted Louis Tomlinson had started becoming a softy. I didn't know if I liked it or not, but I guess that was the influence Harry had on me. He made me go soft with the love I felt for him. I mean, just thinking about him made my heart flutter in my chest, and I knew that was a sign of love.

Mentally smacking myself on the forehead for thinking about him that way, I let out another frustrated sigh. I had to forget about him, and by doing so I couldn't think of how much I loved him.

It only made matters worse that he lived in the same house as me, so it was pretty much impossible not to think about him, but I had to try my best. Otherwise, I would be miserable for the rest of my life.

During the entire afternoon, I stayed in my bedroom and tried to come up with stuff to do that would take my mind off the curly-haired lad. I tried listening to music, but then I remembered that one time when he had come into my room and told me to turn the volume down. I tried taking a shower, but then I remembered that time when I had asked him to go and fetch a towel for me. So, there was simply nothing I could do to make me not think about him, and that frustrated me to no end. I couldn't even go on Twitter because I was only reminded of us being together by all the pictures and stuff that were out there.

At six o'clock, Anne called us down for dinner. Truth be told, I wanted nothing but to stay in my room for the rest of the day without having to face Harry, dad or Anne. I mean, what if they had found out about us and decided to confront us about it during dinner? Don't call me paranoid, everything could happen at any time.

So, it wasn't willingly I got up from my bed and trudged down the stairs to enter the kitchen where everyone was already sitting, waiting for my arrival. Dad looked up and flashed me a warm smile, and so did Anne when she noticed that I had joined them. "Sit down, Louis. We've been waiting for you."

I gulped, flicking my gaze to Harry quickly only to notice that he was too busy plating some spaghetti to look back at me.

Without saying anything, I walked over to the table and sat down beside him seeing as that was the only seat that wasn't already preoccupied. Sitting down on the chair, I glanced at dad and Anne, examining their features to see if they had something on their minds, but they were acting like they normally did. Still, I couldn't help but feel suspicious.

I could suddenly feel someone looking at me, and I instantly noticed that it was Harry. Seeing as he gave me a look of reassurance, I assumed he knew that I was suspicious about the fact that our parents knew about our secret. He placed a hand on my thigh, rubbing it soothingly. I couldn't help but tense at the touch, though. How would I be able to forget about him when he kept doing things like this? It only made me want and miss him even more.

Giving him a warning look, he averted his gaze disappointedly and let out a sigh. Anne took notice of this and looked at her son. "You okay, Harry? You seem pretty quiet today. Has something happened?" She asked worriedly.

He looked at her and shook his head. "Nah, I'm alright. Just had a tough day at school, is all," he admitted.

Mentally face-palming, I shot him another look that I made sure no one noticed. Why did he say that his day at school had been bad? Jesus, how would he be able to explain it without mentioning the truth? Sometimes he was just the worst liar of all time. I was sure he couldn't even lie to save his own life.

"What do you mean 'tough'? Was someone being mean to you?" She wondered, her eyes flickering to me.

Even though I shouldn't be surprised by her action, I couldn't help but feel upset about it. If only she knew that the last thing I would do was to be mean to him these days. I could never hurt him like that anymore.

"Uh, no. It wasn't like that. I just have a lot of schoolwork to do, and one of my teachers keeps pestering us by handing out even more things."

Anne scrunched her eyebrows together. "And you aren't stressed about that, Louis?" She asked, knowing that we shared all of our classes.

I shrugged my shoulders, deciding to put this into my own hands. Someone had to save Harry from this mess. "Well, I usually don't get stressed by school. If I have a lot of homework, I usually push it to the side. I do it at one point, but I don't let it get to me," I explained, giving her a smile.

She nodded her head, the suspicion leaving her eyes. "Alright, but you should know that you can tell me if someone's not treating you right, Harry," she told him, turning her gaze back to her son. "I'm always here if you want to talk."

Harry sent her a smile, nodding his head curtly. The worst part of it all was that Anne was right. He had been treated badly today, and it was probably one of the reasons why he was being so quiet right now. I was probably another one. I could tell it was hard for him not to tell her the truth, and the fact that he didn't just because of me made me want to hit myself yet again. As I said to Niall, sometimes I felt as though I really wasn't worthy of him.

Maybe that was another reason as to why it was better for us to go our separate ways. We were just so different from each other.

When we were almost halfway through dinner, Anne's phone suddenly started ringing. A confused look fell on her face, clarifying that she wasn't expecting anyone to call. Dad looked at her, raising his eyebrows questioningly. "Do you know who it might be?"

Her eyebrows pulled together as she shook her head and pulled her phone out of the pocket of her jeans. Watching the caller ID, the crease between her eyebrows only deepened. Suddenly, she got up from her seat and excused herself before walking out of the room. We could still hear her talking to the person on the other end, though.

"Hello?"

"Yes, I'm the mother of Harry Styles and stepmother of Louis Tomlinson."

"What do you mean 'rumors'?"

That was when the earth stopped spinning for me, and I didn't hear another word she said because all sound faded. Everything went blank, and I was just sitting there, frozen in place. My mouth was as dry as the desert and my eyes were so wide open that it almost hurt. It couldn't be who I thought it was. This must be some kind of wicked dream or something because this wasn't happening. Not like this. Not right now.

I didn't even dare to look at Harry, too scared to see his reaction. But what if I was just overreacting? What if my assumption was wrong?

A few moments later, Anne retreated from the living room, taking slow strides while refusing to meet any of our eyes. She turned to dad as she swallowed hard. "Troy, would you please come with me for a second?" She asked alarmed, making my heart beat faster in my chest.

No, this couldn't be good. Something bad had happened, I was sure of it.

Dad looked a bit confused but nodded his head and followed Anne to the living room, leaving me, Harry and

Gemma alone. It wasn't until then that I dared to turn my head to look at the two siblings. Their faces mirrored my own. They looked terrified, and that was when I knew I wasn't the only one thinking the worst here.

"Do you think...?" Gemma trailed off.

My breathing started getting heavier by the second and I couldn't help but grab the edge of the table, my knuckles turning white from how hard I was gripping it. Harry let out a deep sigh, reaching out to take my hand off the table and lacing our fingers together. He squeezed my hand a few times, giving me a weak smile. This time, I didn't pull away nor give him a warning look. No, because this time, I was happy that he held my hand considering I needed his reassurance. It was the only thing that could keep me from going insane at the moment.

"Whatever it is, it's going to be alright, okay?" Harry said, trying to keep calm himself.

"You don't know that," I muttered, looking down at our hands. "If it is what we think it is and their reactions will be bad, we can't be sure things are going to be alright."

Gemma pursed her lips. "Well, at least you have me on your side. I want the two of you to be happy no matter what. I just hope mum and your dad want that too, but if they don't, I'll defend you guys, I promise."

I snorted, rolling my eyes. "Yeah, as if that's going to make things better. If they don't approve of us, nothing's going to make them change their minds."

Harry knitted his eyebrows together. "But, they can't say anything now anyway. I mean, we aren't even dating anymore, right?" He said, looking at the side of my face.

I pulled my bottom lip between my teeth, my gaze still focused on our entwined hands. "Right," I muttered as I let go of his hand, leaving my own to feel cold.

I knew I was the one who had implied that we shouldn't continue dating, but I just couldn't help but feel hurt when he said the words out loud. It was like the thought hadn't dawned on me until he said that sentence. I mean, sure, it was best if we weren't together. Sometimes I felt as though I didn't deserve him anyway, and considering the consequences, we were better off not dating, but I loved him. How could I not want to be in a relationship with him?

Before any of us could utter another word, dad and Anne entered the kitchen with their lips pressed together in a thin line. They looked up to flicker their gazes between me and Harry, and I knew then that this wouldn't end well. Their faces didn't exactly show happiness, and just their auras made it obvious.

"Harry, Louis. Would you please explain to me why your principal just called and told me that there are rumors of you two dating going around the school?" Anne asked, her voice steady but there was a hint of panic in it.

The two of them sat down at the table across from us. Dad gave me this look that made me want to curl myself into a corner and cry. He was disappointed, there was no doubt about it. His eyes were pleading with me, wanting me to tell him that it wasn't true. I could feel tears well up in my eyes, and I felt frustrated about it. I hated crying. I only did when it was very necessary, and my dad's feelings were a soft spot for me. If I was the cause of him feeling bad, I couldn't help but feel guilty.

"Mum, it's not what you think..." Harry trailed off, inhaling a deep breath.

"Then what is it?" She snapped, glaring at her son.

Harry fell back in his seat, shocked by his mother's reaction. "I... I..."

"We thought you two hated each other. How on earth is it even possible that you two have gone behind our backs and fallen for one another? Or did you never really dislike each other, is that it? Have you two lied to us the entire time?" Anne continued, her nostrils flaring with anger.

But I saw something else. Just like dad, she was disappointed as well. This news was so out of her world that she couldn't help but be angry about it. To be honest, though, I was almost certain it was just her way of handling it. I was sure she didn't mean to be so pissed about it.

"Hey, mum, calm down. I know you're surprised, but don't blame them for this. Do you think it was their choice to fall for each other? Do you think it's easy to like your own stepbrother? You know, there is a reason why they have kept it a secret. They didn't want to feel unaccepted by everyone," Gemma interposed.

Anne swallowed hard, squinting her eyes at her daughter. "So you mean you knew about all this?"

Gemma crossed her arms over her chest and nodded her head. "Yes. I guess I was one of the few people who did, and you know what? My reaction was far better than yours." Her voice was almost as cold as ice, and I had to give it to her. She was good.

Harry's mum turned back to us, shaking her head in frustration. "Just... I just... *How*?" She required, looking at us helplessly.

Refusing to meet my dad's gaze again, I kept my eyes on Anne. "I guess it just kind of happened? As you might know, Harry and I used to be friends back in the days, and I started catching feelings for him then already. It wasn't until a few weeks ago that we started dating, though. I was scared that this would happen, that no one would accept us. That's why I dragged out on it all. Otherwise, we probably would have gotten together a few months ago," I admitted, biting my bottom lip.

Dad got up abruptly from his seat, surprising all of us. His eyes were glued to me, an emotionless look on his face. "Louis, may I please talk to you in private?"

I gulped, looking down at the surface of the table in shame as I nodded my head. Although I could feel Harry giving me a sympathetic look, I didn't turn my head to make sure of it. All I did was to get up and follow my dad to the living room in silence before sitting down on the couch.

He settled down beside me, running a hand through his hair. "Why did you do this, Louis? I thought you told me that you were happy that I had finally moved on from your mother? I just don't understand... Do you want me and Anne to split up, or what is it?"

Letting out a shaky breath, I shook my head frantically. "No. No, of course not. I would never ask you to do such a thing. I am happy that you have moved on from mum, and I'm happy that you have found Anne. I would never get into a relationship with Harry just to break you two apart, I promise. I just... I love him, alright? Of course I want you to be happy, but I want myself to be happy too."

He gave me a thoughtful look, pinching his chin with his thumb and forefinger. "And Harry makes you happy?"

A smile broke out on my face at his words. "Yes, he makes me very happy. Ever since I started dating him, I've actually become a much more positive person. I mean, just thinking about him makes me smile," I told him.

Dad studied my features, and I could see that he was still thinking deeply. "You do realize that you aren't making things easy, right? As your parents, it's not easy for us to accept the fact that our children are dating. People are going to think strangely of us and judge before they know us."

Letting out a sigh, I nodded my head. "Yeah, that's why I told Harry that we should break up. I told him when we got together that we had to keep our relationship a secret because if anyone found out about us, we would be screwed. I knew that you wouldn't be a fan of it, and I was afraid of your reaction. I thought you wouldn't want me anymore, that you would be so disgusted and disappointed that you would disown me or something like that. I knew things wouldn't be easy, but I couldn't keep myself away from him, dad. I just... I've liked him since I was fifteen and the feelings never went away over the years. I do realize now that we shouldn't even have given it a try, though. I mean, our relationship was just bound to never work anyway."

To my great surprise, dad curled his arms around my petite body and pulled me to his chest. The gesture was so unexpected that I tensed in his arms. I couldn't believe that he was hugging me. I thought he would snap at me and tell me how disgusting I was for falling for my stepbrother. Yet, here he was, embracing me like a loving and accepting dad.

Without realizing it, tears started rolling down my cheeks. He had no idea how much this hug meant to me. It meant *everything*. He was the only family member I had left, and knowing he still wanted to embrace me after finding out about all this made me so happy that I couldn't even find the right words to describe it. I just loved him so much.

"Jesus, Louis. I must say that you've really put yourself in a shitty situation this time, but I could never hate you, son. You're my firstborn, my little boy whom I've always loved and always will love. You could probably murder someone and I would still love you. Be disappointed in you? Yeah, maybe, but I would never be able to disown you or something extreme like that. You're my little boy, Louis, and nothing could ever change that."

As if tears weren't already falling from my eyes, I started sniffling like a little baby too. "I love you, dad," I muttered against his shoulder.

He pulled back a little so he could look into my eyes with a small smile on his face. "I love you too, son. And, if Harry is the one who makes you happy, and if what you said is true about him turning you into a more positive person, then he's someone to keep. Sure, it's not going to be easy for you, but if you want to make it work, I'm sure it will."

I just shook my head because I couldn't believe his words. "Why are you so understanding? I don't get it. You should hate me. We're ruining your and Anne's reputation and just... everything. How can you be so accepting of it all?" I wondered, looking at him in confusion.

He put his hands on my shoulders, looking at me sincerely.

"Because, I want my son to be just as happy as I am."

Chapter 42

[Harry]

It had been a month since mum and Troy found out about my and Louis' relationship. It had also been a month since Louis told me we were better off not being together. At first, I had taken it pretty badly. I didn't want to believe it and tried to tell him that we should stay in a relationship due to our deep feelings for one another, but also because Miranda's words had really given me hope. However, after some time, I had started getting used to it.

After Louis' conversation with his dad where he found out that Troy didn't mind him being together with me (as long as he was happy), you probably would have thought that the first thing he did was to get back together with me, but that was not what happened. I was more than happy when I found out about Troy's approval even if it took some time for my mum to accept it. I thought that Louis would change his mind immediately considering he didn't have to worry about his dad hating or disowning him any longer, but no. Things weren't that easy.

I could still remember the day we walked upstairs to go to sleep and he had asked me to follow him to his room. It was just the day after our parents found out about us. I thought he was about to tell me that he had changed his mind about everything and wanted to be with me again, but that wasn't the case. Instead, he had told me what his father had said, and sure, that made him happy, but then he had told me that he couldn't let anyone get hurt because of him. He said that if we were to date, he wouldn't be able to live with the thought of having to see me receive hate every day. He also said that he wouldn't want our family to be prejudiced just because of our relationship.

To be honest, I thought it was all just a bunch of bullshit. To me, it didn't matter what anyone else thought about us as long as I got to be with him. However, I knew that he had always been the type of guy who cared about everyone else's opinions. He did already when we used to be friends two years ago. He had been so careful. No one could know about our friendship because he was afraid of what their reactions may have been if they found out. The same thing went with when we found out that we were stepbrothers. He made sure that no one knew about it and that I didn't tell anyone because he wanted to keep it a secret. Even if he never admitted it, I was pretty sure he was embarrassed by me. Maybe he had gotten over it now, but I wasn't sure.

I'd didn't matter, though, because I still loved him just as much. It was just a little flaw he had. But I mean, who didn't have flaws? I sure did, and according to me, no one was perfect.

After that night, we hadn't talked very much to each other. We ate dinner together with our family, we sometimes stumbled into each other in the mornings when we were leaving the house and sometimes we even managed to enter the bathroom at the same time in the evenings. However, each time it happened, one of us would just excuse ourselves and leave just as quickly.

I hated it, but after a while of having to live with it, I was starting to get used to it. Don't get me wrong. I still missed him. I missed him so much that I had trouble falling asleep at night. And when I eventually did, I would always sleep awfully, and I was pretty sure you could see it as well. I had never looked so tired in my entire life as I did these days. I mean, my mum had even questioned me about it, and that was saying something.

It saddened me that Louis didn't even seem bothered by it, or he was just very good at hiding it. He usually kept to himself, though, going to his room whenever he got home from school and stayed there until it was time to eat dinner. To be honest, it didn't even feel like we lived in the same house anymore. That was how seldom I actually saw him.

Things at school were going better, though, and that was something that made me happy. People started noticing that Louis and I weren't dating anymore considering we never even glanced at each other when we were around one another. To be specific, we weren't any fun to talk about any longer because nothing was going on between us. Of course it made me happy that I didn't have people hating me anymore, but I couldn't help but feel sad about it as well. I mean, I would have happily accepted the hate if it meant I could still be with the one I loved. I honestly didn't care about anything else. Sadly, Louis did, though.

As for Liam, he supported me through it all, and so did Gemma. Our parents also knew that we weren't dating anymore, and I could tell by the confused look on Troy's face when we told them this that he was shocked. They had thought that we would stay together now that they had sort of accepted our relationship, but no, *of course* not.

Sometimes I wished Louis wasn't so stubborn. Sometimes I wished I had a say in things and could decide about our destiny, but no. He was in control of that, and I didn't understand why or how it turned out this way. But, I guess I couldn't force him to be in a relationship with me if he thought it wasn't worth it.

Last week, he had tried something I would never forget. He had brought home a girl. I didn't even know her name, nor did I want to. I just wanted her to get the fuck out of my house and never see her again because she wasn't welcome. It turned out she was a girl from our school, and apparently, she was a cheerleader, which honestly didn't surprise me since Eleanor was one as well.

She had shiny, blonde hair that reached her shoulders and a slim body with close to no curves. She wasn't Louis' type at all, and I honestly had no idea what he saw in her. Maybe she was just the first one he could find or something, I didn't know. However, that night ended up with the girl leaving our house at seven in the evening with tears running down her cheeks because apparently, Louis had told her that things weren't working. Well, good for him that he found that out eventually.

He never mentioned her again, and neither mum nor Troy asked him about her after that. They probably knew that he had sort of used her to get his thoughts off me, which was most likely why they kept their mouths shut. However, you could see the sadness in their eyes when they looked at him during the next couple of days. They just wanted him to be happy, I guess.

Now it was Monday morning and I was sitting in my first class of the day; Math. I wasn't paying too much attention to

Mr. Storm because I was too busy doodling in my notebook. This was pretty much how every lesson turned out these days. I would go to them, but I didn't do much there. The teachers had probably started noticing my lack of focus, but so far, they hadn't said anything about it. Maybe that was because my grades hadn't dropped yet.

Once the bell rang, I gathered my books and picked them up before heading to my locker. I unlocked it and shoved my school work into it, trying to remember what books I needed for the next lesson. Still pondering, I could suddenly hear someone call my name behind me.

Turning around in confusion, I was shocked to see not only Liam standing there but Zayn, Miranda, Niall and Ed as well. My eyes widened as my mouth fell open. "What are you guys doing here?"

Miranda took a step forward, a small smile playing on her lips. "We're here because some of us want to apologize and make up for things, and some want to see you happy again," she explained.

My eyebrows pulled together. "What do you mean happy? I've never said that--"

She rolled her eyes, cutting me off. "You didn't have to say anything because it's pretty obvious by your body language. Not to mention, neither of us have seen you smile in an entire month. Since we also know the reason behind it, we want to make you feel better, you know? We all care about you and we want you to be happy."

My eyes trailed from Niall to Ed, wondering if they honestly thought the same after what they had done. But judging by the sympathetic look on their faces, I assumed they were sorry for what they did. Maybe they were the ones who wanted to make up for things, as Miranda had mentioned. "Okay, but what are you going to do? I mean, what could make me feel better? If you know the reason behind it, you should also know that there's nothing to do. Louis has already made his mind up," I muttered, looking down at my feet.

Liam let out a sigh. "Yeah, he has, but you don't feel the same way. You know, in a relationship there are two people, right? It's not like he is the only one to decide things. You have a say in everything as well," he reminded me.

I knitted my eyebrows together, shaking my head. "But I can't force him to be with me. If he doesn't want me, there's nothing I can do," I explained.

He took a step forward and placed a warm hand on my shoulder. "But he does want you, Harry. I don't know if you haven't seen it, but he's longing for you. Every time we are in class, all of us can see the way he stares at you. He misses you just as much as you miss him," he tried to convince me, but I wasn't too sure.

I was certain Louis hadn't shown any sign of missing me these past few weeks, but then again, I had tried my best to ignore him just like he had told me to do, so maybe I just hadn't noticed it.

Before I could say anything, Niall and Ed stepped forward so they were in focus. "You know, when we posted those tweets, we were certain that Louis was only playing with you. We didn't know that you had so strong feelings for each other, but we do realize our mistake now, and we are so sorry," Ed apologized, biting his bottom lip.

Niall nodded in agreement. "Yeah, and if Louis is the one who makes you so happy, we would do anything to get you two back together because, in the end, all we want is for you to be happy. That's what we've always wanted."

I let a weak smile form on my lips. "Thank you, guys."

To my surprise, Zayn was the next one to take a step forward. It surprised me because he usually didn't say very much, so I was curious to hear what he had in mind. "Louis is one of my best friends. He has always been even if we have never really told each other personal stuff. He is my man, though, and I know him well enough to see that he is pretty devastated right now. I care for him just like Ed and Niall care about you, and I don't think the people at school should stop you from being together. You deserve each other, and you need one another to be truly happy."

The smile never left my face during his speech. I couldn't believe Zayn out of all people would say something like that. I didn't think he cared so much, but it was nice knowing that he did. I hope Louis would find out about it too since they were close friends.

"Alright, but what do you guys suggest I do then?" I asked, raising my eyebrows.

A wide, almost cheeky smile formed on Miranda's lips. "We think that the best thing you could do is to take him by surprise. Go up to him when he's not ready and just tell him what you think. Say that you're tired of not having a say in anything and that you think you guys should get together again seeing as you're pretty damn miserable without each other," she said, but I shook my head.

"That's not going to work. He's too stubborn for that. He'll just turn me down and scold me for gaining people's attention. He'll hate me," I muttered.

She rolled her eyes. "No, he won't. He loves you, Harry, remember that. He misses you just as much as you miss him. He's going to be weak and give in, I promise."

I was about to protest when all the other guys nodded their heads in agreement. "I think she's right, Harry," Liam said, looking at me sincerely. "Louis has been sad for quite some time now, and I don't think it's going to be hard to knock his walls down. I mean, have you guys even made eye contact during the last month? He's going to be putty in your hands, man."

An unwanted chuckle left my lips. "You guys are nuts," I told them honestly. I couldn't believe they actually thought that this was going to work. Just go up to Louis and tell him what I thought? There was no chance he was going to give in.

"Come on, give it a try," Niall urged.

"It's not like it can get any worse, right?" Zayn said, raising his eyebrows at me.

Letting out a sigh, I nodded my head reluctantly. "Alright, I'll do it," I gave in, making Miranda clap her hands together happily while the other guys smiled.

We all just stared at each other for a second until Miranda's smile dropped. "Why are you still here? Go get your man," she urged, hitting me on my shoulder.

I flashed her a playful glare. "Okay, okay. I'm going, but don't follow me. Let me do this alone, okay?" I said, flickering my eyes between all five of them.

They just nodded their heads and told me they wouldn't be a bother. After that, I left them to go find Louis. To be honest, I had no idea where he could be apart from his locker, so that was why I decided to go there first. On my way to the location, I thought about what I was about to do and wondered if it actually was such a good idea. I knew I wanted to be with him but was it really going to work? I didn't want him to hate me, but at the same time, it almost felt like we were back to being enemies anyway.

It turned out I didn't have time to think more about it because, in the next second, I was standing at his locker, right behind his figure. His back was turned to me as he was rummaging through his locker almost frustratingly. He probably couldn't find whatever he was searching for.

Clearing my throat, he turned around abruptly, almost hitting me with his arm in the process. He looked surprised at first, but it quickly turned to confusion when he registered it was me who was standing in front of him. "Harry, what are you--"

"I want to talk," I said, cutting him off.

He turned if possible even more confused. "Talk about what?"

Letting out a sigh, I ran a hand through my brown curls. "I want to talk about us. I mean, I don't want to live like this anymore," I explained, not being able to look him in the eye.

A dry chuckle escaped his lips. "And you just came up with that now?"

For some reason, I got a little irritated by his words. Why did he act so cold about it? It was like he was trying to hide his emotions. "Well, I don't know about you, but I haven't been feeling my greatest during the past month, and I'm tired of it, alright? I'm sick and tired of feeling this way. Ever since we got together, you were the one who made all the decisions. You decided that we should call it quits if anyone found out about us, and you decided it was best for us to break up. I didn't have a say in anything. I just had to agree with it even if it broke my heart. I know I can never force you to be with me, but do you have *any* idea of how much it has all affected me?"

Alright, I probably shouldn't have snapped at him like that, but I couldn't help myself. He needed to know the truth. He needed to know what I thought about it.

He opened his mouth to reply but nothing came out. There weren't many times that Louis Tomlinson was speechless, but now was one of them. It made me feel a little proud of myself, knowing that I had actually gotten to him with my words.

I took a step forward, not caring if anyone was watching us. Reaching up, I cupped his cheek in my hand, caressing his skin as I looked him in the eye. "I know you're scared of people hating us, and I know that you don't want me to get hurt, but I don't care, alright? As long as I get to be with you, I don't care about anything else. So what if people are going to judge our family? I'm sure our parents won't care about it. They just want us to be happy, and I know for sure that I won't be if I'm not with you. I... I love you. You know that. I love you so much it hurts. I mean, I can't even fall asleep at night because all I think about is you and how I can't call you mine any longer..." I trailed off, averting my gaze from him.

God, I was getting emotional. It really wasn't my intention. I just wanted him to know how I felt. Now, he would probably laugh at me and tell me how stupid I was for--

My thoughts were cut off by a pair of lips that crashed into my own. I was so shocked by the action that my eyes sprang open. Was it even possible that Louis was kissing me? I mean, we were standing in the middle of the hallway at school, and he was *kissing* me?

Once my brain registered what was happening, I melted into the kiss and started moving my lips against his. My eyes fell shut as my hands moved to the back of his neck, tugging at the ends of his hair. Louis let out a gasp and pulled me even closer to himself, walking backwards until he was pressed against the wall of lockers. His hands were gripping my face gently, his thumbs caressing the skin on my cheeks.

A smile broke out on my face as his tongue trailed over my bottom lip, asking for entrance. I didn't even hesitate before granting him access, parting my lips so our tongues could meet.

I got goosebumps all over my body at the feeling of his mouth against mine. It had been so long since we kissed like this that I had almost started to forget how it felt.

This was the best feeling in the world, and if I could, I would stay here, at this moment for the rest of my life. I just loved kissing Louis so much. He just made me feel *so* happy.

Once we both ran out of breath, Louis pulled back a little to look me in the eye. "I love you too, Harry. I always have and I always will."

Nibbling on my bottom lip, I gave him a shy smile. "So, does that mean--"

I was cut off by someone wolf-whistling behind me, and when I turned around, I saw a guy on the football team standing there together with some of his friends, smirking at the two of us. "What a lovely scene you made there. You don't wanna show us that again?" He mocked.

Louis dropped his hands from my face and balled them into tight fists at his sides instead. "Ryan, I swear to God. If you don't shut the fuck up, I'm going to make sure you'll end up in the damn hospital," he seethed, his teeth gritted together.

I took one of his hands in mine and entwined our fingers, squeezing them not once but twice to get him to calm down. Ryan, on the other hand, didn't seem affected by the threat but just rolled his eyes. "You don't scare me, Tommo. You're just a weak piece of shit who's in love with your own fucking brother."

This made Louis get even angrier, and if it hadn't been for me holding him back, he would have pounced on him. I had to grip both of his hands to keep him in place. It was a good thing that he wasn't very big or tall. Otherwise, I wouldn't have been able to stop him.

"Look, he can't even get out of his little lover's hold. Did you get weaker when you decided you liked it up the ass?" Ryan chuckled.

"Alright, that's enough!"

My eyes widened at the sound of Zayn's voice booming through the hallway, surprising all of us. If Louis hadn't been just as stunned as I was, this would have been his chance to actually get to Ryan because I lost my grip on him the moment I heard Zayn.

The raven-haired boy stepped forward until he was standing between us and Ryan, glaring at the blonde guy who had talked shit about his best friend. "I thought we were a team. I thought we were all friends with each other, but I'm pretty sure you don't call this being friends," he said coldly, gesturing between Louis and Ryan. "You don't say shit like that to a teammate, especially not your own captain. Hell, you don't even say something like that to *anyone*. I bet you're just jealous that you don't have anyone to call yours."

At first, Ryan just gaped at the raven-haired guy until he composed himself and shot him a glare. "You seriously think I would be jealous of something like that? That's just freaking disgusting," he spat, glaring at me and Louis.

Zayn rolled his eyes. "Well, first off, Louis and Harry aren't even real brothers so there's nothing disgusting about that. Second off, it's pretty sad that you still haven't accepted homosexual people considering you play on a team consisting of almost four of them. Also, it's two thousand and seventeen, mate. Grow the hell up."

I couldn't help but feel proud of Zayn. His words really made me smile because he was so on point. Not only was he standing up for me and Louis, but he was also standing up for every homosexual person out there, and I loved him for that. Who knew that the quiet Zayn had this in him?

Ryan just let out a grunt before gesturing towards his friends to leave. They were all gone only a second later, leaving the three of us standing in the hallway, looking at each other. Louis must be the most surprised one. He was looking at Zayn with wide eyes, and to be honest, he looked speechless once again. This must be a tough day for him, being shocked so many times that he had in only a couple of minutes.

"Zayn, I... I don't know what to say, mate. To be honest, I didn't expect that from you, but that doesn't matter. I just... Thank you, honestly," Louis said, looking at his best friend sincerely.

Zayn placed a hand on Louis' shoulder, flickering his gaze between the two of us with a smile on his face. "No need to thank me, Lou. That's what best friends are for."

Louis returned the smile, nodding to him. The raven-haired boy cleared his throat, scratching the back of his neck. "Alright, I should probably go find Liam now. You two probably still have a lot to talk about, right?" He chuckled, winking at me.

Rolling my eyes, I let out a snort. "Just go already. I'm sure Liam's probably wondering where you are."

He lifted his hands in surrender, walking away from us chuckling. Once he was gone, Louis turned to me in confusion. "What was that all about?" He wondered.

I just waved a hand in dismissal. "Nothing. We just discussed something earlier, but it doesn't matter. Now... I'm quite curious about what's going on inside your head. I mean, I have never really been good at reading your mind."

Louis chuckled, taking a step forward so he could reach up and tuck a stray curl behind my ear. "Well, for your information, I'm pretty sure I'm just as sick and tired as you of having to live with the thought of not being together with you. Every day since I told you that we shouldn't date, I have been miserable. I know that I don't deserve you considering how many chances you have given me, but I just... I was just scared of everyone's opinions, and I couldn't bear the thought of seeing you get hurt for something I could control. I guess I'm just too selfish to keep myself away from you because I know for sure that I can't live without you. And after what just happened, I know that I couldn't care less about anyone's opinion. You are what matters to me, and that is all that's important. They can say whatever they want, but I know that our love for each other is not something disgusting or something we should hide. If anything, we should be proud of ourselves," he admitted, the smile never leaving his face.

My heart swelled with warmth, and I couldn't help but wrap my arms around his neck. "You wanna know what I think?" I asked, making him nod his head.

"I think that you're damn right about that."

With that said, I leaned in to seal our lips together, and yes, I was truly happy when I was with Louis. It was pretty safe to say that he may even be the love of my life.

Epilogue

[Harry]

It was a rainy Friday evening in March, and Gemma, mum, Troy, Louis and I were all gathered in the living room watching TV. Gemma had a grumpy look on her face with her arms crossed over her chest where she was sitting in the armchair, while Louis and I were sharing one of the couches and mum and Troy the other.

The reason why she was so grumpy was that Devon was busy tonight, so she felt 'left out', as she liked to call it, without him. I kind of understood her, though, considering I was lying between Louis' legs while he was carding his fingers through my hair and mum was lying with her head on Troy's lap.

We were being all couply while she didn't even have her partner here with her. I would probably be grumpy as well if I were her. However, I couldn't help but feel content. Nowadays, I did so quite often because Louis and I didn't have to hide our relationship any longer, a relationship that was *real* now. It was the best feeling in the world, finally being able to show my love for him without having to pretend that I hated him.

I could tell our parents were happy for us as well because mum's face would always light up in a smile whenever we walked into the kitchen in the morning on the weekends, Louis' arms around my waist from behind. Once, he had carried me bridal style down the stairs, claiming that his 'princess' shouldn't use her precious legs if not necessary. I had actually hit him in the head that time because one, I was not a girl, and two, I had two feet for a reason, so I could walk without his help. However, mum had cooed at us and laughed, which I took as a good reaction.

Troy made his acceptance obvious by looking at his son proudly whenever Louis showed his love for me. I guess he and mum were just glad that we were finally together and had found someone who made us happy. Nothing else really mattered.

As for the people at school, they had obviously not taken the news that we were back together well. At first, they had started hating on me again, but this time was different because Louis was always there and stood up for me. He usually never left my side these days, and I absolutely loved it. We still had people who still liked hanging out with even if we were dating, so it could have been worse. Liam, Zayn, Ed, Niall, Miranda, Louis and I always ate lunch and hung out together.

Ed and Niall had shown us how truly sorry they were for doing what they did to us so drastically, and both Louis and I had forgiven them by now. Louis was a little hesitant at first seeing as they had betrayed him pretty deeply, but he accepted their apology when he was sure that they knew the real him, that he wasn't just playing with me.

Speaking of Ed and Niall, they had actually started dating. They were taking things slow and trying it all out, but judging by the looks of it, things were going pretty well for them. I was happy that Niall had moved on from me. I always felt so bad when I saw him glancing at me with this sad look on his face, so when he was now back to his normal, smiling self that I had missed, I was nothing but happy. He was a great friend and I would have been sad if we went our separate ways entirely after everything that had happened between us.

On another note, mum and Troy had set a date for their wedding, and they were getting married on the 4th of August this year. It wasn't very long until then, and time literally flew by these days, so I was sure the day would come before we knew it. It was quite weird thinking that they would only have been dating for a little more than a year then, but I guess love had no limits. Why drag out on something that felt right?

What the future had in store for me and Louis, I didn't know, but I was sure we would stay together no matter what. I had applied to a college in London while Louis had gotten a scholarship to play for Arsenal. If I was admitted to my college, it would be perfect. Otherwise, I was planning to move with him anyway, and even if we hadn't told our parents about it yet, I was sure they already knew that we were going there together no matter what.

My thoughts were suddenly interrupted by one of Louis' hands that started moving down the side of my body. The movement was slow, making me wonder what exactly he had in mind. Therefore, I wasn't surprised when it stopped right on top of my crotch. "What are you doing?" I hissed in his ear, turning to look at the side of his face only to see that he had a smirk playing on his lips.

"I'm doing absolutely nothing," he said innocently, grabbing my dick and giving it a squeeze. I suppressed a moan, clenching my eyes shut.

"Stop it before I hit you," I threatened, trying to glare at him, but it was hard when he was subtly palming me through my jeans.

He raised his eyebrows, letting out a chuckle. "Yeah? You sound very convincing."

Rolling my eyes, I reached down to take his hand off of me and intertwined our fingers instead. "I mean it."

The smirk never left his face, though, and the next second, he used his free hand to reach down and pinch my hip under my shirt. "Too bad you decided to lay down practically on top of me then. You were already in for it the moment you did," he winked, making me reach up to flick his nose.

"Ow, what did you do that for?" He whined and lifted the hand that had been pinching my hip to rub his nose.

"You deserved it," I muttered, glaring at him.

He let out a snort and shook his head. "I did not."

"Did too," I argued.

"Did not."

"Did too."

"Did no--"

"Guys, seriously? You're really adorable and all that, but I'm trying to watch TV here, alright?" Gemma complained, interrupting our banter.

Louis and I both broke out into a fit of laughter, which ended up with me muffling it against the crook of his neck. He shivered slightly at the contact, hugging me tighter to his body. I started leaving kisses along his neck, making my way up towards his face. Just as I was about to plant my lips on his jawline, he turned his head so they landed on his warm, pink lips instead.

The angle wasn't exactly the best, but I couldn't care if my neck hurt from the bad position. All I cared about was the fact that Louis' lips were on mine. They moved slowly together, the two of us savoring every second of the moment as he reached his hand up to cup the side of my face tenderly. The kiss was slow, romantic and absolutely perfect if you asked me. These kinds of kisses were the best because they were filled with so much love and passion.

The hand that wasn't cupping my cheek reached down to my hip again. He turned me so I was lying on top of him, my body facing his. It made it easier for us to kiss and it also made it more comfortable. I gripped his hair between my fingers, tugging at it. He gasped at the feeling, placing his hand on my lower back instead.

The touch made goosebumps appear on my skin, and I couldn't help but shiver. If he only knew how he made me feel. It was just insane.

As if that wasn't enough, he dug his fingers into my skin, making me almost let out another moan.

"Alright guys, that's it. Get a fucking room," Gemma snapped, and when I parted from Louis to look at her, I could see that she was glaring at us.

I gave her an innocent smile, shrugging my shoulders. "It wasn't that bad, Gem," I pouted.

She rolled her eyes, looking over at mum and Troy. "You have to agree with me on this."

Mum let out a light chuckle, nodding her head while gazing at me and Louis. "Your sister is right, Harry. Although I think you're adorable, you should probably take it somewhere else. Not that I'm implying anything intimate here, but you get what I mean," she smiled but you could still tell that she was serious about the last part.

I looked down at Louis who was already grinning at me. He wiggled his eyebrows, and I couldn't help but hit his arm gently. I knew what he was thinking, that dirty-minded bastard. With a roll of my eyes, I leaned down to give him a quick kiss on the lips before leaning down to rest my head against his chest, looking back at mum and Gemma. "We won't do anything else, I promise," I said, proving my point by 'zipping' my lips shut.

Troy let out a snort. "I wouldn't be too sure of that, boy," he laughed, giving the two of us a wink.

Mum hit him in the side, glaring up at him. "Hey, don't get them on any thoughts. Let's just watch this movie like we were doing before we started talking."

Troy shrugged his shoulders while looking over at us. I could practically see Louis smirk back at him. He was already thinking 'those' thoughts before he had even mentioned anything. "I think dad's right. Let's go upstairs so we don't have to disturb them anymore, love," Louis said, patting my head to gain my attention.

When I turned my head to meet his gaze, he gave me puppy eyes and pouted his lips to make me give in. It was hard to resist, and I knew if I continued looking at him, I wouldn't be able to say no. The thing was, I couldn't look away from him. He was just so damn beautiful.

"Fine, come on," I sighed, sitting up on the couch and reaching out a hand for him to take.

Mum cleared her throat loudly. "I hope you're not about to do what I think you are," she said sternly, raising an eyebrow at us.

Gemma adjusted herself in the armchair. "Whatever, mum. At least they won't be a bother anymore," she interposed, waving a hand in dismissal.

I couldn't help but laugh, and Louis did too. I could even see Troy's lips turn upwards by her comment. "I guess that's our cue to leave, Harry," Louis chuckled, taking my hand and practically dragging me towards the stairs. "Goodnight, people," he added once we were at the doorframe, and I didn't even have time to open my mouth before we had left the room.

With his hands on my hips, Louis guided me upstairs until we were outside my bedroom door. Reaching out in front of me, he opened it and almost tossed me onto my bed, back first. With a chuckle, I made grabby hands at him because I wanted him to join me, which made him smirk mischievously. "So, now you're up for it, huh?" He joked, crossing his arms over his chest.

I rolled my eyes, sitting up so I could grab his arm and pull him down on top of me. "Well, you asked for it, and who am I not to obey my boyfriend?" I questioned, raising an eyebrow.

The smile never left his face when he leaned in so he was only inches away from me. He reached up to brush my hair to the side so he could look directly into my eyes. "I sure do have a nice boyfriend then, don't I?"

I chuckled, leaning in so my lips were ghosting over his. "The best."

He joined my laughter before leaning in to seal our lips together. It was only a short kiss, yet it was filled with so much love that goosebumps appeared on my skin. I was sure I would never get tired of kissing Louis.

He placed his arms on either side of my head so he could support himself on his elbows, but he made sure to stay very close to my face. "It's quite weird that you actually thought I hated you just a few months ago, don't you think?" He wondered, raising an eyebrow.

I was surprised he wanted to talk about something like this right now, but I decided to go along with it. "Yeah, but when you think about how you treated me, it's not that hard to understand."

He rolled his eyes. "You weren't that innocent yourself, mister. I was quite offended by a lot of things you told me."

Looking at him incredulously, I raised my eyebrows. "I was only standing up for myself," I whined, pouting my bottom lip.

He chuckled, leaning down to give my lips a quick kiss to make the pout go away. He succeeded. "When it comes to what you said, yes, but before that, you started ignoring me, which was the reason I started picking on you," he explained, tilting his head to the side to make a point.

"So you blame it all on me?" I asked.

A wide grin broke out on his face as an adorable chuckle left his lips. He shook his head and looked down at my chest for a second before looking back up into my eyes. "Yes, of course I do," he chuckled.

Hitting him on the arm, I let out a whine. "I hate you."

He cupped my cheek with his hand as he continued laughing. "Too bad I know you don't," he mumbled. "And you wanna know something?"

I nodded my head, staring deep into his ocean blue eyes.

"I don't hate you either. I never have and I never will."

The End

BOOKS BY THE AUTHOR

The Kiss
When Hate Turns Into Love

Printed in Great Britain
by Amazon